CHAIN OF CUSTODY

ANITA NAIR is the author of the novels *The Better Man*, *Ladies Coupé*, *Mistress*, *Lessons in Forgetting*, *Idris* and *Alphabet Soup for Lovers*. *Chain of Custody* follows on from the success of *A Cut-Like Wound*, the first Inspector Gowda novel, published in the UK by Bitter Lemon Press in 2014. Anita is also the author of *Goodnight & God Bless*, a collection of essays, *Malabar Mind*, a volume of poetry, and five books for children.

CHAIN OF CUSTODY

Anita Nair

AN INSPECTOR GOWDA NOVEL

BITTER LEMON PRESS
LONDON

BITTER LEMON PRESS

First published in the United Kingdom in 2016 by
Bitter Lemon Press, 47 Wilmington Square, London WC1X 2ET

www.bitterlemonpress.com

First published in India in 2016 by Harper Black
An imprint of HarperCollins Publishers

A CIP record for this book is available from the British Library

ISBN 978–1–908524–74–4
eBook ISBN 978–1–908524–75–1

Offset by Tetragon, London
Printed and bound in Great Britain by CPI Group (UK) Ltd, Croydon, CR0 4YY

'The only thing necessary for the triumph of evil is for good men to do nothing.'

—Edmund Burke

PROLOGUE
14 MARCH, SATURDAY

7.30 A.M.

A wall of mirrors. He could see himself reflected in it. A big-built man in a pair of mustard-coloured leggings and a navy blue t-shirt that just barely reached the top of his thighs. He had never seen anything more grotesque or disquieting in his life, he thought, staring at the multiple Borei Gowdas. The music began, and the instructor, a tall, thin young man who looked like he had been poured into his clothes and whose limbs seemed attached to his body with double hinges, swayed in time.

'Go on, Inspector Gowda,' he said. 'Get going, listen to the music, let it flow through you. Only then can you tango. Now remember, forward with your left, forward with your right, forward with left ...'

Gowda stopped listening. What the fuck am I doing here, he asked himself, and the many Borei Gowdas in the mirror.

The mobile rang incessantly from the bedside table. Inspector Borei Gowda woke up with a start. What was that fucking dream all about, he wondered as he reached for the phone groggily.

His eyes widened at the sight of the time on the phone. It was almost eight. How could he have slept through an alarm that was set to ring every fifteen minutes from six to seven? But it seemed that he had drunk himself to oblivion last night. Something he had sworn never to do again. He sighed.

'Hello,' he said into the phone.

'Sir, there was a control room call. It was about someone in that gated community near Bible College. I think you should come,' Head Constable Gajendra said even as Gowda heard the Bolero pull up outside his home.

'I will be there in fifteen minutes,' Gowda said, walking to the bathroom. He stood under the shower with a toothbrush stuck in his mouth. The water beat down on his head, stilling the hammering at the back of it. The incidents of the past night ran through his mind in vivid technicolour with Dolby surround sound. He closed his eyes. Later, later, he told himself. For now duty called.

Gajendra was waiting by the gate of the house when Gowda drove up to Shangri La. That was the name etched on the burnished brass plate embedded in the gatepost. The head constable's face was drawn.

A group of people had gathered outside the gate. Gowda nodded in greeting and walked towards the house. A small, thin man peeled himself from the group and hurried to catch up with Gowda. 'Hello Inspector, I am the president.'

Gowda paused and stared at him, wondering if the man was mad. 'President of which country?'

The man flushed. 'President of the association.'

Gowda nodded. 'Oh I see. I will have to ask you to step back.'

The man's face fell as he turned to leave.

The front door had been broken in by two constables. Gowda entered the house and paused. The door had opened into a vestibule like an old-fashioned club. In keeping with the style was a giant mirror in a gilt frame, and beneath it what looked like a table sawn in half. It must have a name. Urmila would know it.

He looked at the man sprawled on the floor on his face. He flinched. One side of his head had been smashed in. A pool of browning blood haloed his head. Near him lay a stone Buddha on its side. The marble floor was cracked like the skull.

The man wore navy blue Crocs on his feet and a t-shirt that had hiked up in the fall. Gowda could see a bruise below his ribs on the left side. Through the lycra shorts he wore, his flaccid penis was clearly visible. Who was this man? Gowda pinched the bridge of his nose thoughtfully.

A towel lay a few feet away. Gowda bent down and hoisted the end of the towel with his pen. It was still damp and smelled of chlorine. The man had gone swimming, he thought. He remembered a glint of blue on the left as he drove into the gated community.

'He was supposed to have a video call with a client at eleven last night. Apparently, the client tried several times and finally called someone else. She couldn't reach him either. When he didn't respond to the calls or messages this morning as well, she had a colleague call the control room,' Head Constable Gajendra said.

'And he lived alone?' Gowda asked. He could see the rest of the room was in order. No upturned furniture. Not even a piece of broken glass or a muddy footprint. It wasn't an intruder. It was someone the victim had known. That much was obvious.

'What about his phone and laptop?' Gowda asked.

'All there,' Gajendra said. 'I don't think it is a burglary gone wrong.'

'Where is the woman who called the control room?'

'She was in Chennai last night. Apparently, she has taken the first flight out and is on her way here from the airport,' Gajendra said, turning at the sound of a car slowing down.

A young man and a woman came hurrying up the garden path. Gowda walked towards them.

'Dr Rathore, is he all right?' the woman asked as the man tried to peer over Gowda's shoulder.

Gowda shook his head. 'I am sorry.'

The woman's face crumpled. 'Oh my god, oh my god,' she whispered, her hand going to her mouth.

'What happened, Inspector?' The man's voice quivered in shock. 'Dr Rathore took care of himself very well.'

'He was a doctor?' Gowda asked.

'Not a *doctor* doctor. A doctor of law,' the man said. 'Can we see him?'

Gowda held up his hand. 'Not now. It's a homicide. Till the forensics team arrives, I can't have the crime scene contaminated.'

'Homicide! But who would want to kill Dr Rathore?' The woman's voice rose.

'Obviously someone did. His skull was bashed in,' Gowda said.

They stared at him, horrified. Gowda held their gaze, not knowing what else to do. There was no easy way of announcing death, be it a suicide, an accident or a homicide. Policemen and doctors knew this. It was their lot to remain unmoved by the toll it took on everyone associated with the victim.

'We need some details,' Gowda said.

Head Constable Gajendra examined the faces of the couple in front of him. He knew Gowda was doing the same.

Gowda figured the two would have nothing to contribute except perhaps what was already in the deceased's planner. He had seen the woman's gaze sweep the garden like she was seeing it for the first time. He saw the man's eyes settle and then linger on the bar counter in a gazebo in a corner of the sprawling lawns. Dr Rathore had never had a drink with his colleagues or invited them home. It seemed to Gowda that the lawyer had a very private life, far removed from what his employees and associates knew of him.

'His family?' Gowda asked.

'His wife and son live in London. She looks after the UK end of the law firm,' the woman said. There was a hint of disapproval in her tone. The young associate, Gowda realized, had been a little in love with the man.

'I'll need to speak with you at length,' Gowda said suddenly.

The woman nodded. Her eyes welled up. 'I still can't believe that ...' The man put his arm around her.

Gowda's eyes met met Gajendra's. Get rid of them, he gestured with a slight tilt of his chin.

Police Constable Byrappa sidled up to Gajendra. 'The security at the gate has a CCTV and a list of visitors.'

Gajendra smiled. He went looking for Gowda. 'I think it will be an open-and-shut case,' he said.

Gowda stared at him. 'You say?'

'Yes, sir. PC Byrappa said there is CCTV footage and a guest register. Once we have the time of death, it's not going to be hard to know who killed the lawyer.'

Gowda said nothing. Deep down he didn't think it was going to be that easy. Gowda turned to look at the dead lawyer one last time. Something niggled at him. He wasn't sure what it was. But it would come to him.

The little man who had called himself the president of the association came in with two other men and a woman. 'Do you think it's the Dandupalaya gang?' one of the men asked in a low whisper.

'Apparently they choose lonely houses with few members. Isn't that the gang's modus operandi?' the woman said, stressing the words with the air of a clever child who has learnt a new phrase. The third man pulled his phone out to shoot pictures.

Gowda frowned. 'No photography,' he said, not even bothering to respond to. the query about the Dandupalaya gang. Ever since the release of the film *Dandupalaya*, based on the real lives of a family in a village in the outskirts of Bangalore, who had gone on a spree of looting, rape and murder, the Dandupalaya gang had assumed a mythical status. He was quite certain that, within the force too, there would be officers who found it convenient to assign this homicide to the resurgence of the Dandupalaya gang. After all, almost 112 cases had been registered against them more than a decade ago.

'Who do you think did it?' the president asked.

'The investigations have already begun,' Gowda said.

How had the murderer entered and exited the lawyer's house? Who else had keys to the house? There was something beyond these obvious questions that he was missing. Gowda reached for his phone. He needed a fresh pair of eyes. He needed Santosh.

Part 1

Nine Days Before ...

5 MARCH, THURSDAY

The smell. Grime, sweat and the unwashed reek of a body dressed in soiled clothes that were threadbare in patches and unravelling at the ends. The pong of desperation.

It was a smell I recognized. For I had lived with it.

In the crowded general compartment of the 18463 Prashanthi Express, scheduled to reach Bangalore City station at 12.05 p.m., desperation hung like a low cloud. The collective breath of the creatures who occupied every seat and aisle.

I looked around. It was a mixed group as always. About ninety people packed into a compartment meant to hold seventy-two. There was barely room to move.

They sat leaning against each other. Three scrawny boys dressed in t-shirts and track pants. Their skin was the colour of clay; their flat noses with flared nostrils and rather prominent brows told me they were from one of the tribal villages of Odisha. Each had a thread around his neck with a little silver charm. One of them touched his charm and rubbed his finger on it. He was frightened of what lay ahead and was willing himself to be brave.

The boys clutched a plastic bag each. It probably held all their possessions: a few worn-out clothes and worthless gewgaws that each would fight viciously to keep. Their feet were bare and only a little dirtier than their faces. But there was something resolute about their expressions that drew me to them.

I knew it all. For I was them, once.

I was six years old when my father sold me to a man for a thousand rupees. That was to be my price for the season. 'You can plant the fields with half the money and the rest will keep you and your family going till the crops are ready to be sold. I'll bring him back once the season is up,' the man told my mother.

My father called the man sardar and I was told to call him the same. The man had five families with him, including my uncle's, and they had offered to include me as part of their group. Men and women like my parents, children like me, two old women, an old man and two babies. My head reeled with all the new names and sensations.

We took a train. I didn't know where I was going. I didn't care. Wherever it was, it would be better than home, I knew. I had never been on a train before or seen running water that came when I opened the tap. Every few hours, the man gave me something to eat. I clung to the window bars of the train and felt the hot wind tattoo my face. I wanted to sing. It felt like my horizon was arced with rainbows. Thousands of them.

We were asked to get off the train at a station called Kazipet, and he took us to a place that made bricks. 'You like playing in the mud, don't you?' my uncle said with a strange sounding laugh.

I nodded as I looked around. At first I thought I couldn't breathe. The heat pressed down upon me and the air hurt my throat and eyes.

'Stop gaping and help me,' my uncle said. We had to build our own little room where all of us would sleep. My uncle, my aunt, his mother-in-law and their two children younger than me. We had been given some straw and a blue sheet. That would be our roof – thatch and plastic. But we would need to build the walls. All of us worked quietly and quickly. That night I lay on the ground outside the unfinished room, staring at the skies. It didn't matter, I told myself. There are others here as well. Somehow that made me feel better.

The days were relentless. At first I was given lumps of coal to beat against each other so they turned into bits that would feed the furnace. Then I was asked to carry small loads of freshly moulded bricks to the kilns. I had to do what I was asked to do. That was what the other children did as well.

I worked through the day. In return, I was given some food, and several beatings. My uncle beat me, my aunt beat me, my aunt's mother beat me, the older boys and girls beat me, the kiln owner's supervisor beat me ... After a while I stopped wondering what I was getting beaten for. All I knew was that there was a furnace with a gaping mouth in my belly. It felt hollow and hot. I didn't know if it was hunger or fear.

I forgot my name. Everyone called me Pathuria. Everyone else was also Pathuria.

The train sped into the day. Soon the ticket collector would make a cursory visit. He seldom went beyond the door. The stench from the bathrooms and from the clogged pores of these vacant-eyed, hollow-cheeked creatures would deter even the bravest man. Once in a while, though, he would pounce on a hapless face and demand, 'Tickets! Tickets!'

Sometimes a tiny runnel of luck would slip into the cloud of desperation, and even if that person didn't have one, the man sitting alongside or someone else from across the aisle would pass him a ticket. And such would be the impact of that jet of luck that the ticket checker would not ask the good samaritan for *his* ticket. Such happenstances occured in the general compartment.

Sometimes though, a face would give itself away. A shifty look, beads of sweat on the upper lip, a tightening of the jaw. The ticket checker was not an idiot. He would see the owner of that face for what he was. Class: Vermin. Category: Vagrant. With the glee of a dog sniffing out a nest of baby rats, he would pounce on him. Ready to toss him out onto the next platform with a growl and a threat. 'Do you want me to call the railway police?'

It was then I would appear. I would have a sheaf of tickets in my pocket. I would wedge my way through the heaving mass of perspiration and fear till I reached the group that I knew was certain to be ticketless and with no knowledge of what to do next.

I leaned against one of the seats now. The boys avoided looking at me as I knew they would. They stared out of the window or at the floor. Look at me, I wanted to tell them. Meet my gaze, let's make this easier for you and me.

You are Krishna, I told myself, thinking of how the thekedar had grasped my shoulders, looked into my eyes and named me. I repeated in my head the words the thekedar had said to me the first time and many times thereafter: Those who come to me go beyond the world of shadows.

I boarded at Chipurupalle station in Andhra Pradesh at 10.58 a.m. It was an hour when no one noticed anything. Sleep weighed heavy on the eyelids and turned all thoughts into a slow, murky stream. At 11.30 a.m. we would be at Vizinagaram with the possibility of the ticket checker turning up any moment. I had a few minutes left to make the boys my own.

They had two bottles of water between them. One of the boys raised a bottle to his lips. His eyes met mine.

'Tame kouthu asicha?' I mumbled in Odiya, hiding a yawn behind my hand. I spoke five languages: Hindi, Tamil, Kannada, Odiya and Bengali, and I had a smattering of Telugu and English. In my line of work, you are nothing if you cannot speak the language of your customers, and mine came from different parts of the country.

His eyes widened and he mumbled something to the boy next to him. This one was the leader of the group. He frowned and then answered my query after a pause.

'Satpada,' he said. 'And you?'

'Puri,' I said. That's my stock answer to anyone from Odisha. I could tell them the truth, that I was from Bolangir, but I don't remember anything about that part of my life. My family, home, or the place.

And if someone probed about Puri, I had another answer ready. My house was in one of the lanes by the temple. I imagined the lane. A dirty, smelly narrow strip of land crowded with people and animals, rickshaws and vendors. The thekedar said that was how it was. But no one ever asked me.

'I have been to Lake Chilka,' I said. It was the truth.

Once, the thekedar and I drove through the villages of southern Odisha. I don't know what caught my breath: the landscape of water beds everywhere or the poverty that lined every face and filled every home.

I touched the thekedar's elbow then and asked, 'What happened here? Why are they so poor?'

He shrugged. 'Who knows? Floods, cyclones, the mining industry, no education, no leftist party ... take your pick!' And then he smiled wolfishly. 'Good for us though!'

I smiled back. It was reassuring to know the well would never run dry.

I saw a gleam in the boy's eye. Was it the relief of meeting someone who knew his village? 'Do you have tickets?' I asked.

The boy's brow furrowed again. But he spoke firmly. 'Yes, yes.' He was lying. How easily they gave themselves away. That little hesitation made all the difference.

'Well then, that's fine. The ticket checker will come in at the next station and the ticketless rats as he calls them will be thrown out onto the platform where the railway police will drag them to jail. A black hole filled with real rats and thrashings thrice a day instead of food. But you don't have to worry. Since you have your tickets, just stay tight and watch the fun!' I winked at him.

I held on to the metal railing and let my face rest against the crook of my arm. I counted under my breath. I needed the security that numbers brought into my life. It probably began at the kiln with the making of bricks. If we made a thousand bricks a day, we were paid eighty rupees. Twenty were mine. And so I learnt to count as we moulded bricks.

At the count of seven, I heard his low voice. 'Dada.'

I shifted my gaze to meet his. 'Yes,' I said slowly. My voice took on the sonorous tone of the big brother, for he had anointed me thus.

'We don't have tickets. What do we do?'

I frowned. 'That's a problem and ...'

Before I could finish, he blurted out, 'Please help us.'

I scratched my head thoughtfully. 'Three of my friends were to have joined me. But their boss didn't let them travel. So we'll just pretend that you three are the friends I bought the tickets for.'

I smiled at them. My best Krishna smile that the thekedar said could light a street, melt ice and open locks. These tribal boys from the middle of nowhere wouldn't be able to resist it.

The tightness around the boys' mouths dissolved. They would go with me to the end of the world, I knew.

'There is something else you must be prepared for,' I told them. Their eyes widened.

I explained what lay ahead. The thekedar had taught me to do so. 'You are Krishna. In the Mahabharata, he is the charioteer. It's your dharma to lead and guide so the others know what to expect.' It made sense then. It made sense now. The thekedar said I had an ancient soul.

'How ancient?' I asked.

'At least five thousand years old.' He smiled.

He said I knew instinctively what others spent a whole lifetime trying to understand.

'You can call me dada, but for all other purposes, we have a thekedar we owe everything to.'

The boys stared uncomprehendingly. They didn't know the word and I couldn't remember the exact equivalent in Odiya for contractor. 'Jamadar,' I said suddenly. 'He is our boss ... You must do as I say. I will be able to help only if I have your faith and obedience.' My voice was firm. The boys nodded. 'Start with your names,' I told them. 'And the names of your parents. Actually, it doesn't matter. The names of your parents will be what I tell you, and don't you forget a word of what I am going to tell you now.'

They made room for me and I huddled with them. Most of the other travellers were asleep, lulled by the rocking of the train and their fatigue. But my boys were wide awake.

They listened.

'Bangalore is not the city you think it is ...' I began. I saw the fear in their eyes, in their clenched fists, in the tautness of their bodies. Fear was good. Fear allowed me to take control. Fear allowed me to rule.

———•———

Rekha couldn't decide what she was going to tell her parents. No parent believed in the myth of 'combined study' any more. And it was not just her parents she needed to convince. Suraj, her brother, would be just as difficult. 'Wat do I say @ home?' she texted Sid.

'Try cmbnd study!' The phone lit up. Rekha glanced at it as she ran a kohl pencil along the edge of her upper eyelid.

On their first date, Sid had suggested that she keep her phone on silent mode at home. 'You don't want your folks wondering who is texting you all the time,' he had said, turning to look at her with a slow embarrassed grin.

She had felt herself melt into him. How could anyone be so considerate? She had marvelled at it. He had placed his hand on the small of her back when they crossed the road. He had offered her his bandana to wrap around her neck when they set out on his bike. He had adjusted the rearview mirror so he could look at her as they spoke. He was hers, hers alone. Like she was his, his alone.

'De won't buy it.' Her fingers raced over the touchscreen.

Her eyes sparkled seeing the reply. 'Gender studies sem @ NLS.'

That would work. The National Law School was some distance away. She would say she was sleeping over at Priya's and slip away with Sid for a long cosy date. Priya would understand and her parents wouldn't mind either, as long as Sid dropped her back by about eleven. And the next morning, if Suraj picked her up from Priya's house, nobody would suspect a thing. She smiled at the thought.

'Why are you smiling at the wall?' Suraj said from the doorway.

'Su, I need a favour. I need to go for a seminar at NLS tomorrow,' she said on a whim.

'Who are you going with?'

'Priya, a few of my classmates and some seniors.'

'So what's the problem?' he asked, turning to leave.

'Wait, Su, it's in the evening, so I'll need to stay back at Priya's. But I'm not sure if the parents will agree. Will you persuade them?'

Suraj gave her a long look. 'You are not involved with some idiot, are you?'

Rekha made a face. 'Do you want to speak to Priya?' She tossed a question back, holding her phone out to him.

Suraj backed off as she had known he would. Suraj had a crush on Priya and the thought of speaking to her was as daunting a prospect as, say, piercing his ear. He was a wonderful brother but a boring one. Not like her Sid, she thought. For a while, she had had a crush on Suraj's friend Roshan. But Sid had soon cured her of that.

She pulled on a pair of black leggings and a long tunic-like green kurta with white paisleys, and went looking for her mother, who was counting a stack of rotis on a plate. 'Are you ready to eat?' her mother asked.

Rekha nodded. 'Amma, I have a seminar tomorrow evening.'

Her mother frowned. She didn't like the sound of it.

'It's at NLS. I was wondering if I could stay at Priya's after the seminar. It would be better than coming back late.'

Her mother shook her head. 'I don't know if your father will agree ...'

'But it's important I go,' Rekha said as she took a plate and helped herself to a roti. She wasn't hungry but her mother wouldn't let her go to college on an empty stomach.

'Is that all?' her mother demanded. 'Shall I pack you a lunchbox?'

Rekha shook her head. 'I'll be home soon.'

In the end, it was Suraj who settled it for her. He told their parents that he would pick her up at 6.30 the morning after and, besides, Priya had been Rekha's friend since Class VI.

Her mother eyed her clothes. 'I like this top,' she said. 'It's smart and decent. Some of the clothes these young girls wear make me want to grab a bedsheet and swaddle them in it.'

Rekha hid a smile. In her bag was a little red top with a deep neckline and a cropped waist. Once she stepped out of the college gates, Sid would take her to a mall and she would change there.

Sid had said that was part of the game: 'You just look sexy and good enough to eat. These guys can't get it up, so you don't have to worry. And you are going to get paid serious bucks just to chit-chat. C'mon, Rex, no harm done. Would I ask you to if I thought it involved any touchy-feely? You know how possessive I am.'

She had snuggled deeper into his side and said, 'Mmm.' They had been in a multiplex. But watching the movie was mostly about canoodling under a dupatta while his hands played with her breasts and he coaxed her to touch his erection.

Sid and she would be together till about 7.00 p.m. Then three hours of chit-chat with the client, who had a late flight to catch and nothing to do between seven and ten. Sid had promised to sit somewhere in the lounge or restaurant to keep an eye on her and make sure she was safe.

Rekha ate her roti quietly. Was she making a mistake? A cloud of yellow butterflies fluttered their wings in the pit of her belly, which suddenly felt hollow.

———•———

Moina stared at the ceiling and thought of the sky that lay beyond it. She didn't know what was above – the sky or another floor. But she chose to imagine a vast blue sky, for only that would allow her to believe that one day this would end. The alternative, an eternity condemned to this hell with no hope of escape, would make her scream and pound her fists and kick her client's shins. The guards wouldn't like that. And their punishment went beyond a mere thrashing. So she lay there, seeing in her mind a sky in which a sun blazed. She had forgotten what the sun looked like. Or the clouds. Or the trees. Or the feel of a breeze.

The client was drunk. That was all she could smell. The stale smell of alcohol and his foetid breath; a body drying from within. It cut through the all-pervasive odour that hung around her, above her and wafted from her – sex, sweat, filth and hopelessness.

When had she last had a bath? She couldn't remember. Was it three days or five? They gave her a small bucket of water to clean herself with. It was left in the corner of the cubicle. There was also the perfume spray she was asked to douse herself with. And a tin of talc. 'The clients don't care what your face looks like when they fuck you. But each one comes here thinking he is having you first ... so don't let them smell a man on you,' the big guard Daulat Ali said. He spoke some Bengali, and so it was he who told her what she must and mustn't do.

Client. Her eyes widened. Five men had fucked her one after the other the first day in the trade. Who or what was a client?

'What?' he asked, seeing her look puzzled.

'Gaard, who is a client?' Moina asked.

'Mokkel,' he said, using the Bengali word. 'All the men who fuck you. It doesn't matter who he is. Black or fair, tall or short, fat or thin ... they are all clients and you address them if you must as bava.'

'Bava?'

'Lover, husband, man, I don't know what ... does it matter?' Daulat Ali snarled at her, reaching across and slapping her hard so she fell against the wall. End of conversation.

Moina had huddled in her cubicle, too afraid to speak. What did it matter, as the guard had said. She would call them whatever she was asked to. Bava. Shah Rukh Khan. Sachin Tendulkar.

Daulat Ali and two other guards she had never seen again had dealt with her in those first days when she had been brought in. They had starved her, beaten her and tortured her in so many ways that she would have done anything to be left alone. The solution was laid out in front of her. She would have to become a khanki. A slut. A whore.

The memory of those horrific days made her freeze. On top of her, the client felt the muscles clench around him. He grunted as he collapsed on her, flooding her with a wetness that she had stopped sensing except as a stickiness in the insides of her thighs.

The client rose, fumbled with his clothes and left. She lay there on her back for a while, cradling her head on an arm. With the other she reached for a rag that was beneath the bed and wiped herself dry. Then she turned on her side and curled into a ball. She sucked on her thumb slowly. Ma, she said. Ma, where are you?

There was a scuffling sound outside the plywood partition that was hers. Another client was on the way. A scream grew within her. Most days, she had as many as seven or eight. On Saturdays the number would go up and on festive days she stopped counting.

Daulat Ali pulled aside the cloth that served as a curtain.

'What time is it?' she asked.

He frowned. 'Why? Won't you fuck if it's two in the afernoon?'

There was a knock on the partition. In five minutes a man would appear. The smaller of the guards, Muniraju, was a local man. He spoke some Hindi and wouldn't meet her eye. It was he who kept the ledger. A long notebook in which he meticulously kept accounts. The clients' names, the time spent and the amount received.

Once, just once, on the second day, when Moina still had some fight left in her, she had padded her way to the open space beyond the four plywood partitions, all empty apart from hers, and fumbled at the ledger. The script was beyond her comprehension but she could read the numbers. She had been fucked by seven men until then and each fuck cost a thousand rupees. On top of each page was a squiggle. She recognized it as something she had seen outside temples in Faridpur.

ॐ

Daulat Ali had slapped her hard for it and allowed her no food. 'That's our thekedar's book of accounts. How dare you touch it?' He had dragged her by her hair to her little hole and hurled her into it. Then he had taken his belt to her. 'You will not step outside this room unless I tell you that you can,' he had said, slashing her skin with the belt, making sure the buckle left its mark. Later he gave her some ointment to put on the welts.

She knew from the sounds that two more girls had arrived. Then she heard a low husky voice. That must be the thekedar, she realized from the note of deference in Daulat Ali's voice. Then two more male voices she didn't recognize.

The second knock. That was Muniraju telling her to get ready. A client was here.

Her mouth was stale and her gudh was painful and sore. Until she got here, she had not once thought about her vagina. But now it was all she could think about. The soreness, the spasms of pain, the violation of her insides. She sat up and hooked the clasp of the bra at her back. Then she went to the bucket on the floor and squatted. She cupped some water in her palm and washed herself. The water felt cold and soothed the stinging ache. She pulled the ends of the lehenga down to her ankles and adjusted her blouse. She reached for the deodorant and sprayed herself again.

Did she have time for a pee? It was excruciatingly painful each time she needed to go, and her body would clench in protest. Only when she could coax her body to relax did the urine trickle out, and then each second felt as if a million razor blades had slashed the passage through which it flowed. All of this took time, and clients couldn't be kept waiting.

———•———

The phone rang almost as soon as the tea-stall owner, Shastri, handed it over to the middle-aged man who had come for it. It was a little past four in the afternoon.

One of Shastri's usual customers had come in, accompanied by another man, an hour ago. They were both taking the bus to Tumkur, the man had said, as Shastri offered them plastic cups of tea.

The other man had kept looking for someone, his eyes scanning the crowds at the Majestic bus stand.

'Any problem, sir?' Shastri had asked.

'My brother-in-law was supposed to meet me here,' the man said with a worried expression. 'Can you do me a favour?'

'What?' Shastri stiffened, a little wary of what might come next.

'Nothing for you to look so worried about.' His customer laughed. 'I'll text my brother-in-law to come here. You just need to give this to him,' he said, proffering a small packet.

'What is it?'

'It's a phone. I can show it to you,' the man said, opening the plastic wrapper.

'No, no, it's all right,' he said. 'It's just that one has to be careful these days.'

The man nodded. He slipped a fifty-rupee note into Shastri's hand. 'My brother-in-law's name is Shankar. And my name is Ramesh. He'll refer to my name so you know it's him.'

Shastri smiled. The tea had cost eight rupees. Fifty rupees for handing over a phone was a windfall! 'Sure. Don't worry!' he called out as the two men left.

The brother-in-law had taken an hour to get there. 'Traffic jam,' he said as he asked for the phone. 'And give me a cup of tea,' he added.

Shastri handed over the phone and was pouring out the tea when the phone began to ring.

'Yes,' the man called Shankar said into the phone.

Shastri pretended to be busy even as he listened.

'My client is a very important man,' Shankar said. 'So we are looking for someone very special too. Good ... Seven in the evening ... What's your name again? Siddharth? I'll text you the name of the hotel. It's a little boutique hotel near the airport. Just Google it.'

Shastri couldn't believe his luck when the man finished his call and left a fifty-rupee note on the table. He watched the man type something into the phone. He pretended to not see him open the back of the phone and remove the sim card within. He looked away pointedly and walked to the entrance of his little booth. He was quite sure that some strange nefarious deal had been transacted in the past few minutes. And yet it had all seemed quite innocuous.

He saw the man snap the sim card and drop it as he walked away.

———◆———

Dr Sanjay Rathore glanced at his watch. It was ten past six. His next appointment was due in five minutes. He frowned. He hoped the man would be on time. He didn't like to be kept waiting. And it wasn't even a client. Merely a middleman, a land broker who had promised him access to the aggregator of the land one of his clients was very keen on acquiring. The clock struck the quarter hour. He had sought to intimidate the broker by asking him to reach at 6.15.

He had seen that in a movie on a flight last week. He didn't remember much about the film or the trip. After a while all international flights, destinations and movies seemed alike. But this had coded itself firmly in his hippocampus. He disliked sloppiness and when people said silly things like 'Keep a memory in your heart,' he was inclined to shake them rudely and say, 'The heart holds no memories. It's just an organ that serves as a pump. Memories are received and stored in the brain.'

All of corporate law was war and he sought for his arsenal any weapon of intimidation hitherto unused. An appointment at the quarter hour was a brilliant manoeuvre. No one would ever manage to arrive at the precise time and he would have the moral advantage of having been kept waiting. That would allow him to set the tone of the meeting. And he needed a decided advantage for this one.

Land brokers were as vicious as sharks, with the tenacity of an octopus, as hard to budge as sea urchins and as slimy as seaweed. Rathore grinned at himself in the ornamental hallway mirror. He liked the neatness of his thought, of how he had stayed within the ocean as he listed out the metaphors.

His eyes swooped on the table in front of the mirror. The stone Khmer Buddha he had picked up in Cambodia had been moved from its place by two inches, skewing the arrangement. The woman who came in to clean was a slovenly creature. It was time to get rid of her, he decided, even as he shifted the Buddha back into place. Then he peered at himself once again and twirled the hair at the arch of his eyebrow.

He was a good-looking man with a strong face of planes and shadows. His eyebrows were heavy and, as if to compensate for them, he kept his face clean-shaven. He played squash twice a week and swam fifteen laps every day. He was considering joining a Krav Maga class to enhance his combat strength.

He knew the impression he made: good-looking, strong, fit and on the go. There was just one thing he could do nothing about. He was short. At 5"4' in his socks, he felt at a disadvantage if the man opposite him was taller. He liked tall women though. He found them sexy.

The bell rang. He switched on the intercom. 'Who is it?'

There was a pause and then a low husky voice enunciated in clear unaccented English, 'Dr Rathore, this is Pujary. I am here about the hundred acres in Hoskote.'

———•———

There were just a few minutes left before the temple closed after the evening puja. He had apologized all the way from the house to the temple until she had put her hand on his arm and murmured, 'It's fine. We can always come back another day.'

'No, it's not fine,' he said, his mouth twisting into a grimace. 'I know you had a reason for wanting to go there this evening, and I shouldn't have cluttered the hour with appointments.'

'Husband, shut up,' she said softly.

He looked at her and smiled. 'Yes, wife!'

She squeezed his arm gently. They had met in school when they were both eight years old. She, the schoolmaster's daughter, and he, the temple priest's son, at a little village near Latur. Since then they had been together, through school and college He had gone on to study further while she waited at home, working on her trousseau until he came to claim her. There had been no one else anyway.

During one of his trips home, they had sneaked out for a bike ride to the Kharosa caves. An oil spill on the road caused the bike to skid; he escaped with minor injuries, she was paralysed waist down. Any opposition her family may have had dissolved when he took full responsibility for the accident and her life. They were only twenty.

They moved to Bangalore a year after they were married. Thirty-two years of marriage and forty-seven years of togetherness. She knew how the hair in each pore of his skin grew. She knew he felt the same way. And that worried her.

'Aren't you sick of this?' she asked.

'What makes you say that?' His hands clenched the steering wheel. 'Do I give you that impression?'

'How can anyone be like you? Every day, and this is the truth, almost every day I ask myself if I have ruined your life, your happiness ...'

'I am the happiest man on this earth. You are all I ever wanted. So stop this silliness,' he said with a mock growl. He had wooed her with it when they were eight. He the prowling lion, she the lost deer.

He parked near the entrance of the temple. Then he lifted her into his arms carefully and carried her inside. There was hardly anyone else there, but the priest was waiting.

He sat her down on the floor against a wall and went back to the car to fetch the offerings.

'Who is he?' one of the devotees asked.

The other man shrugged. 'Somebody very rich. Why else do you think the temple is open this late? I've seen him and his wife here a few times.'

Pujary came back with a platter laden with fruit and flowers, a coconut and a small wad of notes. The priest's eyes widened. Whatever was on the archana plate was for him to take. There were about a thousand rupees in there, he thought, unable to hide his joy.

The priest took the platter from the man. The woman said to the priest, 'Please do the archana in the name of Sharad Pujary, Revati nakshatra, Bharadwaja gotra.'

The priest lit the lamps and rang the bell. He raised the lamp to the deity and began chanting her names, one hundred and eight of them, as he circled the deity's figurine with the lit lamp. Divine powers were invoked to keep Sharad Pujary able, well, prosperous and content.

'Happy?' he asked her as they drove back home.

'When am I not, my husband?' She smiled back at him. 'As long as you are with me ...'

'I have to go to Chennai for the day tomorrow,' he said. Gita nodded without looking at him. She hated it when he had to leave town. 'I'll be home for dinner,' he said cajolingly.

'At eleven p.m.'

'No, our dinner time. Promise.'

Later, when they'd had dinner and he had settled her in bed in front of the TV, he walked downstairs to his study and switched on the laptop and the mobile phone kept there. He sat at his desk, looking for the barrage of mails in his inbox and the log of missed calls on his phone.

The phone trilled. He glanced at it and picked it up. 'I don't want any excuses or explanations. Just give me the report for the day,' he said. His husky voice didn't rise a decibel higher than usual.

The man at the other end of the line felt the hair at the nape of his neck rise at the menace in the tone.

6 MARCH, FRIDAY

The train jerked to an abrupt halt with a long groan and shudder. Gowda opened his eyes and stared at the metal ceiling of the railway carriage, unable to remember where he was.

Then it came to him: Prashanthi Express from Bhubaneshwar, on its way to Bangalore. He glanced at his watch. It was half past eleven in the morning. How long had he slept? He hoisted himself on his elbow and peered down from the sleeping berth. Police Constable Byrappa was studying his mobile phone with great concentration and Police Constable Devraj was playing Sudoku.

Byrappa's eyes rose above the mobile phone and met Gowda's gaze. 'Where are we?' Gowda asked.

'We just pulled out of Cantonment station, sir,' Byrappa said.

Gowda looked at him, incredulous. 'But why didn't you wake me up? We could have got off.'

'I tried,' Byrappa muttered. 'But you told me to shut up or you would shut my mouth for me.' Devraj joined in with a fervent nod of his head. 'Besides, sir, you looked so peaceful in your sleep that we thought we mustn't disturb you.'

Gowda groaned and lay back on his pillow. The PCs ought to have been in the sleeper coach they were eligible to travel in. But he had found two vacant berths in the air-conditioned coach he was entitled to and had organized for them to be upgraded, paying the difference himself. For which the numbskulls, in some misguided sense of gratitude, hadn't bothered to wake him up.

They had got in at Markapur Road station a little past eleven the previous night. Gowda had been unable to sleep till about three in the morning. Once again it had been a wasted trip. And he had known how it was going to turn out even before they left for Markapur. They had received a report of a man apprehended for an ATM dacoity. The MO had indicated that it could very well be the gang that had looted two ATM booths in his station precincts. Assistant Commissioner of Police Vidyaprasad had decreed that Gowda investigate and bring back the accused if he was the one. A sub-inspector could have done the job but ACP Vidyaprasad hadn't forgiven Gowda yet for the egg on his face from the Corporator Ravikumar mess. So Inspector Gowda had to go on a fact-finding mission with two constables in tow. He would have protested in the normal course of things but there had been something else that had to be looked into. And an official trip had been a perfect pretext for some unfinished business from seven months ago.

Every now and then, he thought of it. The series of seemingly unconnected murders, except for the cut-like wound in the victim's throat. And how, by the time he had it all figured out, it was too late. All he needed to do was let his mind wander back to that horrific moment on the factory floor and he would feel again the clammy clutch of fear.

He closed his eyes and held his breath. Slow down, slow down, he told his heart that beat frantically. Seven months had passed but it felt as through the events of that night had just happened. He knew it would be that way until such time as Sub-inspector Santosh was back on his feet, and the murderer was back in jail awaiting trial instead of an accused out on bail and now classified as 'absconding'.

It was a few minutes past noon when the train shuddered to a halt at platform 3 at Bangalore City station. Gowda pulled out his suitcase from the space beneath the lower berth and hurried to the door. His mouth felt furry and his eyes bleary. First a coffee and something to eat. Meanwhile, PC David would arrive with the jeep.

Byrappa and Devraj waited on the platform watching Gowda as he stood at the door of the compartment surveying the goings-on. The Bosco Rescue Unit was just a few feet away from where they were. As they walked past, Gowda peered in. The cubicle was small, crammed with a table, a few chairs and a long bench. A wall-mounted fan stirred the hot air. Two children of indeterminate age were seated and a woman and a man were talking to them. A dog was asleep under a chair.

'The railways charge the Bosco people for the space like they charge a vendor. It's criminal, sir! Twenty thousand rupees a month, I hear. Someone should take it up!' Devraj leaned forward to tell Gowda.

'How do you know?' Byrappa asked, looking at the posters.

'My sister is a staff here. She was telling me.'

Gowda nodded in agreement. Michael, his college-mate, had mentioned it to him as well. Michael Hunt, who had come back to Bangalore seven months ago to sell a house he had inherited in Whitefield, had decided to stay on in Bangalore. 'What's there in Melbourne for me anyway?' he had said when they spoke on the phone two months ago. 'Bob, I need to get out and do something.'

Gowda had smiled at that word, Bob. 'Like what, machan?'

How easily they had slipped into the boy-speak from those faraway years in St Joseph's College. Sometimes he thought that only Michael and Urmila remembered him as he once was. The tall strapping basketball hero who never missed a step or failed to shoot a basket.

'There is this NGO that works with young children. Bosco,' Michael said. 'This isn't the city that you and I grew up in. The Bosco people work with the young at risk and there are so many of them – child labourers, abandoned or orphaned children, victims of drug abuse, victims of child abuse, beggar children, rag pickers. They have seven rehabilitation centres and six street points to locate these children. It's not easy to staff these places or keep them running. So I thought I would volunteer. Besides, I can't just sit at home eating the food Narsamma serves up every few hours.'

Gowda had tapped his fingers on the table as Michael continued to tell him about the volunteer work he was doing. 'Machan, I think you should ask Urmila to volunteer too,' he said softly when Michael ran out of breath.

At the other end of the line, a silence. A studied pause, Gowda thought. 'All well between the two of you?' Michael asked.

'We are fine. But she does have too much time on her hands and too little to do,' Gowda said. 'Besides, it's exactly the kind of thing that will make her happy.'

And give me some breathing space, Gowda thought ruefully. The trouble with women was that they expected the honeymoon to stretch forever. The soaring adrenaline, the excitement, the calls, the texts, the clandestine meetings of the first few months had settled into something more permanent, but sedate.

Urmila, he could sense, wasn't pleased. But he could keep up the frantic pitch, the teenage feverishness, only so long. 'I am a cold unemotional sort of person,' he had said to her again and again.

He saw how her gaze demanded total honesty of him. But he didn't know how to say what she wanted to hear. What words or cadence could he use? The truth was, Gowda hadn't expected his affair with Urmila to last. He had expected that, like most women, sooner or later she would demand he choose between her and his wife. And his inability to do so would end the relationship. But Urmila was loath to even mention Mamtha by name. It was as if Mamtha didn't exist. It helped that Mamtha was a doctor at a primary health centre in Hassan, one hundred and ninety kilometres from Bangalore. A posting she had demanded Gowda organize for her as their son Roshan was studying at the Hassan Medical College and someone had to be there to keep an eye on him. Both of them had known that the truth was she hated the area Gowda had chosen to build their house in. This was her way of protesting.

Urmila asked very little of him except for companionship, and he had thought she would eventually tire of him. Their worlds were so vastly different. And yet, he woke up thinking of her most days; he missed her when he didn't hear from her. It was Urmila he felt protective about. Was this love? He hated categorizing his feelings, so he shut the door on that word.

She had shaken her head almost sadly, watching the play of emotions on his face. 'You aren't cold, Borei. Is it me? Are you no longer attracted to me?' she asked in a flat voice, and Gowda had felt guilt for hurting the woman sitting alongside him.

He took her hand in his. 'Don't,' he said. 'You know that isn't true.'

She needed to do something more meaningful with her time, he had thought then. That's how love survived; by a couple doing their own things instead of turning each other into a project. She needed to have something more relevant in her life than just him.

'You always had time for me. But now, it's almost as though I have to beg to be able to see you,' she had said the last time they managed to spend a couple of hours together.

'It's just that the workload has increased to twice as much,' he tried to explain. But she hadn't been persuaded.

'Call her, machan,' Gowda said again to Michael, knowing that here was the solution to unravel the knots between Urmila and him.

Michael didn't need much prodding. 'It would be good to have someone like her on board.'

Gowda looked at the platform, wondering if either Michael or Urmila was on patrol. Friday was when they came in usually. He looked at the trusted HMT hand-wound watch he continued to wear despite having been gifted three other watches. It was time to go.

'Let's go,' he said, rousing himself and walking briskly towards the staircase.

Outside the station, groups of people were huddled by the pillars of the portico. As David pulled the police vehicle out of the parking lot, Gowda's gaze fell upon a group of migrant workers. Men, women and children with bags, baskets and bundles. Some fast asleep while a few others chatted and a baby crawled amidst the sleeping bodies.

Gowda got into the front of the jeep, Byrappa and Devraj in the rear. He felt his phone vibrate in his pocket. He pulled it out and looked at the screen. Two messages. One from Urmila: 'G, you here?' And the other from Mamtha: 'Reached?'

Gowda swallowed hastily. 'On my way home. Call u later.' He sent the same message to both women. How had it come to this, Gowda asked himself with a little flurry of disgust. How had he become the sort of man who had a mistress and a wife? One who sent them both the same message as if he couldn't even be bothered to type out two separate texts. A great slough of weariness wrapped itself around him.

No one spoke until they stopped at the Adiga restaurant on K.G. Road.

'We may as well have lunch,' Gowda said.

The two constables looked at each other, unable to hide their dismay. 'Sir,' Byrappa said. 'It's been almost five days since we left home. We would prefer to eat at home.'

Gowda nodded. 'In which case I'll take a parcel,' he said, placing his order. 'I didn't let my maid know we were returning today, or she would have cooked something,' he added as they waited.

And again that disturbing thought struck Gowda: how is it that I have become a man who has two women in his life and still no one to share a meal with?

'Sir, why don't you wait in the jeep?' Byrappa said hastily, seeing the sternness in Gowda's expression. It seemed the laidback, almost gregarious and easy-to-be-with Gowda of the past five days was retreating.

Gowda climbed back into the jeep. David put his phone away. I wonder what's going on his life, Gowda thought, seeing a strangely guilty look on the man's face.

'So what's been happening at the station?' Gowda asked.

'There is some good news, sir!' David beamed.

Gowda's eyebrows rose. Unless ACP Vidyaprasad had quit the police force, he didn't think any news would be good enough.

'But I can't tell you, sir!' David said in an almost coquettish tone.

'What do you mean?'

'No, sir, you have to wait till we reach the station. Head Constable Gajendra said I was to bring you back to the station straight from here.'

Gowda frowned. What was going on? They had been sanctioned a water cooler to replace the old one. Was that what this was about? Or had they received a new evidence kit? That was pending too. Or was it the swivel chair he had put in a requistion for?

Byrappa and Devraj came running down the steps and got into the jeep. David, unable to hide his grin, said, 'Shall we go?'

A little fan mounted on the dashboard was turned on. David adjusted the radio controls to find the FM station that played Hindi songs. It was a compromise of sorts. Neither Kannada nor English music; instead, new Hindi songs that sounded like cats yowling while monkeys clanged tin drums. Gowda sat tight-lipped as David sped through the traffic. In the last five days David seemed to have transformed to Ayerton Senna who saw the city roads as his Formula One racing track. When they almost mowed down a scooterist, Gowda finally snapped, 'Slow down ... whatever be the news, it can wait!'

David flushed but didn't say anything.

———•———

It was almost half past one when the jeep turned in through the gates of Neelgubbi station. The green building seemed to be bustling with activity.

Neelgubbi village had changed in the last few months. From a sleepy little hamlet of cowherds and small farmers, it had become one of landlords and real estate brokers. While Bangalore had grown and expanded in all directions, the northeast had remained relatively untouched until the new airport sprung up at Devanahalli and big developers discovered that the possibilities were immense even in villages like Neelgubbi.

In an eight-kilometre radius, a golf village, a thirty-three-floor high rise, a web city, several gated communities and posh apartments were being built. Two colleges and a few international schools had sprung up in the neighbourhood that was speckled with kids from all over the world. Over the weekends the roads were filled with cyclists in their spandex suits and helmets discovering the bliss of cycling through bylanes past sugarcane fields, rose gardens, cauliflower patches, construction sites, vineyards and garbage heaps, all of which existed side by side.

From a quiet outpost, Neelgubbi station had become an important one and the number of complaints that filled the station diary pages often made Gowda think that this must be the crime hub of the city. Gambling, betting, bootlegging, drug dealing, dacoity, rape, murder, burglary, prostitution, and illegal possession of fire arms ... whatever happened, Neelgubbi?

Nevertheless, it felt like coming home. And once again Gowda blanched at the thought: how is it that I have become the sort of man who sees his workplace as home?

But there was no time to brood, for Head Constable Gajendra, on hearing the jeep, was at the door and ushering him into his room. Gowda halted at the doorway at the sight of the person seated with his back to him. His breath snagged in his throat. How could it be?

The man rose and turned. He smiled. A wide grin of joy at having caught Gowda off guard. A white curving scar on his throat echoed the smile.

Sub-inspector Santosh.

The last time Gowda saw Santosh, he had been hitched to tubes and partially sedated to endure the long drive to his home in Dharwad. When his condition had stabilized, the doctors said it was best he recuperate at home. No one was certain how long that would take; there was also the psychological trauma of having survived a near-murder. He hadn't expected Santosh back. He wouldn't have blamed him either, for wanting to put it behind him.

'Good afternoon, sir.' Santosh's once clear and bright voice was now a whisper.

To the astonishment of everyone gathered there and Santosh, who had expected surprise but not such an effusive welcome, Gowda strode forward and clasped Santosh in a hug, muttering, 'I don't believe this! You are here and on your feet!'

The collective gasp brought Gowda back to earth with a thud.

'So this was the surprise?' Gowda asked David. He grinned. So did Byrappa and Devraj. 'So all of you were in on this surprise?'

Gajendra called out, 'Bring it in,' and one of the PCs came in with a box of laddoos.

'SI sir said we mustn't tell you till you reached the station,' Gajendra said, gesturing to the PC to offer the sweet box to Gowda first.

When the laddoos had been eaten and everyone had disbursed, Gowda looked at Santosh carefully. 'How have you been, Santosh?'

'I think I am ready to join duty, sir,' Santosh said, not quite meeting Gowda's gaze. And not quite answering my question, Gowda thought. 'How is madam, sir?' he asked before Gowda could speak.

Gowda was nonplussed. Which madam would that be? Mamtha or Urmila?

'She sent me a get-well card a couple of months ago,' Santosh said, smiling.

'Oh!' Gowda mumbled. It had to be Urmila. Mamtha didn't do get-well cards. 'But how did she get your address?'

'Email, sir. It was an e-card!'

Gowda nodded. It certainly had to be Urmila. But what the hell was an e-card?

'And your son, sir? How is he?' Santosh said.

'Sit down, Santosh.' Gowda sighed. 'Or actually, don't. I'm going home. Come with me. We'll talk there. I need a shower and a shave. And I need my lunch. Have you eaten?'

Santosh looked at the table, unable to decide. 'Sir, why don't you go home? I'll come by in the evening. I have an appointment at the Voice Therapy Institute in Lingarajapuram.'

For the first time that afternoon, their eyes met. They may not have mentioned it but Santosh's husky, whispering voice was a reminder of what had happened seven months ago. The glass-coated thread that had sawn through his throat as it almost strangled the life out of him.

———•———

The boys and I waited in the train for a bit and then got off. I wanted us to blend in with the family groups. This wasn't as simple as it once was. A group of vigilantes stalked these platforms. I wondered if we should have got off at Cantonment station but it was a brief stop of just two minutes and I wasn't sure if the boys would get off in time. They seemed to be sleepwalking. Besides, they would be conspicuous in the not-so-crowded Cantonment station.

A woman walking past us stopped mid-stride and looked at us. She was just an ordinary woman and it wasn't as if she was wearing a uniform, but my boys pressed against each other. I thought of sheep being led out to graze. Not goats, they were too rambunctious, but sheep. Silly stupid sheep who needed to be led and poked and prodded into taking the path you wanted them to follow. 'Keep walking,' I muttered under my breath. The boys continued to walk but they had already given themselves away. I saw the woman call someone on her mobile. At the head of the staircase, two men were waiting for us. 'Remember what I told you,' I said to the boys.

One of the men was tall and burly, dressed in khaki trousers and a navy blue shirt. His hair was short. Something about him suggested that he was in the police or the army. The other man was young and with a small beard. Where did they find them, I wondered, even as the men blocked our path. The other passengers looked at us curiously but continued to walk on. 'Who are these children?' the younger one asked. His Odiya was patchy; coddled from a phrasebook perhaps.

'My nephews,' I replied in Kannada.

'Do you have any identification for them?' he asked.

I pulled out my wallet and handed him my driving licence. He gave it a cursory glance. 'No, for the boys,' he said.

I shrugged. 'They are children. What identification papers will they have?'

'Show me your tickets.'

I gave him the tickets. He examined them. 'You are from Andhra?' the older man asked the boys in Telegu.

They stared at him blankly. They had no idea what language he was speaking to them in. I wondered if I cauld make a dash for it with one of the boys at least. But the man beat me to it.

'Come with us,' he said firmly, grabbing two of boys by their hands. The other man took the third boy's hand in his. They led the boys towards the Bosco Rescue Unit. I had no option but to follow them.

The boys were hungry and tired. I wasn't sure if they would hold up if questioned.

The boys sat at the edge of the black rexine seat in the booth. There were two other children in there. A boy and a girl with coarse hair, pinched faces and threadbare clothes. Their faces were streaked with dirt.

A white man sat behind a desk that seemed nailed to the wall of the booth. He was filling a sheet with the answers the children gave him. They spoke in Tamil. What did the white man understand of what they were saying? I laughed to myself. Then he spoke to them in Tamil. Didn't these fellows have anything to do in their own country? Why did they have to come here and mess around with us?

The children said they had run away from a brick factory near Hosur. Just as I had done, once.

The kiln supervisor gave us provisons for our food but there were a few things everyone needed to buy, and so we were allowed to go to the market once a week. But they kept a close vigil on us even then. Two men were sent along. I had no money to buy anything for myself but my uncle and the others needed someone to carry the goods back. I saw how, after every tenth pulse beat, the watchers turned to look at us. That was all I needed. Ten seconds to disappear.

My boys kept their eyes on the floor.

A man they called the coordinator went to sit beside them boys. He asked in Hindi, 'Where are you from?'

My boys looked at my face. Then Jogan, the leader, said, 'Andhra!'

'Where in Andhra did you board the train?' the coordinator asked in Telugu.

How many languages did they have between them? They were clever, these Bosco people. And they made it difficult for people like me to do our jobs. What was wrong with children working? I started when I was six and look where I got. Going to school was all very well when your belly was full. Otherwise, that was all you could think of: hunger. I wondered if any of them knew what it was to be so hungry that you would forage with street dogs in a garbage bin and fight for a piece of bread that was green with mould. Let me help them fill their bellies first, after which you can take them to school or wherever, I wanted to tell them.

Jogan stared at him, unable to comprehend. These bastards knew how to fluster my boys. He looked at my face again, giving us away completely.

The coordinator asked in a gentle voice in Odiya, 'What's your name?'

'Jogan,' my boy said with relief. He was finally able to answer them.

'So if you are from Odisha, why did you say you are from Andhra?' the man asked in an almost hurt voice.

Jogan finally did what I had asked him to. 'I don't understand you,' he said in Odiya.

The man said nothing for a while. Then he tried again. 'Where is your home? I know Odisha very well.'

'Satpada,' Jogan said. The other two, Ikshu and Barun, cheeped, 'We are from Satpada too. And he,' they said, looking at me, 'is our dada.' And so they anointed me, Krishna, to be their big brother. I knew I had to do the brotherly thing.

'How long is this going to take? The children haven't eaten in two days,' I interrupted, speaking in Kannada. I didn't want to give myself away by speaking in my rusty Odiya.

'You haven't fed them for two days?' another woman asked. I glared at her. I knew all about these do-gooder types. Middle-aged women with empty nests, seeking to fill their lives by trying to be earth mother. They even dressed the part with muddy colours and clothes that hung on their bodies like tents. There was one who found me god-knows-where and brought me to her home in Bangalore. I was seven years old. I became her cause for the season and then I was left in a boys' home to fend for myself.

This one had a shapely bottom which her jeans defined. But I couldn't make out the size of her tits. She was wearing a rust-coloured angarakha. My grandfather used to wear one like that on market days.

Long earrings, bangles of silver and a diamond nose pin. I gave her my head-to-toe appraisal which was enough to intimidate most earth mothers. This one didn't flinch. So I told her with my eyes what I wanted to do to her. When I am done with you, you will be grovelling for mercy. Her gaze dropped. That was when I put on my humblest tone and said, 'The children hated the food on the train. They will be eating their first proper meal when I take them home.'

'Oh,' she said. 'Home food, I see.'

I pretended not to hear the sarcasm in her voice. 'Yes, home-cooked food.' I wanted to slap her across her mouth. See her lips smash and blood erupt.

The boys' eyes darted between the woman and me. Suddenly the man pulled out a wad of one-thousand-rupee notes from his pocket. 'It is very hot here. I am going to get something to drink. Would you boys like some? Jogan, some juice?'

The boys hesitated only for a fraction of a second. They nodded yes. I cursed myself for not having fed them earlier. If they'd had food and drink in them, they would have been less amenable. But now the combination of fatigue, hunger, fear and the sight of so much money overwhelmed them and their loyalties were divided.

The rescue unit was bustling. The woman who pounced on us had just come back with another boy. Didn't these people have anything else to do? The white man and the one called coordinator stepped out with the woman. Only the earth mother was left. I thought of what the thekedar had said to me. All things have their price in this life. It is written in the Bhagwad Gita. Read the Gita, boy. It's all there. How to lead your life and how to get out of a difficult situation.

What would her price be, I wondered. 'Akka,' I said, 'would you be looking for any household help?' She frowned. 'Several of my friends are here in Bangalore and they are always looking for a good place to work at.'

Her frown deepened. 'I don't employ children.'

'Not children. Grown-ups and, in fact, there is a couple. They are from Assam. They would be perfect for you.'

'Hmm ...' she said, writing the number of the rescue unit on a piece of paper. 'Here is my number. Have them call me.'

I dutifully entered her number in my phone. 'Would some money help?' I had to try. She looked at me uncomprehendingly. I added, 'Would some money help to quicken this process? Look at the children. They are exhausted.'

Her face softened. 'This is official work. It will take time. Maybe another half-hour.'

The man came back, speaking into his phone. I heard the word 'shelter'.

I knew then that it was time to switch to plan B. For the flight of arrows begin.

He resumed writing the boys' details on a pink slip. I watched him as I planned my move.

'What did you come here for?' he asked.

'To w—' Ikshu began but Jogan pressed his hand down on his knee to silence him.

'To see the place,' my smart little Jogan said.

'Which class do you study in?'

'They don't go to school,' I said. 'There are no schools where they live.'

The man stared hard at me. The earth mother asked, 'They don't go to school ... what do they do?'

'They work.' I won't be content slapping her, I thought. I would like to bite down on the fleshy underside of her arm.

'Aren't they too young to be sent out to work?' she demanded.

'If they don't work, they won't eat,' I said quietly.

That shut them up.

'We are going to move the children to a shelter. Why don't you ask the parents to come there and fetch them?' the man said. His phone rang again. He answered it and looked at me.

I nodded. We set out towards the entrance where the car would be waiting. Down platform 2 and down the staircase towards the lift.

The man had his arm firmly around Ikshu. Earth mother had Jogan and Barun.

As we descended the steps, I pushed against her. She stumbled and let go.

'Run,' I hollered and scrammed away from the lift. Jogan and Barun stood transfixed for a moment and then they followed me with a speed that surprised me. Who would have thought these little fellows had it in them?

There was pandemonium. Loud voices and scrambling feet. I knew that the police post in the station was on platform 6, but I also knew that there were as many ways to exit the station as there were to exit this world.

We made it to the end of platform 4 and the end of the station. We paused, catching our breath.

I smiled at them. Two out of three isn't bad, I thought.

'What about Ikshu?' Jogan asked.

I shrugged. 'They'll put him in a boys' home if they don't send him back.'

The boys' faces fell. 'You said you would take care of us,' Jogan said almost mutinously.

I touched his elbow and said in the sternest voice I could muster, 'You have to think about yourself first. If you put others first, the world will trample all over you.' They were way too young to understand. So I told them what I knew would make a difference. 'We'll spring Ikshu out of the boys' home. I promise you I will get him out.'

———•———

As the jeep turned into Greenview Residency, Gowda felt a sense of relief. He would be home soon. There was nothing to match the comfort of familiarity: the angle of the showerhead in one's bathroom, the dip in the pillow, a favourite chair, the chime of the clock, the tree outside the window.

The jeep drove past empty plots with knee-high grass and eucalyptus trees.

'It must be lonely without any neighbours,' David ventured to say.

Gowda was too exhausted to snarl a retort. The thought of neighbours and having to say and do neighbourly things made his skin crawl, but it seemed the whole world and Mamtha saw neighbours as vital to existence. In fact, Mamtha had fled to Hassan so she could live on a busy street complete with neighbours and their chit-chat.

Gowda grunted noncommitally. David could take it any which way he chose.

As the jeep drove away, Gowda knew a moment of disquiet, even as he opened the gate to his house.

There was a fine patina of dust on his Bullet. Gowda frowned as he ran a finger along the curve of its petrol tank and onto the seat. Shanthi was supposed to have wiped his bike every day. The car was dusty too, and dried leaves were wedged on the windscreen between the bonnet and the wipers.

She didn't seem to have watered the garden either. The jasmine creeper that wound its way up the pillar at the corner of the verandah looked thirsty, and the potted plants had wilted. Dried leaves lay all over the driveway.

On the doormat were two days' worth of newspapers. Gowda opened the door, perplexed. Where was Shanthi? It was unlike her to not turn up without letting him know. There was a faint musty smell. Of a room shut before the mopped-up floors had time to dry. He opened the windows one by one.

Then he went into the kitchen and turned the tap on. A trickle of water emerged and stopped. 'What the fuck!' Gowda said aloud, slamming his fist on the granite counter. For a moment, he stood there stumped, wondering what to do next.

He dragged himself to the work area behind the kitchen. The switch for the water pump was somewhere in here. He had been one of the lucky ones to strike water when they sank a borewell in his plot of land. At four hundred feet he had wondered if he should ask the borewell operator to stop. 'At this rate, we'll be digging a hole into the White House on the other side of the planet,' he had joked.

The man had stared at him with a blank face. What was the policeman implying? Whatever, it was best to pretend he didn't understand. There was no trusting a man in uniform. But at four hundred and twenty feet, the bore had struck a water table. Water had gushed out with a force that had almost thrown Gowda off his feet. His spirits had soared; it had felt like a personal triumph.

Gowda found the switch and put it on. Fortunately, there was power. Powercuts were part of this new Bangalore. Most homes including his had back-up power but a water pump wouldn't work on it. The humming began. He hoped water was running up the pipes. He opened the door and stepped into the desolate-looking backyard. He found the pipe running up the well to the overhead tank and laid his ear against it. It was a hot afternoon in March and there wasn't a single cloud in the sky but the GI pipe felt cool against his skin and he could hear the reassuring surge of water.

There was nothing for him to do but wait. Roshan had WhatsApped him a word card some days ago. Exhaustipated – too tired to give a shit. That was precisely how he felt now. He pulled out a chair from the dining table. He was hot and weary. He had lain awake through the night on the train and had fallen into a troubled sleep that had left him more exhausted than refreshed. The last five days had been gruelling and it had brought him no closer to tracing the absconding Chikka.

He looked at his phone thoughtfully. He should be calling Mamtha. Urmila would be expecting his call, he knew. However, it was Shanthi he called. There was no response. He looked at the food parcel on the table. But he was loath to eat until he had washed the grime and filth off himself.

Soon he heard the splash of water as the tank overflowed. He switched off the water pump and headed to the bathroom, taking his clothes off as he walked.

Gowda turned the shower on and stood below it, letting the cold jets of water inject life into his weary body. He soaped himself using a daub of shower gel. Urmila had insisted he switch to shower gel.

'Less incriminating when I am here and we need to shower,' she had said. They had stood under the shower, soaping each other, still flushed from having made love. She had sniffed at the cake of soap. Mysore sandalwood. She had put it back on the dish carefully.

He had frowned and appraised her face. Then, unable to help himself, he said, 'You sound like you've done this before.'

She had glared back at him. Then, controlling herself, she said in a voice so cold that it almost made his balls shrivel, 'What are you implying, Borei? I have friends. We talk. Every experience I refer to needn't necessarily be mine.'

Gowda had pulled her to him and held her as a silent apology. How we love is indicative of who we are, he thought. I am that awful cliché that I thought I would never be. A middle-aged man, slack of jaw and spirit, clutching at a straw of hope in the guise of a woman who knew me as I once was. I doubt myself and all that I am, and so I doubt her too. For that is who I have become. A man who doesn't know.

'Say it, Borei,' she had murmured against his chest. 'Tell me what you are thinking, whatever it is.'

He had shaken his head and kissed her on the forehead, feeling a great surge of warmth for her. Love was a word he didn't even use in his head any more. 'I get insecure,' he said. 'I wonder what you are doing with me and then ...'

She touched the tattoo on his forearm and traced her finger along the wings on the wheel. It had been an impulse decision to get a tattoo, and he had chosen one that suggested the open road, the song of the wind, the thump of a Bullet engine, the dream of a lifetime to keep going without pausing. He had had to hide it from Mamtha at first, afraid she would sneer or, worse, prophesize all the diseases he could catch from a tattoo parlour.

'I always wanted to sleep with a man with a tattoo,' Urmila said, straightfaced. 'So you are just part of my bucket list of men.'

He stared at her for a moment. Then he grinned and gathered her to him.

She nuzzled her face into his chest and wrapped her arms around him. 'You give me what no one else ever has,' she said. He noticed that she didn't use the word love either. The shower jet rinsed the soap off their bodies.

A bell rang. Gowda snapped out of his reverie. It rang again. A persistent annoying note that wouldn't allow Gowda to ignore it. He turned off the shower wearily. Who would come calling on him at this hour? He wrapped a towel around his waist and went to the door, dripping water as he walked. He peered through the eyelet in the door. Santosh stood framed in the doorway. Gowda opened the door.

'You have lost weight,' Santosh said by way of greeting.

Gowda touched his chest almost unconsciously. His chest hair had begun to grey.

'And you have been working out?'

Was that a note of approval he heard in the boy's voice, Gowda wondered with some annoyance.

'If you have finished admiring me, may I go finish my bath?' Gowda didn't bother hiding his displeasure.

'Did I disturb your bath?' Santosh said, without a trace of embarrassment.

'What happened to your voice therapy session?'

Santosh shrugged. 'It can wait. I shifted the appointment to later this evening.'

'Sit down,' Gowda said as he padded back to the bathroom.

When Gowda came back to the living room dressed in his habitual track pants and a collared t-shirt, Santosh was looking through a case diary that sat on the table. He put it down.

The beaming Santosh had been replaced by a man whose features were set with the rigidity of a mask. 'He is still out there.' Santosh's fierce whisper filled the silence.

Gowda nodded.

'But why, sir?' Santosh's whisper rose. 'Why is he not behind bars? Why was he given bail in the first place? Section 302 IPC is a non-bailable offence, I thought. Whoever commits murder shall be punished with death or imprisonment for life and shall also be liable to fine.'

Gowda slumped into a chair. He looked at his fingers as he tried to process his thoughts and form the words.

'When we rushed you to the hospital, all I thought of was how I was going to ensure you survived. Chikka was taken into custody. He had confessed to having shot the corporator to save you. Bail, which is never given in 302 cases, was allowed. He had confessed; he was a hero who had saved you, one of our own, from certain death. And he knew which strings to pull. Besides, all of the corporator's property was in Chikka's name. He produced the documents as surety and, given his brother's criminal past, his lawyers claimed that his life would be under threat if we sent him to the undertrial jail in Parappagrahara. And just my bloody bad timing!'

'What do you mean?' Santosh asked.

'It was a Thursday night, if you remember. By the time they had patched you up and moved you to the ICU, it was Friday noon. I hadn't had the time to check your phone. I finally did that evening and went to the PP with fresh evidence. Chikka, however, was out on bail and absconding,' Gowda said. 'The public prosecutor said he had never seen anyone move this fast. It was almost like clockwork.'

'I'll hunt him down, sir.' Santosh's voice rose into a squeak.

Gowda looked at the boy's face. It bespoke a need to exact revenge as much as catch a criminal who thought he had got the better of them.

'You know that I am with you, don't you?' Gowda said. 'We'll hunt him down.'

Gowda's mobile rang. The old-fashioned trilling of a black bakelite phone you dialled with a finger. 'You changed your ringtone.' Santosh grinned.

Gowda shrugged. Then he frowned as he picked up the phone. 'Shanthi,' he barked into the phone, 'where are you? What? I'll come there. Give me a few minutes.' Gowda picked up the Bullet keys.

———•———

Once, there was nothing in Doddegubbi but mango orchards and millet fields. A few farmers lived there, struggling to eke a livelihood out of the land. They grew whatever would grow there. Cauliflowers, cabbage, beans, spinach, snake gourds and chayote that everyone else called 'bengloor kathrikai'. They grazed their cows and in the evening there was the old temple they went to worship at. But the church changed all that in the late nineties with a spate of conversions. It brought people to live in a deserted tract of many acres. Every convert received a piece of land and some money to build a house of their own. The poor from Vasanth Nagar, Lingarajapuram and Vivek Nagar congregated at the land the church had given them in return for converting, and a new village sprang up overnight. It was called Gospelnagar.

The church opened its door, awaiting the flocks of converts. But only a few arrived. Husbands and wives converted but the children remained Hindus. And so, even though a house had a cross fixed to the lintel above the main door, and a photograph of Jesus with his bleeding heart and long melancholic face within, there were also photographs of Ganesha, Lakshmi and Shiva presiding over the household.

Shanthi and her husband had been one of the earlier converts. Shanthi had been unsure about changing her religion but Ranganna, who was now Daniel Ranganna as she was Esther Shanthi, had insisted. Besides, it was the only way they would ever have a house of their own.

A motley group of men, women and children were gathered on the road outside the line of houses in Gospelnagar. They stared as Gowda's bike turned the corner, the duk-duk sound echoing through the street.

Ranganna stood by the side of the road with his hand on his hip. He slammed his forehead with the palm of his hand as he talked to a group of men. At the sight of Gowda's bike, he peeled himself from the group.

Gowda parked the Bullet on its stand. Santosh stood helplessly, not knowing what was expected of him. 'What happened?' Gowda asked with a curtness that surprised Santosh. Gowda, he thought, was very fond of Shanthi.

'I don't know, sir, I don't know!' Ranganna wailed, beating his hands on his head. 'It's all that woman's fault. She is never at home. Who knows what happened to my daughter?'

Gowda quelled him with a glare. 'Stop this playacting, Ranganna,' he snapped. 'If anyone is to blame, it's you; if you didn't drink through everything you earned, your wife wouldn't need to work in three homes. Where is Shanthi?'

From within the house, Shanthi came out. Her hair was unkempt and her face was tear-streaked. 'I am here, sir,' she said, her voice hoarse from crying.

'Tell me what happened,' Gowda said, softening his tone.

'She went to school as usual on Wednesday, sir. It was her maths exam. When she didn't come back by one, I got worried. I waited till two and went to the school. The teacher said she attended the exam but left an hour early on her own. All her friends were still writing the exam at that point, she said. I went to each one of their homes but no one remembered seeing her in the school afterwards. Where could my Nandita have gone, sir?' Shanthi began sobbing again.

'Have you registered a complaint at the station?' Santosh asked, seeing Gowda's discomfiture.

Shanthi shook her head. It was her husband who spoke up. 'We can't go to the police. Once everyone knows about this, who will marry her?'

'She is what, twelve years old, and you are worried about what will happen ten years from now?' Gowda snarled.

Shanthi hastily interrupted. 'I was waiting for you to come back, sir. Some of our close relatives have gone looking for her.'

Gowda sighed. Most people were wary of going anywhere near a police station. Even when they needed the help of the law. 'Go to the station right now and register a complaint. We can't do anything legally till a First Information Report is written,' he said. 'I'll speak to the station writer. You know Head Constable Gajendra, don't you?' He turned to Shanthi. 'Make sure you go too.'

'How will you manage, sir?' she asked as Gowda turned to go.

'Don't worry about that. Let's find your daughter first,' Gowda said gently. 'Shanthi, she will be fine,' he added. 'She must have gone to a relative's house in Kolar. Isn't that where your relatives are?'

Shanthi nodded. 'I have an aunt in Tumkur too.'

'She must have gone there,' Gowda said, starting his bike. He turned to look at Santosh. 'Have you had lunch?'

'No, sir, but ...'

'If I don't eat something soon, I'll pass out. If you don't want to eat, you can watch me,' Gowda growled.

'It seems to me that everything has changed. I was away for just six months but it feels like six years,' Santosh said, gazing around almost wistfully as they rode towards the restaurant.

It was a café-like place with tubular steel chairs and granite-topped tables. A bicyle hung from the stucco-finished wall and each table had a bicycle bell to summon the waiter.

Gowda rang the bicycle bell with an almost imperious note and said, 'Change is inevitable. You can never reverse the past.'

While they waited for the food to arrive, Gowda called Gajendra. 'Have the child welfare officer come in this evening. I need to speak to him.'

Gajendra sighed. 'We don't have one any more, sir!'

Gowda frowned. 'Why? What happened to Manjunath?'

'His father expired and he has gone on leave. I think he'll try and arrange for a transfer to Tumkur,' Gajendra said.

Gowda paused for a moment.

'I think you are thinking what I am thinking, sir,' the head constable said softly.

Gowda grunted. 'Let me talk to DCP Mirza. He would be the best person to speak to. I am sure he'll make it happen.'

'Santosh sir will do a good job as CWO, sir. And it will give him some time to settle in before taking up active duty,' Gajendra said.

When the food arrived, Santosh watched Gowda eat. It seemed he had changed too. Santosh couldn't exactly fathom how, but he had. Where was the man who would have headed to the nearest Darshini restaurant to tuck into a bisibele bath or a karabath? Instead, he seemed to be eating what looked like fat noodles at a place called Bicycle Café. Apart from the bicyle role-playing as wall-hanging, there were no bicycles around and hardly a soul.

'Do you like what you are eating?' Santosh asked. 'Is it Maggi noodles?'

'Pasta,' Gowda said, twirling a strand around a fork. 'It's nice. Do you want to try it?'

Santosh bit his lip, unable to decide. 'Is it beef?' he asked.

Gowda frowned. 'Chicken. But what's wrong with beef?'

'We are Hindus, sir!'

Gowda's mouth twisted into a narrow line. Santosh felt that familiar knot of fear. 'I'd like some,' he said hastily.

Gowda called for an extra plate. He doled out a portion for Santosh and said, 'Don't use your hand. Watch how I eat it with a fork ...'

Santosh stared at his plate of pasta helplessly. Some things never changed, he thought. Gowda still had the ability to fill him with adulation one moment and infuriate him the other. We are Indians and Indians eat with their right hand. Why do we have to use a fork? God knows how many mouths it has been into.

'Are you ready to join duty?' Gowda asked abruptly. A gust of warm air rushed in as the door opened and a group of northeastern students walked in.

Santosh stared at them for a moment and then, meeting Gowda's gaze, he said, 'I am not sure, sir. But if I don't now, I might lose my nerve forever.'

'Countless policemen go through service without anything like this happening to them. It's unfortunate that you had this happen to you on your first case,' Gowda said, choosing each word carefully. 'If you are unsure now, you may never be able to after a few days. For what it's worth, I'll be with you. And ...' Gowda paused. 'I am never going to let you risk your life again. That is a promise I made to myself.'

Santosh felt a lump in his throat. But he knew that Gowda wouldn't like it if he said he was moved. So he said, 'They should have added some dhania podi to this pasta thing!'

Gowda grunted in agreement. He had thought the same but Urmila had almost bitten his head off for saying so. 'What is wrong with you? This is an Italian dish. You should eat it like they do, not smother it with coriander powder and turn it into Udupi Italian.'

'True.' He grinned. He rang the bell again. 'Get me some more chilli flakes and some coriander powder,' he said.

———•———

Moina looked at the packet of food she had been given. It was biriyani again. There was a time when she had dreamt of biriyani – the aromatic rice separated grain by grain with ghee and spice, mutton pieces and the cubes of patato, the whorls of fried onion – but now she was tired of it. Instead, she dreamed of other things: a long leisurely bath with water she had drawn, bucket after bucket, from the well behind her home. Dal chaval and a piece of fried fish and a long green chilli to set her tongue tingling. A walk on the road, feeling the breeze on her face. A full night's sleep. The ceasing of beatings and of the soreness between her legs.

'What? You don't like it?' Daulat Ali asked, seeing the untouched food. 'What does the shezadi want? Do tell.'

Moina felt her heart hammer in her chest. Each time he called her princess, it was followed by a beating. She blinked rapidly. 'No, no, I was just enjoying the aroma of the biriyani,' she said, cramming fistfuls of rice and meat into her mouth and emphasizing her pleasure with loud chewing sounds.

Daulat Ali said nothing. From the partition across came a mewling sound. A girl was crying.

'Oiii, shut up,' Daulat Ali growled, yanking aside the curtain. 'Do you want me to come in there?'

Moina caught a glimpse of the girl before Daulat Ali pulled the curtain back. She was a child. I am sixteen but that is a child, Moina thought. How old is she? Twelve or thirteen?

'Finish eating quickly and you can clean up in the big bathroom. Have a bath. This place smells like a pig sty!' Daulat Ali said as he walked away.

The child is hungry, she thought. She is crying because she is afraid and hungry. Moina shut her eyes tight. She didn't want to think of the alternative.

Daulat Ali returned to stand in front of her. 'Take that girl with you. Show her the lavatory, and explain to her that if she wants to be fed she must do as we ask. No dhandha, no khana. Tell her that!'

Moina scrambled to her feet. There was a tiny stinking toilet at the end of the hall, which was what she was allowed to use. The big bathroom was at the end of a terrace, a few feet away from the back door of the hall. Ten steps away. She had counted. Ten steps, during which she could catch a brief sight of the skies, smell the air and feel sunlight against her skin.

When Moina had finished her tenth standard, back home in Bangladesh, a woman her mother knew had suggested she attend tailoring classes. She can find a job in a garment factory, the woman had said. Two streets away from her home was Noor Tailoring Institute. No one knew who Noor was: the lady who ran it or her plump daughter. Moina did what everyone else did – call the middle-aged woman Aunty. Soon she was Aunty's star pupil. It was Aunty who told her that her sister who worked with a fashion designer needed an expert seamstress. It was Aunty who talked to her mother and made the arrangements. Aunty had paid her mother fifteen thousand rupees as advance against the salary whe would earn.

They had taken a bus from Faridpur to Jessore. Two men had met them there and taken them on a bike to the border. Two men who knew a gap in the barbed wire fencing and held it apart for the women to cross. Moina had looked at the gap and known a tremendous fear clamp her feet. What was she crossing into? It was Aunty who pushed her hard, hissing, 'Do you want to get us shot by those BSF bastards?'

She stumbled in fright. The Border Security Force men were merciless, she had been told. They shot at anything that seemed suspicious – a cat, a crow or a crouching woman. She almost fell and grabbed at the barbed wire. One of the men pulled her hand away, causing blood to spurt from her palm.

Somewhere on that border crossing I left a piece of myself – flesh and blood – Moina would tell Sanya later.

Moina had made it across the border. But after that, everything was a haze of pain. The men had left but there were two others who took them to Habra, where a doctor had sewn up the gaping wound in her palm. From there to Kolkata and a train that brought Aunty and her to Bangalore. They had got off at a station and for the first time Moina felt a surge of hope. The fear and uncertainty that had dogged her began to retreat.

Aunty seemed to know her way well enough. They took an autorickshaw to a house in the middle of a colony of houses. She had heard Aunty say, 'Horamavu'. What did it mean, Moina had wondered.

'This is my sister's house,' Aunty had said. But there was no one there except two men. Moina was too tired to care. She had eaten the rice and dal Aunty had rustled up and fallen asleep. When she woke up, Aunty was gone and the two men had been waiting. They had asked her to pack her things.

'Are we going to the factory?' Moina asked.

One of them nodded. The other one said, 'You could call it that!'

The factory had looked nothing like the factory Moina had built in her head. She had imagined a long hall with many sewing machines behind which many women sat sewing garments. There would be giant tubelights on the ceilings and it would be air-conditioned so their sweat wouldn't stain the garments. There would be laughter and chit-chat and over the weekends, they would go shopping or to watch a film.

Instead, she was led into a narrow street flanked by tenements. At the end of it was a building painted a pale pink that had turned brown in some patches and grey in others. There was a godown on the ground floor, and a staircase went up two floors. There was a curious stillness to the place as they climbed the stairs.

Moina realized something wasn't right. Where were the other girls? The noise and chatter of a factory floor? There wasn't even a signboard. But they flanked her from the front and back, and there was nothing she could do but follow the man who led the way. And at the end of the staircase, Daulat Ali had been waiting for her.

He had led her into a cubicle where another girl stood. They had gazed at each other uncertainly. Sanya had smiled first. 'Where are you from, didi?' she asked.

She had come from Bangladesh too. From Daulatpur. Moina hadn't ever gone beyond Faridpur. That had been her world. Beyond its circumference, she always thought, lay another world which was nothing like her own. But Sanya's Daulatpur, her home and circumstances, seemed different from Faridpur and her life. Sanya had been twelve.

But they had not had much time together. Sanya had been taken a few hours later. She had heard a high-pitched scream and then a silence that had boomed in her ears.

No one had come near her for the rest of the day.

The next day a plate of food was thrust towards her. In the corner was a plastic paint tin. That was to be her lavatory. She had sat huddled, wondering how she could try and escape.

Daulat Ali rapped hard on the plywood wall of the cubicle. 'What? Are you still here?'

Moina grabbed a towel, her soapbox and a shampoo satchet and went to the opposite cubicle. She may as well wash her hair while she had access to water, she thought. She drew the curtain gently and said to the child, 'Come with me.'

The child cowered and clung to the bed she was sitting on. When Moina went closer, she flinched and began to scream.

Moina placed her palm – the wounded palm where a bar of flesh was testimony to the crossing she had made – across the child's mouth. 'Ssh ...' she said.

The child was dressed in what looked like a school uniform. A blue kameez and a white shalwar. A white dupatta was still pinned to the kameez in a V-shape. Her hair was done in two braids with blue ribbons. Her face was streaked with tears and she looked like she hadn't eaten or slept in days.

Moina said gently, 'Where are you from?' The child shook her head. She didn't understand Bengali. Moina touched her lip with a finger to gesture silence. Then she touched her chest and murmured, 'Moina.'

The child gazed at her through eyes filled with tears. 'Nandita,' she said.

———•———

Gowda glanced at his watch. He had twenty minutes to cover eleven kilometres. They were still at Hennur Bande and the traffic showed no signs of speeding up. They still had three traffic lights to get past. 'What were you thinking of, taking this route at peak hour?' Gowda sighed.

'I thought we could take the outer ring road and turn into Thanisandra at Nagawara Lake. I know a way from there to Saharkarnagar. Once we get there, Kodigehalli is not too far. I thought we would get there ahead of time.' PC David thumped the steering wheel impatiently.

Deputy Commissioner of Police Sainuddin Mirza was a stickler for punctuality and he wasn't going to look kindly on Inspector Gowda if he was late for the appointment.

'Is there an alternative route we can take to get past this bottleneck?' Gowda asked, peering at the rearview mirror.

Fortunately, there seemed to be enough space for them to manoeuvre out of the line of traffic gathering behind them.

'There is a route, sir, but the road – if you can call it that – is horrible,' David said quickly. Gowda in a good mood was hard enough to handle but Gowda in a bad mood … David shuddered.

'Just go,' Gowda said, glancing at his watch again.

David turned into a road that led towards Narayanpura. He seemed to be guided by some mysterious satnav located within his skull as he swerved into alleys and raised dust on mud roads. Gowda watched the countryside unfold before him in amazement. A field of cauliflowers here. A field of marigolds there. A stream over which was a tiny bridge. A small temple beneath a giant peepul tree. A makeshift stone bench by a casuarina grove on which an old man sat dozing, leaning against a staff. A flock of sheep grazed while a dog stood among them. Who would have thought such tiny pockets of seemingly bucolic bliss lay hidden just a few kilometres away from the city that was heaving and bursting at its seams? For a moment he wished he were on his Bullet. He would explore these roads one day soon, he decided.

David drove up to the DCP's office with a couple of minutes to spare. Gowda looked at himself in the rearview mirror and smiled in practice. He was ready for all the fake smiles and enquiries of well-being he would have to endure in the brief walk down the corridor and up the steps to Mirza's chamber.

The DCP's room was a paean to minimalism, thought Gowda wryly. A heavy wooden table with a sheet of glass on top sat right in the middle. A table that was conspicuously bare except for DCP Mirza's laptop that was open and humming. Flanking the table on either side were units that he knew held books and an assortment of this and that. A nest of phones sat on top of one of the units and a deep brown leather briefcase sat alongside. A striped Turkish towel draped the back of the chair. It occurred to Gowda that the towel's twin lived on his chair. He didn't even know why it was there or who had placed it. Gowda wondered if that was what differentiated a public servant from a private sector employee – the striped Turkish towel on the chair back that said so much without saying anything at all. Of the complacency born out of job security, the lassitude of babudom, slavery to bureaucracy and red tape. And yet, DCP Mirza was nothing like that. Speaking of whom, where had the DCP disappeared?

A minute later, the DCP emerged from the bathroom attached to his chamber. Gowda stood to attention and saluted.

'You've lost some weight,' the DCP said by way of greeting.

Gowda grinned. 'I've been working out, sir, and I've resumed running.'

'Are you sure running is advisable at your age?' a voice asked from behind Gowda.

Gowda shut his eyes in dismay. How could this orangutan in a uniform arrive just like that? He'd had Gajendra do some discreet probing to check on his schedule for the day and had been told that the man had a hearing at Mayo Hall.

DCP Mirza looked just as surprised and dismayed to see Assistant Commissioner of Police Vidyaprasad. The man was a nuisance and unfortunately had political connections that went high up. Despite the scandal of the corporator case where there had been a great deal of speculation and some evidence of his dealings with the corporator, including steamrolling Chikka's bail, he had sneaked back into his seat with just a rap on his knuckles. In fact, it had made him more smug than before and twice as dangerous. Gowda and Vidyaprasad in the same room was, as his Ammi would say, like keeping a mongoose and a snake together.

'I thought you had a hearing this afternoon,' Mirza said, waving for Vidyaprasad to sit down.

There were two chairs to the left of the table. And it was one of these that Vidyaprasad slid into. He looked at Gowda appraisingly as he sat down.

'It has been shifted to next week. The judge's wife passed away this morning,' the ACP said. 'Bloody nuisance, if you ask me.'

Then, shifting his gaze to Gowda, he asked, 'I say, what brings you here, Gowda? You know, don't you, that all enquiries need to be routed through me.'

Gowda chewed on his lip thoughtfully. What on earth was he going to do? He knew that no matter what his request, the ACP would either turn it down or keep it pending, merely as a matter of routine.

'What about that monastery issue? Have you been to meet the priests?'

'I just got back from Markapur this afternoon and there was a missing case to be looked into. I'll inquire about the monastery issue by this evening.'

'Who went missing? A calf? These rural stations ...' The ACP rolled his eyes and guffawed.

'A twelve-year-old girl, sir,' Gowda said quietly.

'She must have run away to a relative's home. It's exam time, I say. That's what these children do. But the monastery rape could become a human rights and communal issue. So look into it ASAP. And send me a full report,' the ACP snapped.

DCP Mirza took a deep breath. 'Vidya,' he said, using a diminutive rather than the dickhead's full name to soften what he was going to say next. 'I have a confidential matter to instruct Gowda about. Would you excuse us for a few minutes?'

Vidyaprasad's eyebrows rose high as his hairline. 'Confidential matter?' he asked incredulously.

'Yes,' the DCP said in his firmest voice. 'Confidential.' He paused pointedly, waiting for the ACP to leave his chamber.

When the ACP had shut the door, Mirza looked at Gowda who had trained his gaze on a paperweight that sat on one of the units, holding down a sheaf of papers someone had brought in.

'Yes, Gowda, what can I do for you?' he asked.

Gowda smiled. 'It's about Sub-inspector Santosh, sir.'

'How is he?' the DCP asked quietly.

'He's fine. He needs to go for voice therapy. But, sir, I think he's ready to resume duty.'

'So what's the problem?' the DCP asked. 'You don't think he is?'

'He is as ready as he ever will be. But this is a man who has had an almost fatal encounter. So I was wondering if we could assist in the transition from hospital bed to uniform,' Gowda said carefully.

The DCP's mobile beeped. He picked it up and said, 'Let me call you back.'

Gowda saw he had the DCP's full attention. 'Sir, the CWO at the Neelgubbi station has gone on compassionate leave. The grapevine tells me he won't return till he can arrange a transfer to his hometown. So I was wondering if ...'

'Good idea,' the DCP interrupted, smiling. 'I knew I was going to have to sort it out. Santosh will make a good CWO. In fact, there is a smart assistant sub-inspector called Ratna whom I have identified for the assistant CWO post. I'll send the orders out. Meanwhile, they can come in for the orientation tomorrow.'

Gowda rose. 'In which case, sir, I won't take up any more of your time.'

The DCP leaned back in his chair. 'Don't give up on running or fitness, Gowda. I know you are a fine officer and I have great hopes for you.'

Gowda nodded and stepped out. ACP Vidyaprasad stood in the corridor, talking into his mobile phone. A new one, Gowda noticed. The latest iPhone. Where did he find the money for such fancy gadgets? Not on his police salary for sure.

The ACP gestured to Gowda to stop. But Gowda pretended to read the gesture wrong. 'An urgent matter has come up, I just heard from the control room. I'll send you the report by the evening,' he called out, striding away.

Gowda raced down the steps, much to David's astonishment, and ran towards the Bolero.

'What's the matter, sir?' he said even as he ran to catch up with Gowda.

'We need to leave immediately,' Gowda said, clambering into the seat.

'What's wrong, sir?' David asked again.

'I didn't want to talk to someone,' Gowda said as they turned onto the main road.

David grinned. He had seen ACP Vidyaprasad walk in, and everyone knew that Gowda and the ACP were two wrestlers in a ring, sizing each other up all the time. For the moment, it seemed that Gowda was not in the mood to grapple and preferred to flee the spot.

———•———

The Bullet was washed clean. Gowda stood and admired it with the hose still in his hand. The chrome sparkled and even the tyre rims glinted in the twilight. There was a puddle of water around the bike but it would soon dry up, he knew. It was only early March but already summer was on in earnest.

Gowda heard a mew. He turned around, wondering if a cat had dropped her litter somewhere in the premises. He darted a look upstairs. The previous tenants with their dog had been replaced by yet another young couple. A techie couple who worked at Manyata Park. They never seemed to be home except late at night. The mew again. Why would they have got a pet when they were away all day? Gowda frowned.

He was on the patch on the side of the house where, on Shanthi's prompting, the gardener who came once a week had started a vegetable garden.

'You are going to blitz them if you point your hose directly at the plants,' a voice said from behind him.

Gowda turned on his heel abruptly, sending a stream of water all over Urmila. She gasped in shock. He exclaimed in surprise, 'Oh fuck!' and dropped the hose.

She stood on the spot, staring down at her drenched top while he hurried towards the tap to shut the water down.

Gowda came back, trying hard not to grin. 'You caught me by surprise,' he said.

She glared at him.

'C'mon, U,' he said, 'it was an accident. I am not twelve to drench you on purpose. Though now that I see what I can see, I wish I had done this earlier.' He leered suggestively. She glared at him. 'I wasn't expecting you. So I turned around without thinking ...'

'That's the problem. You don't ... I mean you don't think of me. Out of sight is out of mind,' she said, turning away so he wouldn't see the hurt in her eyes.

He went towards her and took her hand in his. 'Let me give you something to change into,' he said, tugging at her hand.

'I am not going to wear your wife's clothes,' Urmila said quietly.

Gowda didn't speak. Instead, he proffered her a clean white t-shirt from a pile in the wardrobe. Then he went to the kitchen and made two mugs of instant coffee.

'Do you think I am such a boor?' he asked, placing a mug by her side. 'I know I am not the sensitive type who cries at a beautiful sunset but I am not a rhino either.'

'Why rhino?' Urmila laughed.

'Its skin is 1.5 to 5 cm thick. And that's how you think of me, as ... a thick-skinned boor. God, Urmila, how could you think I would offer you Mamtha's clothes to change into?' Gowda said, holding her gaze.

She looked away.

'Santosh is back,' he said, attempting to quell the awkwardness that had sprung up between them.

'Oh,' she said, looking up. 'How is he?'

'Well enough. He needs some help with his voice. The injury to his throat has affected it,' Gowda said, dropping into the sofa to sit by her side. 'I missed you.'

She peered at him from the corner of her eye. 'You did? That is a first from you, Borei. I don't remember when you ever said that.'

He smiled. 'When I saw Santosh, I realized how close to death he had come. And it struck me that we go through life without telling the people we care about that we do care about them.'

Urmila leaned towards him and cupped his face in her palms. 'I missed you, my dear Inspector Borei Gowda. Do you realize it's been more than three weeks since we met?'

'Yes,' he said, nuzzling his face into the side of her neck.

She squirmed. 'Don't ... you are tickling me!'

'Do you still feel ticklish at your age?' he murmured.

'Shut up, Borei. You make me sound like I am your grandmother ...' Urmila mock-punched him in the gut.

Horseplay — that was what they were doing, he thought with a secret grin. Did I ever think I would be fooling around with a woman at this stage in my life?

'Borei ... come back ... where have you gone?' Urmila's voice eased him out of his reverie. As he reached for her again, his phone rang. Gowda let it ring till it stopped on its own. It rang again and stopped. When it began ringing again, Urmila sighed. 'You had better take it! Whoever it is won't stop till you do.'

Gowda picked up the phone. It was Head Constable Gajendra.

'Sir, I think you need to come to the station. We've got some information about your maid's daughter.'

Gowda looked at the call log. There were two missed calls, both from his wife. He would have to call her back.

Gowda frowned as the jeep drew closer to the police station. He felt a deep-rooted weariness tug at him. He thought of his bed longingly. It wasn't sleep he craved as much as a soft bed and some uninterrupted silence. A group of men squatted outside the gate under a tree.

'What's going on?' Gowda asked David.

'The boy's people, sir.'

'Which boy?' Gowda's heart sank.

'I don't know, sir. Something to do with your maid's daughter,' David said as he turned in through the gateway.

The tubelight outside the station was switched on, casting a large pool of light. The rest of the grounds were in darkness.

Gowda made a mental note to ask for better lighting of the station area.

Gowda saw Shanthi and her husband hovering by the building. He gestured for them to come in.

Head Constable Gajendra followed him into his room. 'Have someone bring me some tea,' he said to a constable who had tailed after Gajendra.

'Yes,' he said, turning his gaze towards Gajendra.

'Apparently, a boy saw the girl, sir. I have asked him to be brought in for questioning.'

Gowda nodded. 'How old is the boy?'

'I checked. Don't worry, sir; he is twenty.'

Gowda smiled almost in apology to Gajendra. 'You know how it is ... there are half a dozen organizations, both government bodies and social activists, who will descend on us if we bring a minor into the station without a child welfare officer around.'

'Sir, shall I call the boy in?'

Gowda leaned back in his chair. 'Ask Shanthi and her husband to come in first. Gajendra,' he said.

The head constable paused at the door. 'Sir?' he asked.

'Please have this towel removed. I don't want it here,' Gowda said.

Ranganna crept in with downcast eyes. His usual aggression and garrulousness had been replaced by a tongue-tied timidity. Why did police stations do this to people, Gowda wondered. Something about us intimidates people even when they have no need to fear us.

'Sit down, Ranganna,' Gowda said.

He shook his head fervently. Shanthi, who seemed less intimidated, came to stand by her husband's side.

'Tell me about the boy.' Gowda spoke softly.

'He was talking in the angaddi about Nandita,' Shanthi said.

'Why would he discuss your daughter in the market?' Gowda asked abruptly.

'All because of this useless man,' Shanthi sniffed, jabbing a finger into her husband's side.

'I was doing what any father would,' Ranganna growled.

Just then the constable came in with a small cup of tea on a tray. Gowda glared at him. 'Where's my cup?'

'It broke, sir.'

Gowda sighed and looked at the plastic cup. Then he said, 'What did you do, Ranganna?'

'The rascal gave my daughter a love letter. So I thrashed him. And now, sir, do you know what he was saying at the market?'

Gowda gestured with his hand for Ranganna to continue talking. He had little patience for these rhetorical questions and studied pauses.

'He said Ranganna acts as though his daughter is Virgin Mary. If she is such an innocent, why would she leave the exam hall early and take a bus? Where was she going? Now I hear her parents say she's missing. I tell you she's eloped with some boy,' Shanthi said before her husband could speak.

'And ...' Gowda said, knowing for certain that there was more.

'And I thrashed him again and dragged him to the station. That's when his people rallied around him.'

Gowda stared at the man and then snapped, 'Wait outside. Shanthi, I need to speak to you for a moment.'

Ranganna sniffed as he walked out of the room.

'Was Nandita involved with any boy?' Gowda asked Shanthi, not bothering to couch his words.

She shook her head fervently. 'No, sir. She is a child. A good child ...'

'I know, but children these days grow up very quickly,' Gowda said softly.

'No, sir. I am certain. She had many friends, some of them boys, but she didn't have anything to do with boys in that sense.'

'Well then, let me speak to the boy.'

Gowda rang the bell and a constable came in. 'Tell Head Constable Gajendra to take the boy to the room. I'll join him in a few minutes.'

A tall dark boy in a red t-shirt that clung to his skinny frame and a pair of faded jeans stood slouching against a wall. There were several bracelets around one wrist and a glinting silver earring in one ear. The boy straightened when he saw Gowda.

The interrogation cell that they simply referred to as 'the room' had a lone table and two chairs. It was probably meant to be a storeroom. However, it served well as an interrogation room with its narrow confines and lack of natural light. Most first-time criminals blanched on entering it. It was suggestive of police brutality and third-degree torture. There was a hook on the ceiling that was probably meant to hang a stalk of bananas. But to the rookie criminal it was the hook from which the police in movies strung up criminals and caned them. So much of police work was conjecture, Gowda thought wryly as he saw the fear in the boy's eyes. 'Sir, I am innocent. I didn't do anything,' he burst out. 'I am being falsely accused!'

'Aah thoo ... lowde ka baal,' Gajendra spat at the boy. 'Quiet!'

Gowda cringed. There really was no need to get so aggressive or call the boy a pubic hair. But that was what most policemen sought to begin their interrogation with: a large dollop of intimidation by tone and word, and a gesture of contempt.

'What is your name?' Gowda asked.

'Raju, sir.'

'So, Raju, tell me what you saw,' Gowda said softly, sitting on the lone chair in the room.

'I was delivering a package to a house by the Hennur bus depot. There is some roadwork going on there. So I had to wait for the traffic in front of me to clear. That's when I saw her. Nandita, sir. She was in a bus. I knew she had an exam and that there was an hour left for the exam to be over.'

'So you told everyone she had eloped ...' Gajendra said, looking at the boy as if he were a maggot that had crawled out of a cow pat.

A defiant expression appeared on the boy's face. 'Something like that happened two years ago in our village.'

'How do you know that Nandita had an exam and how long it would last?' Gowda asked softly.

The boy dropped his gaze. 'I just know!'

'You can't just know. Do you have a sister or a brother in her class?' Gajendra asked, bringing a steely edge into his voice.

The boy shifted his stance but wouldn't speak.

'Don't make me work on you,' Gajendra said, moving from where he stood leaning against the wall.

'What is it, Raju?' Gowda asked.

'I love her,' the boy burst out. 'So I keep tabs on her. One of her classmates is a boy I know. He tells me everything that is going on.'

Gowda and Gajendra exchanged glances.

'So was something going on?' Gowda murmured.

'Not to my knowledge, sir. But I don't know what she does once she leaves school.' The boy's voice rose as much in anguish as in fear.

'Send him home,' Gowda said, rising to leave. He paused on his way out and said, 'Did you see the bus number?'

The boy nodded. 'It was 292C.'

'And where does it go?' Gajendra asked.

'Up to Majestic ...' the boy said.

Gowda walked back to his room deep in thought. A young girl in a school uniform on her own in the main bus stand. 'What were you thinking of, Nandita?' he asked her photograph on the FIR.

Rekha looked around surreptitiously. The restaurant was plush and the waiters uniformly good-looking. It was a boutique hotel, Sid had said. Mostly used by businessmen. So you don't have to worry that anyone you know will be walking in. Rekha hadn't responded. She had been too overwhelmed by what she was about to do.

Sid had dropped her off at the hotel portico. 'It's best if I don't come in,' he said. 'Just go to the restaurant and wait there. The client will join you. I'll call you by ten. I'll be in the reception lounge. You must excuse yourself by saying it's time for you to leave and slip away.'

'What about the money?' she had asked, horrified at the thought that the man would slip notes into her hand as though she were a whore.

'Not to worry.' He had smiled. 'I've already collected it,' He patted her arm. 'And tomorrow we get the rest, after which you and I go shopping!'

Rekha had smiled at him. The prospect of money to spend filled her with a sudden burst of energy. 'See you soon then,' she said, running up the steps of the hotel.

She glanced at her watch now. It was almost eight. She had been waiting for half an hour and had drunk two glasses of water and texted Sid twelve times. If he doesn't turn up in ten, I am leaving, she texted, and her phone lit up.

Cool it, baby.

'Good evening,' a voice murmured in her ear.

She looked up, startled to see a good-looking middle-aged man at her side. He was almost as old as her father, she thought, a puffed-up little muffin as her English professor liked to say. 'Hi, good evening ...' she stuttered, jumping to her feet. She was not a tall girl, but he was shorter than she was, she realized.

'Sit down,' he said, pulling out a chair for himself. Then he thrust a palm towards her. 'Hello, I am Dr Sanjay Rathore. But you can call me Sanjay.'

She nodded. 'My name is Rekha,' she said.

'Just Rekha?' An eyebrow rose.

'Just Rekha.'

He smiled. 'So, just Rekha, what will you drink?'

She shrugged. Sid had said that she was expected to drink. 'But I don't drink,' she had said. 'I mean, I've had beer and gin, but I'm not really used to it!'

'Ask for a Virgin Mary,' Sid had said.

'What's that?'

'Just tomato juice with celery sticks in it and salt on the rim. Looks like a cocktail but is just a mocktail.'

What was a celery stick? Rekha had let her gaze slide over Sid. How did he know all of this? Sometimes she thought her heart would burst with the love she felt for him. He was tall and had the most endearing dimples. He worked out at the gym so his muscles were well-defined. He should be in the movies, she thought, and sent up a prayer of thanks that he had no such ambitions. She couldn't bear the thought of sharing him. Didn't he mind, she wondered, that she was with another man, sweet-talking him?

'Just Rekha, so what will you drink?' he asked again.

'Virgin Mary,' she said.

His eyebrow rose again. 'Virgin Mary, huh?' She peered through her eyelashes at him. That emphasis on the word virgin – had she imagined it?

Holding her smile in check, she darted a sidelong glance at him. 'Yes, a Virgin Mary,' she said, feeling a rush of excitement.

She watched him as he placed the order. She saw how he twirled the hair at the arch of his eyebrow. It was an affectation, she realized, like the cocking of the eyebrow. He was just as nervous as she was, and something about that made her feel powerful.

'How did you know that it was me waiting for you?' she asked in the silence that hung between them once the waiter had left.

He fiddled with his phone and showed her a picture. Sid had shot it on his mobile just as they left the mall on his bike.

'Oh,' she said, unsure of how she felt. And then, remembering that she had to amuse him, she asked, 'Sanjay, what do you do?'

'I am a lawyer,' he said.

'Oh, where did you study law? I had set my heart on joining the National Law School, but I didn't make the list,' she said. If he had said he was an architect or a pilot, she would have tailored her scope of interest accordingly. Sid had said that she should.

'I was at Oxford,' he said. 'Oxford is in the UK.'

'I know that,' she said. 'I even know London is the capital of Great Britain.'

He flushed. 'I'm sorry, I thought that ...'

She nodded, accepting his apology. She tilted her head at him and asked, 'What's it like living abroad?'

Dr Sanjay Rathore liked the sound of his own voice, she thought as he took her on a tour of the cities he had spent some of his student years in. The waiter brought a plate of kebabs for him and French fries for her. She took a fry and dipped it in the tiny bowl of sauce. She sipped her Virgin Mary and thought, this isn't too bad. I could get used to this. It's like being with one of my uncles ... chit-chat, treats and a gift of money.

——·——

Rathore sipped his Glenfiddich and looked at the girl in front of him. Despite all the innuendoes, Virgin Mary et al, she didn't realize she was flirting with danger. Such innocence, he thought. Had he ever been as naïve? He didn't think so. In a strange way, he was glad that she was with him and not some animal who would have been pawing her by now. With him she was safe. Perhaps he ought to warn her about what she was getting into. The date rape drug was a reality here in India too.

He couldn't believe he was actually sitting here with a strange girl Pujary had sent his way. Or that in the course of the day he had acquired two houseboys.

The night before, when the man had come to his villa, he had asked for a glass of water. Rathore had got up to fetch it, and a surprised Pujary had asked, 'You don't have a servant?'

'I have a maid who comes in for a couple of hours,' he had explained. That seemed to astound Pujary even more, but he hadn't said anything then.

And then this afternoon Pujary had called him. 'Doctor sir,' he had said, 'a friend of mine runs an agency for servants. I spoke to him about you and he has agreed to send two boys to your residence. They will take good care of you. Someone will wait there with them till you reach home.'

He had protested but Pujary had been insistent. 'It is not right that a man of your status has no live-in help.'

That had got to him. It would be nice to have someone tail him when he was home – taking his bag from the car, plugging his mobile charger, pouring him a drink, fetching him a freshly ironed shirt, serving him food ...

'Well, okay,' he had agreed. 'But why two boys?'

'They will be company for each other,' Pujary said as if he were talking of two dogs. 'Try it out for a month, sir, you are going to wonder how you managed before them. And if you don't like them, you can send them back to the agency.'

He had smiled into the phone. He liked deals with exit clauses. In fact, he was beginning to think he liked Pujary. 'Is there anything you can't fix?' he asked.

Pujary's silence had been loaded. 'Sir, you must be lonely,' he said.

Rathore had frowned. 'I am too busy to be lonely.'

'Yes, of course, but take this evening. You have a late flight to catch, you said. What will you do until then?'

'I may meet a friend for a drink,' he had said, wondering where this was leading.

'How about I organize to send someone young and pretty to fill those hours? You need some leisure too, sir ... some R&R as my schoolmaster father-in-law would say.'

'I don't pay for sex,' Rathore had said in his coldest voice.

'Sex! Who's talking about sex? I am not a pimp. You insult me by saying that, sir,' an affronted Pujary exclaimed.

'Look, Pujary, I am sorry ... I wasn't implying anything of that sort. I was just stating my stand.' Rathore had glanced at the clock on the wall.

'Meet this girl, sir. My friend who sets up these things says she is young and pretty. She will make your evening fun. It will cost you just about what you pay for a massage at a good spa. Think of this as massage for the mind.'

On a whim, he had agreed. Besides, he didn't want to antagonize Pujary. The man had access to the hundred acres his clients were panting for. If it went through, it would be a two-hundred-crore deal. And you didn't sniff at money like that.

He had come home to find a tall, thin young man with two boys waiting on the steps of his villa. The young man had jumped to his feet. 'The thekedar sent me here,' he said in Hindi.

Rathore had nodded. He glanced at the boys. 'Are they trustworthy?'

'Yes, sir ... these two boys will do everything around the house for you.'

He looked at the two boys. 'They look very young,' he said, wondering if they were underage.

'They are fifteen, sir. But their poor diet and living conditions have turned them into runts. The truth is that they need your help more than you need them,' the young man said.

He did have a point, Rathore had conceded. It was illegal to employ minors but these were not children. And with him, they stood a better chance of a decent livelihood.

'What are your names?' he asked the boys.

'They don't speak Hindi. Only Odiya.'

Rathore smiled and spoke to them in Odiya, 'What are your names?'

The boys' eyes widened. Then, they fell at his feet and said, 'We are Jogan and Barun and we promise to do everything you say.'

Rathore smiled in memory of the expression he had seen on the boys' faces. Utter disbelief. None of them had expected that he spoke Odiya but he had spent eight years of his life in Bhubaneshwar where his father was once posted.

He glanced at his watch. It was almost nine. 'What about dinner?' he asked.

He made a wager with himself on what she would ask for. If he won, he would see her again, he told himself.

She leaned forward to look at the menu the steward had left on the table. He noticed how she nibbled on her lower lip as she turned the pages. Beneath the perfume she wore, he smelled a hint of sweat. He saw the top of her breasts as she bent over the menu. Somewhere within him he felt a faint stirring. It was ages since he'd had the inclination to be with a woman. A slight hoarseness entered his voice as he asked, 'So have you decided?'

She looked up and said, 'Pizza. But will you share it with me?'

He smiled. He had won the wager. 'Only if you agree to split a salad with me.'

She grinned. 'I will.'

He noticed that she had a mole on her chin. And he thought how much he would like to lick it.

7 MARCH, SATURDAY

Gowda woke up in a sweat. He sat up abruptly, feeling his heart thud in his chest. The power was off and the UPS battery had drained out. He picked up his watch from the bedside table. 3.18 a.m.

He had thought he would fall asleep instantly once his head hit the pillow. And he had. But he kept waking up. The day had been rife with too many emotional eggshells. I am too old for all this, he told himself. At this age I should be checking on the health of my investments, totting up my pension and drinking my Horlicks. Instead of which ...

'Borei, what are you mumbling?' Urmila propped herself up on an elbow.

He blinked, trying to adjust his vision to the darkness that enveloped him. He had forgotten that Urmila had stayed the night.

He had been surprised to find her waiting for him when he returned home.

'I thought you would have left,' he said when she opened the door. It had been latched from the inside.

For an instant, Gowda felt strangely discomfited. Had David seen her? Then he quashed the thought. Even if he had, he knew he had the unswerving loyalty of his men. The handful of them who formed part of his crime team. He smiled as he saw PC David reverse the Bolero, pretending not to see Urmila standing across Gowda's threshold.

'I was planning to, but it's been a while since we had some time together and who knows what you will get busy with tomorrow,' she said quietly.

Gowda sighed and sank into a chair. Urmila had been busy. She had dusted and cleaned the house and cooked dinner. In her own home, he knew she didn't lift a finger except to ring the buzzer that would fetch her minions. Sometimes he thought he was part of a little girl's fantasy of playing house. A middle-aged, sagging-at-the-middle, blurred-at-the-edges Ken to her still sprightly Barbie.

He knew something was troubling her, when she seemed to show no sign of leaving at about ten as she usually did. 'Would you like to spend the night here?' he had asked.

She had nodded. 'I would like that very much.'

And just like that, it had happened. Another rung climbed in their relationship – the first time in nine months they had spent a whole night together. Usually, Urmila would stay on late into the night or come over early, even before sunrise. Neither Gowda nor Urmila had spoken about it but by silent tacit compliance they knew it would be taking a chance. And that this beautiful whatever-it-was between them would fall apart like a house of cards if it was discovered. Right now, Urmila was Gowda's college friend; a social activist who as part of her activism was calling on her good friend's offices; all of that was seen as aboveboard. And if Urmila alone seemed to ease the habitual frown that Gowda wore on his forehead, or if she seemed to enjoy certain liberties with his time or space, no one made too much of it. She was a good-looking woman, well-connected and charming. What man could be impervious to that?

A whole night together in his home. What had he been thinking? But he had needed her to be with him. And it seemed she too had been stricken by that same malaise – a combination of dejection, helplessness, a sense of futility, an abject loneliness. Their lovemaking that night had all the desperation of two survivors on the open seas clutching at each other. A whole night together, spooning each other. A night fraught with strange nameless uncertainties. The only consolation came from knowing 'I at least have this'.

'What's wrong?' Urmila whispered.

'Nothing,' Gowda said. He lay back and turned towards her, draping his arm around her waist. The whites of their eyes glowed in the faint light from the moon, visible through the window.

'Can't you sleep either, Urmila?' he asked gently.

'Yesterday afternoon, two boys I was taking to the shelter vehicle ran away,' Urmila said softly.

'Were you at the rescue unit?' Gowda asked. 'I walked past it. In fact, I stopped by the door ... But I didn't see you ...'

'I must have been on one of the other platforms. The staff brought in a young man with three boys. And two of them escaped. I worry about what will happen to those children now. Jogan and Barun. Those were their names.'

'Don't beat yourself up over it,' Gowda said, drawing her to him. 'They would have been told by the trafficker what to do. And even if it was someone else in charge, the boys would have done the same thing.'

'I know. That's what they told me, but I still feel I failed the boys in some way. What about you, Borei? What's troubling you?' she said, cupping his face in her palms.

He closed his eyes as her thumbs stroked his cheeks with a gentle pressure. 'Too many things. The absconding Chikka. Santosh. And now Shanthi's missing daughter. She is just twelve years old. You know, don't you, that from being a transit point, Bangalore is now a trafficking hub?'

'You are fond of that child, aren't you?'

Gowda nodded. Nandita had often accompanied her mother to Gowda's house. Shanthi would set her little chores to do as she finished hers. 'Don't put her to work,' Gowda had told Shanthi once.

'When did peeling garlic become a job, sir?' Shanthi had frowned. But Gowda had seen that she was secretly pleased.

Just before he left the station, they had printed the missing posters to send to all the stations and uploaded it online. Gajendra had called the CWC home for girls during the day, just in case someone had taken her there, and the Bosco rescue units at the station and bus stands. But they had drawn a blank everywhere.

The fan began turning. The power was back.

'We might as well get up,' Urmila said, clambering over him.

He pulled her down on to him. 'Don't,' he said. 'Don't go yet.'

She lay on him, her face resting on the curve of his neck. He wrapped his arms around her and pressed her into him. 'Nice,' he said, finding something akin to solace in that embrace. 'This feels so nice.'

'Yes, I know.' She nuzzled into the side of his neck. 'When I think of all the time wasted ...' she began and stopped. Borei Gowda, she knew, didn't like dredging up the past. Almost on cue, his hold around her loosened. He slapped her butt lightly and growled, 'Go make me coffee, woman!'

She nipped at the skin of his neck.

'Ouch! What the hell?' he said as she leapt off him and padded to the bathroom. They were using the guest bedroom – again, a tacit unspoken agreement that his marital bed was out of bounds.

He lay with his arms cradling his head, watching her as she dressed. 'Get up,' she said.

Gowda walked into the bathroom and looked at his bleary-eyed reflection in the mirror. The shadow of a stubble speckled his jaw. He ran the back of his hand over it thoughtfully and sniffed at his armpits. He would shave and bathe later. For now Urmila would have to endure his unshaven chin and the odour of sleep. At least he hadn't had too much to drink last night, he grinned. He splashed water on his face and brushed his teeth vigorously.

'They're only teeth, Borei, and not some criminal for you to treat them with such violence,' Urmila quipped to his reflection.

He flicked drops of water on her face. She fled.

He put up the toilet lid and peed into the bowl. He stared at the stream of urine as it tinkled into the toilet. Good boy, he told his penis. You are a good boy to do my bidding even if you have a mind of your own.

'Who were you talking to?' Urmila asked as he walked to the living room where she sat curled on a chair. Two mugs of instant coffee sat steaming on the table. She had placed a plate of Marie biscuits beside them.

'No one,' he said, reaching for a biscuit to dunk in his coffee.

He went to sit by her and they sat there gazing at the skies through the open window.

From within the house a clock chimed the half hour past four. Urmila sighed. 'I have to go.'

Gowda nodded. It was best she left before the tenants upstairs woke up. At least she had come in her Scorpio, which wasn't as conspicuous as the Audi would have been.

Gowda opened the gates as quietly as possible and watched the gleam of her tail lights till the car turned the corner. Then he went back and got into bed again. A wave of longing coursed through him as he smelled her fragrance on the pillow. He closed his eyes and tried to go back to sleep.

He had a seminar to attend. And a missing girl to find.

Nandita shivered. She had woken of her own accord. This was the time her mother woke her up at home.

Her mother would have started the fire and put the cauldron of water on it to heat for Nandita to bathe. Her mother would never let her bathe in cold water, even on the hottest day in summer.

'Do you want to catch a cold?' she would admonish, thrusting a handful of twigs into the mouth of the stove. Nandita detested the smell of the smoky water. No matter how hard she soaped herself, the smell of smoke would cling to her skin. It didn't matter how smoky the water was, she wished now that she could bathe again in the bathroom in her home.

The previous afternoon, Moina had taken her to the bathroom. She had flung a mug of cold water on her. Nandita thought of how Amma washed Gowda sir's car. She would fling water on the car with the same casual violence. 'It will help move the bird shit,' she would tell Gowda when he protested.

Moina had handed her a sliver of soap. Wash yourself, she had mimed. Nandita's hand shook as she ran the soap on herself. It was the first bath she had been allowed after the day she was brought to this place.

The blisters on her legs had burned on contact with the soap. Her legs had trembled. The filthy hole they called a bathroom had smelled of stale urine. The walls were grey and damp. She had thought she would throw up as the water caused the stink from the floor to rise. A dry retching sound had escaped the throat.

'Ssh ...' Moina had held a finger to her lips. 'Jaldi,' she had murmured. 'Hurry up.'

Nandita had been given a rag to dry herself with. Moina had handed her some clothes. A skirt that reached her knees and a frilly top. There were no underclothes. Not even a slip, she had

realized. Nandita had blanched in horror. 'What's this?' she had
protested, peering at the older girl through the sheer fabric.

Moina hadn't replied. Nandita had wondered who she was.
Moina, it seemed, was her only ally ...

Nandita had pulled the top on and the skirt. She didn't feel
safe without her school uniform. She had tugged at the top so it
went over the skirt, offering some modicum of cover. She crossed
her arms over her chest to hide her breasts and hunched her
shoulders as she walked back with Moina to the cubicle that she
had been allotted.

Nandita stood up and peered outside the cubicle. She didn't
know what to expect. She knew, though, that she was in a bad
place. And that the beatings, the starvation, the strange clothes,
the isolation were only a preparation for what would come next.
She trembled again. It was as if she couldn't stop trembling. She
knew that she had no one to blame but herself. She had been
worried about the exams. There was a lot riding on how well
she did. A scholarship had been announced and her mother had
decided that she had to win it. Nandita didn't think she could.
One of the girls at school said she should go to the Infant Jesus
church at Vivek Nagar. 'If you go every Thursday for six weeks
and light a candle there, your wish will be granted. I swear by it,'
Selvi had said. But Nandita didn't think that her mother would
allow it.

'Jesus will not write the scholarship exam. You have to do it,
and for that you need to study. Not moon around in front of the
mirror or watch TV all the time,' Shanthi would have snapped.
Her mother seemed to snap and snarl all the time.

Selvi had suggested the Basilica then. 'Well, what about the
St Mary's Basilica at Shivaji Nagar? She is the mother of Jesus

and will do for one candle what Baby Jesus needs six candles for.'

Nandita had thought that was doable. It had seemed very simple when she thought it through. Sneak out early from the exam hall. Catch a bus to Hennur depot. And a bus from there to Shivaji Nagar. The bus stand was by the Basilica. She would light a candle to Mother Mary, offer her prayers, make a vow of some sort, and catch a bus back to the depot. It would take her less than two hours and she would be home at the usual time. A few extra minutes wouldn't perturb her mother. Nandita had never given her mother any cause for worry until now.

It had all gone according to plan until she had reached the Basilica. She had stood helplessly at the doorway of the church, not knowing what to do.

'Are you alone here, baby?' a voice had asked in Kannada.

She had turned to see a middle-aged woman in a white sari with small blue flowers, the pallu pulled over her hair, standing a few feet behind her. She looked tired, her face etched with lines, her mouth drooping at the corners, her eyes dull. She could have been her mother, right down to the side parting.

'Yes,' she said.

'And you want to make a special prayer to our Mother?' the woman asked.

Nandita nodded.

'Mother Mary isn't inside the church. We need to go to the shrine outside. Come with me,' the woman said.

'What's your name, Aunty?' Nandita asked.

'Mary,' the woman said.

Nandita felt her heart thud. Mother Mary was said to appear to those who sought her with ardent prayer. Was this woman Our Lady in disguise?

The woman helped her light the candle she had brought with her. She knelt with Nandita and they prayed together.

'You are too young to be out on your own,' the woman said when Nandita thanked her.

'I should go now,' Nandita said reluctantly.

'Where is your home?' the woman asked.

'Kothanur area.'

'Where is that?' The woman laughed. 'Never heard of the place!'

'Beyond Hennur, Aunty,' Nandita said, flushing. Her father shouted at her mother every second day for having dragged him to a village for a piece of asbestos over their heads. She looked at the crowded street outside the Basilica, fearful someone her parents knew would choose to pass that way.

'Hmm ...' the lady said. 'I need to go as far as Tannery Road. And I am taking an auto. Why don't you come with me? I'll put you on a bus to Hennur and you can continue to Kothanur from there.' She waved at an autorickshaw.

Nandita clambered in quickly. Now that she had made her petition to Mother Mary, she wanted to go home to her mother.

But she hadn't. She didn't remember much after Aunty had offered her a juice from a bag. She had felt unable to talk or resist and had watched in a sort of stupefied horror as she was taken through roads and alleys she didn't recognize.

The auto had stopped outside an unplastered building. On the ground level were two shops. One had a couple of stacks of tyres and a boy stood beside them. The other had paint tins and cement sacks spilling out of the entrance. Two other shops had their shutters drawn.

She had felt her legs grow heavy and her eyes droop even as the woman dragged her out.

She had felt herself being pushed up a flight of stairs and then they were in a room and she had thought all she wanted to do was lie down. She had tried to curl her tongue around the word 'Aunty' but it had refused to move. She had felt herself slipping away into a grey space where everything turned into shadows.

She had no idea how long she stayed there. Or if she had woken and slipped back into the space. She had visions of prising the bindi off her forehead and sticking it on the door as she usually did, and of her mother holding a glass of water to her dry lips.

When she became fully conscious, she stood up on shaking legs and looked for a way out. A tall burly man had slapped her hard, hurling her against a wall. She had been dragged to this cubicle and left here till Moina was sent to her. How had she reached here? She had no recollection at all.

———•———

PC Byrappa reached the Majestic bus stand a little before noon. If Nandita had got off here, one of the Bosco volunteers would have spotted her. They were very vigilant, he knew. Nevertheless, he thought he would check with them.

The bus stand was not as crowded as it usually was in the morning and evening. Byrappa went to platform 1 where the child assistance centre was located. Ruth Selvi, the Bosco coordinator, looked at him and smiled. 'What brings you here? Work or travel?'

'I am investigating a missing-girl case,' he said, dropping into a chair.

'You look tired,' she said, looking at the police constable who was probably one of the most nondescript men she had ever seen in her life. Average height, average build, average sort of complexion and hair. It probably allowed him to be a good investigator, she thought. He wouldn't stand out in a crowd or draw attention. He would neither attract nor intimidate.

'We just got back yesterday afternoon from Andhra and this has popped up,' Byrappa sighed.

'Who is the girl? Some VIP's daughter?' Ruth Selvi asked, not bothering to hide her sarcasm.

'If only ... this is a housemaid's daughter ... strictly non-creamy-layer case.' Byrappa grinned. That would get her attention, he knew.

She listened to him and looked at the picture he produced of Nandita and then shook her head. 'Very few unaccompanied children escape our notice. We have roped in a lot of stakeholders as we call them – vendors, sweepers, auto and taxi drivers – so an unaccompanied child is immediately brought here or someone informs us. But we could ask around once again.'

Byrappa and Shiju, a volunteer, walked through each of the platforms. The scale of the bus station and the traffic left Byrappa astounded. How would they find anyone here? Accompanied or unaccompanied?

'How many people pass through here?' Byrappa asked in a faint voice.

'About eight lakhs every day. At least, that's what Wikipedia says ...' Shiju grinned.

'Oh my god!' Byrappa gasped.

'Don't look so worried. We rescued 1663 children from here just last year. And a school girl in uniform in the middle of the day would be noticed and remembered. But are you sure she was wearing a school uniform?'

Byrappa nodded. That had been one of the first questions Inspector Gowda had asked Shanthi: if any of her everyday clothes were missing. The woman had been certain that all of her daughter's clothes were at home. 'I would know, sir. I know exactly what she has, right down to the number of hankies.'

'Are you sure you had the right bus number?' Shiju asked.

'We had information that she took 292C,' PC Byrappa said. 'Perhaps that idiot informant got the letter wrong,' he said as a bus drew to a halt near them. D could be mistaken for a C from a distance.

8 MARCH, SUNDAY

Head Constable Gajendra followed Gowda into his room. 'Good morning, sir,' he said, saluting smartly.

Gowda nodded and waved for him to be seated.

'I didn't expect you here on a Sunday,' he said with a slow smile.

'Nor did I expect to see you.' Gowda smiled back.

'It's about your maid's daughter, sir,' Gajendra began.

'Yes …' Gowda leaned forward.

A replacement had been found for Shanthi but that morning she had turned up at his doorstep. 'My staying away is not going to bring her back. And the other children will starve if I lose my job.'

He didn't know what to say. Ranganna must have gone off again on a drinking binge. He did that periodically. There was always a reason. A man had to forget: a slight, a loss at cards, an argument, a death and now a daughter's disappearance.

'How are you, Shanthi?' Gowda asked, taking in her swollen eyes and drawn face.

'I haven't given up hope, sir,' she said quietly. 'I believe my daughter will be found.'

'We are doing our best,' Gowda said. For once no effort was being spared but they hadn't been able to make much headway. Besides, there had been a neighbourhood issue with the garbage trucks and the crime section had been asked to assist with Law & Order to contain the belligerent villagers. And there was the matter at the monastery.

'I know, sir. I know you will do the best you can. I have a request,' she said, peering at the dishes Urmila had washed and putting them back in the sink.

Mamtha did the same, Gowda thought wryly. She examined each dish, plate or glass Shanthi had washed and rinsed them again under the tap before stacking them in the rack.

'I'll need to pick up my children from school. And I'll come in a little later than usual because I need to walk them to the school gates myself. I cannot take any more chances, sir.'

Gowda had handed her the keys silently.

What would he do if Roshan suddenly went missing? It was all very well to speak words of comfort to parents, filling them with hope that a child would be traced. But the truth was something else. The statistics were grim. Of ten children who went missing in the state every day, two remained untraced. In 2012, 617 girls were reported missing. Three hundred and eighty-nine remained untraced. And who knew how many disappearances had not been reported?

'Any leads?' Gowda asked, leaning forward

'Not really, sir. But we know what happened ...'

'Oh.' Gowda sank back in his chair.

'PC Byrappa did as you asked him to and went to the Majestic bus stand yesterday. That's when he realized that we had been given the wrong bus number by that imbecile. It was actually 292D. We managed to track down the conductor of that bus. And we had our first lead, if you can call it that. He remembers Nandita and said she got off at Shivaji Nagar. And she apparently asked when the bus would return,' Gajendra said.

'So she was planning to come back and hasn't run away?' Gowda said slowly.

'Looks like it,' Gajendra said, the worry showing in his eyes.

'So where do you think she could have gone?' Gowda moved a paperweight around. Outside his room, the customary noises of the station house rose and fell. The crackling of the wireless. Low murmured conversations. The loud voices of a squabbling group. The Law & Order head constable shouting them down. A Hoysala jeep leaving the station.

'Not gone as much as taken,' Gajendra sighed.

Gowda's fingers paused. The city had changed beyond recognition in more ways than the obvious. The sleepy city of Bangalore he had grown up in had transformed into a vibrant city luring people with its cool weather, green avenues, its affordable real estate, its pubs and bands. But that Bangalore too had been replaced by a hard ruthless urbanity that allowed trees to be felled with the same heartless ease as lives were dispensed with. This was a city where dog ate dog, rat devoured rat, and everyone would get ahead if they dismissed their conscience as a vestigial organ of the psyche. Real estate prices soared and the city grew taller. Towers of Babel were rising everywhere and men came from all parts of the country to build these edifices that paid homage to human greed. They left behind their homes and families to make good in this city that promised them a living. When a man toils hard and has three square meals, he allows himself a respite and seeks to assuage his other needs.

But this was not Mumbai with its Kamathipura or Kolkata with its Sonagachi or even Pune with its Budhwar Peth or Varanasi with its Shivdaspur. In Bangalore, brothels were everywhere and it wasn't easy to trace them. They mushroomed and disappeared with equal ease. A whole underground city existed parallel to the visible one. A city ruled by pimps, elderly prostitutes and their protectors.

Once, Bangalore had been a transit point, but now it was the destination. Girls were trafficked from Bangladesh and Bengal; young girls from the poorer districts of the state – Gulbarga and Raichur – were picked up by recruiters. And not all of the recruiters were prostitutes too old to sell themselves. They could be anyone. A woman who sat next to you on a bus or a woman who stood in the line behind you at the temple. It wasn't anyone you expected; it was everyone you didn't.

'PC Byrappa is at Shivaji Nagar this morning. I am hoping, sir, that he will be able to get some more information,' Head Constable Gajendra said, rising to leave.

Gowda looked at the station diary. He had spent all of the previous day at a seminar on cyber crime that he had been deputed to attend. It was more Santosh's forte. What the boy didn't know about the cyber world could be written on the back of a bus ticket. Gowda didn't think he would ever be able to handle a cyber crime case. It required specialist knowledge and an understanding of the machinations of the cyber world. But he had made some useful contacts over lunch.

He frowned, looking at the number of complaints. Crime had risen in the city and so had the crime rate in Neelgubbi.

There was a knock on the door. Gowda raised his head to see Santosh standing at the door. With him was a young woman. They were both in everyday clothes and they looked as though they were familiar with each other. Watching Santosh dart a small smile at the woman, Gowda thought, has he got engaged? Then he remembered. This must be Assistant Child Welfare Officer Ratna.

The two of them saluted Gowda. They still hadn't mastered the real-life salute, Gowda thought with a secret grin. There was a language of salutes: the sir-I-am-reporting-for-duty earnest one to the right-I-know-you-are-my-superior-but-it's-only-a-matter-of-rank cursory one to the I-don't-give-a-fuck disdainful one. This one smacked of I-am-happy-I-am-here-and-can-you-please-send-me-off-to-do-something?

Gowda looked at the two of them and thought, when did I get to be like this - an elderly uncle? 'Congratulations, CWO Santosh,' he said, smiling, and turned to the young woman. 'And ACWO Ratna.'

She blushed. Santosh looked at her with concern. And Gowda almost groaned. The boy was smitten.

'How was the training session?' he asked, trying to interject a business-like tone to the meeting.

'Very good, sir,' Santosh said, sitting down.

Assistant Sub-inspector Ratna hesitated for a moment, then sat herself down gingerly. She looked at Gowda, studying him as surreptitiously as she could. There was quite a bit of talk about him in the ranks, and mostly contradictory. She had heard he was an astute IO. Afraid of no one and nothing.

Santosh wouldn't stop talking about him. But there had been others as well. 'If you want to understand what crime investigation is all about, you need to work with him,' an admirer had said. 'I have seen that king-sense at work. Phew! He just looks at what all of us may have dug up and tells us what we missed. And that's the thing that solves the case,' another admirer had murmured in a hushed voice.

'If he is so good, why is he still an inspector? He should have been at least an ACP by now,' the dissenters said. 'Bloody arrogant bastard,' someone had murmured. 'A lazy old drunk,' someone else said. 'Clueless fool! Why can't he look the other way even if he doesn't want a share of the takings?' a voice had added.

So which one of all those descriptions was Borei Gowda, Ratna Patil wondered, taking in the wide, open face and the slight sag in the jawline. He was a big-built man, tall and probably once muscular. But now the edges were blunted and there was a certain weariness in his eyes. And, almost contrarily, there was a saucy dimple on his chin. A hint of insouciance, as though all of him hadn't settled into middle age yet.

'What about you?' Gowda's voice cut into her reverie.

She looked at him blankly for a moment. Gowda's eyes narrowed. It was quite possible she had been told a whole lot of rubbish about him and she was trying to separate for herself the truth from slander.

'Yes, sir, it was very informative,' she said.

'We have a case that I think is going to require the two of you to team up. A twelve-year-old girl, Nandita, has been missing since Wednesday,' Gowda began.

'Sir, Shanthi's daughter is still missing?' Santosh interrupted. Turning to Ratna, he added, 'Shanthi is sir's maid. She ...'

Gowda glared at him and Santosh stopped mid-sentence.

'My maid's daughter, yes, but that's irrelevant. Byrappa traced her till Shivaji Nagar. Gajendra will brief you on what the investigation has revealed until now.'

The phone rang. Gowda picked it up. 'Good morning, sir,' he said. Santosh watched Gowda's face settle into one of exasperated amusement as he listened to what was being told to him. 'Yes, sir. That's wonderful news indeed. And thank you so much for your consideration. Of course I will tell him.' Gowda's eyes met Santosh's when he put down the phone. He said, 'That was ACP Vidyaprasad. He wanted me to know that he had you assigned as CWO so that he can ease your transition from hospital bed to uniform.'

'He's a bloody baboon in uniform. I know you're the one who organized it, and those are your words. DCP Mirza told me that's what you said,' Santosh said, not bothering to hide his outrage.

Gowda shrugged while Ratna looked on with great interest. She was yet to meet the baboon. She cleared her throat. 'What about talking to her friends?' she asked softly.

'We were waiting for you to talk to the children. That's the first thing you need to do this morning. We need to work in tandem. And Santosh, you will be assistant investigating officer on this case,' Gowda said, rising.

They stood up hurriedly.

'Where do you think he is going?' Ratna asked, watching Gowda walk towards his bike. 'Some personal work? He is not in uniform.'

Santosh shook his head. 'I don't think so.' He watched Gowda put on his helmet. I wonder why he didn't ask me to go along, Santosh thought. Once he would have. Santosh felt a wave of dejection sweep through him as Gowda mounted his monster and rode away. Does he think I am no longer fit to do the job? Maybe that's why I've been given this sop – child welfare officer. To handle crimes against children and crimes by children. That's unlikely to get me into any life-and-death situations.

'I don't know what you are thinking, but your face seems to be going through the entire range of navarasas, one after the other,' Ratna said with a little laugh.

Santosh frowned. 'Are you going to stand here discussing my expressions or are we going to get some work done?'

Head Constable Gajendra, who was standing in the vicinity, darted a look at him in amusement. The boy seemed to have absorbed Gowda's brusqueness and made it his own.

Ratna sniffed and tossed her head. Bewarsi, she thought, choosing a mild term of abuse from the several she had learnt from her older brother while still in school. But calling someone a bastard seemed too innocuous, and so for good measure she added another epithet: Arsehole!

Santosh had seemed a decent sort but there was no knowing when men turned into obnoxious creatures. Men and serpents, her aunt used to say, cold-blooded reptiles you can never trust.

Gowda felt a note slip. The Bullet was not an easy mistress. From the smooth arc of her petrol tank to the mudguard that curved just a little over the back wheel, she was a beauty but with a temper. When she was happy, she filled the streets with her distinctive growl, a tigress on the road, her thump-thump echoing her pleasure: 41.3 Nm of torque. Again that slip in timing. He frowned and decided it was time he took her to Kumar. It was only a matter of engine tuning before she was queen again. 'Won't you, Rani?' he asked the bike. The Bullet growled and took the curve with the ease of a heated knife cutting through butter.

Gowda turned towards Shivaji Nagar. He knew that PC Byrappa was here and that soon Santosh would arrive, bringing with him a couple of men. But somewhere in him a voice whispered, what if they left something unchecked? What if they overlooked a contact? What if they are unable to read the pause, the middle-distance gaze, the synapse between truth and a veiled lie?

He parked the bike under a tree and walked with his helmet to a bag shop he knew. Syed, sitting behind the cash counter, looked up and smiled. It was a cautious smile. Gowda on the prowl wasn't good news. At least he wasn't in uniform, he thought.

'Good morning, sir,' Syed said, rising. He waved for his sales boy to bring a chair.

'How is business?' Gowda asked, planting himself in the chair.

'Dull, sir. The schools will close soon and who buys bags then?' Syed affected a weary sigh.

Gowda's eyes narrowed. Syed's bag shop was a front for many things, none of which were illegal, but they weren't entirely legitimate either. He was a fixer. He knew whom to call to facilitate the movement of a file through a bureaucratic corridor; he knew people who could beat up or even kill someone who was proving to be a nuisance; he could help you get dollars or dinars; he would find you a house to rent or transfer a lease; he would organize admission in a school or college and at a pinch get you a ticket on a train that was so full that the waitlist stretched longer than the train. All of this necessitated money or a favour in exchange, but Syed wasn't a criminal. He called himself a humanitarian. That's why people came to him, he said. Syed was as careful as he was astute. So he stayed beyond the reach of the arm of law.

'Any new girls in the whorehouse?' Gowda asked as though he were asking the price of a black bag on which the legend NIKE was stitched.

Syed blinked. 'Sir?' he asked, unable to keep the surprise out of his face and voice.

'You heard me,' Gowda said, tapping a finger on the side of the helmet. 'Has anyone brought a new girl into the whorehouse in the market?'

'There's no brothel in this area, sir.' Syed shook his head. 'That's just a myth.'

'A myth?' Gowda enunciated carefully.

Syed felt a tiny chill run down his spine. With Gowda, one never knew what came next. He was quite capable of organizing a lightning raid or just slamming Syed's face down on the glass top of his table with one swift move.

'It's not really a brothel, sir,' Syed said, trying to wriggle out of the corner.

'Not really a brothel? So what do the girls do there? Play hopscotch?' Gowda's mouth was harder than the granite block that Syed rested his feet on under the table.

'Well, sir, a brothel would mean a place that houses many girls for customers to visit. And ...'

'So you are stating that there are no girls and that no men come to them for sex?' Gowda interrupted abruptly.

'No, I didn't say that,' Syed blurted out, wondering whose face he had seen first thing in the morning. The day didn't seem to be going well at all.

'Syed, cut the crap,' Gowda said quietly. 'Right now I am not here to check on the brothel. What I want to know is if a new girl has been brought in. A young girl ...'

'Sir, many young girls are brought into the profession every day,' Syed began but something about Gowda's face stilled his words. He looked away and then turned his face towards the policeman.

Syed held Gowda's gaze. 'How young?'

'Twelve,' Gowda said.

Syed shook his head. 'No,' he said.

'And you would know if such a child had been brought in?' Gowda asked.

Syed took a deep breath. 'Yes,' he said. 'I don't like it any more than you do. But a twelve-year-old is not an everyday occurrence. A feast for the vultures. Old, pot-bellied balding vultures who like young morsels. I would have heard.'

Gowda rubbed his temple thoughtfully. 'We traced her up to the Shivaji Nagar bus terminus.'

'Is she a Christian girl?' Syed asked.

'Yes. Why?' Gowda frowned.

'Sir, it's exam time. That's when every student becomes extra religious and if she is Christian, she may have come to the Basilica. It's only a ten-minute walk from the bus stand.'

Gowda looked at Syed thoughtfully. He did have a point. Nandita wore a little silver crucifix and Shanthi said the girl liked going to church.

Recruiters came in all shapes and sizes. She didn't always have to be the painted-up version of the madam from the movies. She could be your mother's best friend, a random stranger at a wedding, or the woman who knelt next to you as you prayed.

'There's a watchman there. It's not an official post, you understand, but he helps people park their vehicles if the parking lot is full, and so on. Robert – that's his name. Why don't you ask him, sir? He may have seen the girl.'

'Why would he remember?' Gowda asked curiously.

'He does. He has a prodigious memory. And he is a bloody lech! He will look at anything that has a cloth wound around its legs. And trust me, he will remember.'

Gowda nodded and rose. 'Thanks,' he said softly.

Syed raised his palm and placed it on his chest. In the scorecard of favours, Gowda owed him one.

As a further half-favour, he sent his boy with Gowda. 'Robert knows Imran is with me,' Syed said. 'He is an incorrigible old man and has no family of his own. I slip him a fifty every now and then. What can I say? He is useful ...' Syed added, seeing Gowda's questioning look. 'And that will open Robert's mouth.'

Robert's mouth, Gowda thought, seemed to be stuck around a wad of tobacco. He took in the bald old man in a faded blue shirt, grey trousers and battered plastic slippers.

'Uncle,' Imran called out.

How old was the boy, Gowda wondered. He knew what Syed's answer would be if he queried. 'But, sir, he's my nephew. Can't a nephew assist his uncle in his shop?'

'Uncle,' Imran said, touching the old man's elbow. 'Mamu sent him to you!'

Robert peered at Gowda. 'You are a policeman,' he said softly. Gowda nodded. 'I can tell,' the old man said. 'I can tell a policeman anywhere.'

Gowda leaned forward. 'Where were you in service? You are not from here ...'

Robert allowed Gowda a half-smile. 'Tamil Nadu police. Head Constable Robert Rajasekharan.'

'And?'

'And nothing. Now I am Robert. Worker of the Mother and the church,' Robert said firmly.

What had the old man done, Gowda wondered. Had he been hounded out of town or had he chosen to exile himself?

'Don't bother speculating about me, Inspector. My presence here is irrelevant. But you need something from me. That's why you are here,' Robert said slowly, leaning against a pillar.

'A young girl has been missing since last week. We traced her up to Shivaji Nagar. The bus conductor said she got off here,' Gowda said. Then he added, 'She is a Christian girl. A Catholic. So it's quite possible that she came here.'

'Lots of young girls come here.'

'Yes, I know. But this girl was in a school uniform. A blue kameez and a white salwar. Her hair was in two braids with blue ribbons.' Gowda opened his phone and scrolled the gallery section. Nandita's picture from the FIR was saved in there. He held it towards the old man.

Robert took the phone in his hands and held it at arm's length. 'Hmm ... yes ... I remember. Not the face, to be honest, but the sight of a girl in a uniform. How old did you say she was?'

'I didn't. But she is twelve,' Gowda said, feeling a sudden dislike for the old man.

'Her face is that of a child's but her body is that of a sixteen-year-old. Plump as a broiler chicken.' Robert laughed. Imran sniggered.

Gowda glared at the two of them but bit back his retort. 'So you did see her here?' he asked instead. A steady trickle of devotees went in and out of the Basilica. Women and men of all ages, shapes and sizes.

'She must have come here by about noon. At least that was when I saw her. I remember because I had arranged to meet someone at the gate here. I was waiting for him when I saw her go into the church. A girl in a uniform. When she came out, there was a woman with her. A middle-aged woman,' Robert said thoughtfully.

Gowda felt his heart sink. It was exactly as he had feared.

'I presumed it was the girl's mother. And meanwhile my man arrived.'

'Would you remember the woman's face?' Gowda asked, quite sure what the answer would be.

'Not really.' Robert's face twisted. 'A nondescript woman. No one would look at her twice. And neither did I.'

'Oh,' Gowda said, wanting to slam his fist into something in frustration.

'I did see them again, when they were leaving after lighting candles at the chapel. An auto appeared almost on cue. They got into it and left,' Robert said.

'Do you remember anything about the auto?' Gowda asked.

Robert shook his head and suddenly stopped. 'It was a private autorickshaw and the body was painted a dark blue. It had the picture of a sunset on the back ... that's about it!'

'Teja bhai has an auto like that.' Imran, who had been listening in, piped up eagerly, his voice shrill with excitement. And then he stopped. Syed Mamu would strangle him for this, he realized. 'Keep that mouth shut and ears open,' he told Imran five times a day. 'Or you will get yourself and all of us in trouble.'

'Er ... no ... I got that wrong,' Imran said quickly, trying to correct his slip. 'Teja bhai has a green auto and the photo on the back is of the Taj Mahal.'

Gowda smiled. 'Oh, that's a pity. For a moment I thought you had solved the case.'

Imran's eyes darted this way and that. 'I have to go.'

'Who's Teja bhai?' Gowda asked, popping a note into the boy's pocket.

'Syed Mamu's cousin,' the boy said as he fled.

Robert wondered if he should tell Syed what had happened. Then he shrugged and walked away. None of his buisness.

———•———

I went to the godown in the evening. It was in Sampigehalli. I was yet to see a single champak tree, let alone smell its heavy fragrance. In fact, there were few trees here. Just narrow alleys of dirty tenements a little further from Thanisandra. The godown was a perfect cover. All day, workers stepped in and out. No one was going to notice the difference between a worker and a client climbing the stairs. We called it the godown so that we didn't give ourselves away. I had money in my pocket and it had been some days since I had a woman.

Daulat Ali whickered like a horse when he saw me. 'Look who is here! The chhote nawab himself!'

That was his name for me. The little prince. The thekedar was the boss. And everywhere the thekedar went, I went too. I was the thekedar's eyes and ears; sometimes his arms and weapon of destruction. The thekedar said that to me. 'You are like my discus, Krishna. You are what I send out when I need my path cleared.'

I liked that image of myself. A CD-like discus flying through the air, slicing everything and everyone in its path to reach its destination. I liked to think I was both focused and ruthless. Like the thekedar.

They knew I had the run of the godown. Any girl I chose was mine to have. I grinned and slapped Daulat Ali on his beefy arms. The man was built like a hippo but his size was misleading. He was strong and light on his feet. Apparently, he used to be a wrestler and had trained at the Kale Pehalwan Ki Gardi in Shivaji Nagar.

'So what do you have for me? A nice plump shami kebab?' I joked.

He dropped his voice. 'There is a girl. A little houri yet to be broken. But the thekedar has said that she is to be put into the trade only when he says so.'

I shrugged. That was the usual practice. And I didn't particularly care to bed an inexperienced girl. There were men who got their kicks from women screaming and protesting. Not me. I liked them pliant and willing.

'Is Moina free?' I asked. Daulat Ali nodded. 'Tell her to bathe first,' I said. There were men who didn't care about all that. A woman was just a hole for them to stick their cocks into. They didn't care who she had fucked before and who she would fuck after. Neither did I. But I didn't like smelling another man on the woman I was fucking. 'And ask her to wash her hair and behind her neck; and to shave her armpits,' I added.

Daulat Ali stared at me. 'Do you want me to scrub her back and paint her nails too?' he asked, making a face.

'I wouldn't mind.' I grinned.

'Fuck off,' he said, cheerily walking towards the cubicle.

It took Moina some time to be ready for me. But I didn't mind the wait. I put my feet up on a chair and flicked open and shut my lighter a few times. I wondered how the two boys Jogan and Barun were doing. It was still too early to tell. At this point, both the lawyer and the boys would be tiptoeing around each other like they were stepping on eggshells. I would know when that call came. And it would in a day or two. I closed my eyes.

Moina sat with her head bent demurely as I entered the cubicle. She had even lit two sticks of incense, which swamped the odour of sweat, grime and sex.

'Do you have a dupatta?' I asked.

She looked up then. I saw the fear in her eyes. I could see she was wondering what I needed it for. She nodded slowly.

'Spread it on the bed.'

She stood up and rummaged in a carton under the bed. She had a yellow and red cotton dupatta. It was narrow and didn't cover the bed but it was enough. I saw her look at it forlornly.

'I'll get you another one,' I said on an impulse. 'But make sure you use this only when I am here.'

A small smile lit up her face. 'So you do know how to smile,' I said, lying down on the bed. 'Take your clothes off.'

That was when I heard the whimpering.

'Who is that?' I asked.

'A new girl,' Moina said, pulling her blouse over her head. She was sixteen or so but already her tits were sagging and there was a hardness around her mouth.

'Daulat Ali's houri.' I laughed.

'Is that what he said?' She snorted. 'She is a child. They brought her here dressed in a school uniform.'

'Ask her to shut up,' I snapped.

Moina tugged the curtain aside and went across. A moment later, the whimpering stopped.

'Aren't you taking your clothes off?' Moina asked when she came back.

I crossed my hands behind my head and stared at her. 'You undress me,' I said.

When we were done, I felt a strange sense of dissatisfaction. The whimpering from across the cubicle had resumed.

I dressed hastily, flung two hundred-rupee notes as a tip for Moina and stepped out. On an impulse, I pulled aside the curtain of the cubicle where the houri child was.

She sat crouched in a corner with her knees to her chest. There were tear stains on her face and welts on her calves. Moina was right. She was a child. But most of them were children when they came there.

I didn't know what it was about the girl, but I wanted to be with her. I knew I would not be able to think of anything but her face now.

9 MARCH, MONDAY

Sid stepped out of the ATM. His account balance had been at an all-time low but Rekha's evening with the lawyer had made him flush for now. He hadn't told her the exact amount he had been paid. He had kept most of it for himself and would give her some of it to splash around.

Diagonally opposite the ATM was the college Rekha went to. She had classes till four. She used to like it when he popped in at the canteen and surprised her. But she hadn't sounded pleased when he said he was waiting for her at the college gates. He didn't understand what had changed over the weekend. Rekha didn't message him any more like she used to. He was certain that she was keeping something from him. He glanced at his phone to see if she had messaged.

From the corner of his eye, he saw the cucumber seller push his cart closer to him. He seemed to have added pineapples in a glass case to his wares. The man took a pineapple and began to cut away the shell. 'So it worked out all right last time?' he asked from the corner of his mouth.

Sid leaned forward on his bike, slouching over the petrol tank. 'Yes,' he said.

'There's another one coming up,' the man said, his sharp knife separating the shell from the flesh of the fruit evenly. In about six strokes, the pineapple was shorn of its bristly shell. Sid watched in fascination as the knife sliced through the flesh.

'Are you up to it?' he asked, not lifting his eyes from the fruit he was cutting into discs.

'Same like last time?' Sid asked, tempted by the thought of the money.

'No, more,' the man said, sprinking a few grains of white dust on the pineapple.

'What's that?' Sid asked.

'Salt ... what did you think? Meow meow?' The man grinned. 'Though now that you have put the thought into my head, it may be worth trying ... I hear the White Magic is a big hit in Mumbai. Everybody is into it.'

Sid shuddered. He would think twice about buying fruit from these fellows.

The man began stacking the pineapple slices into the glass box. 'The only thing is, these guys speak English which is beyond me. So I'll give you a number and you could call them ...'

The man pulled his phone out from beneath the plastic sheet on the cart and scrolled through it. He mumbled a number. Sid entered the number in his phone and pressed the call button. There was no harm in making the call, he told himself.

He looked up then and saw Rekha come through the college gates. A secret smile tugged at the corner of her lips. Sid felt his heart plummet.

Rekha shook her head. 'No, I don't want to,' she said.

Sid stared at her, perplexed. 'Why?'

'I just don't want to. Sanjay says that I should be careful,' Rekha said and took a lick of the ice cream cone.

They were sitting on the steps of Garuda Mall with a double-scoop of ice cream each. She her very berry flavour and he rum 'n' raisin. It was one of their favourite things to do. Once in a while they would exchange cones. The thought of tasting each other's saliva was more pleasurable than the cool sweetness of the ice cream.

'Who is Sanjay?' Sid asked, feeling a black curl of jealousy twist around his tongue.

'The man I met last Friday. He is a lawyer and really nice. He said it was fortunate that I got him. Not all men are as decent,' Rekha said, pushing a strand of hair from her face.

'Oh,' Sid murmured and then, unable to stop himself, he asked, 'So have you been in touch after that?'

Rekha shrugged. 'Couple of times. He checked to see if I got home all right. And then just a hello text.'

Sid looked away. She was lying. He could sense that. When she went to the loo, he took out her phone from her bag. He knew the password. It was what she called him: SIDDU.

He opened her message inbox. The lawyer and she had been messaging each other. Since the morning, there had been at least ten messages from him. Tediously typed full texts typical of his age, Sid thought as he read through them. How is my baby girl?/ Don't miss a class. Get an education first./What are you wearing?/ Take notes. There are no shortcuts!/ Why do you need a boyfriend? He will just make you lose focus!

The bastard, Sid thought. Motherfucking bastard. Pretending to be avuncular and drawing her to him like a spider spinning a web. He snapped the phone shut and put it back into her bag. And Rekha, how could she? Shit. Fucking shit. Any man, it seemed, could sweet-talk his way into her heart and panties. Bitch!

'What are you growling at?' Rekha's voice, her sweet cheating voice, whispered in his ear.

He turned towards her. You bitch, he thought. If you are so eager to give it around, give some to whoever I ask you to. 'Do this one more time. It's a lot more money and I am seriously broke. I need you to do this for me, Rex.'

He saw the confusion and fear in her eyes. He squeezed her arm. 'Please,' he said. 'I won't ask again.'

She nodded. 'When?'

'I'll let you know,' he said.

He would ask for 25K this time. 'And she isn't a call girl,' he would say firmly. 'So no touching or feeling. You will need to explain this to your client.'

Who was he fooling? No one was going to pay 25K just to sit across a table and watch a girl suck on a straw. He didn't particularly care any more. He would be out of her life after tomorrow.

He called the number again.

———◆———

In the early evening light, the station house seemed even more decrepit and shabby. Once upon a time, as evening descended, they would have begun to wind up operations. Nothing much ever happened in a rural settlement after dark. Not any more, Gowda thought as he rode into the compound on his Bullet. The size of the station itself had changed.

They had two separate divisions – one to handle law and order and the other to handle crime. He was the station head and oversaw both. But each division had its own set of officers. Two ASIs, two SIs and several constables manned each division. And two station writers. The tight ship he had run had become a cruise liner, he told himself. He glanced at his watch as he walked into the station. It was a little past four.

A group of men huddled in front of the station writer's table stared at him curiously.

'Is there any point in approaching him?' one of the men asked.

The station writer grimaced. 'Pointless! It's all about rules for him.'

'What's to be done then?' The man frowned. It was a clear case of trespass but the trespasser claimed he had papers to prove that his claim on the land was as valid.

'It's about how the FIR is lodged,' the station writer murmured.

The man peered into the station writer's face. 'Oh,' he said after a pause.

Somewhere a phone rang. The man sat up to make an offer to the station writer but before he could speak, a constable appeared. 'Gowda sir wants to see you,' he said.

The station writer pushed his glasses up his nose and stood up.

Gowda had a stack of brown files in front of him. He waved to the writer to sit down. Gowda had had a long and frustrating afternoon trying to chase Teja bhai. He had drawn a blank among his informer networks and his most trusted informer, Mohammed, was unreachable. He would have to get a couple of constables to scour the streets. In times of acute staff shortage, it was going to be hard. When people complained about inadequate policing, they needed to remember that there was one policeman for every thousand citizens of this city.

He had begun examining the case diaries almost as a matter of routine but he felt his foul mood worsen when he noticed something was awry.

No one knew better than Gowda just how crucial the role of the station writer was. Some of them could teach High Court judges a thing or two about points of law. They knew exactly how to lodge a complaint depending on who was bribing them. And Zahir, the new station writer, was a pro at what he did.

'What's going on?' he asked without any preamble.

'I don't understand, sir,' the station writer said.

'Don't play the fool with me, Zahir.' Gowda frowned. 'I've been keeping an eye on you. I am talking about the FIRs you lodge. Somehow it's always the accused who gets the benefit of the doubt and not the complainant.'

Zahir put on his most aggrieved look. 'Sir, I don't know who is gossiping about me. But you must realize that because of my religion, I am a target.'

'Stop it,' Gowda snapped, leaning forward. 'Don't you dare play the religion card here. I don't know how it was in the station that you were in before, but here I make my decisions based on what I observe. Do you understand?'

Zahir flushed.

'I see that the Muddelmal register shows that most of the recovered stolen property is still here at the station. Why is that?'

Zahir looked at a point above Gowda's head. 'The owners haven't come to collect it.'

'Let them know, Zahir. Until you do, how will the complainant know that it has been recovered?' Gowda looked at the file pointedly.

Zahir stood for a moment, then left. As he went out, he passed Santosh, who was walking in. He heard Gowda snarl, 'What?'

Santosh felt the insides of his belly descend to his knees. How could someone do this to him at his age, he asked himself. It was like going to the school headmaster's room all over again.

'Sir,' he said, pulling himself together.

Gowda stared at him, waiting for him to go on.

Something about the stare tied his tongue and thoughts into knots. 'Sir,' he tried again as his mind raced to form an opening sentence that would get Gowda's attention.

'Are you going to stand here sirring me or are you going to say something more?' Gowda growled.

It had occurred to Santosh in the past two days that Gowda had mellowed. The cantankerousness that had been such a part of him seemed to have retreated. Obviously it hadn't. 'Sir,' he said. 'We had a breakthrough in the Nandita case investigation.'

Gowda waved for him to sit. 'Tell me.'

'Ratna met a few of Nandita's classmates today and one girl who seems to have been Nandita's confidante said that she may have gone to the Basilica to pray. Something about a scholarship she was hoping to get,' Santosh said, watching Gowda's face for a glimmer of a smile.

Instead there was curious blankness.

'So we went there this afternoon, and Ratna who knows a flower seller there made some enquiries,' Santosh continued.

'And ...' Gowda asked, again that curious flat note in his voice.

'The woman remembered her. She said that she had wondered about a girl in school uniform all by herself. But then she saw there was a woman with her.'

'And they got into an auto and left,' Gowda concluded for him.

Santosh stared, too surprised to speak. 'How did ...' he began after a pause.

Gowda leaned back in his chair. 'I was there yesterday and I heard from another source just about the same details. The auto belongs to a man called Teja bhai who suddenly seems to have disappeared from the face of earth.'

'I wish you had told us,' Santosh said. 'We could have saved so much time.'

Gowda flushed. 'I should have,' he admitted. He hadn't meant to keep the team out of the loop but he was used to doing things on his own. It had been unprofessional of him.

It was turning dark outside, and through the window mesh the hum of mosquitoes had grown into a steady drone. One of the constables knocked and came in bearing a lit mosquito coil. The heavy acrid smoke swirled through the room. Santosh coughed. Gowda pushed the glass of water on his table towards him. Santosh, eyes streaming, grabbed the glass hastily and drank the water to quell the irritation in his throat.

'What were you saying?' Santosh asked, shoving the coil to a distant corner of the room.

'Nothing of consequence.' Gowda shrugged.

'There's more, sir.' Santosh's voice wobbled.

Santosh cleared his throat. 'The flower seller said she thought she recognized the woman. Which is why she didn't ask Nandita what she was doing on her own. That's what she told Ratna.'

Santosh paused and swallowed.

'Her name is Mary, sir, and apparently she is a recruiter.'

'You are certain about that?' Gowda asked.

'Mary is well known in those areas, sir, and it isn't as if the flower seller is an innocent woman. She used to sell ganja along with her flowers and that's how Ratna knows her.'

'This Ratna is smart. What do you think?' Gowda asked with a small smile.

Santosh had mentioned Ratna's name about six times in the past twenty minutes.

'She is very smart, sir. And, sir, she is a Gowda like us and she is from Hassan.' Instantly realizing that he was treading dangerous territory, Santosh hastened to add, 'Her grandfather is Veerendra Gowda, the freedom fighter and poet.'

Gowda's eyes narrowed. Santosh flushed. Why had he mentioned that she was a Gowda? Once, he had thought that Inspector Gowda would accept him and make him one of his own if he knew that Santosh belonged to the Gowda caste as well. He had hoped that would cut him some slack even. That was what he had been told – that the police force was built on tiers of caste. You could be sure of unswerving allegiance and loyalty from your castemen. Except in the case of Gowda. Any reference to the caste equation only annoyed him. Santosh reached for the glass of water again.

Gowda waited for him to put the glass down. 'And you think she is smart because she is a Gowda?' he asked, his voice dangerously soft.

'Yes, sir … no, sir,' Santosh blubbered. Then with an effort, he collected himself and said, 'Sir, she is very intelligent. I just mentioned she is a Gowda. It's not connected to the case. I was just passing on a bit of information. Inconsequential trivia, actually.'

Gowda smiled. 'Good! And,' he continued, 'if you believe in something, stand by it. Or you will never get ahead in life. You can't let someone browbeat you into changing your mind simply because it's not their point of view. Gowdas are strong people, you know,' he added with a twinkle in his eye.

Santosh flushed. He didn't know whether he wanted to hug the man or strangle him.

'And now there is something we must get done right away,' Gowda said, reaching for the phone. 'Get the flower seller to describe the woman to the portrait artist. Not the one we will be allotted but a friend of mine who used to be at the forensic lab.'

'Sir, won't we be breaking rules?' Santosh asked.

Gowda took a deep breath. Santosh bit his lip nervously, waiting for the explosion. Was Gowda counting under his breath, he wondered in dismay. He was known to do that or drink a glass of water, when he was trying to curb his irritability.

'Sometimes we need to get around the rules in the interests of the victim,' Gowda enunciated, as though speaking to a particularly slow dog. 'Our priority here should be the missing child and not whether we are following the rules. If we put this request through the official channels, Nandita will be in some brothel before the artist here decides to switch on the system. If we have a reasonable likeness, we can show it around.'

'You mean, send it to other stations?' Santosh asked.

'Hmm ... not really, but to some others as well. Fixers, pimps, prostitutes, touts ... I am sure that Ratna has a few contacts too,' Gowda said, dialling the number of the forensic artist.

'Shenoy,' he said, 'I need a favour.'

Santosh saw Gowda smile. The man knew how to smile after all.

Ratna and Santosh sat in the back of the jeep while Gowda got into the front with PC David. He pressed a button on the dashboard searching for an FM station. There was one that played Hindi music all day long. Neither David nor Santosh spoke even though their eyes met in the mirror. Gowda generally didn't approve of music being played in the official vehicle. What was going on in his mind, they wondered. Only

Ratna looked pleased as a lilting song came on, '*Sheela ki jawani* ...' Gowda adjusted the volume and slumped into the seat, brooding at the traffic as they headed towards Shivaji Nagar.

'You like this song?' Santosh asked, seeing Ratna mouth the words silently.

She nodded. Santosh swallowed. He had imagined her taste would veer towards the semi-classical or even the Kannada Bhaavageetha, not this cacophony from Bollywood masquerading as music.

As if on cue, Gowda reached across and turned off the music, mumbling, 'Rubbish!'

The streets of Shivaji Nagar were bustling as usual. In the evening, it became an exotic bazaar of colour, scents and sounds. People teeming everywhere; some who had come in for a quick bargain before heading to the bus stand; earnest shoppers with a list; tourists who had been told the best bargains were to be found here. This was a Bangalore far removed from the plate glass malls of branded merchandise and credit-card-flashing customers. This city within a city didn't distinguish between clerk and tout, pimp and priest. You were not judged by your accent or clothes, your haircut or the bag on your shoulder. You were here because you had something to pick up. And there they were: the push carts of gewgaws, clothes, sweets, vegetables, dry fruits, plastic basins, flowers, fruits, teacups, porcelain jars, shirts and factory-reject shoes. You could pick up anything you wanted by wandering through the streets of Shivaji Nagar. You just needed to know where to look and then bargain as if your very life depended on it.

Summer had begun in earnest and the heat pressed down on man, animal, building and tarmac. The fruit sellers and kulfi vendors did brisk business. Some of the stalls offered fruit juices, milk shakes, faloodas and lassi in tall cold glasses. People thronged around, allowing the cold sweetness to quench their thirst and dull the edge of the heat. Some others drank tea. The old timers knew that worked better than the cold drinks. The hot tea made you sweat and kept you cooler longer.

David manoeuvred the jeep carefully through the evening traffic, finally finding a parking spot near the Basilica.

Gowda turned to Santosh. 'So we are here again.'

Santosh nodded. It had all begun here: Bhuvana and what followed. He stumbled as he walked away from the jeep.

Gowda grabbed his arm, 'Are you all right?' he asked softly.

'I am,' Santosh said. 'I tripped, that's all.'

———•———

Santosh turned abruptly and walked back to the Bolero. He opened the door and leaned inside.

'Looks like he has forgotten something,' ACWO Ratna said.

Gowda nodded. For a fleeting moment, their gazes met and both of them looked away. Neither wanted to acknowledge that Santosh stood with his back to the Basilica.

They heard a door slam. PC David had stepped out of the Bolero, giving Santosh the space to compose himself. Gowda felt a rare sense of pride. Such tacit understanding from his men filled him with a glimmer of hope.

He thought of a film he had watched a long time ago, in which a policeman had proclaimed: 'There is a heart beating beneath this khaki uniform.'

The theatre had erupted in a sound cloud of boos, jeers and cat calls. Policemen were expected to be boors, and most of them lived up to that image with no real effort.

Santosh gripped the edge of the seat to steady himself. He felt a flutter in his chest. For the last seven months, he had told himself that when he went into Shivaji Nagar next, it wouldn't affect him. The place had nothing to do with what had happened to him. In the sanctuary of his home, he had sipped his herbal concoction and told himself that when it was time, he would hold himself upright and let everyone see that Santosh may have been scarred in the battle but he hadn't lost the war.

But now that he was here, the horrific events of the evening of 8 September came back to him. Bhuvana and he in the autorickshaw. The still factory. The manja thread cutting into his throat. He shuddered and felt beads of sweat pop up on his brow. Get a grip on yourself, he muttered again and again like a mantra. Within his head, his inner voice that had taken on Gowda's cadence and timbre drawled, 'Are you going to make us wait here all evening?'

He clenched his muscles and turned around. He shut the vehicle door gently, took a deep breath and walked towards Gowda and Ratna. 'I just needed a moment,' he stated baldly.

Gowda nodded. Then he wiped his forehead with a handkerchief. 'Where is the flower seller?' he asked.

Santosh felt Ratna dart a glance in his direction. He pretended not to see it as he matched his stride with Gowda's. He soon felt her at his side. 'This way,' she said, leading them towards a line of handcarts piled with vegetables and a mountain of pineapples. The flower seller, a thin woman with a beaky nose and her hair pulled back in a bun-like knot, sat amidst them on a stool with a slightly larger upturned crate in front of her. On it were balls of jasmine garlands and one of bright yellow chrysanthemums. She was talking animatedly to a man who stood by her side even as her fingers worked on their own, weaving a garland of jasmine buds – two buds in one hand, and with the other hand knotting them in place with banana fibre. The man disappeared as he saw them approach.

She frowned when she saw Ratna.

'Let me speak to her,' Ratna said under her breath to the two men, afraid they would say something that would make the flower seller mutinous and uncooperative.

Gowda nodded. He paused near the cart of pineapples, close enough to hear what was being discussed. Santosh hovered by the cart of vegetables. Gowda saw Santosh examine an eggplant. Did the boy really know how to buy vegetables? But taking a cue from him, he picked up a pineapple.

'What now?' the flower seller said through clenched teeth as she bit through the banana fibre.

'I want you to describe the woman to the police artist,' Ratna said.

The flower seller's eyes narrowed. 'What if I don't remember?' she said, starting on another mound of buds.

'Are you saying you don't remember or you choose not to remember?' Ratna's voice was hard.

Santosh flinched at her tone. Gowda smiled. The girl had balls. Sweet-talking her wouldn't get Santosh anywhere.

The woman shrugged.

Ratna leaned forward and hissed, 'You really don't want me poking around your buds and flowers, bra and petticoat, do you?'

The woman's eyes darted this way and that. It wouldn't do her reputation any good to have a young girl talk to her in that tone of voice.

Ratna straightened. 'Get someone to sit here and mind your business.'

The woman sighed. 'It's peak time ...'

Ratna folded her arms. 'Your peak hours are from 8 p.m. onwards. You know that as well as I do. No one's going to buy your little pouches of ganja in broad daylight. Neither you nor they are so stupid. We'll have you back by the time your real customers turn up.'

Santosh expelled his breath in admiration. She was only as old as he was, perhaps a few months younger, but she seemed to have all the worldliness of Gajendra when dealing with criminals. In a strange way, her feistiness excited him.

What did she have on the woman, Gowda wondered.

The portrait artist Shenoy was on his way to a restaurant nearby that Gowda had decided on. It looked more like a park with gazebos and a garden space around, Ratna thought as she and the flower seller walked towards it while Gowda and Santosh followed in the police vehicle. She realized that Gowda had chosen it for that very reason. They wouldn't be noticed.

'I knew they were with you!' the flower seller sniffed as she saw the two men draw closer to the table they were seated at. 'The older one was looking at the pineapple as if it might bite him. And the younger one was fingering the eggplants as if they were his goolies.'

Ratna flushed. 'Watch your mouth,' she snapped.

'Why? Don't policemen have balls?' the flower seller persisted, enjoying Ratna's discomfiture.

'Whether they do or don't is not your business,' Ratna said in a furious voice.

Gowda's eyebrows rose. 'What are you talking about?' he asked as he pulled up a chair.

'Nothing,' Ratna murmured.

'Policemen's goolies,' the flower seller said, waiting to revel in the embarrassment that would pop up on the men's faces. Santosh spluttered and choked on the water he was sipping.

Gowda's eyebrows rose higher, but he didn't allow any emotion to show on his face even as Ratna hissed, 'Shut up!'

'What would you like to drink?' Gowda asked, beckoning to a waiter who didn't seem very interested.

'Rum and water,' the woman said with a bland expression.

'Oii Kamala, do you realize who you're with?' Ratna said, her eyes narrowing in anger. 'This isn't your wine shaap and we are not your cronies you share a quarter with.'

Santosh looked at Ratna. Was Ratna really as worldly wise as she sounded? He had met other women ASIs, women inspectors, but they had all spent years in the force. How did Ratna know about such things? What had she done before she entered the service?

Gowda waved an arm airily. 'A Khoday's triple X and water for her. What about you, Ratna and Santosh? Whisky, brandy, gin?' he asked.

Ratna smiled. Santosh swallowed.

'Three coffees,' Gowda said, wanting to reach out and box Santosh's ears. Couldn't the boy understand a joke?

The artist and the drinks arrived together. Shenoy looked at the tableaux before him and his eyebrows almost disappeared into his hairline.

'I wouldn't do this for anyone but you, sir,' the portrait artist said, before pulling a chair out.

'I know,' Gowda said, holding out his hand to the man. The portrait artist shook Gowda's hand. Santosh wondered what the story was. The flower seller took a deep drink of her rum and water. She wiped her mouth and said, 'Can we get started? Some of us have to get back to work ...'

Gowda frowned, and the flower seller's mouth gulped air. Good, Ratna thought. Time he stopped being so easy on her. That was the trouble with petty criminals. Their sense of self-importance made them forget they were there on sufferance more than anything else.

'Quiet!' Santosh said. Ratna darted a look at him. Maybe he wasn't as meek as he made himself out to be.

Shenoy, as if on cue, opened his bag and pulled out a sheaf of cards.

'What were her eyes like?' he asked, taking out a pad and a thick, flat pencil.

The flower seller frowned. 'Like everyone's, I guess.'

Ratna opened her mouth. Gowda held up his hand.

'Kamalamma,' he said. 'There are four of us around the table here. Do all of us have the same kind of eyes?'

Shenoy looked at Gowda in amazement. The Gowda he once knew would have hollered. This was a new Gowda, an improved version. His fingers itched to draw him.

The flower seller peered into each one of their faces.

'Her eyes are like his,' she said, gesturing to Santosh with her chin. 'Wide and quite big. Like a calf's ... if you know what I mean. Just about to be led to slaughter. Her eyebrows are thick.'

Shenoy handed her a sheaf of cards. She picked the ones that she thought were the closest.

'Her face is like a mango seed that's been sucked on,' the flower seller said, beginning to enjoy the process.

Shenoy looked at Gowda as if to ask, what have you got me into? But he continued to sketch as she chose a nose like a pig's and lips that were like Ratna's. For a moment all of them stared at Ratna's lips. Santosh, who hadn't looked at her so carefully until then, saw she had nice lips. Not too full or too thin, with the ends curling upwards. Actually, he thought, she was nice everything.

Shenoy held up a sheet of paper. 'Anything like this?'

The flower seller peered. 'Make her older. She is an old woman, almost fifty.'

Gowda looked away, glad that Urmila wasn't anywhere nearby. Ever since Urmila's fiftieth birthday, she hadn't stopped talking about fifty being the new thirty.

'And give her a side parting,' the flower seller said suddenly.

Shenoy made the changes and held it out to the flower seller.

'Yes ... this could be Mary,' she said, shaking her head in amazement. 'But you haven't seen her. How did you do that? There was this man who walked away with my gold chain. Three sovereigns. The bastard pretended he would be there for me, wriggled into my life and home, and ran away with my gold chain. If I describe him to you, could you make a picture? I don't need the police to take care of the rest ...'

Shenoy gazed at Gowda helplessly. Gowda looked at Ratna. She nodded and stood up. 'Kamalamma, I think it's time to go. We'll take you back to your shop.'

The flower seller made a face. 'What was I thinking of, expecting you to help me? It's always like that. Police or thieves, they want to be your best friends till they get what they need from you and then psss ... you are a banana skin to be tossed aside.'

'Kamalamma,' Ratna's voice rose in warning.

Gowda leaned forward and looked at the flower seller. 'When this is all sorted out, I'll make sure that you get a picture of the man who cheated you. And we'll help you find him.

Now I need to get down to work. There is a missing child, Kamalamma, so if you hear anything ...' He gestured with his hand for her to leave.

Santosh stood up to go with Ratna.

'Don't bother,' the flower seller said. 'Do you think I don't know my way back?'

Then, turning to Gowda, she said, 'Thanks.'

The English word hung like a beacon between the two of them. You can count on me, the light flashed.

Santosh had a moment of epiphany. Gowda had gathered yet another recruit to his fold of informers. How smoothly it had been done.

They waited as Shenoy did a fresh sketch of the face of the woman.

'And check your personal mail tomorrow,' Shenoy said as he was leaving. Gowda nodded, wondering what was coming his way.

'Why did he leave the police force, sir?' Santosh asked, looking at the sketch again.

'Death threats. But he didn't take them that seriously. He has a young daughter. Someone knocked her down as she rode her bicycle to school. Fortunately she fell on a heap of sand and not under the van that was approaching from the opposite direction. Maybe it was an accident or maybe it had been planned ... But Shenoy put in his papers. He wasn't going to take any chances, he said,' Gowda said, remembering the fear in the man's eyes. 'We lost a superb portrait artist. The pity is that no one in the force even tried to hold him back ...'

'Except you,' Santosh said.

Gowda smiled. A narrow smile of resignation. 'Except me ... He had drawn an exact resemblance of a man who hadn't been identified until then. It hadn't been entered into the system when the accident happened. The drawing disappeared when Shenoy left.'

'And no one pursued the matter?' Ratna asked, watching Santosh wave frantically to the waiter.

'They did but the next portrait artist came up with a face that resembled the Indian prime minister's,' Gowda said.

The gate lights were on; as were the lights in the verandah and within the house. Who was in? Urmila had a key but she never came by without letting him know. It was an implicit understanding between the two of them. And even if it was her, she was not given to lighting up the house like the Mysore palace at Dussehra.

He pushed the gate open and drove his Bullet in. Mamtha, he thought, but how had she got in?

He rang the bell. The door opened after a whole five minutes. Mamtha stood beaming at the doorway. He had a strange sense of déjà vu. Had it been only three nights ago when Urmila had stood there, beaming, the light behind her picking on the brown and gold hints in her hair?

'You didn't say you were coming,' Gowda said.

He saw the smile slip on Mamtha's face and almost bit his tongue in remorse.

'What a surprise!' he tried again.

'You don't look too happy to see me,' Mamtha said quietly.

His gaze dropped. Then, with an effusiveness that sounded horribly false to even his ears, he said, 'Why do you say that, Mamtha? I was just surprised ...'

If someone used that fake note of joy in their voice, I would reach across and slap them, Gowda thought. But apparently it seemed to satisfy Mamtha because she smiled and took his hand.

'Why don't you shower and change? And for once, can you not sit with a bottle till midnight? I am hungry too.'

Gowda nodded and went meekly to their bedroom. He stood under the shower, telling himself, I must not. I must not compare Mamtha with Urmila. It is not fair to either woman.

But only Mamtha could combine tenderness with censure, concern with the rasp of shrewish petulance, all in one breath. For as long as he could remember, it had been so. He sighed, turning the shower off. Why did he even expect something would change? Nothing would. Ever.

When he had poured himself a drink, Mamtha came in with a sheaf of takeaway menus. 'What's happened to this area?' she said, waving it at him. 'Panda Express. Subway. Kabab Plaza, Koel's Pizzeria.'

Gowda smiled. 'I told you the city will catch up with us one of these days.' And then, remembering to say the right thing, he added, 'Are you sure you don't want to get a transfer back to Bangalore?'

'Except that we still have no neighbours,' she said, putting her glasses on.

Mamtha, Gowda observed, had dyed her hair and made an effort with her appearance. She was wearing a pale pink cotton churidar kurta and had even painted her nails. What was going on?

Over dinner Mamtha told him why she was here. He had been too afraid to ask. A two-day conference, she said. And Roshan would be coming too.

'We can do things together like a family. Go to a mall, eat out, go for a movie. What do you think?' she asked, leaning forward to touch his hand.

Unbidden, a lyric floated into his head: 'So, so you can tell ... blue skies from pain.'

What was that? A line from Pink Floyd. Urmila and he used to listen to it together. Sharing a Walkman, the right earpiece in his ear and the left one in her left ear. Oh fuck, he thought, he had promised Urmila that they would have dinner at her home on Wednesday. What now?

'You don't look like you want to,' Mamtha said, glaring at him.

'No, no, I was just running the case load through my head,' he said quickly.

'It's not as if Bangalore city has just one policeman!' she snapped.

'Mamtha,' he said. 'I didn't say no. I was just scheduling stuff in my head.'

'Hmm ...' she said, rising. As she cleared the table, Gowda told her about Nandita. Mamtha listened quietly. When Gowda was done, she said thoughtfully, 'Poor Shanthi, I can't even imagine what I would do if our Roshan went missing.'

A moment later, she added, 'I did wonder at the state of the house. Shanthi is lazy, but not this slovenly. The house was a mess when I walked in. I guess this explains it.'

Gowda looked at her for a long second. Then he went to the verandah and lit a cigarette. He inhaled deeply, telling himself: Gowda, calm down. Calm down. There's still the night to get through.

Later in bed, he made the mandatory move. She lifted his hand away from around her waist gently and said, 'I am tired. It's been a long day.'

They slept. Man and wife. The oak and the cypress.

10 MARCH, TUESDAY

Shanthi looked at the printout. 'So this is the woman who took my daughter?' she asked Gowda.

'That's what we believe,' Head Constable Gajendra said.

'Do you know if it's her or not?' Shanthi snapped. Gajendra frowned. Gowda saw it was time to step in.

'Shanthi,' he said in a tone that hinted at censure. Watch it, don't cross any boundaries, it said. 'The portrait is done based on a description we were given by someone who saw her with a girl who matched the description of Nandita. That's all we have to go by.'

'It's been seven days, sir. My child is out there in the hands of god knows who ...' Shanthi's eyes filled up.

'Have you checked the morgues?' Mamtha asked Gowda, walking in from the kitchen where she had been inspecting the contents of the cupboards.

Gowda glared at her. Shanthi wiped her eyes with the pallu of her sari. 'That's what her father said too. But I know my child is alive. Within me I would know if she wasn't.'

Mamtha looked a little shamefaced. She hadn't meant for it to sound like it had come out. Sometimes, she thought, no matter what she said to Borei, she would never get it right.

Shanthi looked at the printout. 'You can keep it if you want,' Gowda said, more to puncture the awkward silence in the room.

Shanthi nodded. 'Thanks,' she said, turning to go back into the house where chores awaited her.

When Gajendra had left, Gowda turned towards Mamtha. 'You ...' he began.

'Yes, I know I shouldn't have said that,' she said quietly. 'I was thinking like a doctor and not as a mother. You know how it is. You are a policeman. Sometimes, in our line of duty, we have to say the most unpleasant things because that is the truth.'

Gowda's jaw almost dropped. This was a first for Mamtha. To admit to a mistake. 'What time is your conference?' he asked.

She glanced at her watch. 'There is an orientation at 11 a.m. It's going to be a long day. Then cocktails and dinner.'

Gowda's eyebrows rose. 'Who is hosting it? Surely not the health department?'

Mamtha made a face. 'If it was them, it would be bhajis and coffee. One-by-two coffee.'

Gowda smiled. A queer sadness filled him. This side of Mamtha was something he had never seen before. The less-than-perfect Mamtha who admitted to mistakes and could make a joke or two.

'Do you want me to drop you?' he asked.

'That would be helpful. It's at the Ritz. I don't even know where that is.'

'The Ritz,' Gowda guffawed. 'Wow ... what kind of medical conference is this?'

Mamtha smiled. 'Pharma companies have a lot of money to flash around to dazzle provincial doctors like me.'

'We should be going then,' he said.

When Mamtha stepped out, Gowda looked at her, dressed in a blue silk sari with a deep yellow border and said, 'You should wear bright clothes more often. You look nice.'

Mamtha rolled her eyes. 'A compliment from Inspector Gowda. I don't believe this ...'

They didn't speak much in the car. Gowda cleared his throat a few times to start a conversation but couldn't find anything to say. Eventually he began. 'This case is really worrying me, Mamtha.'

'Which case?' she asked.

'Shanthi's daughter Nandita going missing. This city is not what it used to be. I ...'

She held up her hand, mouthing, 'Just a moment' as her mobile rang.

For the rest of the drive, Mamtha was on her mobile. Do we ever really know anyone, he asked himself as he heard her morph into several women over the fifty-five minutes it took them to reach the Ritz. Different Mamthas he hadn't encountered before: jocular, teasing, gossipy, giggly ...

'If you let me know an hour in advance, I'll have you picked up,' he said as they drove into the hotel.

'In a police jeep?' she asked.

'Don't be silly ...' he said and wished he hadn't when he saw her face. She had been joking. What on earth was she on? Anti-depressants?

He turned onto Museum Road and went towards Lavelle Road as he knew he was going to. It was best that he explain to Urmila in person rather than on the phone about cancelling dinner on Wednesday.

She would be home, he knew. It was her book club day. Though why on earth people had to get together to discuss a book after they had read it was beyond him.

Urmila opened the door with a little gasp of joy. 'G, what brings you here?'

He saw her glance at his hand. Had she expected him to bring her flowers? He wasn't that sort of man. She knew that.

Gowda had meant to lead up to it gently but the chaos in his head made him blurt it out. 'I had to drop Mamtha at the Ritz.'

'Oh,' Urmila said. But it was Lady Urmila who added, 'How nice of you.' And then after a pause, 'Would you like to come in?'

He followed her into the living room that took his breath away, each time. It was a room out of a magazine, just like the rest of the flat. The leather sofas that invited you to sink into them; the plump silk cushions and what she said was a Persian carpet; the coffee table strewn tastefully with silver thingies; the occasional tables and the table lamps. And on a gatelegged table a giant glass vase of flowers.

His eyes took in the indoor plants and the paintings on the walls – Achuthan Kudallur, Yusuf Arakkal, B. Prabha, S.G. Vasudev, and even a Hussain. She had pointed out the paintings to him the first time he had visited her. He saw there was a new painting and the child-like squiggles suggested she must have paid a fortune for it. Didn't artists paint landscapes or people any more, he wondered as he walked towards a sofa.

'Would you like coffee? A drink?' she asked.

Gowda paused and touched her elbow. 'Don't be like this, Urmila ...'

'Don't be like what?' Her eyebrows rose with a hint of scorn.

'Don't mess with me. You know what I'm talking about. I came over because I wanted to see you,' Gowda said, his voice hardening of its own volition.

'It's not easy, G ... it's not,' she said softly. 'I didn't know being the other woman would feel like this.'

He wrapped his arms around her. He could see she was hurting, but he didn't know how to make it go away.

'How long is she here for?' she said against his chest.

'I don't know ...' he murmured. He felt her hold on him tighten. 'Baby,' he said.

She tilted her chin and stared at him. Then, giggling, she said, 'Baby! Where did that come from?'

He smiled sheepishly. He didn't know either. 'May I have that coffee?' he asked, dropping into a sofa.

'Just coffee?' She smiled.

He looked at her. She was wearing a yellow shirt in some clingy material and white trousers. 'You look like an egg,' he said.

'What?' she asked, sitting by his side.

'Good enough to eat.' He smiled.

Urmila pinched his cheek, and in his head Michael muttered: Bob, you are getting really good at buttering up the ladies!

'There is someone I want you to meet,' Urmila said suddenly, going into the bedroom.

Gowda stared after her. When she returned, she bore a stuffed toy in her arms.

The dog leapt from her arms and danced at his knees. 'He wants you to pick him up.' She grinned. 'He was meant to go to a friend but I couldn't resist him.'

'Does he have a name?' Gowda asked as the dog settled on his lap.

'Mr Right.'

———•———

'Where's PC David?' Santosh asked, glancing at the new man in the driver's seat.

'He is more familiar with the place we are going to,' Byrappa said, getting into the backseat. 'This is PC Shafi,' he said by way of introduction, looking at him meaningfully, though Santosh would understand the point of that gaze only much later.

'Are you sure you have the right autorickshaw?' Ratna asked, as she got in beside Santosh.

Byrappa nodded.

'It didn't take you very long.' Santosh frowned.

'Gowda sir knew exactly whom to call ... so all I needed to do was follow up.'

'Whom did he call?' Ratna asked.

'He has informants and connections everywhere,' PC Byrappa said.

'Who was it? Mohammed?' Santosh asked.

'How did you know?' PC Byrappa asked.

Santosh shrugged.

'Mohammed led us towards an auto mechanic in that area,' Byrappa said.

The jeep pulled up outside a small block on a little road off Shyampur near Dr Ambedkar Hospital.

Byrappa stepped out and walked towards a block of low-cost housing-board flats. Santosh and Ratna followed him. A little boy was riding his tricycle up and down the enclosed verandah of the ground-floor flat of G Block. He saw the approaching strangers and burst into loud sobs as he fled.

'What happened?' Santosh said, rushing towards the verandah.

Byrappa stood transfixed. 'I didn't do anything, I didn't even speak a word.'

Ratna shook her head with a wry smile. 'Weren't you told as little boys that the police would come to get you, if you didn't behave?'

Byrappa grinned at the thought of his uniform frightening the child. 'I just wish my uniform had the same effect on some of the hooligans I have to deal with.'

'Why are you wearing a uniform anyway?' Santosh asked Byrappa.

'Special duty at the airport this morning,' Byrappa replied.

'The only thing is, if his father is at home, the boy's cries would have sent him into hiding,' Santosh said.

'Do these flats have back doors?' Ratna asked.

Byrappa nodded. 'I would think so.'

'The two of you go in. I'll wait in the lane behind. If he pops out from the back entrance, I'll grab him,' Ratna said, thrusting a file into Santosh's hands.

'You shouldn't ...' Santosh began, but Ratna was gone.

A middle-aged woman with a dupatta over her head came into the enclosed verandah. The little boy peered at them from behind her.

'We are here regarding an enquiry. We think that the autorickshaw that belongs to ...' Santosh began in Kannada.

The woman's eyes widened.

'Is Tejuddin here?' Byrappa interrupted in a language that seemed to be a mixture of Urdu and something else.

'This is the Urdu they understand,' he said when the woman went back in. 'The Shivaji Nagar Urdu. So all that flowery Kannada was wasted on her.'

She returned with an elderly man. 'I am Tejuddin,' he said, leaning on a Zimmer frame.

Santosh opened his notebook.

'You're the owner of autorickshaw vehicle number KA-03-1585.'

The man nodded.

'Do you have a driver?' Santosh asked.

'No ... we keep the autorickshaw for personal use. I call in one of the local boys to drive it when we need to go out.'

'Your son?' Byrappa asked, trying to peer over the man's shoulder.

'He's in Saudi Arabia,' the elderly man said. 'Why? What's wrong?'

'We had some information that your autorickshaw may have been involved in a kidnapping,' Santosh said, ignoring Byrappa's frown.

The elderly man shook his head. 'You are mistaken. We don't do such haram. Besides, I know when my autorickshaw is used and by whom.'

The little boy was tugging at the old man's kurta, urging him to come in.

'Where is the autorickshaw?' Santosh asked.

'My nephew Rafiq has taken it for the day,' the old man said, tousling the hair of his grandson. 'Stop it, Abbas,' he said sternly.

'So who lives here?'

'The two of us, our daughter-in-law and our grandson,' the woman said.

Byrappa nodded. 'We'll be back,' he said cryptically, turning to leave.

'The old man is speaking the truth, but she is hiding something,' he said as they walked down the lane.

'Yes, I thought so too,' Santosh said, wondering where Ratna was.

Santosh's mobile rang. It was Ratna. 'You had better hurry this side,' she said in a low voice.

Santosh gestured for Byrappa to follow him. Next to the block of flats was an empty piece of land hemmed in by a five-foot-high wall with a locked gate. Santosh hoisted himself over the wall. The ground was overgrown with tall grass and bushes.

A guava tree stood laden with fruit. At the farther end of the ground was an extraordinary sight: scooters with dented sides and one with a half missing, as though it had been sawed in the middle; autorickshaws in various stages of disembowelment. A couple of cars that were recognizable as cars only from their shells.

'What is this place?' Santosh asked.

Byrappa smiled. 'This is where vehicles come to die.'

Santosh darted a quick look at him. Who would have thought there was a poet in PC Byrappa!

The plot was open on the other side, facing the railway line. Ratna was standing near a tree by a tender-coconut vendor.

The coconut vendor stared at the sight of the two men emerging from the graveyard of autos. That's what the ground was called – Auto Kabaristhan.

Santosh walked towards Ratna. Under the next tree on the dirt road was a vehicle swathed in a blue plastic sheet.

'He jumped over the wall at the rear of the flats and hid himself in the autorickshaw beneath the tarpaulin,' Ratna said softly.

'It looks like a car,' Santosh murmured.

'They have pushed a cart beneath it so it looks bigger at first glance. But one end of it doesn't touch the ground and I could see it's a cart,' Ratna said, opening her bag and peering into it.

Santosh turned his head carefully to his left. Byrappa nodded almost imperceptibly. In one swift motion they moved towards the swaddled auto. Byrappa pulled away the plastic sheet from the front of the vehicle. Within sat a young man. He looked barely nineteen. He leapt to his feet but Santosh grabbed his arm. 'Are you going to come with us without making a fuss or do you want me to handcuff you?' Santosh growled. A very Gowda-like growl, Byrappa thought with grudging admiration.

'I didn't do anything wrong,' the young man said, not bothering to hide his anger as he tried to pull his arm away.

'In which case, why are you hiding?' Santosh asked.

Ratna stepped forward.

'You,' said the young man. 'It's you ... I thought you were a fucking whore and I felt sorry for you ... standing under the tree in the middle of the day.'

Santosh raised his arm to smack the boy.

'Don't,' Byrappa said. 'He's trying to rile you so you slap him. That's exactly what he wants. Look across ...' A boy stood with his mobile phone aloft, capturing the goings-on. 'Every motherf ...' Then, realizing it was Ratna he was talking to, he changed it to, 'every street rat is a citizen journalist now!'

The coconut seller was watching them. He had his mobile out too.

Ratna walked towards him. 'If you don't erase what you've recorded, I'll have you taken into custody,' she said under her breath. The man did as he was told. He waved to the boy across the road, shooing him: 'Ja, ja!'

Byrappa hooked a finger through the loop in the young man's trousers. 'Take your hands off me,' he snarled.

'It's either this or handcuffs,' Byrappa said in a conciliatory voice that made Santosh glance at him. That's experience, he thought, suddenly out of his depth.

'Walk,' Byrappa said. 'Let's see what Tejuddin has to say ...'

A small group of people followed them back to Tejuddin's house. A small group of militant young men.

One of them hollered, 'It's all planned by them. They are taking one of us away for no reason.'

Santosh turned his head to look at them. A young boy screamed, 'That policeman, it's he who grabbed Rafiq bhai ...'

Ratna's face was pale, he noticed. 'Should we ask for reinforcements?' She asked nervously.

PC Shafi stepped out of the Bolero. He walked towards the mob. 'Kya so ... what's going on?' he asked the young man with a skull cap who was turning a shade of vermilion from the heat and his rising fury.

'You think you can come here and take one of us just like that?' Skull Cap bristled.

Shafi frowned. 'Don't turn this into them and us, you idiot. This is an enquiry about a kidnapping case.'

'Kidnapping?'

'Yes, a twelve-year-old girl. And as a devout Muslim, you should know that nowwhere in the Koran does it say that it's all right to kidnap a young girl.'

'You harami,' Skull Cap said, raising his hand to slap the young man.

'Stop it,' Byrappa said, lapsing into Urdu. 'No need for you to play the police. That's what we are here for!'

Skull Cap turned and waved his hand to disburse the mob. 'Ja, ja,' he called out. 'This is police business. No need for us to get involved with what this harami has done.'

Santosh and Ratna exchanged glances. There was nothing as frightening or as fickle as a mob.

The commotion had brought Tejuddin back to the verandah. 'What's going on?' he asked, his voice trembling at the sight of the police and a crowd of curious neighbours. 'Rafiq, what did you do?'

'Who is he?' Byrappa asked, thrusting the young man forward.

'I didn't do anything, mamu,' the boy mumbled. 'I am being accused. It's because we are Muslims.'

'Shut up,' Shafi said. 'Do you know what he did?'

It was time for him to step in, Santosh decided. 'Shafi, I suggest you take care of the crowd. We'll handle this.'

'What did you do?' Tejuddin asked again.

'Who is he?'

'A relative. My son thought we needed a young man around to help us; I am not what I used to be.' He gestured to the walker he clutched, his knuckles turning white as he gripped it tightly.

'Sit down, Tejuddin,' Santosh said gently as he led the elderly man to a bench in the verandah.

'What have you done, Rafiq?' The old man's voice shook as he sat down.

The young man's belligerence had drained away. His head drooped. 'I just wanted some money of my own. Not handouts from Mami and you.'

'And?' Santosh probed. He was little more than a boy, he realized, seeing the faint dusting of hair on the boy's upper lip.

'One of the boys I met at the petty shop said he knew how I could make some money. All I had to do was drive an auto, preferably a private one. Mamu's stood under its tarpaulin. I didn't think I was commiting a crime.'

'This boy's name?' Ratna interrupted.

'Vasu,' Rafiq said.

'So this Vasu is your contact.' Santosh leaned forward.

'No, not Vasu. He gave me a number. I called the number and I was told where to go,' Rafiq said and suddenly stopped. The enormity of what he had done struck him. It had been only duplicity at that point, and not a real crime.

'Give me the number,' Ratna said, opening her notebook. Rafiq took his phone out and scrolled down the contacts list.

He began reading out a number, and then another, and then one more.

'How many are there?' Ratna asked, looking up from the notebook.

'Five. Each time I am given a new number.'

'So you have used the auto five times ...' Santosh said.

'You son of a pig, you filthy dog ... is this how you repay me for taking you in?' Tejuddin burst out. 'What have you used my auto for? What? What?'

'The girl and the woman you picked up at St Mary's Basilica. Where did you drop them?' Byrappa asked impatiently.

———•———

This time Santosh took the front seat for himself. The sense of power it gave him filled him with a confidence he had thought was lost to him forever.

Shafi darted a quick look at Santosh's face. There was a grim set to it which was faintly reminiscent of someone he knew. His eyes widened. Santosh was pretending to do a Gowda. Wait till he told Byrappa and David about that.

'What's so funny?' Santosh frowned.

Shafi almost choked with laughter. The boy had even made Gowda's tone his. He shook his head. 'Nothing, sir, I just remembered something ... a joke.'

Santosh allowed his mouth to twist a little in a Gowda-like grimace.

None of them spoke as Shafi followed Rafiq's directions, which were all over the place.

'Do you know where we are going?' Ratna glared at him. 'Or are you just messing with us?'

'Boli magane,' Byrappa murmured into his ear. He paused. 'Oii chinal ka, you know what we do to smart boys, don't you?'

Rafiq swallowed and suddenly remembered the precise location, down to the granite blockyard adjacent to the building. When the police vehicle pulled up outside the old unplastered structure, a young boy was working on a tyre. The boy stood up hastily. From the shop next door, a man peered out.

Byrappa stepped out. Rafiq sat still, unwilling to step out. 'This is the place?' Byrappa asked, looking at the floor above. It seemed vacant.

Rafiq nodded.

Santosh and Ratna followed Byrappa as he climbed the staircase that led to the top floor. It was an unfinished room and there was nothing there except a blue plastic barrel, a mound of bricks and an alcove with a makeshift door.

'Did he get it right?' Santosh asked Byrappa.

Ratna darted towards the blue barrel. Something had caught her eye. She peered at it. A bindi was stuck on the side of the barrel. A teardrop of a bindi with a sparkling stone.

'He did get it right. Look at this ...' Ratna pointed.

'It could be anyone's.' Byrappa leaned forward to look.

'Don't touch it,' Ratna said. From her handbag she pulled out a clear plastic sleeve and drew the bindi into it.

Santosh looked at her and the handbag in admiration. What else did the bag hold, he wondered. Suddenly a thought struck him. 'Byrappa sir,' he hollered across the room. 'What's chinal ka?'

Ratna turned her head to hide a smile. Byrappa flushed. He walked towards Santosh and muttered, 'Did you have to shout it? It means backstabbing dick.'

Santosh swallowed. 'Chinal ka,' he said under his breath. It had a nice ring to it.

———•———

The Member of the Legislative Assembly was busy, his PA had said on the phone. But Pujary wasn't going to be deterred by that. The MLA needed people like him to continue his reign.

MLA Papanna was in an enviable position. He had stood as an independent candidate from Bangalore North and won. Now he was being wooed by all the major parties. And so Papanna had begun to grow bigger than the white sandals he wore as part of his white attire – white shirt, white trousers, white sandals and a wristwatch with a white strap. The black hue of his skin glistened against the white and made him unforgettable and hence invincible. Pujary watched the MLA hold court in the outhouse attached to his residence.

In the long hall with a high roof and open sides into which an aluminium mesh had been placed, the MLA met everyone who came to see him. He called it his open house and Pujary realized why the man had won with an overwhelming majority. He sounded sincere, he sounded like he really meant to help in every possible way and he sounded like he expected nothing in return but goodwill. When he smiled, his rather large plank-like teeth with a visible space between the front two gleamed with kindliness.

Across the room, MLA Papanna's gaze met Pujary's. The man tilted back his head and said something to his PA. The man nodded and walked towards Pujary.

'MLA sir will see you in ten minutes,' he said softly.

Pujary nodded. The PA was a new man. Whatever happened to the old one, he wondered.

Pujary glanced at his watch. He knew the MLA would see him do it. He leaned back in the red plastic chair and closed his eyes. He was exhausted.

The lawyer was hard work. He had thought the offer of the college girl would soften him up. But it seemed to have had the reverse effect. In fact, he had taken it upon himself to lecture Pujary.

'I don't know what you think you are doing but this certainly is not the way to go about it,' he had said when Pujary had gone to meet him. The way to deal with an offensive attack was not to retaliate, Pujary knew.

'What are you talking about, sir?' Pujary had used his silkiest voice, a swish of incomprehension and a swash of innocence.

'That girl ...' Rathore had frowned. 'She was a college girl and a minor. Do you realize the trouble I could have got into?'

'Oh, I was told she was twenty-two,' Pujary had replied.

'No, she wasn't. An innocent child like her ...' The lawyer had pulled at the arch of his eyebrow in consternation.

Pujary had put on his most penitent expression. 'Yes, if it had been anyone else ... but Vittala took care of her, sir ... what else can I say?'

'Vittala? Who's that? I took care of her,' the man said, standing up.

'Vittala is another name for Lord Krishna, sir,' Pujary said. 'The keeper of the universe.' Then, in an almost sly tone, he added, 'I hear the boys are not working out.'

'Oh yes, useless idiots!'

'What can I say, sir?' Pujary threw up his arms. 'These boys, one tries to help them but ... I tried to get the contractor to talk to them but they say they want to leave.'

Rathore flushed. Pujary was clever. He knew how to kick a man in his balls without lifting his foot from the ground.

Stalemate having been achieved, Pujary had brought out the land document and the lawyer had pounced on the one name that was in the original deed but missing in the list of current heirs put together by the aggregator. Pujary had known he would. He was too sharp a lawyer to miss it. And it seemed that they couldn't go forward till the descendant of that man whose name was in the original deed provided a no-objection certificate. MLA Papanna had access to that man, he had heard. But MLA Papanna would require something in return. What would it be?

MLA Papanna listened to him. 'My PA will tell you about the commission,' he said, his plank teeth flashing.

Pujary nodded. He had expected that. There was no such thing as free service among politicians even if they were your best friends. And MLA Papanna was just an acquaintance.

'By the way, isn't there a lovely morsel you can send my way?' the MLA asked.

'I am not a pimp ...'

'I know that. But you have contacts. Someone like you would, I know.'

'I have to call the concerned people to make it happen,' Pujary said in a flat voice.

'Do that. I need it to happen tomorrow,' the MLA retorted as he turned to leave.

11 MARCH, WEDNESDAY

Sometime in the wee hours of the day, Gowda woke Mamtha and made quiet husbandly love to her in that zone hovering between sleep and consciousness. A warm body, a pair of arms clasped around his neck, a familiar rhythm and a slaking of need. When he rolled off her, spent and wide awake, a deep shame filled him.

The night before, they had made desultory conversation as they prepared to go to bed.

'How is Roshan behaving these days?' Gowda asked Mamtha as she sat on the edge of the bed coiling her hair into a topknot. He remembered his mother doing the same when he was a child. The clink of bangles and the rustle of hair; a fragrance that was an amalgamation of talc, turmeric, and toothpaste. His mother wore flowers in her hair; jasmine, he remembered, but Mamtha didn't. That was the only difference.

'Roshan?' Gowda asked again, when Mamtha didn't respond. 'When did he go to Goa? And in the middle of a term? What's happening there?'

'He went three days ago. He said there was a college fest,' Mamtha had said, turning on her side and curving her bottom towards him. Gowda had felt his heart sink. Mamtha was in the mood to make love and he didn't think he was up to it. All he wanted to do was lie there, processing his thoughts and day, and go to sleep.

'Oh,' Gowda had said, crossing his arms beneath his head as though oblivious to her invitation.

He had felt Mamtha snuggle deeper into him. What on earth was the woman on? Usually he would have had to beg and plead with her to get her into the mood. He had thought she would be relieved when he didn't put his arm around her waist. Which was usually his cue for telling her that he wanted sex.

He stroked her arm warily. 'It's been a long day, Mamtha,' he said softly. It hadn't been, save for a whole lot of paperwork, but he didn't think he was the sort of man who could make love to his mistress and wife in the span of a few hours.

He had felt her go still and then stiffen. He groaned in his head. Then he fell asleep.

By morning, though, the sense of remorse had softened to a stoic acceptance – ultimately all marriages were such. A matter of routine. And Mamtha seemed happy enough, husbandly and wifely duty done and dealt with. She was humming as she poured hot water into the coffee filter, he noticed as he hid himself behind the newspaper.

The call came just after breakfast. The health minister was planning to make a surprise visit to the primary health centres in Hassan district. Mamtha decided it was prudent that she return immediately. 'I am going to need at least two days to spruce up the place,' she said.

Gowda was glad he had done whatever it was he had when he noticed Mamtha was still humming under her breath as she packed.

'Roshan?' he asked. 'What time is he getting in?'

'Sometime during the day,' Mamtha said. They were sitting in the verandah, waiting for the cab to take her to the bus stand.

'Should I call him and ask him to come to Hassan straight?' she said suddenly. 'If you are busy with this Nandita case, won't it be a nuisance having him around?'

'No, let him come. I hardly see him,' Gowda said, lighting up a cigarette.

'Why don't you give up this disgusting habit?' Mamtha said.

Gowda felt a snarl grow in him and was fortunately saved from fracturing the peace of the moment by the cab drawing in. When Mamtha had left, Gowda continued to sit there, feeling a sense of disquiet. Mamtha's arrival and departure, all of it seemed a little forced and feverish. Had she been checking on him? Someone had been talking. He wondered who.

Santosh and Ratna were huddled together when Gowda walked into the station. They looked cosy as they sat sipping from their plastic cups of tea. Santosh felt Gowda's gaze flick past them.

'Shall we?' Ratna asked, seeing Gowda go into his room.

'Give him a few minutes to settle down,' Santosh said, blowing the top of his tea. A thin layer of skin had already formed.

Ratna's eyebrows rose. 'That's what my mother would say when my father came in from work – don't go to him till he settles down with his cup of coffee. Or he won't give you a patient hearing. We are going to discuss work, not ask him for a favour.'

Santosh glared at her.

Last evening, he had thought Ratna and he had connected in a way that went beyond just two colleagues sitting in a little restaurant with a plate of Mysore bonda and two cups of coffee. She had told him about herself. A childhood that was just like his, in a small town. She had gone to college and opted for a master's in social work.

'What made you join the police force?' he asked.

She shrugged. 'I started working for a small organization that dealt with child drug addicts. The first few days I couldn't eat or sleep; I found it hard to even breathe. Have you ever seen a child addict, s ... Santosh?'

She had called him by his name, not the habitual 'sir'. A little dove flapped its wings in his chest.

'No,' he said. 'I haven't, Ratna ...' He spoke her name as if it were an endearment.

Her eyes met his. Then she dropped her head into her hands.
'Six- and seven-year-olds who learned to sniff glue watching
their parents or siblings do it. That vacant gaze, the slackness of
jaw ... everything becomes bearable for them. The hunger, the
lack of joy, the scrounging through garbage, the sexual abuse ... I
met Kamalamma during those days.'

Santosh nodded. He had his answer now about Ratna's
familiarity with that world.

He had dropped her home, feeling like they had taken a step
forward together.

Santosh took a deep breath. 'No, we'll wait,' he said in his
firmest voice. It didn't do to get too chummy with your juniors,
he told himself. Give them an inch and they'll want to run your
life. She needed to know her place. In the official hierarchy, he
outranked her. 'You wait here. I'll call you when Gowda sir and
I have discussed a few things first.'

Gowda was on the phone when Santosh walked in and saluted
him. Gowda gestured for him to sit.

Santosh gazed at a point on the wall just above Gowda's head,
trying to look disinterested in Gowda's end of the conversation.

'Did you find a good seat?'

'Let me know when you reach. Take care ... and ... I wish you
hadn't gone back so quickly.'

Santosh's eyes met Gowda's at that. Gowda blinked, a hint of
mischief lighting up his gaze.

How did he do it, Santosh wondered. Manage to keep two
women happy while he couldn't even seem to make one smile.

Gowda put down his phone and asked, 'How did it go?'

'Let me call Ratna in, sir.' Santosh stood up.

Gowda cocked his head, watching Santosh almost race to the door. Was the boy in love with Ratna or in awe of her?

———•———

Gowda looked at the disappointed faces. 'So we are back to square one,' he said, playing with the paperweight.

'Yes and no ... we at least know what happened to her,' Santosh said.

'That's not going to do her or us any good, knowing that she was in that room,' Ratna snorted with an impatience that made Santosh frown.

Gowda gazed at her with a sense of déjà vu. The two of them reminded him of his earlier self split into two.

'Did you speak to the tyre shop people?' he asked.

Santosh nodded. 'They said they didn't know anything. They have leased the shop from someone. They were quite surly, in fact.'

'PC Byrappa wanted to bring the man in, and I am inclined to agree with him,' Ratna said darkly. The tyre shop man had given her a head-to-toe dekko, returning to linger on her breasts. She didn't wear a dupatta; never had. She found slinging a roll of gauzy cloth around her neck a frivolity and a nuisance. But for the first time, she wished she had worn one.

Gowda said, 'Get the details of the landlord. We'll make a beginning there. And ...' His voice hardened. 'No slacking. I want it ASAP. Do you hear that? As soon as possible, which means right now.'

Gowda stood up. He took his Bullet keys from the tray on the table. Ratna and Santosh stood up. 'I'm going out,' he said, walking out.

Neither of them said anything. They looked at each other.

Ratna opened her mouth to speak.

'Don't,' Santosh said softly. 'Don't say it. Actually, don't even think it. You don't know.'

Ratna looked at the paperweight as if she would like to hurl it at him.

'Don't,' she said in her iciest voice. 'Don't second-guess me. All I was going to ask was, how can we track the landlord?'

Santosh had seen Ratna and the station writer chatting and wondered what Zahir had filled her head with about Gowda.

He thought then of the story his brother the writer had told him. Of the Sufi and his acolyte. The two men had met a woman waiting on the banks of a river. She wept that she had no way of crossing it and if she didn't, her life would fall apart. The Sufi carried the woman on his shoulders and waded across the river. For the whole of the next day the acolyte wouldn't speak to his master. Eventually the Sufi asked him what was wrong. 'You who said we must be celibate carried her on your shoulders. How could you?' the acolyte snarled. The Sufi smiled. 'I let her off once we had crossed the river and forgot about her. It seems to me that you are still walking with her on your back.'

That was him, carrying the burden of his past and his assumptions.

Gajendra frowned, seeing their faces. Santosh looked unhappy and Ratna annoyed. The two of them, he thought, were like nursery school children. Best friends for a while and then hissing and spitting at each other like angry cats ... it was time he brought this to Gowda's attention. They were working on a case that needed the two young officers to be at their best, and not expending time and energy besting each other.

The sun was fierce on his back, but on a bike the heat was tempered. Gowda felt the headiness of velocity that came with the sheer girth of the Bullet ploughing through distance and time. At traffic lights, when he paused, he felt eyes rake him. No other bike, the Harley or the Ducati or even the Triumph, drew the Indian eye as much as the 500CC Bullet. He knew that in his black Royal Enfield helmet he made an impressive sight – a 1991 Bullet was a coveted one with its right-hand gear. With the number plate draped over the front wheel, it made the newer model and their riders seem like me-too men. Gowda looked at himself in the mirror and thought he looked rather like Urmila's Mr Right. He wore the smug expression of a creature fed on gourmet food and treats, went for walks twice a day wearing a bowtie and slept on silk cushions in a sunny balcony.

The great sense of contentment evaporated as he drove past Manyata Tech Park. With the advent of tech parks, the rural districts of Bangalore had slowly become satellite towns. High-rise buildings, a gated community, an international school, restaurants, spas, a liquor store and a multiplex, so the techies didn't have to travel into town to spend their hefty pay cheques. The god of disposable incomes had a soft corner for techies and they, in turn, propitiated him by buying up almost everything in sight, without a second thought. Bloody upstarts, he thought, stopping to look at the notes he had made.

A road to the right and down a dirt track, to a tract of empty land. Where was he? Gowda kick-started the bike again and drove down the dirt track, towards the lone building that Santosh and Ratna had described. There was nothing on either side of the road. Just vacant plots of land fenced with barbed wire and a yard with stacks of granite slabs.

He chugged to a halt just outside the building. A boy was sitting by a heap of tyres, trickling water from a tube onto a tyre.

Gowda cursed loudly at his bike and began examining it. He walked towards the boy. 'Where is the nearest petrol bunk?'

The boy looked up. 'Two kilometres away.'

'Sule magane,' Gowda growled, kicking a tyre with his boot. 'The man I borrowed the bike from didn't tell me it had no petrol ... What the fuck am I going to do?'

The boy grinned. 'I can go get the petrol for you,' he offered. 'But ...'

'But what?'

'Will you give me a ride on the Bullet? I've never been on one.'

Gowda frowned. 'I was thinking I'll give you a twenty for the effort.'

'That and the ride,' the boy said, flinging the tube down.

'Hmmm ...' Gowda pretended to think. 'All right then.' He pulled out two hundred-rupee notes from his wallet. 'Get me petrol for 180 and the bill. And keep the twenty'.

The boy whistled as he grabbed an empty two-litre Pepsi bottle from a sack in the shop and ran towards a bicycle leaning against the side of the shop.

Gowda climbed the stairs and stepped into a narrow open verandah that ran from end to end of the first floor. One day it would be rented out as an office or divided up into several small shops. For now it was an empty room with a door and windows and a tiny toilet with an Odisha pan. The walls were distemper washed and the floor was mosaic. Someone had made an effort to clean it but not very hard. Gowda walked from one end to the other of the dank sour-smelling space with a few paint tins and a blue barrel strewn to one side. He looked at the blue barrel thoughtfully. They had sent the bindi to a forensic lab. But he was quite sure it would come to nothing. Could a bindi provide tissue for a DNA or fingerprint match? He didn't even know that. Clutching at straws – that was what they were doing.

He heard the boy call. 'Sir, sir ...'

Gowda went back. There was nothing much to do here.

The boy stood holding up the Pepsi bottle.

Gowda smiled. 'That was quick,' he said. He hoped the boy hadn't bought half a litre of petrol and peed into the bottle to make up the rest of the amber liquid.

The boy grinned.

Gowda opened his petrol tank and began trickling in the fuel. 'You like Pepsi, do you?' he asked.

The boy nodded. 'Very much. When I get it. Why?'

'This bottle?' Gowda said.

'Oh, that ... some people left it behind.'

'Customers? And they didn't give you any?'

The boy made a face. 'I don't know who they were. They spent an afternoon and an evening in the hall upstairs. A man, a woman and a girl. They were the building owner's friends, my boss said. I was asked to bring them biriyani and a bottle of Pepsi. They left exactly so much of the Pepsi,' he said, holding up a narrow sliver between his thumb and forefinger. 'Just enough for one swallow. I kept the bottle. I was going to fill it with water and drop it from the roof. Have you tried it? It explodes with a splash.' The boy had a cheeky grin and Gowda reached out and tugged at the cowlick on his head.

'Shall we go for that ride?' he asked.

The boy's face fell. 'I don't know if the boss will let me go.'

A man drove in on a scooter and parked. He eyed Gowda curiously.

'Oi, what are you up to?' He glowered at the boy.

'Does he know how to remove a flat tyre?' Gowda asked.

'Yes. Why?' The man frowned.

'My car has a flat. Let me take him with me and we'll bring the tyre back.'

The man looked at the boy. 'That will be extra,' he said.

Gowda shrugged. 'Give him your helmet,' he said. 'I don't want the cops catching me.'

The man made a face as he gestured to the boy to take the helmet. 'Put a newspaper on top of your head. I don't want the grease in your hair messing up my helmet.' He watched the boy strap the helmet on. 'Do you have lice?' he asked suddenly.

'No, only camels,' the boy murmured under his breath.

Gowda grinned at his cheek and pulled his phone out and made a call. 'Shenoy, where are you?' he asked. 'I am coming over. Don't leave till I get there.' As an afterthought, he added, 'Please.'

He started the Bullet and gestured for the boy to climb on to the back seat. 'Hold tight,' he said.

In the rearview mirror, Gowda looked at the boy. His face, smeared with dirt, was a picture of happiness. Gowda smiled. He took a small lane that led towards the Airport Road. He saw the boy's eyes widen as they went up the flyover; the sparkle of delight as he raised the accelerator, causing the Bullet to reverberate with its classic note: duk-duk-duk. Another one to the fold, Gowda thought ruefully.

At Sahakarnagar, he pulled into the service road and turned into another lane. He drew up outside a barber shop. Shenoy was seated in a chair, flicking through a magazine. He looked up. His head and jaw bore clear signs of the barber's touch.

Shenoy walked to the door. 'How did you know I would be at this very barber shop?'

Gowda grinned. 'Didn't you tell me you have been coming here for the last six years? Why would you change now?'

Shenoy gestured with his freshly-shaven chin. 'Who is that?'

'A young friend. Is there somewhere nearby we can go for a coffee?'

Shenoy looked at his watch pointedly. 'Coffee?'

Gowda grinned. 'Lunch then, and it's on me!'

Shenoy got on to his Kinetic Honda. 'Follow me,' he said, putting his helmet on.

On the main road was a vegetarian restaurant that Shenoy seemed familiar with. It had mirrors on one wall, festooned with artificial vines and grapes and flowers that would have made a botanist and an oenologist bang their heads on the mirror in puzzlement: How did a lotus grow on a grapevine? There were granite tables with plush red velvet banquettes. There was an industrial-sized pedestal fan at the entrance and an overpowering smell of incense that was guaranteed to take your breath away just in case the decor didn't. The boy's eyes widened, as though Gowda had taken him to a five-star hotel. A matter of perspective, Gowda thought. That's all there is to what amazes us or tires us.

'What do you want to eat?' he asked.

The boy shook his head.

'Have you had lunch?' he asked. The boy shook his head again.

Shenoy watched amused as Gowda had the boy sliding onto the bench and then seated himself at the edge. Shenoy slid into the seat on the other side of the table.

When the waiter came, Gowda ordered a paper dosa for the boy and a curd rice for himself. Shenoy wanted a full thali.

'Are you really that hungry or just making me pay for dragging you here?' Gowda drawled.

Shenoy sipped his water and didn't bother responding.

Gowda looked at the boy and said, 'If there is something else you want to eat after the dosa, let me know.'

The boy nodded. His fingers were sliding along the edge of the red-velvet bench in wonder.

Gowda continued, 'This man is a great artist. He can draw a face just from a description you give him.'

'Really?' The boy's eyes shone. 'Can you draw my brother?'

Gowda shook his head. 'That's too easy. He has you as a reference point. What about the people who stayed upstairs? The ones who left no Pepsi for you.' Gowda turned and clicked his finger at the waiter who had taken their order. 'A Pepsi,' he said.

The boy smiled. 'I saw the woman. I can describe her. I didn't see the man or the girl.'

'That's fine,' Gowda said. Shenoy sighed.

The dosa had been folded to look like a conical hat. It was fragrant with ghee and was accompanied by three small bowls of green chutney, red chutney and sambhar. The boy looked at the plate of food before him and the can of Pepsi, and swallowed visibly.

Gowda opened the can.

'Can I keep the can?' the boy asked. Gowda nodded. 'Start eating,' Gowda said gently.

Shenoy cleared his throat. 'So describe this woman to me.'

The boy cocked his head. 'How do you describe someone?'

Shenoy looked up from his plate lined with several small dishes. 'You tell me if she has a narrow or big forehead, the shape of the eyes, if her nose is thin or fat ...'

The boy smiled. Shenoy pushed aside his plate and pulled out a pad from his sling bag. 'Helli,' he said.

Gowda watched as the pencil flew over the paper. A couple of times Shenoy looked up to meet Gowda's gaze. When it was done, the boy's face split into a wide grin. 'This is exactly the woman.'

Gowda and Shenoy looked at each other. It was the same woman the flower seller had described.

Gowda looked at the boy thoughtfully. 'Have you seen the building owner?'

The boy shook his head. 'He comes to the shop once in a few months, I am told. I am new to that shop.'

'If he ever comes, will you take a good look and call me?' Gowda asked.

The boy nodded. He didn't know what it was all about, but he didn't really care. As Gowda and Shenoy finished their meal, he drained his Pepsi to the last drop. A belch grew in him and erupted with a satisfying hiss of bubbles in his nasal passage. He clutched the Pepsi can as Gowda started the bike.

At home, Gowda was greeted by the sight of a wide open door and a son who looked stoned even with his eyes closed.

The boy was in the living room with one of his legs hooked over the back of the sofa he had sprawled himself upon. He looked like a rabbit, Gowda thought, with his earphones on.

Gowda felt a familiar surge of irritation. 'How did you get in?' he asked, looming over the boy.

There was no response.

Gowda bent down and yanked the earphones off. Roshan almost leapt in the air. 'What the fu ...'

The word was never finished when he saw his father's frown.

'Hello, Appa,' he said, unhooking his leg and sitting up. He smiled.

Gowda managed to turn his grimace into a smile. Who had taught the boy this? He remembered his mother whispering in his ear when his father growled at him. Smile at him when he frowns at you. He will smile back. That is what a smile can do.

Either his mother had returned as a ghost to whisper in the boy's ears or he had been reading one of those self-help books or he was on some substance.

Gowda dropped into a chair. 'Where's Amma?' Roshan asked.

'She had to go back,' Gowda said.

'Why? Did you quarrel?' Roshan asked, as if he were enquiring about the water table, not of any particular consequence to him.

'No, we didn't quarrel. She had to go back because the health minister may come by to the hospital and she needs to make sure that the medicine vials are dusted and the X-ray machine dressed up,' Gowda said.

Roshan grinned. 'Thank god.'

'Why? She wanted us to go to a mall, watch a movie, eat at a restaurant, etc.'

'Exactly. I was dreading it. She asked me if I wanted to go to Amoeba. I wish she'd remember I am twenty, not four, to be taken to a gaming arcade for kids.'

Gowda shrugged. Then he asked again, 'But how did you get in?'

'Amma gave me a key.' Roshan grinned.

Gowda nibbled on his lip. The boy smiled too much. What was he on? There was a new cockiness to him as well.

Gowda glanced at his watch. He would go to the station, he decided. There was nothing else for him to do.

Gowda sat at his desk feeling a strange restlessness gather in him. The files on his desk needed to be dealt with. Neelgubbi had changed. No one saw it more than a policeman. It wasn't just the new high-rise apartment blocks and the arrival of fast-food outlets; the gyms and spas, the sports centre and the liquor marts – it was the nature of crime. Where once the police were called in to settle a squabble between two neighbours about a wandering cow or solve a petty burglary, large-scale gambling, extortion, drugs and prostitution were the new order of crime that Gowda and his station had to contend with.

From the window he saw the head constable talking to two men who looked like they had stopped by on their way from an evening stroll. One wore a t-shirt, shorts and Crocs. The other wore a t-shirt pulled over loose track pants. Who were they?

Across the yard, Gajendra's eyes met his. A few minutes later, he was knocking at his door.

'Who is that Laurel and Hardy team?' he asked.

Gajendra smiled. He could see Gowda was in a curious mood, wanting to scratch an itch without knowing where the itch was.

'They are from that gated community, sir, by the lake. They want to know if they can plant trees here.'

'Plant trees. Why?' Gowda asked.

'They have some extra saplings and no place to plant them.'

Gowda nodded. 'Let them.'

'But sir,' Gajendra said, looking distinctly unhappy, 'who will water them? Besides, aren't we moving from here?'

Gowda pulled at the skin of his nose. 'The trees will be here when we are gone. And I am not talking about the new police station. As for watering them, tell Laurel and Hardy to handle it till the saplings grow three feet high. After which we will figure out something.'

Gajendra went out, wondering where Santosh was. Gowda might want to take up a puppy adoption drive if he didn't move ahead with the Nandita case.

By the time Gowda had read through the fourth file on his desk, the phone was ringing. It was Santosh.

'We haven't been able to get anything on the landlord, sir. Apparently the shop in the building is leased for two years. There is a rental agreement. The tyre shop owner will bring it to the station on Saturday.'

'Why not later today?' Gowda growled.

'He says it is in the bank locker in Dharwad,' Santosh said.

Gowda muttered an expletive that must have caused Santosh to flinch. He could hear Ratna ask, 'What's wrong?'

'Are you coming back to the station?' Gowda asked.

'We are on our way to Bagaluru station, sir,' Santosh said. 'There is a juvenile offender there we need to question.'

'Let's meet tomorrow, first thing in the morning. We need to discuss what to do next,' Gowda said as he hung up. He needed a smoke.

As he stood under the mango tree by the almost dried-up lake, away from the comings and goings of the frontyard, Gowda was struck by a thought. The MLA's name had already appeared in three files. The man was a lowdown bastard. But perhaps he had something that might lead them to Nandita. It wasn't the orthodox thing to do, ask a criminal for help, but Gowda didn't play by the rulebook anyway.

Gowda parked outside the MLA's house. It was called Bella Manne. The white house in which the man who dressed only in white lived. Outside, in the driveway, was a fleet of white cars, including a Jaguar. The gates were wide open and a few feet beyond them was an arch from which a huge bell was strung with a bell rope. Gowda gaped. Who on earth did the MLA think he was? The Mughal emperor Jahangir with his bell of justice?

Gowda saw the MLA get into a car as he walked through the gate. He stopped, unsure what to do next. He had come on a whim. The car pulled up alongside him and a window rolled down. 'What can I do for you, Inspector?' MLA Papanna asked.

'I had a few queries about the landfill on the north of Rampura lake, the garbage truck accident outside the school and the assault on one Gopal Reddy in Bilishivale,' Gowda said without any of the mandatory preamble.

The man looked at him and said, 'You needn't have come all this way yourself. You could have sent a constable and my PA would have given him whatever information was required.'

Gowda shrugged. 'I wanted to meet you, sir.'

The man flashed his plank teeth. 'In which case, do make an appointment with my PA, Gowda sir, and you can ask me whatever you want. My life is an open book. Like my doorway. All you need to do is ring the bell and I will make myself available.'

When the MLA drove away, Gowda was inclined to do what Head Constable Gajendra did as a preamble to all interrogation, to suggest total contempt: pretend to spit on the floor with an aa-thoo and snarl, 'Lowde ka baal!'

Instead, he decided to go home.

The house was empty when Gowda arrived. The gate lights were on and the porch light too. He must have missed Roshan by a few minutes. Usually, Gowda came home to a dark house. That was what he hated most about living alone. He hadn't thought Roshan was the caring kind. But surprise, surprise ...

Gowda changed into track pants, pulled on his running shoes and set off on a brisk walk. If he walked for an hour, he would pour himself a drink. That would be his reward.

Fifteen minutes later, he paused in his tracks. Would Urmila be free to see him this evening? He had cancelled their dinner plan. Did he dare turn up at her doorstep, expecting to be fed, indulged and loved? Gowda sighed. He didn't blame her for getting Mr Right. At least he was constant.

———·———

I went back to the godown in Sampigehalli. I needed to see her again.

'Ah, the chhote nawab is back!' Daulat Ali said, his mouth twisting into a smirk.

I tried to hide the sheepishness I felt. But Daulat Ali wasn't going to let it be.

'Can't keep it in your pants, huh?' he said, reaching to cup my balls with a laugh.

'Take your hands off me,' I said, moving back. 'And don't ever do that again!'

He flinched. I had learnt my lesson from the thekedar well. I knew how to melt ice with my smile. I also knew how to freeze the marrow with a certain look and tone of voice.

'Who is it? Moina again?' he asked, turning away.

'What about the new girl?' I walked towards the cubicle she had been in.

He put his hand on my arm. 'No, not her. The thekedar has said he will decide when she is to enter the business.' I was not quick enough to hide my dismay. Daulat Ali seized on it and added, 'I think he's keeping her for some big fish.'

'Ah, all right.' I shrugged. 'A cunt is a cunt ...' I feigned a nonchalance that I didn't feel. I didn't want Daulat Ali reporting to the thekedar what he had seen on my face. In this world you cannot trust anyone. Not even your shadow. For even that changes with the light.

'Tell Moina to clean up,' I said, walking back to the main door. 'I'll be back in half an hour.'

When I returned I had a few things in a plastic bag. The metal shutters were down. What the hell was going on, I wondered, banging on them.

Daulat Ali appeared it. He looked grim.

'What's up?' I asked.

'That new randi ki ladli ...' he murmured. 'She tried to run away.'

'How do you know she's a whore's daughter?' I asked with an artlessness that I knew would set his teeth on edge.

'Oii chhote nawab.' He glowered at me. 'Don't be so fucking literal! You are so good at teaching people lessons, aren't you? Go in there and teach her a lesson. If I do, she won't have any teeth left.'

I walked into the cubicle. She was crouched on the floor, her cheeks wet with tear stains. She stared at me defiantly.

'Get up,' I said in Kannada. Moina had said she was from Bangalore.

'Anna,' she said. 'Help me, please.'

'I will.' I sat by her side. 'But you have to do as I say.'

She nodded.

'Do you trust me, Nandita?'

I saw her eyes widen in surprise. She hadn't expected me to remember her name. 'I don't know,' she said. I smiled then. I would have to teach her to trust me.

'Scream,' I said. 'Scream as if you are in pain.'

She stared at me. 'Why?'

I lit a cigarette with my lighter. I saw the fear in her eyes. I brought it towards her. She whimpered.

'Scream,' I said under my breath.

But she wouldn't. So I stubbed the flaming end of the cigarette on the inner side of my upper arm. The smell of burnt skin. The charred flesh.

She screamed then. Again and again. Three long screams followed by one that stopped suddenly.

Her eyes filled with tears. 'Anna, what did you do? Why?'

'Because I cannot hurt you. And because I want you to trust me,' I said, feeling the burn sting. I reached across and caressed her cheek. 'Nandita, my name is Krishna. I will always be here for you.'

'I'm scared, anna,' she said.

'I know.' I took her hand in mine. 'When you're scared, recite the multiplication tables ... It will make you feel less scared.'

I got up and left the bag behind. I had meant to ask Moina to give it to her. It had a bar of chocolate, a magazine and a hair band. I had no idea what girls liked. But something told me she would like these.

'I'll be back,' I said.

She looked at me wordlessly.

'Don't worry,' I said. 'I'll make sure no one does anything to hurt you.'

She smiled then. My girl.

Moina frowned. She smelled chocolate when she entered the cubicle. She saw Nandita shove a book behind her. 'What is that?' she pointed.

Nandita shook her head. Then she held out the magazine and the last bit of chocolate.

'Where did you get that?' Moina gestured, popping the chocolate into her mouth. It slid like silk down her throat.

Nandita flushed. 'Anna!' she said, gesturing to suggest someone taller than her.

'Krishna?' Moina asked. So that was what had happened. Daulat Ali had asked her to get ready for Krishna. She thought she had heard his voice. And he had come to see this brat instead of her.

Nandita nodded.

'Did he fuck you?' Moina asked.

Nandita looked at her uncomprehendingly.

Moina exhaled and smiled. 'I suppose not. He is mine. Do you hear me? Don't try and take him away.'

Suddenly the curtain was pulled rudely aside. Daulat Ali stood there looking at them.

'Where did that chocolate come from?'

Nandita shrunk into the corner.

'K—' she began when Moina butted in.

'One of my customers left it behind with the book. I gave the book to her and we shared the chocolate.'

Daulat Ali looked at her for a long moment. 'Get back to your cubicle. There is someone coming in.' Daulat Ali turned to look at Nandita. Something about the girl bothered him. He couldn't put his finger on it but it would come to him sooner than later. Nothing escaped Daulat Ali for too long. Runaway girls, non-paying clients, debts or wandering thoughts.

———•———

Sid glanced at his phone. Where was she? She was late by twenty minutes. They needed to get to a service apartment in Indiranagar. In the rush-hour traffic, there was no way they would get there in time.

Bitch, fucking cunt, he thought as he messaged her: Rex, where are you? He would have to park his bike somewhere on Church Street and take her on the metro.

He saw the double-tick appear. Received. He saw the double-tick turn blue. Read. What the fuck! Why wasn't she responding?

He called her number. The phone rang but she didn't pick up. The money in his wallet burned. It was the advance he had received. He was to pick up the balance once he dropped her off.

He slammed the petrol tank of the bike with his fist. Money was one thing, but the person he had talked to was not going to like it if he didn't deliver as promised. Displeasure was shown in many forms, the cucumber seller had warned him. 'Don't get into it if you can't keep your word. At this point, saying no won't cost you anything. But once you take up a job, if you don't finish it, you'll be screwed. Royally. Left and right. Up and down. In and out. You won't know if you're breathing through your nostrils or your arsehole.'

Sid had laughed at the man's rhetoric. Only now he thought he was going to cry. What had he got himself into? What was he going to do? If she didn't turn up, his arse was fried.

Where the fuck was she? And why wasn't she taking his call?

Rex ... Come on, baby ... he whispered, calling her again. And again.

———•———

They were sitting in the living room watching a DVD. It was one of their favourite things to do. He peeled an orange and gave it to her segment by segment. When his phone vibrated on the coffee table, he looked at it, frowning.

He put the orange down and rose. Then he picked up his phone and walked to the next room. She gazed up at him.

'Why do you leave the room each time you have to use the phone?' she asked. 'What is it that you don't want me to hear?'

'Wife, I don't want to ask you to lower the volume of the TV.' He smiled and whispered, 'Back in two minutes.'

She paused the film. He walked out into the verandah.

'Pujary, where is the girl?' the MLA barked into his ear.

'Isn't she there?' he asked softly.

'If she was, would I call? You fucking ruined my mood ...' the man grumbled.

'Let me sort it out,' he said, trying to placate the man.

'Ah, forget it! I'm going home. You are a useless fellow, I say.' The phone went silent.

Pujary felt his heartburn begin. He walked back into the room.

'Who was it? Your girlfriend?' Gita asked. 'Why did you leave the room to take the call?'

'Gita, don't ever say that to me again,' he snapped. 'Do you hear me?'

She stared at him, unable to hide her fear and dismay. 'I ...' she said, 'I was only joking.'

He dropped to the floor and laid his head on her knees. 'I am sorry ... I am sorry ... I don't know what came over me.'

'Everything all right?' she murmured, running her fingers through his stubble-length hair.

He rubbed the middle of his chest. 'Acidity!' he said, making a face. 'And that call didn't help.'

'You shouldn't have had so much of that mango pickle at lunch!' she scolded.

'I know.' He smiled.

He felt his heartburn turn into a lump of cold rage and fear.

Gita knew something was troubling him even though he tried to hide it behind that wornout excuse: acidity.

She was not a fool even though he liked to think she was naïve. That her world was all black and white with the two of them firmly entrenched in the light of white. Government servants, as he often referred to himself in the early years of their marriage, had limited means. When their first house and car were acquired, she knew that he had stepped into the grey zone of compromise. They had more than what a government servant could afford. But she had looked away like she did when he touched himself under the sheet with his back to her. He needed his release like he needed challenges to shape his day. Besides, she knew that he wasn't a bad man. He wouldn't do anything that moved from the grey zone into the midnight space of black. She knew that about him. Sometimes she thought she knew him better than he knew himself.

Gita took his hand in hers and began cracking his knuckles one by one. He smiled at her.

12 MARCH, THURSDAY

Mavelli Tiffin Room was crowded. But that was to be expected, Pujary thought as he left the car running and rushed in. They knew him by sight and name. He had been doing this for almost three decades now.

Old Bangaloreans like him saw in MTR one of the last links to the past, while the new Bangaloreans, he thought, throwing a contemptuous look at a group that sat wolfing down their tiffin. They came here for the food as much as to be able to mention breezily their visits to MTR. That way everyone else would see them as true-blue Bangaloreans and not those upstart immigrants with software degrees, overpaid jobs in one of the IT companies, pseudo trans-Atlantic accents that slipped every few minutes, and no roots.

Pujary paid for his order. He had ordered breakfast in advance.

'Idlis, chutney, vada and chandrakala.' It was Gita's favourite breakfast. Every Thursday they went to Lal Bagh and picnicked there. He would push her wheelchair for a little stroll along the paths on which it was possible to do so. They would return home by lunchtime.

Gita would have liked something else once in a while. And another place. She was bored with the Thursday routine. But he was a very busy man and yet he kept aside this time for them. So she said nothing and played along. Besides, that was the only time they reverted to being the madly-and-recklessly-in-love couple they had once been. They chatted, they laughed, and for once he stopped treating her like she was fragile China.

But that morning there was something unsaid between them. Who would speak about it first, each of them wondered as they sat silently in the car.

Eventually, Gita said in a small voice, 'I would like to go home.'

Pujary nodded. He took a U-turn at the Lal Bagh gate and they drove back in almost total silence.

She felt his gaze on her as he put the food away. 'We'll have it for tiffin in the evening,' he said.

She smiled. It wrenched at his gut. He had never seen her look so forlorn or unhappy. Not even when she had been told she would never walk on her own again.

'We need to talk,' he said.

'Yes.'

When his phone buzzed, it was a welcome reprieve. 'I have to go, wife,' he said. 'There is something I need to deal with right away.'

She watched him leave without once asking her if she needed to be helped upstairs. It had never happened before.

———•———

She had been awake when he came into their room last night. She couldn't sleep. The sleeping pill had slipped out of her hand and fallen on the floor, and she had decided to go without, rather than ask him for another one. He had been troubled all evening and she didn't know what she could do to help. It was on days like this that she wished he had walked out on her. She could see he was fretting about something, a worry that he couldn't toss into the air and make it disappear like he always did. But he had pretended everything was wonderful as always. She had lain in bed, wondering what was wrong as he straightened the quilt over her. But she hadn't asked. And she wouldn't.

Once upon a time they had shared a bed. Once upon a time, every few weeks, he would make love to her as if she were the most beautiful creature on earth. He would kiss and caress her so her breasts tingled, but she felt nothing below her waist and lay there like a log spliced into two halves. God, that lazy woodcutter, gave her at least that much, she told herself. She could give him an orifice to expend into.

A few years ago she had suggested that they have twin beds rather than share one. She hoped he would take that as a cue that she no longer wanted intimacy between them. It was time he had a real woman in his life.

Did he have another woman? Gita had often wondered. She wouldn't blame him, she thought, looking at her shrivelled legs and caved-in cheeks. She wouldn't grudge him anything. She would kill for him; she would die for him.

And he would do the same for her, she knew.

Usually he joined her in an hour, by which time the sleeping pill would have taken effect and she would feel his lips press down on hers as he whispered, 'Good night, my love.'

That night, he had done the same as always. Turning her on her side so she faced his side of the bed, smoothening the side of the bed she had been lying on. Tucking the quilt under her chin, and then turning off the bedside lamp. He kissed her on the lips and got into the twin bed. She had pretended to be asleep. She would ask herself again and again why she had not let him know that she was awake.

He had ordered a special mattress for her to make sure she didn't develop bedsores. But once a night, he woke up and shifted her position. He didn't see it as a chore and when she suggested they bring in a carer – 'You aren't getting any younger, husband' – he had been upset.

'Have I ever reneged on my promise?' he had asked.

'No, but you need to sleep, a full night's sleep,' she had replied. Some days his love for her stifled her.

He was propped up against the pillows, reading the Bhagwad Gita, when the call came. She saw him reach for the phone and look at it. She felt him glance towards her. Then he murmured softly, 'Yes ... I am setting it all up for the weekend. One of the girls is already here. The other girl will reach tomorrow ... Yes, they are both twelve years old like I said.'

Suddenly he had looked her way and met her gaze. She closed her eyes. He had cut the call then.

'Gita,' he had whispered.

But she hadn't stirred. Her eyes were pressed shut.

'Gita, I ...' he began and then said nothing.

He must have a reason for talking about the children. What was he going to do with them?

All these years, the climb to prosperity had seemed a natural progression for someone as ambitious and hardworking as her husband. He was a businessman. But what was the nature of his business?

She had asked a few times and he had said, 'Property. Commodity. Security. You name it and I have something to do with it. But you wouldn't understand, wife. Don't worry about it. I am here to do all the worrying for you!'

She had felt him continuing to look at her. For the first time in all the years they had been together, she felt uncertain. Who was this man? What did he really do? What did he need two twelve-year-olds for?

When she heard Pujary's car drive away and the creak of the gates as the watchman pulled shut, Gita pressed the button on her motorized wheelchair and rode into the study.

She opened the drawers of his desk and began looking at the files he kept there. She put her glasses on and started reading.

Pujary realized that he was being kept waiting. And that when MLA Papanna decided to see him, it wouldn't be an easy conversation.

He wondered what the politician's tone of voice would be: Angry? Sarcastic? Condescending? Dismissive? Abusive?

Whatever it was, he had no option but to take it without fuelling his rage any further.

'I thought I was sitting on a gold mine; now it's just a kakoos because of you,' MLA Papanna said by way of greeting.

Pujary flinched. The MLA was a crude man and he had expected nothing less from him. But he hadn't heard the colloquial term for a hole-in-the-ground toilet in a long while.

'It was 200 crore ... do you hear me? That's what the lawyer agreed to and now he has changed his mind. Who got to him? One of your rivals?'

Flecks of spit splattered Pujary's face. He drew out a handkerchief and wiped himself calmly. 'We'll find another buyer ...' So MLA Papanna was the man behind the aggregator.

The MLA calmed down. He took a long gulp of water. 'What happened to the lawyer?'

Pujary shrugged. 'I don't know. He agreed to everything and suddenly changed his mind. '

MLA Papanna asked slyly, 'Are you losing your touch? The lawyer's gone off the deal and you know nothing about it. And that lovely morsel you promised me didn't turn up either. Are you up to playing this game? Or have your teeth and talons blunted, Pujary?'

For a few moments, Pujary asked himself the same. Had he turned soft?

At first, crime had been his way to survive and make life better for Gita. Then it became a profession. And now the rush of it kept him going. Manipulating lives and deals; it let him forget that he had little control over his own life or the slavish love that he had for Gita.

'There is another party,' Pujary said. 'But he needs to be coaxed.'

'So what are you waiting for?' the MLA snorted.

'Two young girls,' Pujary said, remembering what he had heard about the mining baron's preferences. 'Someone I know is setting it up.'

The MLA's eyes lit up. 'Virgins? How young?'

'Twelve, I am told. Apparently they are the same height, same size, everything, the only difference is that one is ebony and the other ivory ...'

The MLA almost smacked his lips. 'And when he's done, I want them. I want an orgy too.' He used the English word orgy, only he said it like 'froggie'.

'You will have your orgy when I receive my commission.' Pujary mimicked the MLA with a straight face.

Pujary thought of the girl he had set up for the lawyer and how that had misfired. He was going to fix that arrogant bustard. But before that, there was one more thing to take care of.

———•———

I woke up with a start. My mobile was ringing. It was by my pillow. I picked it up. It was a little past ten in the morning and the thekedar was calling.

'Saab ...' I said, sitting up.

'We need to talk,' he said.

'Yes, saab ...' I wiped the sleep from my eyes with the back of my hand.

'I have a job for you,' The thekedar said.

I swallowed. What was going on?

The previous evening, I had called the thekedar. I was his trusted lieutenant and I thought he would listen to me. He did, and then said no.

'Why?' I asked.

The thekedar was silent. Then he asked, 'Do I hear some rumblings of dissent? All for a girl. The scriptures teach you that again and again: Kingdoms fall for the love of gold and lust for women. Who would have thought you, my Krishna, would succumb too?'

'She is worth a lot,' he said when I didn't respond. 'I can't let her go just like that.' Then, for the first time ever, the thekedar spoke almost as if to justify his decision. 'It's not really in my control. There are others who have a greater say in what we do. And they will not allow it.'

I imagined I was looking straight at him and said, 'What if I pay the price?'

'They may consider it then. But it will be a lot of money ...' I heard the surprise in his voice. 'What has got into you, boy?'

'How much?'

The thekedar pretended not to hear the belligerence in my tone. 'Two lakhs. Do you have that much?'

'I will by the end of the week. I have never asked anything of you, thekedar. Will you wait that long? Please ...' I kept my voice low and imploring.

'I can't promise anything but I will do my best,' he said. 'What's so special about the girl?'

I shook my head. 'I don't know.'

I squashed the fugitive hope that he may have called with a solution. The thekedar wasn't given to grand gestures. He would extract every single drop of my blood, sweat and semen too, before he let me have her. But I was prepared.

———•———

Across the city, at a watch shop in Safina Plaza, Gowda stared at the watches on display. 'Is there something you like?' he asked Roshan, who was staring at his phone again.

'Oh, what?' he asked, looking up. 'Appa, I told you I don't want a watch. No one in my generation wears one.'

'But you are studying to be a doctor. Don't you need to time the pulse rate?'

The sales clerk behind the counter suppressed a sigh. Each time a fond father wanted to buy his son a watch, the brat always wanted something else.

'My phone is better. It has a stop clock. So if you really want to get me something, please make it a hard disk,' Roshan said. 'Or a set of new headphones. Actually what I would like are boots.'

Gowda rubbed his forehead. 'Why would you need to wear boots in Hassan? It's so hot there ...'

'I thought we were here to buy Thatha a gift,' Roshan said.

'He doesn't want a watch either,' Gowda growled.

The sales clerk sighed. 'It seems to me, sir, that neither the young nor the old perceive any value in watches. It's only us middle-aged who wear them. We have a very fine everyday wear range. Would you like to look at it?'

Gowda was tempted, but he knew he wouldn't feel right without the old HMT on his wrist. 'I'll be back,' he said as they stepped out.

Gowda had taken the day off. It was his father's birthday, and his brother Nagendra had insisted Gowda and Roshan join the family for lunch.

Gowda had said he would drop by in the evening. But Nagendra, who seldom said much, snapped at his brother, 'It's once a year, for heaven's sake, Borei. Do you think he is going to live forever?'

Gowda had been mortified. Urmila was right. He didn't see the forest for the trees. 'I'll be there,' he said. 'I'll bring Roshan along.' Even if I have to handcuff him and drag him by the scruff of his neck, he thought.

So here they were, on the way to the birthday lunch. And Gowda, who was doing his being-a-good-son bit, had tried to extend it to being-a-good-father. Except it seemed to him that he had not a clue how to be either. His father looked at the shirt Gowda gave him and grimaced. 'Why do you waste money like this? Do you know how many shirts I have in my bureau?'

His sister-in-law Meena touched Gowda's elbow, warning him not to snap back. 'If I had come in bearing no gifts, he would have sulked. What does he want from me?' Gowda whispered furiously to Nagendra and Meena.

Nagendra led him towards the paved frontyard where two coconut trees stood sentinel by the gate. 'He planted these trees when we were born, one for each of us,' Nagendra said.

'So?' Gowda mumbled.

'Most days he talks to the tree that is supposed to be you. He misses you, Borei. So when he sees you, he doesn't know how to react. Come see him more often. After a certain age, that's all parents expect from children – their presence.'

Borei Gowda lit a cigarette. Nagendra had a gentle way of stating facts that made Gowda want to bury his head in the ground in shame. 'I know I should,' Gowda said. 'But work ...'

'If you think it's important, you'll make the time, Borei,' his brother said firmly. 'We are going to get there as well, Borei, and our children will learn from us.'

His cigarette felt like ashes in his mouth.

A neighbour waved as he drove past. 'Isn't that Shankar?' Gowda asked.

'Yes.' Nagendra made a face. 'He's just come back from the Sringeri mutt; that man is at some holy place or the other every week!'

Another neighbour came towards the gate. Someone Gowda hadn't met before.

Jayanagar too had changed. The property next door had been sold to a real-estate developer who was going to build a block of flats there. In time Nagendra might want to do the same. There would be nothing left of his childhood home, except the trees, perhaps, and memories. Gowda knew why he didn't find the time to come here more often. His childhood home made him maudlin; stirred up emotions he didn't like to feel. The inevitability of time going by and the certainty of the death of loved ones.

At fifty, what man can beguile himself into thinking life and its possibilities are forever? Only a fool would go on tilting at windmills and fighting shadows. In his home, in his station house, time seemed to stand still, making him feel in control of his hours if not his destiny. He stubbed out the cigarette and went back in.

Roshan was showing his grandfather how Instagram worked. The stern expression on his grandfather's face had been replaced with one of wonder. 'You mean to say that total strangers around the world can see our photograph?'

Gowda peered at Roshan's phone. So this was the Instagram thing he had heard Santosh and Ratna refer to.

'Let's shoot a picture of the three of us,' Gowda suggested in a voice he had heard fun-loving fathers use on TV commercials.

Soon Gowda had the app on his phone and Roshan helped him put up the photograph with appropriate tags: #FatherSonGrandfather, #HappyFamilies, #BirthdaySurprise and #LifeIsForLiving.

Was there one called #fuckingwastedtime or #joblessidiots or #neveragain or #notevenifiampaidforit? This would be his first and last Instagram, Gowda decided, trying to mask his discomfort at such blatant exhibitionism.

They were sitting in the living room, making desultory conversation after an enormous birthday lunch.

Gowda had frowned, watching Roshan shovel the food into his mouth hungrily as though he hadn't eaten for a week. Was the boy stoned?

'Why are you frowning?' his father asked. Gowda plastered a smile on his face and mouthed something inane to Meena. 'Are beans in season now? These are very tasty.'

Nagendra had stared at him amused but said nothing.

And now Roshan lay on the sofa with headphones plugged into his ears. Why did the boy need headphones when he already had a pair? Suddenly Roshan sat up. 'Tell you what,' Roshan said. 'Why don't you give me the money instead?'

'Instead of what?' Gowda asked. His face ached from all the smiling he had to subject it to.

'Instead of the hard disk that I asked for instead of the watch,' Roshan explained patiently.

'He was always a little slow,' the indulgent grandfather pitched in.

Gowda mumbled a noncommittal huh.

He had done all that was expected of him. Played son, brother, brother-in-law and father. Now it was time to get back to the station house and his desk. That was one place where he knew who he really was.

Borei Gowda was ready to leave. But how was he going to get away without ruffling feathers?

When his phone rang and DCP Mirza's image popped up, Gowda grabbed it like a drowning man clutching at a straw.

———•———

Gowda and Santosh drove up in the official vehicle. For once Gowda's shoes shone and his uniform appeared to have come straight from the drycleaner's. Santosh darted secret looks at Gowda. He had never seen him so spruced up or as relaxed.

David turned onto a narrow tarred road alongside a eucalyptus grove. 'But isn't this the way to MLA Papanna's house?' Gowda asked.

'Yes. And the home is in the next compound,' Santosh said.

DCP Mirza had called, asking Gowda to attend the inauguration of the home. 'Our official presence is required there. I hear the home minister for the state may come in. And the women and children's welfare minister will certainly be there.'

Gowda chewed on his lips thoughtfully. The MLA had his fingers in too many pies and connections that seemed to spread like the roots of a ficus tree. He was yet to make the appointment with the PA. He would try and fix it first thing tomorrow morning, he decided. And would let Santosh handle it. The PA would have his guard up if Gowda spoke to him. He would see him for who he was; a policeman on the prowl. Santosh was very good at weeding out details and his clear-cut boyish looks made him seem more earnest than shrewd.

'All of this area is his,' David said. 'He buys up all the access routes around and the small landowners are trapped within, with no entry or exit points. He then buys them out at half the market rate.'

'You seem very bitter,' Gowda said.

'My cousin lost all his earnings,' David said.

The road to the girls' home was lined with cars. The building was outlined with serial light bulbs and the gate was festooned with marigold garlands. Two plantain trees were tied to the gateposts.

'I wish he had used the money on the girls' home,' Santosh snorted.

Gajendra patted down his moustache. 'How will the locals know about the home he has funded if he doesn't make a song and dance about it?'

Gowda smiled and then worried if his cynicism was contagious.

'I don't know if you heard, sir, but when he had his housewarming ceremony, he had a helicopter shower rose petals on his house. That's the sort of man he is!' Gajendra added.

'All he needed to do was have someone shine a torch on his teeth. It would have lit up the place,' Byrappa said, looking at Santosh.

Santosh grinned. He was beginning to like Byrappa more and more.

When Gowda's phone rang, he saw it was an unknown number. He wondered if he should pick it up.

Santosh called Ratna. 'Where are you?' he asked.

'Home. Why? Is there any news of Nandita?' she asked.

'No, but something else has come up,' he said. 'I'll pick you up in twenty minutes, if not earlier,' he added.

She opened the door as soon as he rang the bell. Her flatmate watched them leave. Ratna and she had planned to watch a movie. 'Where are you going?' she asked.

'I'll be back soon,' Ratna said.

Santosh watched her put on her helmet. 'I'm not so sure about that.'

She swung her leg over the pillion seat. 'What's going on?'

Santosh met her eyes in the rearview mirror. 'Gowda sir received a piece of information. There is somebody at the place where Nandita was taken to. The room above the tyre shop.'

Santosh didn't want to reveal more than that to her. He knew it had taken all of Gowda's goodwill, built over the years, and considerable machination to set up the operation in forty-five minutes. Gowda had made sure that the rulebook had been followed to the exact clause and word.

'The station head of that outpost, Basavappa, used to work with Gowda as a young SI and worships him. Which is probably why he is stuck in that outpost,' Gajendra had said ruefully.'We need to keep this very quiet. One careless word could change everything.'

Ratna was trustworthy, Santosh's heart told him. But they had known each other less than a week, his head warned him. 'We'll know more when we get there,' he said.

Santosh rode his bike to the end of the road where the building was. Ratna and he walked towards a car parked at a little distance from the building so as to not draw attention to themselves.

They waited quietly in Gowda's car. Twenty minutes later, Basavappa and two constables arrived in a jeep and parked a hundred feet away from Gowda's car.

There was a low wattage light in the top floor; otherwise, the building was wreathed in darkness. Gowda and Basavappa, followed by Ratna, climbed the stairs as quietly as they could. Byrappa and Gajendra covered the back of the building. Santosh stood at the foot of the staircase with the constables, who looked bored and grumpy. The T20 series between India and Australia was on and Virat Kohli had just come in to bat.

'What do you think B-report Gowda is chasing now?' one of them grumbled.

Santosh glared at them. 'Hush,' he whispered furiously.

They crept along the narrow verandah towards the doorway that Gowda remembered from his exploration. In the light of a naked bulb, Gowda saw through the door a young girl dressed in clothes too grown-up for her, a little boy and a middle-aged man. The man stood up and walked towards them. 'Did the thekedar send you?' he asked Gowda in Hindi.

Then he saw the man in uniform. Gowda saw the panic on his face replaced by a sullen expression as he demanded, 'Yes, what can I do for you?'

'Who are these children?' Gowda asked softly.

'Children?' The man laughed. 'That's my woman. My new wife. And he is my son from my first wife who died last year.'

'She can't be more than fourteen,' Ratna said, bristling. 'It's a crime to marry a minor girl.'

'Who said she is a minor? She is nineteen.' The man stood his ground.

'Do you have proof?' Basavappa growled.

'What proof do you want? We are here in Bangalore to visit relatives. We are from Bombay,' the man said.

'If you are here to visit relatives, why are you in this unfinished building?' Gowda asked, his gaze lingering on the children. The boy's face was a mess. The girl had a healing bruise on one cheek. The children looked like they would never smile again.

As the man began a convoluted explanation, the girl stood up and came towards him. 'I is Tina,' she said in English. 'I is twelve years old. I is not his missus. Abdul not his son.'

There was a moment of silence. Then the man tried to race past them towards the balcony.

Gowda stuck his leg out and tripped him. Then he sank his fist into the man's face. As the man crumpled to the ground, Gowda saw joy flare in the children's eyes even if their faces stayed resolutely grim.

———•———

'How did you know?' Gajendra asked as they drove back after dropping PC Byrappa home.

The man had been taken to the station lock-up by SI Basavappa, and the children to a shelter by Ratna. Santosh had gone with her.

'The boy ... Muthu ... I had asked him to call me if there was any activity in the first floor of the building.'

'And he actually did? What did you give him?' Gajendra couldn't hold back the surprise in his voice.

'A can of Pepsi,' Gowda said.

'Are you serious?'

'I have never been more serious. He is eleven years old. The usual story – stepfather beat him every day till he fled. He should be in school; instead, he is working for a pittance in the tyre shop.' Gowda spoke as if he were speaking to himself. 'He's a smart boy ... and it's sad that he'll get nowhere. Unless ...'

'What are you thinking, sir?' Gajendra was worried. What new scheme did Gowda have germinating in his head now?

'Nothing as of now ...' Gowda drew up outside Gajendra's home.

'Good night,' Gowda said. 'Actually, good morning. It's 1.00 a.m.'

13 MARCH, FRIDAY

I glanced at my phone. It was 3.00 a.m. I couldn't sleep. I didn't know what to do.

The previous evening, the thekedar had wanted me to pick up three items from K.R. Puram station. I had thought nothing of it and did as he asked.

Then the thekedar said I should come to the godown. He was already there when I reached.

'There is something that has come up,' he told the men. 'A party,' he elaborated.

'At the farmhouse?' I asked.

'Where else?' the thekedar said. 'I need it to go right from start to finish.'

I nodded. I had helped out at a few parties before. Kebabs and booze, music, the lights on trees, cocaine for those who wanted it and viagra for those who couldn't get it up, porn on pen drives, all leading to the bedroom with the waterbed, mirrors and screaming girls. That seemed to excite the men until the girls turned into pliable orifices.

'What about the girls?' I asked, my mouth going dry. I knew what was coming.

'There's the one you picked up this evening. And we have one girl here. Together they'll make my client very happy.' The thekedar's face and voice betrayed no emotion.

I gazed at the floor. 'Thekedar.' I tried to choose words that wouldn't form. 'Isn't there anyone else?'

He sighed. 'No ... I can't wait. The client said he didn't want Nepali or Bangladeshi girls. He wanted a Kannadiga girl, he said. He insisted.'

I felt the lump in my chest grow. He patted me on my back. 'Krishna, these things happen.'

He looked at Daulat Ali. I saw the beefy guard give him an imperceptible nod.

We drove back in silence. Just when it was time for me to get off, I asked, 'Won't you reconsider?'

'I cannot,' he said softly, almost apologetically. 'There is much at stake. Besides, once I make an exception for you, the rest of them will expect the same.' His fingers tapped the steering wheel impatiently.

'But I am not everyone. I am Krishna.'

He stared at me. 'I made you Krishna.' The chill in the car made me shiver. 'Without me, there would be no Krishna.'

I stood watching the car turn the corner.

Then I waved down an auto. 'Sampigehalli,' I told the driver.

Daulat Ali wouldn't let me in. 'The thekedar said no one is to be allowed to see her,' he said.

'The thekedar didn't mean me,' I said, grinning.

'He said especially you.'

Daulat Ali, I noticed, wasn't calling me chhote nawab as he usually did.

'Oh, keep that little lollipop for yourself. What about Moina? I can fuck her, right?' I said, sighing. 'I am going to explode if I don't.' I made a gesture of shoving my thumb into the fist of my other hand.

But he didn't grin. Instead, he said, 'She is busy.'

'Rubbish,' I said, trying to go past him. But he wouldn't let me.

'Go away,' he said. 'Don't make this worse for yourself.'

'What do you mean?'

'I asked you to teach that girl a lesson, and instead you bought her chocolates. Do you think my name is Stupid?' he asked.

'No, I know your name is Daulat Ali,' I tried to joke.

'Go,' he said.

I tried to shove him. He shoved me back. I slapped him then. He slapped me back. Two others I had never seen before came to his aid.

'Get out,' Daulat Ali said. I left.

I lay on the bed, hearing the thekadar's words in my head: I made you Krishna. These things happen.

I had thought I was special. The chosen one. I had thought that the thekedar would make allowances for me. But I realized I was nothing more to him than one more element in the grand scheme of things.

When I fled the kiln as a young boy, I had no idea where I was going or what I was going to do. I didn't want to go home. My father would only send me back. So I hid in a truck. I didn't know where it was headed. I didn't particularly care. When the truck stopped, I saw it was a rest point. There were shacks on the roadside and loud music, and I knew that way lay the prospect of work and food.

I worked in a dhaba. I cleaned. I fetched water. I cleaned the toilet that wouldn't be clean no matter what one did to clean it. I washed dishes. I chopped vegetables. I kneaded dough. I plucked the chickens someone else killed. In a few weeks, I killed my first chicken. I didn't feel anything. It was just a job to be done.

I wasn't paid anything but once in a while the truck drivers would leave a few coins for me. Once, one of them left a lighter behind, which I pocketed. It was a metal lighter.

I don't remember how long I was there. But the day I had a hundred rupees, I took my lighter and cadged a ride with another truck driver. That was how I arrived in Bangalore. For a while I lived with a bunch of boys and girls on the streets. We begged, stole, foraged through garbage and we survived. Then, one day, I was hit by a car while darting across the road with a wallet I had picked from somebody's pocket.

A woman took me to a hospital. When she discovered I was a street child, she took me home. I was given a bath, new clothes, food to eat and a name – Rakesh. She was apparently a great admirer of some man called Rakesh Sharma who had gone to space. She told everyone that the sky was my limit.

When the photographs had been taken and the news item had appeared in all the newspapers about the child who had set her on the path to child welfare, I was sent to a home. I went to school by day and sucked the warden's cock at night. I didn't feel anything. Anger, disgust or sorrow. It was something that needed to be done to get the biggest piece of meat, the extra sweet and two hardboiled eggs every day. Fair is fair, I thought.

But one night, he wanted to try something new. I slashed the kitchen knife across his belly and fled. I jumped the wall and saw a car parked on the road. I thought the doors would be locked but for some reason, when I tried the rear door, it opened. I slipped in and lay down in the space on the floor between the front and back seat. A little later, a man came and started the car. He put on some music. I felt him slowing down; I heard him slam his fist on the steering wheel. Bloody thullas, I heard him mutter.

I felt a grin grow on my face. If the sight of policemen bothered him so much, he had something of value in his car. Something that wasn't entirely legal. When the car stopped, I was seated on the back seat. A policeman peered in. He looked at the man and me and called out, 'Not the one we

*are looking for. This is a father and son.' He waved at us to keep going,
'Hogo, hogo ...'*

*When the man moved away from the police blockade, he stopped the car
and looked at me. 'Who are you?' he asked.*

I smiled. 'I can be anything you want.'

He gave me a strange look. 'Who taught you to say that?'

*I shrugged. And so I became Krishna and he my thekedar. He was a patient
teacher and I was eager to please; and I wanted him to be proud of me. Soon,
everywhere he went, I went too. Anything he wanted done, I did it, or made
sure it got done.*

My rage grew. I didn't know what I was angry about. That the
thekedar thought I could be dispensed with? Or that he was
going to take away my Nandita even though he knew how I felt
about her? Or that he had let even that scum Daulat Ali know
that I could be treated with such disrespect?

I touched my jaw. It hurt where his fist had landed. I probed
my mouth with my tongue. I could still taste the blood.

I stopped at a bar and picked up a half of Original Choice
whisky. I needed something to numb my anger and my pain.
All these years I had done everything he asked me to, without
question or complaint. Clearly, none of it had mattered to him.

And he had the gall to quote the Gita to me.

Suddenly I felt light-headed. There is a way. There is always
a way. Well, here's one for you, thekedar: The heat of the sun
comes from me, and I send and withhold the rains. I am life
immortal and death; I am what I is and what I is not.

Two lakh rupees, he had said. I had twenty-five thousand. I
could raise another twenty-five. I needed a lakh and fifty. And I
knew how to get it.

———•———

Jogan and Barun looked at me wide-eyed. They reminded me of bedraggled kittens. If I were to shine a torch into their faces, they would stare at me with the same helpless fear I would see in the kittens' eyes. 'Dada,' they said. 'What is this place?'

The bus ride from Hennur to Hosur took us more than two hours. The boys had been quite relieved to leave the lawyer's home.

When I took them there, they thought they had stumbled into heaven. The lawyer's house was beautiful and enormous. There were no children or pets to mess it up and everything stayed in its place. The floors were a pale marble and the walls an endless white. And when they lifted the dusty sheets and peered beneath, they could see dark wood furniture upholstered in real silk. The coffee table in the sunken living room was as big as a bed and there was a giant glass on it that could quench the thirst of a whole family for a day. In it were tall flowers that looked like crab claws. And this was just the front room. There was a dining room, a room with three walls of books, a giant kitchen that was as big as the shelter that they had been relocated to during the last cyclone in Satpada. And on the floor above were four bedrooms, each one with a big bed and a TV and its own bathroom. How rich the lawyer must be, they whispered to each other, we will live like princes here.

They were then shown the room allotted to them in the back of the house with its grey-washed walls, cement floor and two camp cots on which were a mattress and a thin pillow rolled up. And they thought, even if we don't live like princes, we will have three full meals every day and just as much work as we are capable of. They had it all chalked out in their heads. They wouldn't have to pay any rent and the food would be free. They would save every rupee of their salary. Half to send home and the rest to keep till they had enough to open a small shop in Satpada. They told me all this when I went to visit them the day after I took them there as per the thekedar's instructions.

'Don't forget my commission,' I had said pleasantly enough.

'No, dada, every month, one-fourth of our salary is yours,' Jogan had said.

He hadn't known that the salary would be paid directly to me and that I would decide if it was to be one-fourth, one-third or half.

I was busy for the next three days. One of my contacts had been pestering me to source some boys for him. There was a man in MLA Pappana's employ, who had tentacles in Gulbarga. He would be able to provide me with a group, he had said. On my way back from meeting him, I had called in on the lawyer's house to check on my boys. I waited for the lawyer to leave before knocking on his door. The boys greeted me with sullen faces.

The lawyer had returned from Delhi and the easy time the boys had the first day had changed into a nightmare of excessive demands and miserly portions of tasteless food.

'He keeps saying, don't do this, don't do that, don't touch this, don't sit there ...' Jogan said.

'And gives us very little food, dada,' Barun added. 'We may as well have stayed home if we have to starve here.'

They thought me responsible for their plight. I wanted to tell them that no one was responsible for the life we led and the situations we got ourselves into. Just ourselves.

You can rest your head on another person's arm for a while, after which they will shrug you off. The only arm you can rest your head on for as long as you live is your own. Who told me that? I don't remember.

My contact had asked for eight boys and I had been able to source only six.

'I have found you something else. But it will be hard work,' I said.

'Anything would be better than this!' Jogan muttered. The previous evening, the lawyer had given him an old sock, a mug of water and asked him to clean the leaves of the plants within the house. 'Change the water in the mug after you finish a plant,' the lawyer had said, twirling his eyebrow. 'And don't snap a leaf or tear one!'

Jogan had wondered if the lawyer was mad. Barun had been given a toothbrush and asked to work on the grouting of the tiles in the kitchen. It was spotless but the lawyer seemed to see lines of dirt and specks of dust everywhere.

'What time does he leave in the morning?' I asked.

'By seven-thirty,' Jogan said.

'He starts eating his nashta at seven,' Barun had butted in. 'A whole papaya that has to be chopped into cubes. A hardboiled egg and a big bowl of some grain he pours milk over. And we get to eat the previous night's rotis and a glass of black tea. No milk! No sugar! Black tea!'

Jogan cuffed him. 'Is that all you can think of? Food?'

'Get ready. Let's go.'

The boys put on the new t-shirts the lawyer had given them. I could barely hide my disgust. Ungrateful wretches, I thought. They deserved everything they got. I had told the thekedar that the boys were unhappy at the lawyer's.

'It's the nature of that class,' he had said. He had forgotten that I was and perhaps still am of 'that class'. I saw it as a compliment that he had forgotten how I had pulled myself out of the gutter I had been born in.

'The first few days they are eager to please, then nothing satisfies them. But in this case, I am not surprised. The lawyer is an asshole too.' Had he even met the lawyer, I wondered. But the thekedar was like that. Sometimes he would take a violent dislike to people for no real reason.

It was a dusty road and the heat of the noonday sun was relentless. But the boys seemed unmoved by the heat or dust. Instead, they drank in the sight of the eucalyptus groves and the open spaces. I wondered what was going on in their minds.

There was a barbed-wire fence around the compound. The building itself was some way from the gate. From the distance nothing was visible. It looked run-down and unoccupied. A burly man peeled himself from the shadow of a tree and came towards the gate where I stood. 'What do you want?' he asked. The brusqueness of his tone scared the boys. I smiled. My smile that can melt ice, open locks and douse a fire. His next question was less abrasive. 'Who sent you?'

'Nagu Reddy,' I murmured.

His brow cleared and he went back to a little room by the gate. A room made of unplastered concrete blocks and a tin roof. It was probably baking in there, which was why he had chosen to sit under the tree. He came back with a bunch of keys and opened the lock on the gate.

'Where are the boys from?' he asked, giving Jogan and Barun a cursory look.

'Odisha,' I said.

The man made a face. 'Sneaky bastards! All of them! The moment they come in, they are looking for a way to run away!'

Jogan and Barun looked at my face, trying to read my expression. Not a muscle on my face moved. The watchman and I could have been discussing the weather for all they knew.

'What about Ikshu dada?' Jogan asked.

'Can you bring him here to us?' Barun asked. All three of them had grown up together but Barun and Ikshu were cousins.

'Let me see. I'll do my best,' I promised them, knowing very well that I would never see them again.

I led the boys towards the building. It was a child's drawing of a factory – a long low shed with a tin roof and boxes cut out for windows. The windows were boarded up on the side that faced the road. And the door opened to the other side, where there was a high wall. Beyond that was a quarry. I could hear the sound of machines at work.

A green tin door was set into the wall. It was latched from within. I rapped on the door. The metal made a hollow noise. The door opened and a man stood framed by the shadows.

'Nagu Reddy sent me,' I said. 'I have two boys.'

I felt a slight tug on either hand as the boys stepped back. 'Maybe we should go back to the lawyer's house,' Jogan said. 'I think we were too hasty.'

I pulled in the boys. 'It's a big factory,' I told them. 'A place where they make school bags. The more bags you make, the more money you'll earn.'

I could hear a humming, the whirr of sewing machines, the rustle of plastic sheets, the shadows. But not a human sound. They were ordered to not chat or laugh. I pushed the boys in towards the man.

'They get scrawnier by the day,' the man said, eyeing them.

I shrugged. 'This is the best of the lot.'

The man shut the door and I walked back to the gate. I had made thirty thousand rupees for a morning's work. Once upon a time, fifteen would have gone to the thekedar. But this was mine. Every rupee of it.

Once, someone asked me if I felt guilty about what I did. No, I said. Guilt is a luxury for the poor. When one seeks to survive, a man has to put his interests first. It is his breath he safeguards before he thinks of anyone else. That was what the thekedar taught me. It was in the Gita as well. To die in one's duty is life; to live in another's is death.

I needed to make another lakh and forty-five in twenty-four hours. That was all I could think of now. I began counting the number in my head. By the time I reached 1,45,000, I knew I would have a plan.

———•———

Pujary glared at the TV as he ate his lunch. Gita still wasn't speaking to him beyond the bare essentials. But at least the tension between them had simmered down to an uneasy silence. In a few days, she would come around. He knew that.

When he had finished his lunch, Gita said, 'I want you to tell me what is going on.'

'What's going on where?' He put on a mock frown as he laughed.

'What you are doing?' she began and stopped. 'How can you?'

'All of this ...' He waved his hand around to indicate the 55-inch LED TV, the enclosed garden, the marble floors and the cunning little elevator she could use to go upstairs if he was not around to help her. 'Where do you think it comes from? I do it for you, for us,' he added in a gentle voice.

She shook her head furiously. 'I don't need any of this. Neither should you. We have each other. Isn't that enough?'

He smiled. His Gita was such a naïve child. Her body may have given up on her. But her mind was that of a young girl's. Radiant with hopes and ideals. Except that he knew when you were trying to make a life for the one you loved, you tossed out ideals and did what you had to do. Nevertheless, he had given in as she wanted him to and caressed her cheek. 'That is enough, wife!'

'You will stop what you are doing?' she had persisted. 'Husband, you must ... we don't need the money you earn this way.'

'Gita,' he said quietly, moving to sit by her side. 'What is it you think I do? I am not a bloody pimp.'

She flinched.

'I deal in real estate. That's all.'

'The girls you were referring to ...' she said haltingly. 'The twelve-year-old ...'

'Vittala, Vittala,' he guffawed, 'is this what you are so perturbed about? Those were girls I had said I would help locate for someone I know who is making a video.'

She looked at him for a long moment. He held her gaze. She said nothing thereafter. He knew she was ashamed of having doubted him. But that too would pass.

She pressed the button of her wheelchair and rode into the kitchen. She returned with two small bowls of shrikhand.

He smiled. She knew it was his favourite sweet. This was a peace offering.

'Husband, what is this business with the lawyer and the girls?'

He looked at her. She met his gaze. 'The lawyer was supposed to help with the sale of a land but he changed his mind. The MLA is furious. It's a really huge deal. Two hundred crores. If it had gone through, I may never have needed to work again. So I spoke to a few contacts. One of them knows a buyer but he said the buyer is a strange man who likes watching young girls play. Hopscotch. Skip. On a swing. Down a slide. Up and down a seesaw. People, eh?'

She frowned. 'Just play?'

'Just play,' Pujary said. 'I am corrupt, Gita, but not evil.'

'It doesn't sound right,' she said.

'What can I do to convince you?'

'Nothing. But there's something else you can do,' she said, spooning the shrikhand and holding it to his lips. He licked the sweet off like a cat. She smiled.

'What?' he asked, smiling back.

'Take me to the lawyer. Let me talk to him,' Gita said.

Pujary stared at her in surprise. 'He won't listen to you, wife. He is a shark. A shark with the soul of a python, wanting to swallow everything whole.'

'Please,' she said. 'Let me try and persuade him. I would prefer it if you had nothing to do with this girls business.'

———•———

I went to the building where I had left the three items last evening. There was no one there. I called the thekedar.

'What do you mean they are not there?'

'There's no sign of them. Neither Mohan, nor the girl and boy he brought with him. I asked the man who runs the petty shop in the corner. He says he doesn't know. He mentioned that a police jeep was there last night,' I added.

'Mohan is an experienced man. He knows how to handle situations.' The thekedar exhaled. 'He'll get in touch. He knows what to do. Where are you now?'

'Near the shop.'

'There is something else I want you to do,' he said.

'What's in it for me?' I asked.

I heard the silence at the end of the line. But I refused to be intimidated. He was the one who taught me that there's no such thing as a free lunch.

———•———

Sid sat in the food court of the mall. He hadn't been here before. He glanced at his phone. It was almost two. The person he was supposed to meet was late.

A man had called him in the morning.

'What happened?' he had asked. A polite, concerned, avuncular voice, almost as if it were enquiring about his ailing grandfather in Thrissur.

Sid had felt his heart beat faster.

'I don't know, sir. I really don't know. She promised to meet me outside Koshy's, but she didn't show up,' he stammered. 'I really don't understand, sir.'

'Did you call her?'

'I did. At least twenty times. I messaged her. WhatsApped her. I saw she had read the messages. After a while her phone was switched off,' Sid had tried to explain his helplessness. 'Sir, I think the lawyer she went to meet the last time must have told her not to take my call.'

The voice at the other end of the phone had sighed. 'These things happen!'

Sid had felt the knot in his chest loosen. 'I am really sorry. She does everything I ask her to. I don't know why she didn't turn up last evening. Maybe ...'

'Maybe ... what?' the voice had asked.

'I don't know if her periods started. She acts weird then ...' He had added quickly, 'Sir, I'd like to return the advance.'

'Yes, you must,' the voice said.

'Where can I drop it off?' Sid asked, swearing to himself this would be the last time he did anything like this. And then, not wanting to take chances, he had decided to ask that they meet at a public place. 'What about a mall, sir? With so many people there, no one will notice the money changing hands.'

'Hmm ...' the voice had said. 'That's rather clever of you. One of my boys will come and pick it up. Make sure you are at Elements mall at the food court by 1.30 p.m.'

'How will I know him?' Sid had asked, wondering where on earth Elements mall was.

He had hoped they could meet at one of the more central ones.

'Don't worry about that. He'll find you. Just make sure you are there,' the voice had said and the phone had gone silent.

Sid looked at his FB timeline. He had posted a selfie yesterday afternoon and the number of likes had crossed 235. There was a whole bevy of friend requests as well.

'Siddharth,' a voice said softly. He looked up to see a boy his age, if not younger. A thin dark boy with hair cut short and wearing a t-shirt and jeans.

'Siddharth?' the boy said again.

Sid nodded.

'I am here for the money,' the boy said.

What had he been so worried about, Sid asked himself as he twisted around to take his wallet from the back pocket of his jeans.

'Not here. Let's go to the bathroom. You can give it to me there. Malls have security cameras,' the boy said, walking off.

Sid followed him. He looked around nervously to see if two hulks or three were following him. That was how it happened in the movies.

Two girls walked past, licking their ice-cream cones. They looked at him. He looked back, allowing a half-smile to settle on his lips. The girls giggled and looked away. Sid felt a little rush of triumph. Forget that bitch, there were other chicks who would do what he wanted.

He walked into the men's room and entered a stall. When he came out, the washroom had emptied out except for the boy who stood by the row of sinks. Sid pulled his wallet out.

A fist landed on his face. He saw an arc of blood spray across the wall and slip down the mirror.

'I explained to your boss,' Sid tried to protest through a mouthful of blood.

The boy pushed him down and kicked him, aiming precisely so each blow landed where it hurt the most.

'No, no,' Sid whispered, curling into a ball.

The boy bent and retrieved the wallet. He took out all the money in it and flung the wallet at Sid's face.

'These things happen,' he said as he washed his hands and slammed the door after him.

———•———

He had been unable to sleep after the adrenaline surge of the rescue. It was almost five in the morning when he fell into a deep slumber. It was Roshan who woke him up.

'Are you all right?' he asked.

Gowda stared at him, not knowing where he was. 'What time is it?' he asked. Almost as if on cue, the clock struck twelve. Gowda groaned. 'What do you want to do this evening?'

Roshan shrugged. 'I am going out. We are going to Humming Tree.'

'Do trees hum?'

'Ha ha,' Roshan said politely.

'Do you need dinner?' Gowda asked.

'I don't know.' Roshan frowned, looking at his phone that was pinging once every thirty seconds.

Gowda had a sudden urge to box the boy's ears. 'What kind of an answer is that?'

'I don't know, Appa. But if it makes it easier, I don't need dinner. I'll grab a bite with my friends.' Roshan was still peering at his phone while his thumbs danced on the surface.

When he had showered and shaved, Shanthi asked him what he would like to eat. Gowda shrugged. Shanthi smiled and served him dosas with mutton curry. And a tall mug of filter coffee.

Roshan sat across from him, watching him eat.

'What about you?' Gowda asked.

'I had breakfast at nine,' Roshan said with an almost smug smile.

Gowda glared at him. Tomorrow he would wake up at six and give the boy a lecture on waking up early and exercising, he decided.

Gowda parked his bike and went towards the lake. He lit a cigarette and took a deep drag. What had happened to the children? And the trafficker? He was quite sure that someone would appear soon to bail him out. That was how it was.

Gowda squashed the cigarette butt beneath his foot and buried it under a mound of leaves. Smoking in a public area was an offence. They slapped a fine of two hundred rupees on you. This segment of land between the police station grounds and the lake, what did it qualify as? No man's land, Gowda told himself with a grin, feeling better for the smoke.

There was a change in the air when he stepped into the station house. The station writer stepped out of Gowda's room and walked past him with a smug smile. What had transpired in the time it took to smoke a cigarette?

ACP Vidyaprasad was in Gowda's room, staring at the soft board that was already curling at one end. Gowda had several sheets of paper pinned to it. Santosh stood alongside with a worried expression. Gowda saluted. The ACP responded with a nod.

'What's this? The school bulletin board?' the ACP said with half a laugh. 'I don't think even schools have one any more.'

Gowda didn't answer. His reluctance to let a tablet plot his day would have the ACP start on how he had to move with the times.

Suddenly the ACP frowned. 'What did you go to the MLA's house for?'

'I was asked to by DCP Mirza. He said the home minister may be there. And I should be there as per protocol.' Gowda's face was as bland as a potato peel.

Santosh looked away, trying to hide his smile. Protocol was a favourite word in the ACP's dictionary. And that particular expression of Gowda's appeared when he was in a playful mood.

'I don't mean yesterday. MLA Papanna said you wanted to talk to him about a few cases.'

'Oh that. Some routine enquiry, sir. In fact, Santosh will handle it. He'll talk to the MLA's PA and get the details,' Gowda said, moving towards his seat.

'Next time you need to speak to the MLA, you route it through me. That's the protocol.'

When Gowda didn't respond, the ACP glared at him. 'And where did you disappear to last night? I caught a glimpse of you and then you were gone.'

Gowda schooled his face to not reveal what he was thinking. 'There was an emergency, sir.'

'What emergency are you talking about, I say? A stolen hen? This is not a mofussil station any more. Get that into your head.'

Gowda said nothing. Instead, he imagined the corner of a room. Only, this time he saw in his head the toilet in the hall above the tyre shop. The walls were filthy and it had a stink of clogged manholes and careless flushing.

ACP Vidyaprasad was a fastidious man but in that moment of fear and horror, he would press himself against the wall that had probably been peed upon or spat on. And Gowda, whose boots were the kind that always gleamed, the spikes sparkling with a diamond edge, would stretch his leg backwards at the knee as if he were aiming a kick at a football. He would know the sheer triumph of his boot making the impact; all of him slamming into the weevil in the corner. The shredding of bone; the ripping of flesh; kicking till the weevil was a pulverized mess of bone and meat. His Messi moment, Gowda thought with a secret laugh.

'Sir,' Santosh began.

Gowda frowned at him. Then he said, turning to the ACP, 'I understand, sir.'

The ACP stared at him, wondering what this suddenly compliant Gowda was actually up to.

'I hear an arrest was made. A suspected child trafficking case at Sathanur. It was a night raid. Inspector Basavappa thinks we may have a breakthrough in the trafficking racket.'

Gowda nodded but didn't speak.

The ACP's mouth twisted. 'Gowda, you need to be better informed, man.'

When the ACP left, Santosh blurted out in exasperation, 'But why didn't you tell him, sir? It was you who set up the raid. Why are you letting someone else take the credit?'

'Does it matter who gets the credit as long as we manage to apprehend the criminal?' Gowda said, reaching for a file.

'Sir, I think you should have mentioned it to the ACP,' Gajendra said, walking into the room.

'Were you listening outside the door?' Gowda glared at him.

'I don't need to. His voice is loud enough for everyone in the station and all of Neelgubbi to hear,' Gajendra mumbled, not quite meeting his eye.

'It's best he doesn't know my role in it,' Gowda said cryptically, refusing to elaborate any further.

Into the sudden silence that crept into the room, Gowda asked, 'Has Ratna called?'

Santosh nodded. 'She is taking the girl, Tina, that's her name, for the medical examination. The boy too. The children are in a bad way, sir.'

Gowda was not surprised. The bruises he had seen on the children were just a small part of what they must have been subjected to. He looked out of the window for a moment. He was running out of time. It was already ten days since Nandita had gone missing. If they weren't able to trace her soon, they may never be able to.

Nandita, where are you?

'What about that woman, Mary? Anything on her?' Gowda asked.

Santosh shook his head. 'PC Byrappa managed to get an address for her. The house was locked when we went there last evening. The neighbours said she had gone away just that morning.'

'Absconding, that is.' Gowda's mouth drew into a narrow line.

'Yes. Absconding,' Santosh said, not bothering to hide his anger or dismay.

'You think someone tipped her off?' Gowda asked.

'The thought did cross my mind.' Santosh's face was grim.

There was a knock on the door. Ratna came in. 'The children won't talk to any of us,' she said. 'When I speak to them, they look away.'

Santosh frowned. 'They probably don't understand Kannada.'

Ratna glared at him. 'I am not stupid. I spoke to them in Hindi. They understand that.'

Gowda raised his head from the notes he was making. 'The children have probably seen money being given to the police. Why would they trust us? We are as vile as the traffickers in their eyes.'

'Sir, what do we do?' Ratna had a worn out expression.

'We'll have to bring someone else in. Maybe a social worker from a child welfare organization. Someone they'll be able to trust.'

'That's what I thought,' said Ratna, looking distinctly unhappy. 'Whom do we call? The truth is, sir, I am not sure it will be treated with the attention it deserves if it goes out of our hands. The doctor let me in when he was examining the girl. She is twelve and has been abused so badly.'

The room went quiet.

'What's surprising, sir, is that the child's vagina is intact. The abuser has been having anal sex with her,' Ratna continued.

Santosh reddened. Gowda pretended not to see his embarrassment. He tapped his pen thoughtfully and said, 'A twelve-year-old virgin would fetch a higher price. But the trafficker wasn't going to let her go without branding her. What do you understand from this?'

Santosh and Ratna looked at him dumbstruck. What did Gowda mean?

Gowda sighed. 'She is being kept for a higher transaction. And the man we found is not the kingpin; he is just a stooge and probably someone who resents his boss. This is his way of getting even.'

'Don't these guys have a conscience?' Santosh said, unable to hide his consternation.

'No,' Gowda said. 'They don't see children as children or women as women. They are just commodities; products they supply to meet a demand.'

'Still,' Santosh persisted. 'How do they sleep at night? How do they tell themselves it's all right to do what they're doing?'

'Does the vegetable vendor lose sleep over how the tomatoes he sells are sliced? Does the butcher cry for the goat he sold part by part?' Gowda said.

Gowda was angry; upset and frustrated. Gajendra knew that from his voice. And he knew too that recklessness would follow. He wiped his forehead with a handkerchief.

'Ratna,' Gowda said rising, 'I have friends who work with children. They'll be able to help. Santosh knows them, so he can help take this forward.'

Santosh looked up, startled. This was the second time in a few hours that Gowda had made an announcement of his confidence in Santosh's ability to take charge. It felt good.

Santosh and Ratna looked at each other as they followed Gowda into the lobby. The indoor plants and a huge sculpture made it seem more like a corporate office than an apartment building. Looking at the panel of name boards, Santosh wondered at the name Lady Deviah. Everyone could see she was a lady, so why was it being declared on a name board?

'Must be very rich,' Ratna muttered. 'It's ten thousand rupees a square foot in this area, I am told.'

'Maybe she has rented it out. She has none of the airs of the super rich. I've met her. She is very friendly and sweet.'

Ratna snorted. Super rich and sweet. They didn't go together. You didn't get to be super rich by being sweet. Sometimes she wondered if Santosh had crawled out from under a stone in a well in the Hampi ruins.

Gowda pretended not to hear them. Had he made a mistake by bringing them here? But he was afraid the case would slip out of his hands once the Child Welfare Committee got involved. It would come under the jurisdiction of people who may or may not pursue it.

The girl was young and seriously abused, but she was feisty and angry. She would speak to someone she could trust. And if she did, the boy would too.

Michael opened the door and ushered them in. 'Been a while, Bob,' he said to Gowda.

'You are the busy one.' Gowda smiled.

'Let's meet up this Sunday,' Michael said as Urmila entered the room.

Gowda almost sighed. She looked good enough to eat. Urmila smiled at everyone but him. He got a frosty glance. She was furious at him, he realized. But what had he done?

Gowda watched Urmila as she talked to Ratna. Santosh watched Gowda watching them. Michael watched Santosh watching Gowda. He cleared his throat, causing everyone to drop their gaze. 'The children must have seen the police being paid money. How do you expect them to trust the police after that?'

Santosh's mouth tightened. Gowda smiled. Santosh had accepted the truth when Gowda had said it but he was not going to let a member of the public get away with it. He was at that point in his career when any slight to the police force was taken as a personal insult. This too shall pass, Gowda thought ruefully. Meanwhile, he didn't want Santosh getting Michael's back up. So he leaned towards Michael and said, 'Well, that's why we need you to speak to them.'

'The children won't open up in the first meeting. We are going to have to earn their trust,' Michael said.

A maid came in bearing a tray of glasses of juice. Gowda took a glass and gulped it down. Then he stood up and said, 'Mind if I smoke?'

Urmila threw him a dirty look but she rose to open the balcony doors. Gowda suppressed his grin as he followed her.

'What did I do now?' he asked her under his breath.

'We were supposed to have dinner last night. That was what you said when you called me on Wednesday night. You said we would go out like a proper couple and drink a pitcher of beer between us. Do you even remember that? I waited for you at the pub for over an hour. And then I went home. Your phone wasn't reachable. Why do you do this to me, Borei? I deserve better. Do I have to be a victim to earn your time?'

Gowda hissed, an indrawn breath of remorse. 'I forgot, Urmila. You know what happened last night ...'

Urmila shook her head. 'I do. But is it too much to expect that you would call to let me know? Courtesy, Borei. Is that too much to ask?'

'I'll make it up to you,' he said, touching her elbow.

'I don't know, Borei. I really don't know what you feel about me. Or if I am even relevant to you,' she said, stepping back into the living room and joining the others, who pretended not to be curious about the furious whispering in the balcony.

Gowda stayed in the balcony, trying to compose his thoughts.

Why couldn't he leave well alone? There was no need for him to have gone on that raid. Basavappa was someone he had implicit faith in. And yet, when he had heard about the young girl, he had wondered if it was Nandita. Even if it wasn't, he wanted to be there. He wanted to make sure nothing went wrong. Did that make him a control freak? Or was not being able to delegate a congenital flaw?

A stuffed toy hurled itself into the balcony and clambered at his knee. Gowda looked at Mr Right, and unable to help himself, smiled. 'You ridiculous looking thing,' he whispered, bending down.

The dog leapt into his arms.

'At least I can do no wrong in your eyes,' he murmured in Mr Right's ear.

———•———

Gowda left the bedroom and bathroom door ajar so the music would reach him. He had turned off the living-room lights and put a CD on. It was music that he hadn't listened to in a while, but Urmila had given it to him and suddenly he felt like he needed to hear something that reminded him of a time when there were no suspicious wives, furious girlfriends, hostile and patronizing bosses or missing children – his maid's and his – to clutter up his thoughts.

As he stood under the shower, he wished he had called her; gone out for dinner with her, perhaps. Done the right thing for once. Almost as if on cue, Wishbone Ash burst into '*Error of my ways*'.

The shower rained hard on his back. Urmila had replaced his old one with a giant shower nozzle. 'So you feel me on you,' she had said. 'Twice a day.'

He had watched her fix the shower head as if she were a professional plumber. The woman had her own toolbox and a can of WB40 in her car at all times.

'What are you reading these days?' he had guffawed. 'Mills & Boon?'

'No, *Fifty Shades of Grey*,' she said, tweaking his nipple gently with her pliers.

He had gasped. The eroticism of the pleasurable pain gave him a sudden hard-on. 'Urmila!' he hissed, grabbing her.

Gowda smiled as he thought of that day. He missed her. Not in that savage, gut-hollowing way of his youth but with a gentle ache that was harder to deal with.

He raised his face to the shower and let the hard spindles of water knock out everything but the need to breathe.

When Gowda had slipped on his habitual track suit bottoms and t-shirt, a strange restlessness filled him. He poured himself a drink even though he had told himself he wouldn't drink alone. Just a small one, a tiny voice in his head wheedled. Just a teeny one.

He texted Urmila. But there was no response. Where was she?

He walked listlessly through the house and stopped at Roshan's room, as he knew he would.

Things were strewn around, but that was how Roshan was. There was order in his chaos, he claimed. Gowda smiled. He wished the boy were home. They could have talked. Gowda would have offered him a drink. Did the boy drink, he wondered. There was so much he didn't know about his son. Was he still a virgin? Or was it just a tug job under the covers? Actually, had he even kissed a girl? Condoms – what about that? The boy was a medical student and should know better than to take chances. But doctors were ruled by a misguided notion that disease always bypassed them. Some day soon, he would need to talk to his son. There were enough true-life accounts of boys going whoring without adequate protection and contracting HIV. Gowda shuddered.

His eyes fell on the rucksack. For a moment, Gowda hesitated. Just for a moment he felt ashamed of what he was about to do; this callous violation of privacy. Then he remembered the boy's face; that easy, happy-go-lucky expression, that everything-in-the-world-is-so-cool-right-now smile, and he unzipped the rucksack.

There was a laptop in it; they had bought him one for his birthday; headphones, a hard disk and power cables. In another pouch there was a notepad and a pen. In the secret pocket, he found a pouch that contained a coconut shell bowl, a little round metal tin, like the one his mother had kept her kumkum in, a box of rolling papers and filters. Gowda frowned, wondering what it was for. He opened the little round tin – it was a crusher. Gowda could smell weed. His heart sank. Roshan didn't just take a drag from a joint once in a while. He was a regular marijuana smoker and this was the paraphernalia he used to justify his habit. To make it seem as if it were just as serious as smoking a pipe.

Gowda gnawed at his lip. He wasn't perturbed by the marijuana itself. It probably wasn't as harmful as tobacco. What worried him was Roshan's dependence on the substance. How deep was he into it? And would he stop with this or move on to hard drugs?

Gowda slid his fingers into the secret pocket. In a little resealable bag he found what looked like rice grains. Gowda opened the bag and sniffed. It smelled like vanilla. What on earth was it? It looked like solidified baby goop. He touched it and licked his finger. It tasted of nothing.

He tapped the bag into his mouth. Three or four grains fell on his tongue and it tasted like everything bitter he had eaten; all at the same time and magnified a million times. He took a hasty swallow of his rum and Coke. The bitterness stayed resolutely on his palate. What on earth was it, Gowda wondered as he put the bag back and packed Roshan's paraphernalia away. Should he leave it exactly as he had found it? Or should he make it apparent that he had been sniffing around? Should he be cop or father? Gowda sighed loudly. The truth was, he couldn't stop being either.

He had thought he wouldn't ever have to worry about the boy once he got past the age of sticking his fingers into plug points, falling off trees, and accepting dares to take condoms to school. It seemed with every year, the magnitude of worry only increased in both scope and intensity.

Gowda let the cop in him prevail.

He walked back to the living room, puzzled about the substance he had tasted. What was it? Some kind of aphrodisiac or an upper?

He threw himself into his favourite chair. Then he got up and went to the music system to change CDs. He knew what he was going to play. A curious lassitude unfurled in him as Mukesh sang '*Kabhi kabhi ...*'

Gowda felt his eyes smart.

He scrolled down his text messages and checked his call log. Suddenly he felt a great yearning to speak to Stanley Sagayaraj, his basketball captain from college and now ACP at the CCB – 'Central Crime Bureau that is, and not City Crime Bureau', Gowda had heard a vexed Stanley explain to a wet-behind-the-ears reporter from a local rag.

Gowda grinned.

Stanley picked up on the third ring.

'How're you, machan?' Gowda said. He felt a slight furring of his throat even as he spoke.

There was silence at the other end and then Stanley said, 'Everything all right, Inspector Gowda?'

'Can't I call you just like that?' Gowda heard the petulance in his tone, but couldn't help himself. 'Just wanted to connect, machan. What, you don't like me calling you that?'

'That was a long time back, Gowda. But you can call me machan as long it's just you and me.'

'So who else is here now?' Gowda guffawed.

'I'm at an official dinner. Is there something urgent?'

'Nope,' Gowda said, stretching out the word. 'Just wanted to say I miss those days, machan. Remember Pink Floyd? We don't need no education, we don't need no thought control,' Gowda sang.

'Is anyone at home with you?' Stanley asked gently.

'N...o...p...e,' Gowda said. He liked this nope. NOPE. 'Gowda, always on his own, that's me, Borei Gowda and his attitude ... Someone told me you said that – that I am a good guy, a good cop, but I have an attitude problem. But you know what, I don't mind, machan, you can say anything to me, you can ask me to fuck off ... FUCK OFF! And I will take it from you because you are me captain!'

'Gowda, I have to go. Let's catch up one evening,' Stanley said.

'Let's do that. Love you, machan. You were always the best in this heartache city. But remember to leave on time.' Gowda burst into song again. When he had finished singing the chorus two times over, he realized that the call had been disconnected. Would that bastard hang up on him? N...o...p...e... Gowda thought. He must have moved into a black hole. Stanley was a good cop and a great man.

An amazing sense of happiness rushed through Gowda. He had to tell Urmila how he felt. When she didn't pick up, he recorded a long message of love and sexy endearments and what he would like to do to her inch by inch with his tongue, and finished it with his best rendition of '*I just called to say I love you*'. He then sent it to her on WhatsApp.

Gowda heard someone open the latch. He frowned. Head Constable Gajendra appeared in the doorway.

'What are you doing here?' Gowda smiled.

Gajendra blinked at the expansive all-encompassing smile, the kind you might expect to see on the faces of babies, godmen and lunatics. What had happened to Gowda, he wondered.

When ACP Stanley Sagayaraj had called and asked him to check on Gowda, he had thought that Gowda was ill. At least then, he would have known what to do. But what could he do with this beatific Gowda except persuade him to go to bed? And it would be easier to put a porcupine to bed!

Dr Sanjay Rathore rested his head on the edge of the pool and looked at the stars in the night sky. He knew that overhead was Jupiter, blazing bright, and a little to the west was Sirius, diminished by Jupiter's magnificence. And that was how it should be, he told himself. Jupiter was a planet and Sirius was a star. Not just in life but among heavenly bodies too, each ought to have its place. And as long as each kept to its designated orbit, there would be neither anarchy nor chaos.

The community association had rules about how long the swimming pool could be kept open. He broke the rule anyway. If they protested, he would take them to court. They knew his reputation, so nothing more than a tiny protest had been voiced.

He had returned to an empty house. Both the boys were gone. He had called the security guards at the gate.

'They left around ten this morning,' one of the guards said.

'Why didn't you stop them?' Rathore snarled. 'What if they have stolen stuff from my residence?'

'We checked their bags. There was nothing in them. Besides, they returned their ID cards to us. So how could we stop them? This isn't a prison, sir.' The guard had sounded sullen.

All the other residents gave the security guards a gift for Diwali. An envelope with Rs 500 in it or a shirt. But the lawyer didn't. 'We pay them. Why give them a bonus for doing their job?' he argued. He sent a box of sweets that they were all expected to share.

The bastard guard was probably paying him back for that. He slammed the intercom down.

From the farther end of the pool, he heard a plop. A frog. He shuddered. He loved swimming in the night and apparently, so did the frogs. While he could tolerate a pool with shrieking children, he drew a line at frogs. He hauled himself up. The pool ladder was for kids and women; men didn't use ladders unless they were decrepit. And that he wasn't. He dried himself briskly, put a t-shirt on, drank all the water in the water bottle he carried to the pool and walked back to his house.

He looked at his watch. It was a quarter to nine. He had a conference call at eleven with a colleague in London before they closed for the weekend.

The villa in the gated community had been a good idea. The one hour it took him to drive from the city put a physical and mental distance between work and him. And a man needed respite. Especially someone like him, a true-blue workaholic who was inclined to work through every waking moment.

The gate lights were on and so was the portico light at Shangri La. His heaven on earth.

He latched the gate and paused for a moment in the driveway that wound alongside the lawns to the house. The rose bushes were heavy with flower. The champak tree across the road was in bloom. Their fragrance filled the warm night. The hollyhocks his gardener had planted were almost as tall as him and so laden with deep pink flowers that the darkness turned them into burgundy. He stopped to look at his garden of fragrances and shadows. He was filled with a strange emotion. What was it? Happiness or well-being? He didn't know and didn't particularly care as long as it felt like every knot in his shoulders had opened out. The new masseuse was good. He made a mental note to book an appointment at the spa for Sunday morning. Get a facial, manicure and pedicure too. Maybe touch up up the grey in his hair as well. He had seen Rekha glance at it.

Friday evenings were customary three-drinks days. He would pour himself a single malt as he walked to the bathroom and keep it on the cabinet. He would take little sips as he showered and dressed. The second single malt, a more peaty one, was for when he sat in his sunken living room with some music on. He was going through a Nusrat Fateh Ali Khan phase. The man may have eaten himself to death, displaying a complete absence of self-restraint, but he had a voice that caused curlicues in his chest. In recent times, he hadn't come close to that feeling except when he listened to music with a drink in his hand. The third drink, after dinner, was cognac taken sitting in the balcony off his bedroom. He allowed himself a smoke then.

His phone beeped. He had called for a team meeting at eleven in the morning. He checked for messages. There were ten work messages and that text he had been hoping for. He smiled. Was he being a callow teenager? He didn't feel his age and he was as fit as a man of thirty years. He stood on the garden path and texted back: What time are you coming? Can't wait to see you. (⸚)

As he opened his door, he heard the creak of the garden gate. He insisted that the gardener didn't oil the hinges of the gate. That way he knew when someone entered his property. There was nothing to fear in this neighbourhood. The gated community had 24-hour security and CCTV. He turned. 'Oh, it's you!' he said with a frown. Then his eyes widened in surprise.

Part 2

14 March, Saturday

9.30 a.m.

Gowda felt the beginning of a headache; a low thump in the back of his skull which he knew would soon become a nasty pounding.

Who was this Dr Sanjay Rathore? And why had someone bashed his head in? Even at first glance he could see this wasn't a burglary gone wrong. Was it a crime of passion or an act of revenge? Had someone bumped him off because he knew too much? Or because he hadn't budged enough?

'Are you all right?' Head Constable Gajendra asked.

He wondered if the inspector remembered that he had helped him into bed, put the fan on and drawn a sheet over him. What had Gowda been drinking? He had never seen him so amiable or incoherent.

Suddenly Gowda saw a familiar couple outside the gate. 'What are Laurel and Hardy doing here?' He turned to Gajendra.

'They live here.' Gajendra smiled.

'I would like to speak to them.'

'Now?'

'No, at their clubhouse. I want to see what that looks like as well.'

Gowda and Gajendra walked towards the clubhouse. The
streets were lined with trees and at every street corner was an
old-fashioned street lamp. The houses were gigantic and the
gardens mostly manicured. Mamtha would have approved and
gushed about 'neighbours like us' and the amenities. Urmila's
eyes would have widened and dropped with a hint of disdain.
She was too toffee-nosed to approve of gated communities. As
for himself, he would have felt under scrutiny all the time.

'Nice layout,' Gajendra said, pausing to pick a flower.

'Don't.' Gowda pointed to the little board that said 'Don't
pick flowers by order.'

'Whose order?' Gajendra frowned.

'Laurel and Hardy's,' Gowda said with a straight face.

Gajendra guffawed and converted it to a cough.

At the clubhouse, a granite-clad building, a reception
committee awaited them: Laurel and Hardy and two others.
Gowda recognized the man from the group outside the gate.
The man who had said he was president. A portly man stood by
his side. The prime minister?

'Sit down, Gajendra,' Gowda said to the head constable, who
hovered at his elbow like a curious aunt.

'Dr Sanjay Rathore,' Gowda said, clearing his throat.

'A gem of a man,' the president finished. 'A well-known
lawyer, and an asset to our community.'

'Save the eulogy for his funeral,' Laurel mumbled. 'He was a
first-class bastard.'

Gowda darted a look at Laurel, who seemed to live in t-shirts
with strange captions. This one read: I am Page 3 in Kazakhstan.

'And tight-fisted. He owed us three years' maintenance,
Inspector. And the committee was scared to censure him. He
had a reputation for saying, I will see you in court,' Laurel said,
looking at Hardy to corroborate.

But Hardy was gazing at his fingernails as if they held the secret to the anti-matter theory.

'Vinod ...' The president touched Laurel's elbow. 'Calm down. The man is dead; murdered.'

He turned to Gowda. 'Inspector, the lawyer refused to join the Green the Neighbourhood movement we started. Since then, Vinod has disliked him. Gentlemen,' he continued, 'this is a murder investigation and they are really not interested in the politics of our layout.'

'Oh, but I am,' Gowda said, tilting his chair back. 'Each one of you here is a potential suspect unless you have a cast-iron alibi.'

The men's faces paled. 'Suspect!' Hardy said in almost a whisper. 'You think I murdered that lawyer?'

'I didn't say that, Mr ...?' Gowda's voice was soft.

'Chatterjee. Dibakar Chatterjee,' Hardy said. 'Retired from IRS in 2010. I am a retired government servant. A Class I officer,' he added as an afterthought. Unlike the others, his tone implied.

Gowda nodded. 'We are going to examine the CCTV footage and the register. One of my officers will speak to each one of you to ascertain where you were last night. And speak to the live-in help and security guards in the layout. It's routine in any investigation.'

It was Laurel who croaked, 'But they could have come by the north wall ...' and abruptly stopped. He turned to the president. 'If you had fixed the wall when Dibakar and I asked you to, there would have been no breach of security.'

Gowda sighed. Where was Santosh? He didn't think anyone in the gated community had anything to do with the murder. But you left nothing to chance in a murder investigation. Santosh could be trusted to weed out every detail from each one of the residents. PC Byrappa would work on the live-in help and the security guards. He would ferret out every piece of gossip. All he needed was a glint in someone's eye.

Gowda glanced at his watch. The forensics team should be here soon. He lit a cigarette. His first for the day. As he inhaled, he felt a familiar sense of ease flood his system. Who was he kidding? He was never going to be able to give up. From twenty a day, he had brought it down to ten. But that was it, he decided as he tapped the ash from his cigarette.

Santosh stopped his bike and rushed towards Gowda. 'What's happened, sir?'

'Gajendra will brief you. I need you to step in, Santosh,' Gowda said. And then, after a pause, 'There's some CCTV footage.'

Santosh nodded. 'I have my hard disk. I'll get it transferred to that. How long back should we go?'

'As far back as is available,' Gowda said. 'Will your hard disk be able to hold that much?'

Santosh grinned. 'It's 2 TB.'

'Oh,' Gowda said, not knowing what he was saying oh to.

'I'll bring it to the station house, sir,' Santosh said, fumbling in his rucksack.

'Remind me again, how old are you, Santosh?' Gowda asked.

'Twenty-four, sir.' There was a question in his eye which Gowda chose to ignore.

Santosh was just four years older than Roshan but he was already an adult unlike his son. Speaking of which, where was the rascal? He hadn't come home last night. Or had he?

Gowda felt his headache resume again. When the forensics team returned, he would go home for a nap. He needed a clear head for what lay ahead.

'Anything on the landlord of the building?' Gowda asked.

'No, sir. The rental agreement is via a lawyer in Pune. I've got the number.'

Gowda nodded.

———•———

4.00 p.m.

Gowda rode into the Neelgubbi police station. He had gone home when the headache threatened to split his skull. He had left Gajendra with the forensic team and had PC David drive him home.

All he remembered was taking a swill of water before dropping into his unmade bed. When he woke up three hours later, his mouth was dry but there was that curious stillness in his head that said the headache had ached itself out.

He stepped out of the room. The door to Roshan's room was ajar. The rucksack was still there; the bed had been made even if sloppily. Where was he?

In the kitchen Gowda found a set of covered dishes. Shanthi had come in at some point to cook and clean. How many people had keys to his home?

That was the other thing, he thought, as he heated the bisi bele bath. Who else had keys to the lawyer's home? They needed to get a list.

He opened the small container of mixture. There was also a bowl of kachumber. If Gowda's mother had been around, this was exactly what he would have demanded of her. Comfort food, he told himself as he served the heated rice and vegetables onto a plate.

Somewhere out there was that child, Nandita. They had a whole set of leads but were nowhere close to knowing where it would take them and if it would end in Nandita. Meanwhile, this was what they called a high-profile murder and everyone's attention would be diverted towards it.

Gowda stood under the shower after he had eaten. His mother used to say, you mustn't bathe after a meal. But he had no more time to lose and Amma would have to be content with the fact that he didn't soap his belly as he stood under the cold water. As he dressed, he was glad that neither Mamtha nor Urmila was around to distract him. He would call Roshan in a bit to check if he was fine and then he would go to work.

Gowda walked into his room to see a distinctly harassed-looking Santosh, a vexed Ratna and a very smug ACP Vidyaprasad.

Gowda saluted, wondering what the ACP was doing in the police station on a Saturday afternoon.

'Good afternoon, sir,' Gowda said.

Vidyaprasad looked at his watch pointedly. 'I say, Gowda, this is highly irresponsible. Where were you?'

'I had a migraine, sir, and needed to rest,' Gowda said quietly.

'Migraine or hangover?'

The smirk made Gowda want to reach out and sink his fist into the man's face.

The ACP's gaze lingered on Ratna. Gowda saw Santosh bristle. Then his phone buzzed. He picked it up. 'Take this,' he said, offering his phone to Santosh. 'Put it on speaker so Ratna can join in too. It's from the shelter.'

ACP frowned. He didn't like the idea of his audience dissipating. There was no point in tearing Gowda apart if there was no one to witness his humiliation.

'This is a high-profile murder case and you go off for your siesta. Highly irresponsible,' he said again.

'I wouldn't have been able to function, sir,' Gowda said. 'Migraines are very debilitating.'

'The TV crews are on their way and I need to make a statement,' the ACP said, turning his chair this way and that. 'You don't mind my using your chair, do you?'

'No, sir.' Gowda shook his head. And then, unable to resist it, he added what Urmila said to him on and off, 'Mi casa es su casa!'

'Come again?'

'That's Spanish for my house is your house.'

ACP Vidyaprasad pretended not to hear him. Instead, he asked him, 'So, what am I going to tell them?'

'The usual.' Gowda didn't bother hiding the disdain in his voice. 'We are investigating. We have some very strong leads. We expect to close the case and apprehend the murderer shortly.'

'Are you mocking me, Gowda?' Vidyaprasad said, sitting up straight.

'Why would I?' Gowda said in his most artless voice.

The ACP went back to swivelling the chair from left to right, right to left. The creaking began.

'And what is this Nandita case? Your maid's daughter, I hear ...'

A missing girl wasn't something that came under an ACP's purview. Who was the mole in the station, Gowda wondered. Someone who thought it necessary to inform both Mamtha and ACP Vidyaprasad about the goings-on his life. Someone who tipped off Mary before an arrest could be made.

'A twelve-year old girl has gone missing,' Gowda began. 'She has been missing since 4 March.'

'Ten days! What are you doing here? Anyway, if you haven't traced her by now, she's probably in some brothel or dead.'

'We are doing our best.'

'Save your best for the lawyer murder case. One of the SIs can follow up on the missing girl. If you ask me, it's best that she stays missing. Easier on the family and us,' the ACP said. He paused his swivelling and leaned forward. 'The commissioner is taking a personal interest in this. So ...' The ACP resumed his swivelling and Gowda waited.

At the next turn of the chair, the extendable stem of the single leg sank into the groove and the ACP felt himself sinking. A hand shot up, groping for something to hold on to – table edge, in-tray, paperweight.

Gowda stepped forward to extricate the man from beneath the desk he was wedged under. He dragged the table away to ease the ACP out.

'What nonsense!' the ACP fumed, trying to wriggle out. Gowda offered him a hand. The ACP took it reluctantly and hoisted himself up. 'This place is a mess.'

'I sent a request for some office furniture months ago,' Gowda said, pretending he didn't understand.

'Humph ...' the ACP said as he strode away. At the door, he turned. 'I want results. Soon.' He didn't bother hiding the implied threat – or you are going to be in serious trouble.

———•———

5.30 p.m.

Rekha gnawed at a nail. She didn't know what to do. She looked at her phone screen. Her friends had said she must block Sid. But she was too afraid to do that either. As long as he knew she was reachable, he wouldn't do what he threatened to: tell her parents about her or put up pictures of her on social media, But something told her that if she made herself unreachable, he would.

She looked at the messages again. He had called her just about every foul word he knew in English and Kannada. Even reading it made her flinch. She looked at the last message and shuddered.

Sanjay was right. She was messing with fire. He had said that she was to go to his home that afternoon. They would watch a movie in his home theatre, hang out together and he would call her a cab to drop her back.

'You will be home by half past six, latest,' he had added. 'Like a good college girl!' He had touched her cheek with the tip of his index finger.

She felt safe with Sanjay. She thought of the narrow escape she'd had from Sid. He was nothing more than a pimp. And he was frightening her.

Sanjay would know what to do, she thought.

Except when she got there, she discovered there had been some kerfuffle in the gated community with the police coming and going. She sent Sanjay a message saying she was going back. Why hadn't he texted her back? Was he angry with her?

Her mother was surprised to see her back early but she was pleased as well. She thought all nefarious things happened in the cover of darkness. If her daughter was back home before dusk, all would be well.

'I thought you had an extra class,' her mother said.

'It got cancelled,' she said.

Rekha wanted to weep and confide in her mother. But she was afraid of the consequences. Her phone would be confiscated and she wouldn't be allowed outside without a chaperone. Worse, they would send her away.

'What's wrong, Rex?' her brother asked. He had come into the room without her even realizing it.

Suddenly she knew what she must do.

———•———

6.00 p.m.

Nandita sat on the bed. All day she did nothing but sit and wait. She wished Krishna would come. But the day before, there had been a scuffle when he wanted to see her. Daulat Ali had said no. The thekedar had said no one was allowed to be near her.

'The thekedar didn't mean me,' Krishna had insisted loudly.

But the man wouldn't let him. She had heard sounds of slapping, groans and a door slamming. Moina had sauntered into her cubicle. 'Are you satisfied now that you have got the two of them slapping each other?'

Nandita had blinked. 'What did I do?'

Moina had snorted and walked away.

Nandita buried her head in her hands. What was happening? Krishna had said he would take her away from here.

From one of the other cubicles, where she knew there were more girls, though she hadn't been allowed to see any of them, she heard the sounds that seemed to fill the space periodically. A rhythmic splat-splat on the plywood of the beds; the grunting and then the muffled groan. It scared her, that sound. Everything scared her here. She had thought Moina was her friend but now Moina seemed to hate her.

She heard a scream. Again. There was a frantic drumming of heels against the partition. What was going on?

She cried softly.

'Stop your sniffling ... What are you weeping for? Who died?' The big man glowered from the doorway.

She bit her sobs down and began reciting the multiplication tables. One sixteen is sixteen, two sixteens are thirty-two ...

7.00 p.m.

Gowda, Gajendra and Santosh sat together, watching the footage on Santosh's laptop. Suddenly Gowda stood up. 'Let's take this to my house,' he said. 'Will you be able to connect it to my TV?'

Santosh thought of the ancient TV in Gowda's home. 'I don't think so, sir,' he said, not knowing how to keep the embarrassment out of his voice.

'Oh,' Gowda said.

Head Constable Gajendra cleared his throat. 'I have a 32-inch LED TV at home.'

'That will be fine,' Santosh said.

Gajendra's home took Gowda's breath away. He had a 32-inch LED TV, a double-door fridge, a showcase full of assorted brassware and stuffed toys – a cross-eyed teddy, an inebriated dog and a constipated cat, rotund distended belly and all.

Gowda made a note to himself in his head: CHANGE TV.

There was also a row of interlinked steel chairs. Like the ones dentists seemed to have a proclivity for. And a sofa that would have been more appropriate in the Mysore palace. How did he manage to pay for all of this? Was the man on the take?

Gajendra looked at him, waiting for the compliment that first-time guests festooned him with. Gowda cleared his throat. 'What an amazing house,' he said.

Gajendra beamed and dusted the already spotless sofa for Gowda to sit on.

'When did you shift here?' Gowda asked curiously.

Gajenrda's previous house, he remembered, had been smaller and sparsely furnished.

'I sold some land, sir, and decided to buy this house. It was a distress sale. That tailor's ...' he said.

Gowda nodded. There had been a case of a tailor and his wife killing themselves. The tailor's brother had sold the house at a throwaway price, he had heard.

Santosh had meanwhile started looking for the USB port to plug in the hard disk.

Gowda felt breathless. The room was stuffy and in honour of their arrival, Gajendra's missus, as he referred to her, had lit a handful of incense sticks. 'Please come in for coffee and tiffin,' Gajendra said, beckoning them to the dining room where a chrome and glass table stood laden with covered dishes.

How had Gajendra's wife managed to put all of this together in half an hour? Gowda hoped they were not eating the family's dinner.

Kara bath and kesari bath; salt and sweet; piping-hot filter coffee. Gowda would have fallen on his knees and wept in gratitude another time. This evening though, he was in a strange mood. A butterfly kept fluttering on one of his eyelids for no specific reason.

Santosh had the CCTV footage running by the time Gowda had eaten. 'Do you want to watch the whole thing or should I fast-forward the footage?' he asked.

Gowda took a deep breath. 'Let's start from two hours before the lawyer returned home and tally the register entries. Do we know if each of the visitor entry passes carries the plot owner's signature?'

Gajendra nodded. 'I had PC Byrappa verify that first. He has started talking to the security and staff as well.'

'Something very curious happened this afternoon, sir,' Santosh said. He had stepped into the dining room and filled a plate with enough food to feed a cricket team, Gowda thought. In a strange way, he envied the younger man's ability to make himself at home no matter where he was. Everywhere Gowda went, he stood out like a sore thumb, separate and mostly left alone.

Gowda turned to look at Santosh. 'Like what?'

'I was talking to the guard at the gated community when this young woman turned up in an auto. I think she left when she saw the commotion at the gate. One of the guards said he had seen her with the lawyer earlier in the week.'

Gowda frowned. 'Did you get her details?'

Santosh shook his head. 'She didn't enter and went back in the same autorickshaw she came in. But the camera got a frame of her face and I took a picture of that.'

'Get a printout. What about the lawyer's phone?' Gowda asked. 'We'll find something in it surely.'

'It's password-protected and has a fingerprint sensor,' Gajendra said. 'I have requested the mobile phone company for call, text and WhatsApp records ...'

Gowda nodded and turned his attention to the footage.

'Did he have just one phone?' Gowda asked suddenly.

'We didn't find any others in the house,' Gajendra said. 'I'll check with his office and the security at the layout.'

Fifteen minutes later, Gowda had enough of watching the guava vendor outside the gate scratching his testicles. Another mental note: if you buy guavas, leave them in water for at least half an hour.

'Speed it up,' he said.

A pizza delivery man and two service men from Samsung came on motorbikes. A dog came running, and stood thoughtfully at the gate. Two young girls came on bicycles. A line of maids left and then a group of construction workers. Soon the pizza man and the service men left. At half past seven, a dusty Mercedes honked at the gate.

'That's the lawyer,' Santosh said.

The lawyer's car window was down and he took delivery of a few letters. 'He lived alone?' Gowda said.

'Yes, there were two boys for two or three days last week, but they left. One of the security men said the boys ran away. They'd had enough.'

Santosh butted in. 'That's the thing, sir. Apparently the boys left on Friday morning ...'

Gowda frowned. 'You realize we need to explore that angle too.'

Santosh nodded. 'I've already started on that. The boys had work passes which they left back at the house. I have them at the station, sir. I checked the CCTV. They left with a young man. I am getting a printout of his face as well.'

Gowda grunted. Santosh was shaping up better than he had expected. He had seemed lost when he first returned to work but he seemed to have got a grip on himself.

'Excellent,' he said.

'Thank you, sir,' Santosh said, careful to hide the glee in his voice.

Gajendra hid his smile. Gowda and his acolytes – it was like watching a reality show. The young SI would go places or stay in the rut Gowda and he had dug up together. You didn't know which way it would end till it happened.

———•———

9.00 p.m.

Daulat Ali called. I let the phone ring till it stopped. He called again. This time, I picked it up on the very last ring.

I listened to what he had to say.

'So, will you?' he asked me.

'What about my girl?' I retorted.

'Krishna, be reasonable ....' he said. 'I cannot go against the thekedar.' I stayed silent. 'It's not in my hands.' He sighed. 'I am just another employee like you. Even the thekedar, he is just a few rungs up the ladder.'

'I thought he is the boss!' I was astounded.

'He has bosses too!' Daulat Ali's voice was low. 'I'll do my best,' he said.

So I went to the godown. Daulat Ali was waiting for me by the steps. 'Bhai, I am glad you are here,' he said.

Was the deference in his voice real or put on for the occasion? I gave him a brief nod.

I climbed the stairs. He followed me quietly. 'Where is she?' I asked.

Daulat Ali led me to one of the cubicles. I looked at the dead girl. Moina.

'It was an accident,' Daulat Ali said. He didn't look at my face.

Every death is an accident. Yours, or someone else's. Moina looked like she had been strangled.

'I only meant to frighten her. But she kicked out at me and I lost my temper,' Daulat Ali said.

'Put her into the auto.' I turned away, not wanting him to see my face. She didn't deserve to die like this. And yet, it was probably better than dying of disease.

I drove the auto to a secluded stretch alongside a railway line. I heard the train. 'Now,' I told Daulat Ali.

We took Moina's body and left it on the railway line. The speeding train would do the rest.

There would be a newspaper report, an enquiry, and then the file would gather dust somewhere.

I got off once we entered a road with streetlights. I was a man with a plan.

I tried the woman's number from the phone I had stolen last night. She didn't pick up. I tried again. I didn't know what else to do.

Eventually, after eleven attempts, a man picked up the phone.

'Sir,' I said.

'Who is this?' he asked. 'Do you realize what time it is?'

'I know it's after midnight but listen to me ...' I didn't hide my vexation. That shut him up. 'There is a brothel where minor girls are being forced into prostitution.'

There was silence for a moment. 'Who is this?' he asked. 'And how did you get this number?'

'I am Krishna,' I said. 'Urmila madam gave me the number.'

'What? When? And why should I believe you?' he asked. 'How do I know you are not playing a prank? If this is true, why don't you call the child helpline? It's 10924 and it's 24/7.'

'I am the man from the railway station. With the three boys,' I said. 'I ran away with two of them.'

'You have some cheek calling us then,' he snarled.

'Which is why you should listen to what I have to say.' I gave him the brothel whereabouts. 'Sir, if you wait too long, the girls won't be there.'

'Why are you doing this?' he demanded. 'And where are the two boys?'

I cut the call.

I wiped the phone and tossed it into an overgrown plot of land.

———·———

15 MARCH, SUNDAY

9.00 a.m.

Gowda raised his eyes from the newspaper as Roshan came into the living room, bleary-eyed.

'What time did you get in?' Gowda said, taking care to curb the parental displeasure in his tone.

'About two.' The boy yawned, raising his arms. He had giant tufts of hair in his armpits. Gowda blinked. When did that happen?

'Party night, huh?' Gowda offered in his best buddy-daddy voice.

'Hardly. The scene here is quite dull, Appa. After Goa, this seems like a sleepy hole.'

Gowda wondered if it was a good time to bring up the smoking paraphernalia he had found in the boy's rucksack. But Roshan was suddenly sitting across from him with a serious expression. 'Appa, there is something I need to talk to you about.'

Gowda nodded.

'Don't frown.' Roshan smiled. 'It's not me. It's for my friend Suraj. His sister seems to have got into a mess and he doesn't know what to do.'

'What sort of a mess?'

'I don't know. He seemed reluctant to speak about it over the phone.'

'Ask him to come by this evening,' Gowda said, rising. He was going to the station house. He had asked Gajendra to hire a TV so they could watch the rest of the footage. 'Best if we do it here,' he had said the night before. 'It's a Sunday and your missus will need to watch the Sunday programmes.'

The thought of going back to that house made him want to reach for an antihistamine.

'ACP sir called. I said you were still at home,' the station writer said as Gowda walked in.

Gowda cocked an eyebrow. 'Is that so?'

Could this fucker be the mole, he wondered. And where had everyone else been when the ACP called?

'I suggest that Santosh and Byrappa proceed with the interviews after we view the footage. Have we got a time of death yet?' Gowda began as soon as everyone assembled in his room for the briefing.

Gajendra nodded. 'Between 9.30 and 10.30 p.m.'

'Right, so let's take a look at the footage. Fast-forward, pause, you know the routine, don't you?'

For the next hour, hardly anyone spoke. The lawyer, it seemed, had just two visitors. However, ten non-residents had entered the gated community. 'Looks like an open-and-shut case, sir,' Santosh said.

'I wish,' Gowda said. 'Something tells me it won't be such an easy case to crack.'

'You do like to complicate things; or you wouldn't be Borei Gowda,' a voice said from the doorway. ACP Vidyaprasad in his Sunday best – a pale yellow linen shirt, navy blue denims, loafers, his moustache twirled and his eyebrows daubed with vaseline. He smelled expensive. 'What's this TV doing here?' He frowned.

'We were watching the CCTV footage,' Gowda said.

'Now? Couldn't you have finished it last night?'

'We were ...' Santosh began.

'Gowda sir's TV at home isn't compatible with the system and we began watching it last night at my home,' Gajendra butted in.

'Listen to me, Gowda,' the ACP said impatiently.

Gajendra and Santosh stood up. 'Where are you going?' the ACP demanded. 'Look at the time of death; look at who visited the lawyer then ... and you have the assailant. Don't overthink things,' he said, giving his moustache end a tiny twirl as he left the room.

Gowda watched him leave, bemused. Was the man a born idiot or was he pretending to be one to save himself from having to actually do some work?

Santosh erupted as soon as the ACP left. 'It's just not right,' he snarled.

Gowda raised an eyebrow.

'All of us know about his involvement in the corporator case and here he is as if nothing ever happened. The system sucks, sir.' Santosh's voice quivered with righteous indignation.

Gowda stood up and walked towards Santosh. He poured a glass of water and offered it to the young man.

'The system sucks but we must do what we can. Much as I hate the system, there would be anarchy without it. So we must hope for the best.'

Gajendra looked at Gowda in surprise.

'I can't stop thinking of the children we rescued. We fail them if we give up on the system,' Gowda said.

Gajendra had never seen Gowda as affected by anything. He cleared his throat.

'Have you got the names and details?' Gowda asked, turning towards Santosh.

The young man nodded.

Gowda glanced at his watch. It was a few minutes past two. 'Start the interviews of the residents and check the guest register with them.'

'But sir, each guest has to sign the gate pass when they leave,' Santosh said.

'Have you seen the gate passes? The signatures look like crows strutting on the page.'

Gowda's phone rang. He peered at it thoughtfully. 'I need to step out,' he said.

———•———

3.00 p.m.

Michael's face was ashen and his eyes red-rimmed when Gowda walked into the office room he had been allotted by the Sunshine Home for Children. They had decided to bring the children here rather than interview them at the shelter.

'You look shaken, Bob,' Gowda said without any preamble.

'The children began talking to me this morning,' Michael said and dropped his head into his hands.

'How bad is it?' Gowda asked. Outside he could hear the children playing in the yard outside the home. They were kicking a ball and raising little puffs of dust.

'Listen to this,' he said, switching on the voice recorder app on his phone.

The recording began with Michael coaxing the children. 'Tina, it will help us if you tell us what happened to you.'

'Tina, do you hear me? Do you understand what I am saying?'

'Would you like some water or a cup of tea?'

The sound of a squirrel chirping on a tree outside punctured the silence.

Then a low voice spoke as if it were reciting a lesson by rote.

It was a Thursday. The date was 5 March. Tina stood before the mirror, adjusting her t-shirt, fluffing it out so it didn't cling to her breast buds. She wore a slip beneath the t-shirt but it didn't help. Mummy had said she would buy her a brassiere soon. Tina had been embarrassed and had dropped her gaze. Everything made her flush these days, especially when the boys looked at her. And sometimes men ...

Tina picked up the purse and counted again the two hundred rupees in it. Mummy had said she would have to buy the BP tablets and other medicines as Mummy would be late that evening. The sari factory she worked in had a big order and Mummy wanted to make the most of the overtime. 'It's more money,' Mummy had said and Tina had nodded.

Tina was a smart girl. That was what everyone said. She will go places, they said. Just you watch!

She had thought out everything. She would lock the door, leave the key with the next-door aunty, cross the road, buy the medicines, come home and chop the vegetables and prepare the dough so Mummy only had to make the rotis later. Then she would do her homework. Tina glanced at the timepiece on top of the TV. It was a quarter past four. The medical shop would open soon.

Tina wondered if life would have been different for Mummy and her if Papa was still with them. Mummy said Papa died. But Tina had heard that Papa had another woman and he lived with her in Borivali.

Tina looked at herself in the mirror, fluffed the t-shirt again and shut the door. The one-room tenement was part of an old building and Mummy had to struggle, first to get it and now to keep it. The landlord raised the rent every few years. 'This is Mumbai. If not you, there will always be someone else,' he had said when all the tenants including Mummy had gone to plead for clemency: 'If almost 40 per cent of our wages go to pay rent, how are we to manage?' they said.

But Mummy never complained, even if she had to work extra hours. The sari factory was in Matunga, not far from where they stayed in Wadala, and it allowed her to keep long hours. And now that Tina was twelve, she could be counted on to help with the household chores.

Tina walked down the steps to the paan wallah. He would let her make a call from his mobile for a rupee. She called her mother. 'Mummy, I am going to the medical shop. The key is with Aunty. Do you want me to buy some vegetables?'

There was a grunt in response. Mummy was not allowed to use her mobile. But they had worked a system of codes. A grunt was a yes. A cough was a no.

Tina returned the mobile. The road was crowded as always. She looked both ways and stepped forward to join a group of people who were waiting to cross the road. The din of traffic hurtling this way and that filled her ears. She would buy some spinach, she thought. It was good for the blood, the science teacher at school had said.

Tina felt something or someone whizz past her. The strap of her purse snapped. 'What?' she cried, turning and seeing a little boy dart through the traffic. Tina ran after him. Yes, Tina did that. She cut through the traffic, not bothering about the screech of tyres and the blaring of horns.

The boy ran and so did Tina. Her heart almost popped into her mouth. But Tina wouldn't stop till she got her purse back and cuffed the boy for trying to steal from her. The boy seemed to have wings for feet. Tina panted, trying not to lose sight of him. There was a little park up ahead. If he went in there, Tina knew she would catch him. The boy ran into the park. Tina followed.

A hand grabbed Tina by her waist as she stopped to catch her breath. Just as the hand snaked around her waist, she felt something smash into the side of her face, but she moved her head so only a glancing blow grazed her cheek. A man stood with a rock in one hand. He raised the rock and brought it down on her face again. She felt her cheek tear open and her mouth split. Her teeth bit down on her tongue and something rang in her ears. She felt her mouth fill with blood and an excruciating pain tore through her.

Through a haze of pain, she saw the boy come towards her. She saw the man slap the boy as he said, 'Why did you have to run so far?'

The man and the boy took her towards a waiting taxi. Her feet had gone numb and so had her mind. She whimpered. He slapped her other cheek and said, 'You want me to smash this side of your face too?'

The taxi drove up the short distance to Wadala station. Tina tried to cling to the seat of the taxi through the pain. But the man prised her fingers off the seat and hoisted her into his arms. The boy followed wordlessly.

As always, the Wadala station was packed. She didn't know what she could do to escape but she knew she had to try. She squirmed but the man's grip held her in place. Through the pain she saw her captor was a smooth-faced man with a full head of hair. He could have been her papa. 'What's wrong?' a woman asked as the man hurried towards the platform with the boy in tow.

Tina whispered, trying to speak. 'Help,' she tried to say. 'Help! He hit my face with a rock!'

A red-tinged bubble escaped her smashed mouth. The man looked at her and said, 'She fell off a ladder and I can't afford a taxi to take her to the hospital!'

No one questioned why he wasn't taking her to a hospital in Wadala. No one had the time. They made sympathetic noises and made way for him to get into the crowded local train. Two men even gave up their seats so he could lay her down while he held a blood-sodden cloth to her face. No one was bothered about what didn't concern them. Tina understood that now.

They changed trains. Again someone asked: What happened?

This time he said that Tina had fallen from the train. Silly child! Wouldn't listen! And now I have to take her to the hospital, the man said.

Who wouldn't believe him? He looked like a concerned father hastening to find medical help for his daughter, with the younger child in tow. A poor man who couldn't even afford a taxi. Bechara, someone said under his breath. Tina passed out then.

When Tina was conscious, she was in a hovel and an old woman was bathing her wounds. 'Lie still,' the woman said as she applied a salve. Tina flinched. A strong smell of antiseptic filled her nostrils. A familiar smell that she knew. Tincture of iodine. Mummy kept a bottle to apply on cuts and bruises.

'I am going to give you an injection,' the woman said. Tina's left eye widened. The other side of her face was so swollen that she could not open the eye. Perhaps the old woman was a nurse. Perhaps she would help. 'I,' she tried to say.

'Shut up,' the old woman said. 'Don't talk. Do you want the wound to open up further? What was the fool thinking of, smashing your face? The thekedar isn't going to like it. What will he say when he finds out?'

'I,' Tina tried again.

'Shut up, I said,' the woman snapped. 'So you want him to teach you obedience as well? He's mangled your face already and if you are going to be headstrong, you are finished.'

Tina closed her eyes. What was the old woman garbling about? Through the half-opened tin door, she saw the arc of a street lamp. Where was she? What time was it? Mummy must be home. Would Mummy go to the police? What then?

This was a nightmare. She would wake up any moment now. A chill ran through her. She began shivering. Soon the shivering wouldn't stop.

When Tina woke up, an IV was attached to her arm and there was a bandage on her face. Tina stared at the ceiling of the hospital ward. The old woman sat at her side and the boy came in with a glass of tea and two maska paav.

'I've had enough of this hospital duty,' the old woman said, dunking a piece of the bun into the tea and popping it into her mouth.

Tina's stomach rumbled. Hunger gnawed at her. She licked her lips. They were dry and cracked but it didn't hurt to open her mouth any more.

'I ...' she croaked. 'My mummy ...'

'Forget that you had a mummy, daddy, bhai, behan, whoever ... you are here now and if you do as they say, they will treat you all right,' the old woman said through a mouthful of soggy dough. 'Ask chooha here if you don't trust me,' she said, pushing the boy towards the bed Tina lay on.

Rat. Was that the boy's name?

The boy's eyes met hers and then his glance dropped. Tina turned her head away. The little rat was the reason she was here.

'Didi,' he mumbled. She refused to look at him. Go away, rat, she thought.

'Didi, sorry,' the rat said. 'My name isn't chooha. It's Abdul.'

Tina turned to glare at him. 'Why did you do it?'

Abdul darted a glance at the old woman. He didn't speak.

Tina had a new home. Platform 4 on the Kalyan station. And a shadow, Abdul. There were other girls. They were in the trade. They get fed and paid, he told her.

Tina stared the old woman down. 'No,' she said. 'I won't. You can't make me.'

The man came back. He had a name. Mohan. He wasn't from here, Abdul said. He was from Bangalore. Tina sat still, refusing to move. She shoved the plate of food away even though she was faint with hunger. 'Let me go,' she said. 'I won't tell anyone. Just let me go!'

Mohan stared at her impassively. 'What about all the money I spent on you at the hospital?'

'My mother will give it to you. Twice the amount. Just let me go. We won't tell anyone.'

'For a little girl you are very bold,' the man said.

'I am not little. I am twelve years old. Did you hear what I said? Let me go.'

The man's eyes narrowed. 'No, not until I recover my money.'

'I said my mother will give it to you.' Tina's voice was shrill as she leaned towards him.

'If your mother is so concerned, why aren't the police out looking for you? It's been five days since you went missing. Do you think your mother cares?' the man said softly.

Tina stared at him. What was he implying? 'No,' she said. 'My mother loves me.'

'Does she?' His voice was a whisper now. 'You are still in Mumbai. Why aren't the police knocking on my door yet? I have been accused before of abducting girls. Why aren't they questioning me?'

Tina didn't know what to say. Or think. Was he right? Her mother loved her. The man was just trying to rattle her.

She sat with her head pressed to her knees. She would pretend to do whatever he asked. And at the first chance she would flee. She was still in Mumbai. She would find her way home.

'What do you want me to do?' she asked. 'I'll do anything but what the other girls do. I'll scream if a man comes near me.'

'How old did you say you are?' There was a reluctant note of admiration in his voice.

'Twelve,' she said.

'Twelve going on thirty.' He laughed. 'And no, my dear, you don't have to do that. Not yet.'

Later that evening, when he asked her to go with him, Tina went quietly. Abdul dogged her steps. They are taking us away, the boy whispered. Tina's heart stilled. But she ignored the boy. She hadn't forgiven him.

'Where are we going?' She plucked at Mohan's sleeve.

'You'll know when you get there,' he said. It wasn't the train station they went into but another room where a man in a white shirt and brown trousers waited. He had a high forehead and a beaky nose. Tina thought he looked like the priest at the Hanuman temple.

The man looked at her and smiled. 'You are Tina,' he said in Marathi.

'Uncle, please take me home,' she cried.

'Ssh ...' he said, patting her head. 'Don't worry. I'll take care of you.'

'Make sure you don't touch her,' he said, turning to Mohan. 'Light brown eyes and dark skin. She is a rare commodity, too precious for you to fiddle around with.'

Mohan dropped his gaze. 'I wasn't going to,' he said almost defiantly.

'What?' the man in white demanded.

'Nothing, saab,' Mohan said.

'Good. I will let you know when to start for Bangalore,' the man said, walking to the door. He turned to look at Tina. 'Be a good girl!'

The door slammed. Tina felt tears cascade down her cheeks. How was she to escape if the man took her away to Bangalore?

'Stop crying,' Mohan snapped. But she continued to howl. 'Stop it,' he said, twisting her arm. 'I won't let you go.'

She stopped abruptly. 'You will help me?' she asked.

'The thekedar thinks he is a big shit. But he doesn't know me. He doesn't know what I can do,' the man said.

Then, with a small smile, he grabbed her hair and slammed her face into the wall. Once. Twice. Thrice. Tina cried out.

Abdul whimpered in fright.

'Shut up, you chooha! Watch ... just watch without a squeak!' the man growled.

Then, with few words and an economy of movement, he unbuttoned his jeans, pushed her skirt up and held her against the table the man had perched on. He spat on his palm and smeared it in her anal region, separating her buttocks.

Through the pain in her skull and the blood trickling down her forehead, Tina knew a greater excruciating agony. She felt a hard object split her. Tina screamed.

Mohan continued to ram the hard object into her while the boy Abdul watched, biting on his hands to stop the scream from escaping his mouth. He was too afraid to scream.

———·———

'How did they get here?' Gowda asked.

Michael sighed. 'I don't know. We haven't got that far. She stopped talking. Tomorrow I'll try again. I've asked Urmila to join me. Perhaps with a woman in the room, she may be less frightened.'

Gowda nodded. The girl had spoken in a flat monotone as if she were recounting what had happened to someone else. She had used the word 'I' just once.

Gowda stood up and went to the window. The children at the home were the children of convicts serving their sentences. For no fault of theirs, they were ostracized by the society they were part of. But they had a chance of reprieve. They would be able to shrug off the stigma. But this girl and the little boy ... would they ever survive this? What could any counsellor say to these children to help them move on?

———·———

5.30 p.m.

At the station, Gowda told Gajendra, Byrappa, Santosh and Ratna what he had heard.

None of them spoke. Instead they all went back to what they had been doing. A dead lawyer was easier to deal with than the story of children entombed alive.

Ratna said she had to go. She was meeting an NGO friend.

'We have managed to take screenshots of the lawyer's two visitors. One was a young man and the other a couple,' Santosh said, opening the images on his laptop.

Gowda looked at the grainy pictures. There was nothing to suggest anything out of the ordinary. What was he missing?

Santosh stretched and yawned.

'The station seems a little quiet?' Gowda said.

'It's Sunday, sir,' Gajendra murmured.

Gowda smiled. He had forgotten. So much had happened in the span of a week that the days had merged into one breathless moment.

The fatigue began deep in his bones and weighed him down with a weariness that made him close the files and rise.

'I'm going home,' he said.

The others looked at him, but said nothing. Gowda saw it on their faces, that they felt it too. On an everyday basis, they dealt with human culpability, but in a matter of three days, they had seen human depravity and the extent to which it could descend had left them all with a sense of hopelessness. Neither law nor its enforcement seemed to have made any real impact.

'I think all of us need to go home and get a good night's rest,' Gowda said. 'The two children are at the shelter. And there is nothing we can do for the lawyer now. As for Nandita, we are doing everything we can.'

Santosh opened his mouth to protest, but Gajendra beat him to it. 'It helps to look away for a moment; we'll come back with a clearer gaze,' he said, rising.

7.30 p.m.

Roshan was waiting for him at home with another boy. 'Appa, this is Suraj,' he said as Gowda entered the house.

Gowda gave him a curt nod, and then remembered to stretch his lips into smile. Roshan had complained as a child that he was reluctant to invite friends home.

'Why?' Gowda had asked. He had been polishing his shoes at the time.

Roshan had brought a small mirror and held it to his face. 'Look at yourself,' he said. 'You look at everything, whether it's your shoes or my friends or me, as if we have done something wrong. You frown and glare as if we are guilty.'

Gowda had learnt to smile after that. He smiled at his shoes, after that Roshan's friends and Roshan.

'Give me a few minutes,' Gowda said, going into his room. He closed his eyes and turned the shower on. The water rained on him and washed away some of the greyness he felt within. Gowda dried himself and stepped into a fresh pair of clothes.

'Yes,' he said, walking into the living room and dropping into a chair. What had the boy done?

Roshan cleared his throat, signalling for his friend to speak. Suraj twisted his fingers and said, 'Uncle, there is this boy who is troubling my sister.'

Gowda looked at the boy's anxious face. 'How old is your sister?'

'Seventeen. She just turned seventeen and she's got involved with this bastard who's threatening her.'

Gowda's eyebrows rose at the epithet.

'He's got some photographs of him and her and he's threatening to put them up on Facebook,' Suraj said. He made no attempt to hide the fact that his sister had shamed him and their family. But as her older brother he had to do what he had to do.

The boy swallowed. 'If that happens, my parents will murder her and probably kill themselves.'

Gowda nodded. Was there a season for crime as well? Everything in the past few days had to do with girls in trouble.

'Which is why I am afraid to write a formal complaint. My parents ... they are very conservative,' Suraj mumbled.

'Appa ...' Roshan leaned forward. 'I think you know Suraj's father. They live a street away from us in Jayanagar. And his father works in the same bank as Doddappa.'

'My father's name is Shankar,' Suraj said.

Gowda groaned. He couldn't think of a more dyed-in-the-wool conservative family from Mysore; the kind that believed in the healing and holy properties of cow pee and observed a fast every second day.

'Do you have a picture of this fellow?' Gowda wondered if it was too early to pour himself a drink. He needed one like a bee needed nectar.

'Get me a glass of water,' said Gowda, turning peremptorily towards Roshan. 'Have you seen the photographs?' Gowda asked when Roshan was out of earshot.

'No, Uncle.' The boy avoided his gaze. Then he added, 'I saw two or three, but not everything.'

Roshan came back with a glass of water and a serious expression. 'He is a sick asshole, Appa,' Roshan said.

Gowda frowned, wondering if he should ask his son to mind his language. But Roshan probably wanted his friend to see this as one of those man-to-man chats, and Gowda didn't want to show the boy up.

'Do you have his address and his photograph?' Gowda asked. A friendly warning should do, he thought. 'And one of your sister?' he added as an afterthought.

'I'll send it to you, Uncle,' Suraj said.

Gowda glanced at his phone as Suraj's message arrived. For a moment, he couldn't believe his eyes. Suraj's sister was the girl who had come to meet the lawyer in the afternoon. The boy who had been blackmailing her had visited the lawyer the evening he was murdered. What were they up to? He didn't want to go further with that thought. Where did this end, this need to accumulate? Was nothing sacred any more?

Suddenly he felt he had to get away. Gowda looked at his watch.

'I have to go,' Gowda said, rising.

'He is investigating a murder case,' Roshan explained to Suraj. Gowda heard the pride in his son's voice, the subtext being, my daddy is bigger and better than yours. I wish I were, Gowda thought as he shrugged into a half-sleeved shirt and pulled on a pair of jeans.

What did Roshan actually think of him? And then Gowda was struck by the irony of it. All through his youth, he had worried about what his father thought of him. And now he was worrying about what his son must think of him. Did either his father or his son ever wonder what he thought of them? He didn't think so.

Gowda spritzed some cologne on himself and patted his pocket to make sure he had everything – phone, wallet, keys and cigarettes.

'Don't wait up for me,' he told Roshan as he stepped out.

Gowda thumped the seat of his Bullet as if it were the rump of a horse. 'Now, don't you dare stall on me,' he whispered sternly. He needed to feel the wind in his face; he wanted a pair of arms to gather him in an embrace; he needed to feel for himself that love wasn't a commodity with a price. He needed to believe in happily-ever-afters at least for a few hours.

Urmila glared at him. 'How do you know I'm not busy?'

'Are you?' he asked, allowing the weariness in his voice to show.

'No. But ...'

'Urmila, I am so tired. I am worn out in my head and I don't have the energy for this. Didn't Michael tell you what the child said?'

She nodded.

'Do you want me to leave?' he asked, leaning against the door.

'Borei,' she said and held him.

She poured him a drink and sat next to him as he drank his rum in silence.

'Human greed,' he said after a long while. 'Is it ever satiated?'

Gowda clinked the ice in his glass.

'I would like to stay the night,' he said. She laid her cheek against his. It had never happened before. Neither had she seen Gowda in such a state before.

Urmila's phone rang just as they slid into bed.

'Don't answer it,' he murmured against her neck.

'No, I have to,' she said, glancing at the name of the caller.

Urmilla sat up and answered the phone. 'Yes,' she said. Gowda watched the play of emotions in her eyes.

'What's going on?' he asked.

'A social worker I know. They've set up a raid and they want me to be a part of it.'

'Now?'

'Yes, now. Borei, why don't you sleep? I'll be back,' she said slowly.

'I am the policeman here and you are the citizen,' he said.
She paused as she pulled on her clothes. 'So?'

'So I am going with you.'

---·---

10.00 p.m.

The two of them reached the meeting point that had been fixed
by the NGO. Urmila let the car engine run as they waited. She
called the NGO coordinator.

'They are at the junction ahead,' Urmila said, switching off
the engine.

'Don't slam the door when you get out,' Gowda said quietly.

A dog barked. Another one took up. Urmila opened her
handbag and brought out a few slices of bread.

'Here, here ...' she whispered, flinging a piece of bread at the
side of the road. The dog snuffled as it wolfed it down.

It wouldn't have occurred to him to do that, Gowda thought.

The NGO coordinator, Tessa Martin, was short and stout. But
she bounced with an energy that would make a rubber ball feel
inadequate, Gowda thought as he saw her approach them. He
tried to hide his frown as he saw Santosh and Ratna following
her. What were they doing here?

Santosh walked towards Gowda. 'You didn't mention this to
me,' Gowda said, not bothering to hide his annoyance.

Santosh held his gaze steadily. 'Tessa called after you left to
say that they were doing a raid tonight. I have to be here. It's
under my purview. Ratna too.'

'Which station?' Gowda asked.

'Sampigehalli,' Ratna said, joining them.

The three of them walked quickly. Gowda realized they were unsure of having him with them. And yet neither of them dared say anything.

The inspector of Sampigehalli station had no such qualms. He frowned, seeing Gowda, and clenched his jaw.

'Do you have a toothache, Inspector Narayanaswamy?' Gowda had his most genial expression on.

Santosh said hastily, 'There is a missing-girl case we are investigating. Gowda sir is the IO.'

The inspector said nothing. He looked at his men.

'Our volunteer is in there. The moment he calls, let's go in without any delay,' the coordinator said to Gowda.

The inspector growled, 'Madam, this is my station, he is not in charge. I am.'

She snorted. 'And you didn't know about the brothel. How far is it from here? One kilometre?'

The man frowned. Gowda grinned.

Ratna touched her arm and said, 'When did your man go in?'

'About twenty minutes ago.' The coordinator glanced at her watch.

'When did you receive the tip-off?' Gowda asked.

'Actually, Urmila was the one,' the coordinator said. 'Someone called for her at the Bosco rescue unit in the railway station. Apparently he asked for her, saying he had information about minor girls in a brothel. And Urmila seemed to know who he was.'

And you didn't come to me, Gowda thought furiously. But he said nothing.

'Madam called me late last night,' Santosh murmured. 'I said this was outside our station jurisdiction.'

'Tessa was the one I went to meet early this evening,' Ratna said. 'We had to prepare the ground. We needed to find a pimp who could lead us here.'

Gowda felt Urmila's imploring gaze. But he avoided meeting her eyes. There would be time, he decided, to ask her why she hadn't called him. For now it was important to make sure everything went right.

A few minutes later, the coordinator's phone rang. 'Now,' she said.

'I suggest you wait here,' Gowda told Urmila.

'No, we need her. We need as many women as we can get on an operation like this,' the coordinator hissed.

They walked down the narrow alley. Most of the doors of the tenements were shut and the windows were dark. As they approached, a man sitting on the doorstep got up and went in. He shut the door and turned off the light.

Inspector Narayanaswamy strode up the stairs, followed by two constables. The coordinator and Ratna ran behind them, followed by Santosh, Gowda and Urmila.

The shutters were drawn halfway down. The inspector pushed it up, making enough noise to wake up the dead in the distant cemetery. The coordinator and Santosh hissed, 'What are you doing?'

But he sauntered in unheeding, calling out, 'Police.' For effect, a constable blew a whistle.

Gowda felt the blood go to his face. 'You fucking bastard!' he muttered as he saw the raid turn into a farce.

Half-naked girls; men with their briefs around their ankles; screaming and shrieking; the sound of upturned boxes; a few slaps ...

A slender young man met Gowda's gaze for a moment and then began running. Gowda tried to dive for his ankles but the boy escaped his clutch and leapt towards the staircase. 'Get him,' Gowda hollered and chased after him. The boy's feet barely touched the stairs as he leapt over four or five steps at a time.

The boy ran into the alley. Gowda followed him. He saw the police jeep parked at the end of the alley. Gowda leapt into it and said, 'Follow him. We have to get him.'

The police driver looked at him questioningly. 'Go man, go!' Gowda shouted.

The driver turned the key. But the engine wouldn't start.

'What are you playing at?' Gowda said as the boy became a speck in the distance.

The jeep wouldn't start. 'I am sorry, sir,' the driver said with a contrite expression. 'I don't know what happened.'

Gowda stared at him and got out. He had been played. All of them were in it.

Then he saw Santosh run down the stairs and towards him. 'Sir, she is here,' he said, his voice hoarse with excitement.

Nandita sat on the edge of the bed in a cubicle. She looked dazed. Ratna was sitting at her side. Urmila stood alongside. But Nandita wouldn't speak. She just stared unseeingly at the wall opposite. When she saw Gowda, a flicker of something showed on her face.

He went to sit by her. 'Nandita, do you know me?' he asked gently. She nodded. 'Shall I take you home?' he asked.

She nodded again. Then, as if struck by a thought, she said, 'Amma will be angry.'

'No, she won't,' Gowda murmured. 'She will be happy to see you,' he said, gesturing to Urmila to take her.

The inspector stood examining an account book he had found in a little cupboard. It was just a few days old. Gowda looked at it. 'How convenient,' he said. 'None of the major monthly payouts.'

'What do you mean?' the inspector said.

'You didn't buy this on your salary ... I am not a fool.' Gowda tapped the heavy gem-encrusted ring the other man wore on his index finger.

'Let's go,' Gowda said as Urmila walked out with Nandita.

'You can't just take her like that,' the inspector protested. 'There are formalities to be followed.'

'Try me,' Gowda said, shutting his protests down with a stare.

'Apart from Nandita, there are four girls here. Two are from Assam. One is from Gulbarga and one is from Bangladesh. Apparently she was brought in just this morning.'

'Where is your volunteer?' Gowda asked, looking towards the NGO coordinator who was talking to the girls.

An elderly man stepped forward. 'He is one of our staff members,' Tessa said. 'He helps with the clerical work.'

'These are the two guards,' Santosh said, gesturing to Daulat Ali and his stooge. 'We should be able to get some information from them about who owns this place and how the operation is run.'

Tessa snorted. 'They probably know nothing, which is why they didn't run like the one that got away. Anyway, they will be out or they'll esacape when being transported to the station. Isn't that how it happens?' She glared at Inspector Narayanaswamy. 'When you grab a young man from the streets for some petty crime, you keep him in the lockup for a whole week before producing him in front of a judge. But then these scums walk free in twenty-four hours.'

Gowda looked away. Everything Tessa said was true. He looked at the girls. Not one of them was over sixteen.

'Sir,' Santosh asked, 'what will happen to the girls?'

Gowda took a deep breath. He hated having to be the one to tell Santosh, but he was bound to find out sooner or later.

'The Gulbarga and north-eastern girls will go to the government shelter. Once the authorities in the places the girls are from are reached, the girls will go to a home there or, if they have a family to return to, they will be sent there.'

'And so the girls will be home soon.'

'No.' Gowda shook his head. 'It might take anything from six months to a year. These things have a way of stretching out.'

Santosh's face fell. 'What about the Bangladeshi girl?'

'She will be sent to prison,' Gowda said quietly. 'They usually have no papers and that's what happens to illegal immigrants.'

16 MARCH, MONDAY

6.30 a.m.

Gowda could hear murmurings from the kitchen.

Shanthi came into the living room when she heard the bedroom door open. Gowda blinked. He saw a shadowy form behind her. He had thought she wouldn't come in to work that morning

'Namaste,' he said.

'Namaste, sir.' She smiled. 'Would you like some coffee? I have put the hot water on for your bath.'

Gowda smiled. She had probably polished his shoes as well and laid out a freshly laundered and ironed handkerchief.

He walked to the front door and saw it was locked. 'Shanthi, why have you locked the door?'

'Nandita is with me.'

'How is she?' Gowda asked.

'She won't let me out of sight. She held my hand all through the night and wouldn't stop crying. I don't know what to do, sir.' Shanthi's eyes filled.

'At dawn, she demanded I bring her here. She feels safe here,' Shanthi said. 'But even here she is afraid someone will come and grab her. She wanted me to lock the door so that if anyone comes here, they'll think there's no one at home.'

Gowda nodded. He moved towards the shadowy form. 'Don't be afraid, Nandita. Nothing will happen to you,' he said gently.

He hoped that the many million gods in the Hindu pantheon and Jesus and Mary would ensure that Nandita survived her ordeal. The scar tissue, he hoped, would form thick and soon.

'Shanthi,' Gowda called out from the living room as he sipped his filter coffee.

She came to the door with a worried expression.

'There are formalities to be followed. I'll ask Ratna madam to come here. It may not be easy for Nandita to answer the questions, but it needs to be done,' he said, as he walked into his bedroom.

The previous night, Ratna had gone with Tessa and the girls, while Urmila, Santosh and he had taken Nandita to her home in Gospelnagar. Shanthi had opened the door. When she saw Gowda, she had blinked in surprise. When Gowda moved aside and she saw who was with him, she had burst into tears. She had stumbled over the threshold to gather her daughter in a tight embrace even as she pressed kisses on the girl's face. The younger children came out at the commotion and so did some neighbours. From within the house, Gowda heard Ranganna snoring loudly in a drunken stupor. Gowda had glared at the man in disgust. 'Shall I go prod him awake?' Santosh asked.

'Don't,' Gowda said. 'He will beat his daughter, wife and children and create a scene. It will be all about him and I don't have the stomach for it after the day we have had. I may end up breaking his nose ...'

Santosh had smiled and the two men waited while Urmila reassured Shanthi that Nandita was unharmed.

'I'll drop you both home and go back to mine,' she said as they got back into the car.

'No,' he said. 'I'll drive you back and return with my bike.'

'I'll go with you, sir,' Santosh said.

It had been almost half past two when Gowda entered his bathroom for a quick shower before crawling into bed.

8.00 a.m.

'Something has come up,' Gowda said when the team were all assembled. He looked at their curious faces – Santosh, Ratna, Gajendra and Byrappa. Between the five of them they would have to untangle the knotted mess of this case.

Gowda opened his phone and showed them the photograph Suraj had sent him.

'This is the second visitor,' Santosh said.

They listened as Gowda explained to them about Rekha, Siddharth and their connection with the deceased.

Ratna kept shaking her head. 'What's wrong?' Santosh asked.

'At the NGO I was first with, there were cases of many such girls. Some who get into it because of their boyfriends ... and some' – Ratna looked embarrassed that there could be women who valued their bodies so little – 'who do it for the spending money. The ones who came to us didn't know what to do. The boyfriends had probably disappeared and there wasn't anyone else they could turn to. And you know what, most of them wouldn't even remember what happened. Or even what the person who had been with them looked like.'

'Rohypnol?' Santosh asked.

Ratna nodded. 'Is he the one?' Ratna asked, pointing at Sid's photo.

'That's what we need to find out,' Gowda said, looking at Gajendra's face. The head constable had been silent. 'What do you think?' he asked.

'Is it that simple? I am not sure,' the head constable said thoughtfully.

'Exactly. But we will know only when we bring the boy in,' Gowda said, reaching for his phone as it beeped.

Last night, as they had driven back, Gowda had asked about the call that had come for Urmila at the rescue unit. 'Could you get the number?' he had asked.

Urmila had promised to send it to him first thing in the morning. And so she had.

Gowda dialled the number. It was switched off.

He wrote the number on a piece of paper and gave it to Gajendra. 'It's switched off. We need to trace it to see who it belongs to.'

10.00 a.m.

Santosh and Byrappa stood outside the house in Shanthi Nagar. The boy's address had been easy to locate. Except that there was a lock on the door.

'Where do you think he's gone?' Byrappa said, staring down the lane.

From the corner of his eye, Santosh saw a tiny movement at a window. 'I think he's here,' Santosh said.

Byrappa frowned. Then he walked to the door and thumped on it loudly. 'You can either come out or I can drag you out. Which do you prefer?'

They heard a side door open. Byrappa hurried towards it while Santosh stood by the front door.

'I didn't do it,' the boy mumbled. 'I didn't do it.'

Santosh walked up to the boy, who seemed to have shrunk. He was all bones, eyes and an unshaven chin. He had a massive bruise on his face and his arm was in a sling.

'Why are you hiding then?' Byrappa asked.

'I am afraid they'll come for me,' the boy said, his eyes darting beyond Byrappa and Santosh to see if anyone else had followed them.

'Who?' Santosh asked.

'Can I go with you, please?' the boy pleaded. 'Please take me away from here, please.'

Santosh and Byrappa exchanged a look. What was he so frightened of?

12.00 p.m.

Just another boy like Roshan and Suraj, Gowda thought, looking at the boy huddled in the interrogation room.

'How do you know Dr Rathore?' Gajendra asked.

'I didn't kill him, sir.' The boy turned towards Gowda. 'He was already dead when I got there.' He rubbed his eyes.

'Answer my question,' Gajendra growled.

The boy sunk his head in his hands. Then the words emerged; a sordid torrent of events. Rekha. The cucumber seller. The easy money. 'It was just once, but she began having this fling with the lawyer.'

'And so you decided to kill him?' Gajendra demanded.

The boy raised his head from his hands for a brief moment. 'If I did kill him, why would I come here, sir?'

Gowda looked at Gajendra. It was time to move onto the next phase now that phase one of the interrogation had been accomplished.

He tilted his chin at Gajendra to indicate he was taking over. Gowda dragged the chair to the other side of the table so the boy would have to raise his head to look at him.

'Sid,' Gowda said.

The boy's eyes widened.

'Siddharth,' Gowda said again. 'What did you do when you discovered Rekha – Rex, that's what you called her, right – was involved with the lawyer?'

'I was angry, sir. I was furious that she was cheating on me. So I decided to set up another escort evening, get my money and fuck off ...'

Santosh growled, 'Watch your language!'

'I am sorry,' the boy said. He took a deep breath. Gowda and the others listened: the call; the date that didn't happen; the beating.

'You knew what that evening was going to be like ...' Gowda said softly.

The boy nodded.

'She was your girlfriend and you still went ahead. Are you a pimp?' Santosh said, placing his palms down on the table and glaring.

'But she didn't go. And the man who set it up said it was all right. Except he didn't mean it. He had me beaten up.'

Gowda leaned forward. 'And ...'

'So I called her and said I was going to upload our chats and pictures on Facebook and WhatsApp.' The boy's voice was defiant. 'But she said she would go to the police. Everyone knows the police only listen to the woman's side.'

Gajendra boxed his ears at that. 'It's usually because they are the victims ...'

Gowda glared at him. 'Go on,' he said.

'I thought I would go to the lawyer and show him what his baby girl had been up to with me. I wasn't thinking straight, sir. I was angry at what she had done; and I was angrier that I had been beaten up because of her. She treated me like dirt. She ...'

Gowda touched his arm to interrupt the boy's diatribe. 'What did you see when you got there?'

'The door was closed, but there was a glass panel by the door. I peered in and saw a man lying on the floor. When I saw blood, I fled.' Sid shivered.

'You didn't think of alerting the neighbours or the security or calling the police?' Santosh asked from the shadows.

The boy shook his head. 'I was sure that if I got involved, I would get into a deeper mess. I had mentioned to the man who beat me up that the lawyer was responsible for Rekha not going on that date. I thought they had got to him as well. Except that I didn't know they had killed him. I saw it on TV later that night. That's when I locked my front door and stayed inside.'

Gowda stood up. 'Take his statement and keep him here since he is happy to be remanded.'

Gowda sat at his table with his hands laced beneath his chin.

'Do you think he is speaking the truth?' Santosh asked.

'We'll know when we do a fingerprint match,' Gowda said. 'But I don't think he is lying. He is petrified of what will happen to him.'

The station was abuzz with activity. Mondays were always busy, but Ugadi was drawing close and pre-festival times saw a strange spurt of petty crime.

'Have you got the postmortem report?' Gowda asked.

'It's on your table, sir,' Santosh said. He had been afraid that he would need to go to the morgue again and witness a postmortem. The first one was still fresh in his mind and the taste of bile that flooded his mouth after. But Gajendra had gone in his place.

Gowda glanced at his watch. 'Why don't you and Ratna finish taking Nandita's statement? She and Shanthi are at my place.'

And for once I can file an A-report – case solved and closed, Gowda thought ruefully.

———·———

Ratna and Santosh walked towards the police jeep. PC David was standing under a tree, rubbing his forehead furiously.

'What's wrong?' Santosh asked, taking in the man's wan face.

'Sinus headache. And not getting better. I think I have a fever too.'

'But we need to go out.' Santosh's bike was at the service station. He didn't think Gowda would take kindly to him asking if he could borrow the Bullet.

'I'll drive,' Ratna said.

'You can drive a jeep?' Santosh queried in surprise.

'I can drive anything except a train, tank and plane,' she said airily.

'I don't think I can let you drive the jeep,' David said unhappily.

'C'mon, PC David.' Ratna opened her palm to him. 'It's just to Inspector Gowda's house. And you can sit in the jeep.'

David dropped the keys into her palm.

Santosh wondered if he should offer to drive instead. But he was curious to see how good a driver she was.

Ratna got into the jeep. Santosh followed and stopped himself from telling her to check if the handbrake was on. David got into the back seat and closed his eyes.

Ratna reversed defty and drove out of the gates with a fluidity that made David sigh in relief and Santosh look at her in admiration.

'May I ask you a question?' He glanced at her face.

She met his gaze with a swift look. 'Ask away!'

'You chose to be an assistant sub-inspector. Why?' His voice was low. 'You have a postgraduate degree. You could have joined at the sub-inspector level or even written the civil services exam.'

'And do what? Push a few papers this way and that?' She smiled at him. 'I wanted to be hands-on; haven't you seen how it is with women and children?' She spoke quietly. 'I didn't want to be stuck with administrative work which any fool sub-inspector can do. I didn't mean you,' she added hastily.

He smiled. 'I know what you mean, ASI Ratna. And what do you think now?'

'I don't know,' Ratna said, turning into Green Fields. 'It feels like we are at the visible end of the garbage dump; the rest of it is cloaked in darkness and deceit.'

Santosh placed his hand gently on hers. That was all he dared. 'For what it's worth, you can count on me,' he said.

2.00 p.m.

The postmortem report said what Gowda had already deduced. The lawyer's skull had been smashed in, Dr Khan had written. There was nothing in the contents of the viscera to suggest he had been poisoned or drugged. In fact, it seemed the lawyer's last meal had been several hours earlier.

Meanwhile, there was the other visitor to check on.

'Do we have an address for him?' Gowda asked Gajendra.

'It's incomplete,' Gajendra said. 'These security guys are perfectly useless fellows.'

'They may be, but not the security camera. Get the vehicle number and we can track the owner's name and address,' Gowda said, his eyes pausing on a line in the description of the injury.

A typical signature fracture. A localized depressed fracture where the outer table had been driven into the diploe. The inner table was fractured irregularly and to a greater extent comminuted. A spider's web with no displacement of fragments of the skull. The roughly triangular depression indicated that it was possibly caused by an uneven object made of stone or metal. There was bleeding from the ear, suggesting the transverse sigmoid sinus had torn and there was a posterior fossa haematoma. However, he hadn't been dead yet. The sudden nature of the attack had caused him to fall so heavily on his face that he had broken his nose and drowned in his own blood. The fracture line suggested that the assailant had been a little taller than the victim and left-handed. Gowda thought of

Sid. The boy was at least 6"2' and the angle of the blow would have been different.

He thought of the weapon. The stone Buddha they had found on the floor? Could a child have done it on his own? He thought of the two boys who had run away. Had they returned? But how had they entered the gated community without the guards spotting them?

'In the rains we had three weeks ago, a section of the wall fell. But there is a quarry on the other side of the wall. Quite a deep one,' Byrappa said. 'So the security must have been lax there.'

'Let's take a look,' Gowda said, rising. The three men drove into the gated community. There was a group of people near the broken wall. Gowda groaned. 'Oh no,' he said, 'Laurel and Hardy.' Gajendra hid his smile.

'We were getting a quote from the contractor,' Laurel said, and Hardy nodded his head.

'How long has this wall been down?' Gowda asked, climbing the rubble to see what lay beyond.

'Three weeks,' Hardy mumbled.

'It should have been built the next day, but the association is filled with retired bureaucrats,' Laurel said, following Gowda up the rubble.

Beyond lay an abandoned quarry, deep and dangerous, with its sides jagged at some points. There was a pool of green water at the bottom. 'Only a fool would attempt to climb the wall this way,' Laurel said.

Or a very desperate person, thought Gowda. There was a narrow lip of land abutting the wall and edging the quarry. It was possible to walk by holding on to the wall and enter through the broken section. But who knew about the breach in the wall? Beyond the quarry was a barbed-wire fence, behind which were a few low-slung tile-roofed buildings. 'What's there?' Gowda asked.

'A pig farm. Bloody nuisance. They slaughter every few days and the residents complain of the squealing,' Laurel said.

Suddenly the case was acquiring dimensions that even Gowda hadn't anticipated. Could someone who worked on the pig farm have come in?

'We need to check on the farm employees,' Gowda told Byrappa as they entered.

He glanced at his watch. Michael had messaged asking him to come by late afternoon. He would have to leave as soon as Ratna and Santosh returned.

Gajendra's phone beeped. He stared at the message and looked at Gowda with a dumbfounded expression. 'You are not going to believe this. The number you asked me to trace? It was the lawyer's.'

'What?' Gowda sat up.

What did Nandita's disappearance have to do with the murdered lawyer? What was he not seeing?

4.00 p.m.

At the Sunshine Home, Gowda was greeted by the sight of Mr Right, Urmila's ridiculous dog, on Tina's lap. She was murmuring into the dog's ears and he was licking her face. Urmila stood alongside, smiling and talking to the girl.

Michael stepped out of his room. 'Urmila dropped in on her way to the vet and when the girl saw the dog, her eyes lit up. Over the last three days, I haven't seen her react or show a single flicker of emotion. Usually she won't even look at any of us.'

Ridiculous as he was, Mr Right could be the perfect Mr Right.

Michael looked at Gowda. 'I don't know if she will talk when she sees you in uniform.'

Gowda whistled through his teeth. But Tina remembered Gowda from the rescue and her lips stretched a micro-millimetre in recognition. When he walked towards her, he saw her stiffen. He stopped mid-stride and pretended to look at a picture on the soft board.

'Tina,' Gowda said. 'Do you remember me?'

She nodded.

'Do you remember Ratna and Santosh? We were the ones who rescued you.'

Tina didn't speak. Instead, she stroked Mr Right.

'I need you to tell us how you came here. Only then can we catch and punish the people who did this to you,' Gowda said, careful not to step forward.

She continued to fondle the dog. Michael cleared his throat.

'Tina, we can do it another day if you don't want to talk now,' Urmila said, sitting down beside her.

'No, I'll tell you what happened,' she said softly. 'Does he understand everything we say?' She looked at Urmila and then at Mr Right.

Urmila smiled gently. 'Even if he does, it won't matter to him.'

'Will he still like me?'

Urmila squeezed Tina's hand. 'He will. He loves unconditionally. Do you know what that means? He just loves. He doesn't wonder why and how.'

Tina nodded and laid her cheek against the dog.

'What about Abdul?' she asked suddenly. 'Where is he?'

'We'll talk to him separately,' Gowda said.

Tina nodded. 'How is he?' she asked. 'He was taken away from his home too.'

Michael put on the voice recorder on his phone. 'Whenever you are ready,' he said quietly.

Tina took a deep breath and looked at the wall opposite as if it were a white screen. When she began speaking, Urmila's eyes met Gowda's. The tone was tinny and flat. And there it was again, the third person. This was not her but someone else called Tina, stuck in a nightmare that she would never escape.

Tina began observing Mohan. She thought if she did, she would know how to protect herself till she escaped.

Mohan was clever. He gave nothing away. He watched her all the time. Tina realized they were playing a cat-and-mouse game. And the mice were Abdul and she.

Tina saw the sim he retrieved from his pocket and inserted into a phone to make a call. One afternoon, he brought her new clothes. A brilliant blue salwaar kameez with a dupatta edged with tinsel. 'Cover your head with it and don't show your face. And put these on,' he told her, thrusting a card of stick-on bindis and a dozen glass bangles into har hand. She didn't understand. Why was he suddenly being nice? What other horror awaited her now?

It all fell into place when Tina saw the three tickets he had got them. Second-class tickets for a man, his young bride and his son from his first marriage.

They boarded the train. 'Not a word to anyone, do you hear me?' Mohan said as he shoved a little suitcase under the seat. The chooha barely spoke. Tina saw he had a fresh bruise on his face. After the first time Mohan had slammed her face into the wall, he had stopped doing it. Instead, he slammed the chooha's face into the wall. He made her watch, and though she steeled herself not to flinch, she did. And then with a grin that wasn't a real grin, he would thrust her against the table, spit on his palm and slather the saliva between her buttocks, and shove his lund into her anus. The pain was excruciating each time and she could tell that her whimpering excited him as much as the sight of Abdul's bloody face.

What had Abdul got it for, she wondered. She reached out and took his hand in hers. He didn't look at her but his fingers tightened around hers. It was the first time she had acknowledged his presence. They held hands till Mohan got up to go towards the door for a smoke.

'How did you get here?' Tina asked.

'I was taken outside my home like you were,' the boy whispered through cracked lips.

'Where is home, chooha?' she asked. His Hindi was not the Mumbaiyya Hindi.

'Don't call me that,' he said.

'Sorry,' she said, stroking his face.

'Muzaffarnagar,' he said.

'Where is that, Abdul?'

His fingers tightened around hers. 'Uttar Pradesh. I went out to play in the evening after school. We were playing near the railway tracks ... the other boys went back. I waited for them to leave so I could go see if my magnet was ready.'

Tina frowned. 'I don't understand.'

'I had heard one of the older boys at school say that if you placed a piece of iron on a railway track, it would become a magnet once a train ran over it. There was a man there. He held up my magnet and asked if I wanted more. I went with him and he offered me a sweet on the way.'

'How could you have been so stupid?' Tina asked.

'And you were not? They got you too! It doesn't matter. They know how to get us.'

'Yes,' she said. 'What are we going to do?'

'I don't know. I don't know, didi,' he said, and she felt a teardrop on her hand. It was the first time she had seen him cry. Tears filled her eyes too.

They didn't dare cry. Mohan would be angry if he saw tears.

'We'll make a plan,' Tina said.

'And what plan would that be?' Mohan asked, sitting by her side.

She didn't reply. But she felt Abdul's fingers clasp her tighter.

A vendor came by with a metal tray stacked with food packets. The man signalled to him. 'Two,' he said.

The vendor put the tray down in the middle of the aisle. 'What about you? Aren't you eating?' he asked. 'There will be no food till the breakfast stop at Raichur or Guntakal Junction.'

Mohan saw the other passengers look at him. He had forgotten that the gaze of the long-distance co-passenger extended beyond mere curiosity.

Mohan smiled and shook his head. He didn't want to draw any attention to them. If he said the boy and girl would share a packet, there would be questions. Polite words of enquiry, but questions nevertheless.

He thrust the packets of food into their hands. Abdul tore open a packet and stuffed his mouth. He ate in a frenzy, afraid the food would be taken away from him. It was the first time in many months that he was eating more than the leftovers from someone else's meal.

Tina ate slowly, chewing one grain at a time. She feared what would come next. But as she looked around her, a small sense of relief grew in her. He wouldn't dare do anything to her or Abdul with so many people in the compartment. A couple of hours passed. Then Mohan gestured for her to get up. When she stood up, he said loud enough to be heard by anyone who was listening and understood Marathi, 'Beta, come, use the bathroom before you go to sleep.'

They walked down the aisle towards the end of the compartment where the toilets were. There was no one there. The rest of the passengers hadn't begun on their dinner yet. He unlatched one of the toilets and shoved them in. It was a tight squeeze but Mohan didn't seem to think so. Tina stared at the toilet. Now what, she thought. The train had started at Surat and had been running for many hours before they boarded at Kalyan. It had been hosed down, but the toilet still bore the stench of a bathroom used repeatedly.

She heard him unzip his trousers. When she looked up, he had his thing in his hands. 'Hold it,' he told Abdul.

The boy looked at him blankly.

'Hold my lund, you madarchod,' he said. 'Unless you want me to slam your head against the sink.' He reached for Abdul's head. Tina reached out and took it in her hand. It came alive.

'Stroke it,' he said. 'Up and down.'

She did as he asked.

'Now take it between your fingers,' he groaned.

The biriyani she had eaten heaved into her mouth. A retch escaped her lips.

'You don't like it, do you, cunt?' he growled. 'I'd stick it down your throat except I don't want you biting it off. Looks like you are enjoying it. Or dear chooha's head will go bang-bang against the steel sink.'

Tina saw the fear in Abdul's eyes. She bit down on her lip and told herself that she would think of the time her mother and she went to see a film at a multiplex in Bandra. The tickets had cost a lot of money, but her mother had said that for once they were going to splurge and have popcorn too. Caramel and salted popcorn. Make sure you mix them well, her mother had told the boy at the counter. He had smiled and added an extra spoon of caramel popcorn, giving her a wink. Sweet and salt. She didn't know what each handful would bring to her mouth. Sweet or salt. Or sometimes a combination that made her feel that this must be what Jesus ate in heaven.

She felt something splatter into her hand. The sticky fluid that his thing spat into her when he shoved it up her shithole. So this was what it was. She looked at her fingers, not knowing what was expected of her next.

'Wash your hands and let's go back. The next time I gesture, you come here. I'll follow you in a while,' he said, opening the door and stepping out.

'Didi,' Abdul said.

She glared at him. 'Don't say a word. Don't say anything. Or I'll scream.'

When it was time to sleep, he offered his lower berth to an elderly woman. 'The boy can climb to the top and so can my wife. I'll take the middle berth,' he said.

He wound Tina's dupatta around Abdul's leg and stretched it across the space between the berths to tie it to her leg. Then he fastened the other end around his wrist.

'Just tug it if you need something,' he said.

Tina saw the elderly couple glance at each other, hiding their smiles.

At first she thought she would have a few hours of reprieve. A few hours later he tugged at her leg and she got up. He followed her with Abdul in tow. This time he made Abdul do it while she watched. Next time he made the two of them do it together. He left them alone after that.

But they didn't know that. All they knew was, as long as they were on the train, one more ordeal had been added to the list of what they would have to endure.

'Get ready. We are getting off at the next station,' Mohan said.

Tina felt Abdul press into her. She touched his shoulder.

The train ground to a halt and they got out.

Tina read the station clock. It was 4.30 p.m. and the station was called Krishnarajapuram. All railway stations looked alike, she thought. It didn't matter where she was as long as it was not on a train. She shuddered. The last twenty hours must have been the worst hours of her life.

Now what, she thought. Could there be anything worse awaiting her?

No one spoke. What could they say?

The five of them collectively would have known only a fraction of what she had endured in a few days' time.

Michael sat frozen in his chair. Santosh stood as if he had turned to stone. Ratna went to sit by Tina. She put her arm around her. The girl pushed it away.

Urmila rose slowly and walked to the door. Gowda followed her outside. She turned to him wordlessly and he held her. The two of them clung to each other.

Something clicked in Gowda's head. He remembered Santosh narrating to him the brothel guard Daulat Ali's conversation.

He had said 'thekedar'. So had Tina. Who was this mysterious thekedar who seemed to be everywhere and yet nowhere?

Gowda moved Urmila gently away from him. 'Tina,' he said, going back in. 'Do you remember the thekedar man?'

She nodded.

6.00 p.m.

Shenoy looked at Gowda in disbelief. 'Are you serious?'

Gowda didn't smile. 'Hear me out,' he said.

When Gowda finished what he had to say, Shenoy rubbed his eyes. 'When do you want me to see her?' he asked after a pause.

'I will get both children in the room so we get a definite portrait of this man,' Gowda said. Then he added, 'Thanks.'

Shenoy shook his head. 'How do you do this, Gowda? How do you live without losing your faith in humanity?'

'Who said I had faith in humanity?'

'If you didn't, you wouldn't be doing this, trying to make things better,' Shenoy said, preparing to leave. 'The layers are way beyond what you and I can fathom, Gowda. You know that the traffickers will have clout that extends high up in the world. That they will do everything possible to make it go away?' Shenoy continued as he gathered up his pencils and sketchpad.

Gowda nodded.

'And you still want to do it?'

'I don't have a choice,' Gowda said. 'I have to live with myself.'

8.00 p.m.

At the station, Santosh sat with a disgruntled expression, reading a report. 'The fingerprint reports are here,' he said.

'And?' Gowda said, dropping into a chair.

'Sid's fingerprints are on the door, glass and gate. But not inside,' Santosh mumbled.

'What about the vehicle number?' Gowda asked, looking at his watch.

'We'll get a trace on it first thing in the morning,' Santosh said.

Where had the day gone? It was past eight. He saw he had a missed call. Stanley.

Gowda picked the phone up and called him. What had come up?

'So what was all that about on Friday night?' Stanley asked.

Gowda flushed. The truth was he didn't remember much. Urmila had played for him the audio message he sent her. 'I didn't know you cared for me so much.' She grinned. 'I especially like the bit about comparing my teeth to Basmati rice. Are they really that long?' She had prodded him in his ribs.

'I really don't know what happened,' he had told her and she had accepted it just like that.

But Stanley wasn't so easy to placate. 'I'm in Kothanur to meet a relative. I'll drop in at your place in about half an hour.' Stanley hung up before Gowda could make an excuse to put him off.

Gowda was showered and dressed when the bell rang. He had given his teeth a good brush as well.

Stanley Sagayaraj stood at the door, eyeing Gowda curiously.

'Good evening, sir,' Gowda said.

Stanley nodded, continuing to look at Gowda.

'What,' he asked, 'is wrong?'

'Let's say I am relieved more than anything else,' Stanley said, following Gowda in.

'Why?' Gowda frowned as Stanley lifted the ashtray and sniffed at the butts. 'What's up, Stanley?'

'Do you remember calling me on Friday night?'

Gowda smiled sheepishly. 'No ...'

'Between that call and what the ACP has been saying, I came here expecting to see you drunk and lolling on your side along with empty bottles of Old Monk,' Stanley said.

'I don't drink like I used to,' Gowda said quietly.

'I can see that. You have lost some weight too.'

'What were you sniffing at the butts for?' Gowda said, wondering if he should offer Stanley a drink. He needed one very badly after the sort of day he'd had. 'Having said that, I am going to pour myself a drink. Do you want one?'

Stanley smiled. 'Sure.' Then he looked at Gowda and asked, 'Were you stoned on Friday night?'

Gowda paused. 'What did I actually say and do?'

Stanley grinned. 'You don't want to know.'

Gowda said nothing. He placed the glasses on a table and brought a small bowl of peanuts and Bombay mixture from the kitchen.

Then he went into Roshan's room and pulled out one of the rice grain-like things from the inner pocket. He held it out to Stanley. 'I took two or three of these on top of two drinks,' he said.

Stanley held it between his thumb and forefinger. 'That explains it,' he said, his eyes suddenly grim.

'What is it?' Gowda felt a huge ball of dismay and worry fill his chest.

'Molly. Love drug. Or just E. It's a party drug,' Stanley said. 'Your son's?'

Gowda nodded. He was going to have a serious talk with Roshan. Weed was one thing, but the moment Roshan moved to hard stuff, it was time Gowda stepped in and told him a few home truths.

'How is the murder investigation coming along?' Stanley asked.

Gowda shrugged. 'ACP Vidyaprasad would like us to wrap it up on circumstantial evidence. But I can't do that. There are more horrifying things buried underneath.'

Stanley held Gowda's gaze. 'You think so? Do you have any evidence to support it?'

'Both, sir,' Gowda said. His one-time college basketball captain wasn't someone who needed to be convinced. But Gowda wanted to explain to someone the case he was building.

Stanley listened without interrupting. Neither of them was new to the world of trafficking. Stanley had in fact set up a few raids. But children as sex slaves was something else. It made them feel hopeless. For each child rescued, there were ten children who were lost.

'Let me know if you need me to step in,' Stanley said as he rose.

---

17 March, Tuesday

3.00 a.m.

Gowda woke up in a cold clammy sweat.

He turned the fan regulator as high as it would go but an incisive heat spread under his skin.

Global warming, he thought. Trees cut in the Amazon basin were leading to climate change, Urmila said. You don't need to look that far, he thought, propping the pillows against the headboard. Trees being cut all over Bangalore and the buildings that seemed to pop up overnight like mushrooms after a thunderstorm, they caused it too. Climate change. And not just change in weather patterns but human behaviour too. There were over five lakh migrant workers in Bangalore, most of them men. They would do whatever it took to satiate their needs and feel in control instead of languishing as lowly pawns in the fabric of society.

Gowda shut his eyes. He needed to go back to sleep but he couldn't. He wished he were at the station with all the information at arm's reach. Gowda swore to buy a laptop and learn how to use it. He needed to. The society that he had to deal with was racing ahead at a speed that defied time, and if he didn't keep up, its crime and criminals would outrun him even before he began to comprehend what was happening.

There was a sound from the living room. Gowda stiffened. He rose and pulled out the sturdy Maglite flashlight he had got a friend from Dubai to bring him. He picked up the hockey stick he kept in his bedroom.

He padded quietly towards the living room. He hadn't forgotten how he had been ambushed and beaten up a few months ago while working on the Bhuvana case, and he wasn't going to be caught unawares again.

When Gowda's flashlight swung towards the face of the intruder, he heard a yelp. It was Roshan walking on tiptoe, trying not to walk into a wall or furniture. He put his hand up to cover his eyes from the bright light. Gowda reached for the light switch. The boy shrank into himself. Gowda looked at him for a moment. 'Go to bed,' Gowda said.

'Appa ...' the boy began, seeing his father's grim expression.

'Roshan, we'll talk in the morning. Go to bed now.'

He watched his son kick off his sneakers and drop into his bed fully clothed.

A few minutes later, he heard a retching sound.

Gowda ran into his son's bedroom.

He sighed. He fetched the plastic bucket from the bathroom and placed it on the floor. Then he found a face towel, dampened it and wiped his son's brow and face. He pulled the covers over Roshan and then lay down beside him. He didn't want Roshan choking on his own vomit.

What made one an exemplary father? One who hectored his son and forbade him from experimenting or excess? Or one who let his son be and cleaned his vomit and hoped the boy would learn from each experiment? Gowda stared at the ceiling, wide awake. From the trees around, he could hear birdsong and the rolling notes of the crow pheasant.

He would let Roshan sleep it out, Gowda decided when the clock struck six. He would go as early as he could to the station.

9.00 a.m.

'What have you got for me?' Gowda asked when he had settled at his desk with a cup of tea.

Gajendra and Santosh sat across him. Santosh pushed a file towards him. 'We have the vehicle details, sir.'

'And PC Byrappa talked to the pig farm people. The watchman said they don't bother about the quarry side because "what idiot would risk it at night?" But he did say that he had heard the dogs bark at nine in the night and then again around eleven.'

'What do the fingerprints reveal?' Gowda asked, taking a long sip of the tea.

'That's the curious thing, sir. Various fingerprints in the house. But nothing in the living room or on the weapon used.'

'It's been wiped down.' Gowda's mouth turned into a grim line. It was early in the day but already the heat was pressing down and causing the particular brand of summer warmth that was distinctly Bangalore – still and stifling, like being trapped between two sheets of glass in the sun.

'What time did the vehicle return?' he asked.

'It came in at about 9.00 and left at 9.40,' Santosh said, referring to his notes.

Gowda opened the file and looked at the sheet of paper. 'In which case, let's go pay Mr Sharad Pujary, whoever he is, a visit,' he said, rising.

'Why don't we ask him to come here?' Gajendra frowned.

'Look at the address. RMV Extension. Those sorts of people won't come to the station without a lawyer and anticipatory bail. Apart from which a minister or at least an MP will be brought into the picture,' Gowda said quietly. 'It's best we go there as if it's part of the investigation routine.'

Ratna rode in on her Scooty as they left. She waved at them and David braked abruptly.

'I've got a lead about the two boys who worked at the lawyer's house,' she said, peering into the vehicle.

Gowda nodded. 'Keep me informed,' he said.

He didn't think there would be much to it. But in a murder investigation, every lead had to be pursued. It could take them to another lead even if the first one was of little significance.

None of them spoke much as they drove towards RMV Extension. Gowda wondered how Roshan was. He was going to have to confront his son. Before he became an exemplary father, he was going to have to a be father.

Increasingly it occurred to him that in trying not to be his father, he had gone to the other extreme. Where did one draw the line between being involved and intrusive; concerned and overbearing?

Gowda's phone rang. It was Urmila. She didn't call him often during working hours.

'Are you all right?' he asked.

'Yes, Borei,' she said. 'I just needed to hear your voice for a moment. The children are back here with the portrait artist.'

'Are you all right?' he asked again.

'No,' she said. 'I would like to see you. Please.'

He heard the forlorn note in her voice. 'I am heading out to meet someone. I'll come over when I am done,' he said.

'Thanks,' she said.

'You take care,' he murmured softly.

Gajendra and Santosh stared ahead, pretending not to have heard Gowda's side of the conversation.

Gowda knew that they knew he had been talking to Urmila. So he didn't speak either.

It was a bungalow which, on that road of well-appointed homes, looked no different. It wasn't conspicuously new, nor was it a crumbling old house. When the jeep pulled up, the watchman came out of his sentry box.

'Is the owner at home?' Gajendra asked.

The watchman nodded and asked, 'Who should I say has come?'

'What do you think we look like?' Gajendra growled. 'Circus clowns?'

'Open the gates,' Gowda said quietly.

The watchman opened the gates. As the jeep drove up, Gowda saw there was a rectangular lawn in front, onto which a tarmac pathway had been laid. There were a few trees close to the perimeter of the wall. Edging the lawn was a low wall on which were potted plants. Roses, mostly, and an occasional hibiscus.

There wasn't the gazebo or barbecue pit that was de rigueur in this part of town, no overweight Labrador lolling in the grass. Quiet money, Gowda decided, looking at the car parked in the portico. A spotless black BMW.

A tall elderly man came to the door. He had a long, austere-looking face with a high forehead, and wore a cream linen shirt over beige trousers. There was that same squeaky clean aura around him, just like his car, Gowda thought, taking in the discreet Rolex, the white star of the Mont Blanc pen in his pocket and the narrow gold band on his ring finger.

'Yes, Inspector,' he said, peering at Gowda's breast pocket. 'What can I do for you?'

His smile was cordial, but not welcoming.

Gowda said in the most pleasant voice he could muster, 'Good morning, Mr Pujary.'

The man lowered his chin and touched his chest with the tips of his fingers. It was the gesture of the supplicant. Ask of me what you need and I will do my best.

Gowda could smell incense from within the house. 'This is regarding the lawyer Sanjay Rathore's murder.'

'I heard. What a terrible thing to happen!' Pujary said softly. 'I saw him just that evening.'

'So you know why we are here.' Gowda's voice was even.

'Yes. I was quite sure you would be reaching out to me sooner or later, though if you had let me know, I would have come to the station myself. Please come inside,' Pujary said, leading them into the house.

'This is my colleague, Sub-inspector Santosh,' Gowda said, gesturing to him.

Pujary smiled, but there was no sign of deference, Gowda noticed.

The living room was filled with straight-backed wooden sofas, low tables with little artifacts on them, and a giant Nataraja in bronze.

Across them was a wall made of giant plate glass. On the other side of it was an exquisite enclosed garden. 'You have a beautiful home,' Gowda said.

'It's my wife. She is the one with the taste. I am just a boring businessman; a real estate wallah.'

'Is there a dancer in your family?' Santosh asked, pointing to the dancing god.

'No,' Pujary replied shortly. Then he said, 'You have a sore throat. Would you like warm water or ginger tea?'

Santosh shook his head. Gowda stepped in. Any reference to his voice upset Santosh. 'Have you been living here long?' Gowda asked, sitting down. He waved to Santosh to seat himself.

A buzzer echoed through the house. Pujary stood up. 'If you will excuse me,' he said, going up the stairs that curved gently onto the top floor from the end of the living room. It reminded Gowda of the movie sets used to portray the rich in the Bollywood movies of the eighties.

A few minutes later, Pujary appeared at the head of the staircase with a woman cradled in his arms. He descended the stairs carefully and sat her down in one of the sofas. Then he smiled at her as if there was no one else in the room.

'This is my wife, Gita,' he said.

Gowda and Santosh rose to their feet. She smiled at them. A quiet little smile that only emphasized the grey pallor of her skin and the black circles beneath her eyes. Once she must have been an exquisite-looking woman.

'Yes, Inspector, you were saying ...' Pujary he gestured for them to sit.

Gowda took a deep breath. 'The CCTV at the gated community showed us that you had visited the lawyer just before he was murdered.'

'Yes,' Pujary said and clasped his hands. 'Dreadful business that.'

He paused for a moment. 'My wife and I had gone to MLA Papanna's shelter for girls at about seven. We are family friends. My wife wanted to give the girls a new set of clothes each. We don't have children of our own. So my wife sees all destitute children as our children to cherish. Right, Gita?' He smiled at her. 'And then, since we were in the neighbourhood, we went to Sanjay's house. He is a family friend too. We didn't stay long. The next morning, it was my wife who saw the news on TV9.'

The wife sat with her head bent. Gowda noticed that she hadn't spoken a word.

'Was there anything unusual that you noticed, ma'am?' Gowda turned towards her.

'No,' she said softly. Her gaze darted towards Pujary. 'I'd like my chair,' she said.

Pujary rose and walked to an anteroom. He pushed out a wheelchair and moved his wife into it. She pressed a switch and steered it towards an inner room.

'Were you business associates?' Santosh asked.

Pujary frowned. 'Not really. I told you, we were family friends, but there was a piece of land he was interested in that I was trying to negotiate for him.'

Santosh went to the plate glass window. 'This is a very beautiful garden,' he said.

'Gita's garden. That's what I call it,' Pujary said. Gowda saw
the softening in the man's gaze. 'She does everything. From
choosing the plants to potting to watering and pruning.'

Gowda saw the woman's pinched face in his mind. He
wondered what it was like to be trapped in a wheelchair.

The whirring sound of the battery-operated chair made him
turn. She came in with a tray on her lap on which were three
coffee mugs and a plate of biscuits. She placed them on the table
and went back to fetch the coffee jug.

None of them spoke as she poured the coffee into the mugs.
'Please have some coffee,' she said.

Gowda and Santosh accepted the mugs and sipped slowly.

'Have you found any leads, Inspector?' Pujary's voice cut
through the silence.

'Yes, we are working on a few leads, but ...' Gowda said. He set
the mug down abruptly and rose. 'Thank you, sir and madam,'
he added, turning to the woman who sat quietly. Her fingers,
Gowda saw, were restless as they clasped and unclasped each
other.

Pujary followed Gowda's gaze. 'Gita,' he said. Her fingers
stilled.

'The coffee was delicious,' Gowda said into the uneasy pause.
She smiled at him.

As they left, Gowda turned for one last glance at the couple.
There was a combination of relief and fear on her face, and
intense concentration on his.

'Yes, Inspector,' Pujary said.

'We will need to take a statement. We'll have someone come
by,' Gowda said.

'We can come to the station,' Pujary said, walking towards
them.

'I wouldn't want to trouble madam,' Gowda said.

'No trouble at all, Inspector. She is very mobile thanks to the wheelchair. Just tell us when and we'll come by.'

Gowda nodded. The woman in the wheelchair had a strange expression.

'Nice couple,' Santosh said as they went to the jeep.

'So, what did he say?' Gajendra asked.

Santosh explained.

Gajendra frowned. 'Either he is lying or the watchman is. According to him, they left that night at eight and were back by ten.'

'Why would they lie?' Santosh asked.

Gowda looked ahead. A snarl of thoughts – observations, evidence, findings, conjectures and a hunch that told him the jigsaw would fall into place if he found that one last piece.

'Drop me off at the children's home,' he said.

12.00 p.m.

At the Sunshine Home, all was grey and bleak. Tina and Abdul had arrived, and so had Shenoy. But Tina wasn't talking. When Abdul opened his mouth, Tina clamped her palm over his lips. 'Shut up, shut up,' she snarled.

Gowda saw the little girl huddled in her chair. There was a manic gleam in her eyes and her nostrils were pinched with rage. She was clutching the edges of the chair with her hands, and rocking steadily, back and forth.

Michael sighed.

'What's wrong?' Shenoy asked.

He shrugged. Gowda watched the simmering rage in the child for a while. 'She's probably been bullied at the shelter,' he said. 'And she sees us as being responsible for it. We sent her to the shelter.'

Ratna looked at him in surprise. 'How did you know?'

'I know how these places function. She is a newcomer. She needs to be taught a lesson. And she's getting a lot of attention. What did they do?' Gowda said, leaving the room and gesturing for the others also to do the same.

'They tried to cut her hair off,' Ratna said. 'So she smashed her fist into the girl's face. The rest of them fell on her and beat her up. Some of them are just hooligans in skirts.' Ratna's face bespoke her confusion and disgust.

Gowda took a deep breath. 'None of us know what these children went through, so let's not judge them ...'

Shenoy cleared his throat. 'Should I come back another time?'

'No,' Gowda said. 'Where's Urmila?'

Michael gestured to a room. 'She's helping with some correspondence,' he said.

'Shenoy,' Gowda said, 'will you go back to the room and start sketching? Try and turn it into a class like the kind you conduct at the club. Meanwhile, let me see what we can do to bring Tina back to us.'

'Hi,' said Gowda, walking into the room where Urmila sat working on a desktop.

She looked up and smiled. 'Borei,' she said. It was a greeting and an endearment.

He went to her and caressed her cheek with a finger. How could one word say so much? 'Urmila,' Gowda said, 'I have a favour to ask of you.'

Her eyes widened.

'Can we bring your Mr Right here for a bit?'

'Who?'

'That ridiculous dog of yours. Tina ... she's clamped up again, and I need her to describe to Shenoy the man she called thekedar.'

'Yes, of course,' she said, rising.

'I'll go with you,' he said.

She smiled at him. What was it about Borei, she wondered. A new gentleness had crept into him.

Mr Right insisted on sitting on Gowda's lap. Urmila looked at the two of them in amusement. 'He adores you,' she said, giggling, as she drove up the ramp of the basement.

Gowda snorted, but his finger found the scratching spot near Mr Right's left ear.

The Audi inched along. Gowda glanced at his watch. 'Step on it, U,' he said softly.

'Are you sure?' she asked. 'What if I get pulled up?'

'I'll handle it, I don't know why, but I think this portrait is the key to so many things.'

Urmila smiled, pressed down on the accelerator and changed gears. They jumped red lights, went down the wrong way on a one-way street, and narrowly escaped being mangled by a giant truck.

Gowda exhaled when they pulled up outside Sunshine Home. 'Remind me to never say step on it,' he said, trying to shift the frozen grin on his face.

Mr Right walked ahead and, as if he had been briefed, danced at Tina's knees. Her face lit up. She bent to pick him up and he hurled himself into her arms, craning his neck to lick her face. Tina turned her face this way and that. Her hairband came undone and Gowda heard Urmila gasp at the sight of her butchered hair.

Gowda's phone rang. It was Gajendra. 'Sir,' Gajendra said, the agitation in his voice buzzing in Gowda's ear.

'Yes, what happened?' The last time he had heard Gajendra so agitated was when they were rushing Santosh to the hospital.

'You have to come back, sir. A man has confessed.'

4.00 p.m.

When Gowda walked into the station, it was abuzz with excitement. OB vans and press vehicles were drawing up and there was a palpable air of expectation.

'The murderer has come forward and surrendered,' Gajendra said.

'And he chose to do it here?' Gowda asked curiously.

Gajendra shook his head. 'He went to the MLA's house saying he needed to confess. As the MLA and the ACP are buddies, he called the ACP, who came as quickly as he could. It's exactly what he must have been praying for. Ah, here's the hero,' Gajendra mumbled.

The ACP strode out from the direction of the cells. An impromptu press conference was going to be held shortly. His uniform was crisp and his chin newly shaved. The moustache gleamed and his cologne could be smelt a mile away.

The ACP saw Gowda and frowned. 'I say, Gowda, you heard the news, didn't you?'

Gowda nodded. 'Sir, but are you sure?'

Vidyaprasad shook his head in dismay. 'What's wrong with you? A man has come forward and his story corroborates with the findings, all of which have been kept confidential. So what's your problem, Gowda? When you hear hooves, you don't have to think zebras.'

And neither should you think asses, Gowda thought, but wisely kept his counsel.

'Where is the so-called murderer?' Gowda asked when the ACP had left to speak to the media.

'He's in the cell,' Byrappa said, coming towards them.

Gowda walked towards the cell. In a corner sat a young man, cross-legged. There was a hint of a smile on his lips and an almost unnatural calm on his face.

Gowda stood still. The man looked back at Gowda without dropping his gaze. He had confessed, and so he was absolved, his eyes said.

'Seen enough?' he asked.

Gowda frowned and turned away. Then he turned again to look at him.

He knew he had seen him somewhere before. But he couldn't remember where or when.

Gowda decided to go for a ride. It was either that or get drunk. And he didn't want Roshan to see him drunk and angry.

He started his bike with one swift kick and rode out of the gate. Instead of making his way down Kalasanahalli, he decided to take the long route through Bilishivale. At the Association of People with Disability nursery gates, a lorry was backing up. Gowda halted. On a whim, he parked his bike and walked through the nursery, looking at the potted plants and greenhouses. A few minutes later, he was back on the road that would take him to Kothanur and beyond, as far as he would go.

He came back two hours later when he felt the rage in him had dwindled to something else. A resolution to find out more. It was as if the confession had been stage-managed to ensure that the investigation ceased before any real damage was done.

7.00 p.m.

Roshan sat in the living room, poring over what looked like a medical text. Gowda looked at him and asked, 'How are you?'

'I am sorry, Appa,' the boy said, flushing.

'What's going on?' Gowda asked. 'I found Ecstasy in your rucksack and last night you were, what's the word, wasted?'

Gowda sat down beside him. Roshan took a deep breath. 'You fucked me up, the two of you,' he said.

Gowda said nothing. He had thought as much about his parents when he was Roshan's age.

'All you do is snarl at each other, Amma and you. Because of you, I don't believe in marriage or long-term relationships.'

'So how is your getting drunk or doped out of your head going to change that?' Gowda asked quietly.

'My girlfriend broke up with me. She said I was a commitment-phobe ...' Roshan wiped his eyes furiously.

Gowda put his arm around his son. He didn't know what to say or how to make his son feel better.

'Does it feel like more than you can handle?' he asked. Roshan turned into his shoulder and wept.

Gowda felt his eyes smart. He wrapped his arms around his son. 'There, there,' he said. 'Every generation thinks this. That our parents fucked us up. But we need to get a grip on ourselves, Roshan, you and I, we don't realize how fortunate we are that our troubles are the type that can be dealt with, surmounted even ...'

'What do you mean?' Roshan asked, raising his tear-streaked face to see a tear trickle down his father's cheeks.

Gowda told him then of the goings-on, leaving nothing out so Roshan would know the extent of real evil and depravity. And that parents who snapped at each other were not the end of the world.

Roshan listened and said nothing. He had expected his father to rage at him. But this man who seemed as lost as him was a new sight. And he wasn't too sure if he liked this vulnerable man who, despite the bike, the tattoo and the gruff manner, was clearly hurting.

'Appa, what can I do to help?'

Gowda shrugged. 'Just go easy on yourself. That's all I ask. And on me. I may be your father, Roshan, but I am not infallible. I make mistakes too.'

Roshan nodded. 'Appa,' he said suddenly. 'Somebody dropped off an envelope for you.' He rose to get it.

Gowda opened the envelope. It was a scanned image of the portrait Shenoy had drawn as per Tina and Abdul's description.

He looked at it for a long while and then he knew. The last piece had fallen into place.

9.00 p.m.

Gowda walked into the station that seemed curiously lifeless after the excitement of a few hours ago. The play had been performed to a standing ovation and the audience had left. The actor sat in his cell and elsewhere the director was patting himself on the back over how he had managed to pull it off. Not for the first time, perhaps.

'Bring the boy to the interrogation room,' Gowda said to one of the PCs on duty.

The man dithered. Another one of the ACP's footsoldiers, Gowda thought, seeing the man's hesitation. 'The ACP ...' the PC began.

'Do as the inspector tells you to,' Gajendra snarled. He had been on his way out when he saw Gowda stride into the station.

The young man was handcuffed for the short walk from the cell to the interrogation room. Gowda sat across from him at the table. There was a particular glint of amusement in the young man's eyes. He knew for certain then. 'Sit down, Rakesh,' Gowda said.

'My name is not Rakesh. It's Krishna,' he said.

Gowda held his gaze. 'Sit down.' Turning to the PC, he said, 'Take the handcuffs off. He is not going to run. The man surrendered, if you remember.'

The PC twisted his mouth to indicate displeasure, but did as asked.

'Please wait outside,' Gowda said. 'And close the door after you.'

The young man waited for him to speak.

'Rakesh,' Gowda began.

'I am not Rakesh. I am Krishna.'

Gowda took a deep breath and said, 'You were the informant who led us towards Nandita.'

The young man smiled. He leaned forward and asked eagerly, 'How is she?'

'Krishna, I know you didn't commit the murder, so why are you here?'

Krishna snorted. 'What do you know?'

Gowda held his gaze. 'I know that Pujary, or thekedar as you call him, went to see the lawyer.'

'So?'

'And that Pujary's wife was with him. And that she killed the lawyer. So why have you confessed to something you had no hand in?' Gowda said.

'Because I am Krishna.'

Gowda wanted to reach across and smack him. Instead, he said in an even voice, 'You are Rakesh. You are not Krishna and you do not know what you have taken on. Do you know that we have the death penalty in India?'

The young man threw his head back and laughed. 'This is India. When that man who raped and killed a girl in Kerala, what's his name, Govindaswamy, and that Delhi girl's rapists are still alive, why do you think I'll be hanged? And I confessed on my own and surrendered.'

Gowda stared at the table. It was an old one and the patina of age had worn the surface to a satiny smoothness.

'Why, Krishna?'

'Good. Now that you accept me for who I am, we can talk. I am curious. Why do think Gita-di killed the lawyer?'

'Krishna,' Gowda said, rising. Was the boy out of his mind? Or pretending? 'This morning, I went to meet your thekedar and I met his wife as well. They said they had gone to visit the lawyer. They said they were family friends. Except that no one in the lawyer's office had ever heard of them. Dr Rathore, they said, had no friends.'

'And so you decided that helpless lady in a wheelchair killed him?' The young man's eyebrows rose.

'I don't arrive at conclusions on mere conjecture. So tell me, Krishna, what really happened? Nothing is going to change. You will go to the gallows or rot in jail. But that's your choice. I just want to know what really happened.'

Krishna smiled. 'You did rescue my Nandita. But once I step outside this room, I will deny everything I told you and say you forced me to retract my confession.'

Gowda sat back in his chair and said, 'Go on, Krishna.'

The thekedar wanted to know what was special about Nandita.

I didn't have an answer. Do we ever know why we fall in love? But once we do, wouldn't we move heaven and earth to make sure that the one we love is safe and happy?

The thekedar would understand this, I thought. After all, he had devoted himself to caring for his crippled wife. I had watched them together and I knew he wasn't pretending. She was everything to him.

I tried talking to him once again. 'I will find you other girls,' I told him.

But he wouldn't agree. 'There is too much money involved,' he said.

And I thought perhaps if I arranged the money, he would let me take her away. The only person I could think of who would have that kind of money at home was the lawyer. My boys who had worked there had told me about a cupboard in the lawyer's bedroom which he wouldn't let anyone else touch.

I knew of the breach in the compound wall. I went in through that and entered the house through a ventilator in the servant's bathroom at the back of the house. The lawyer was a cheapskate. He had put a ventilator with glass slats instead of a proper window. I took the slats down one by one.

I was waiting in the kitchen for him. I had my face wrapped in a cloth and in my hand was a cleaver I had found in the kitchen. The edge of the blade was sharp. German steel, the boys had mimicked him. If you look after it, it will serve you for life, he would tell them if one of them left a knife unwashed.

I was going to make him give me the money, then I would tie him up and leave. I knew he lived alone and by the time somebody came to his aid, I would be long gone.

Then I heard voices. I stepped into the passage from where the entrance was visible. I saw the thekedar come in. I saw him hold the door open for Gita-di's wheelchair. I heard the thekedar speak to the lawyer about some land. But the lawyer was refusing to hear him out.

'Look, Pujary,' the lawyer said, 'I told you the deal is off.'

'Sir, I can sort out that non-encumbrance certificate. There won't be any problem, I assure you. The MLA has assured me that he will handle it.'

'No.' The lawyer was adamant. 'This isn't going to work. I have a reputation and your deals are murky. I can't take the risk.'

I could see Gita-di's face change. Her body was beginning to tremble and her face had turned red. The lawyer was waving his hand as he gave the thekedar a lecture. The water bottle in his hand dropped. I saw him bend down to pick it up from beneath that half-moon table. That was when she reached for the stone Buddha on the table and slammed it on his head. Just above the left ear. One heavy blow. And then again. 'You won't let him change. You and others like you have turned him into this monster. You are evil. Not him,' she screamed again and again at the lawyer, who had fallen face-down on the floor. I could see blood pooling around him. I could see the thekedar's aghast face. I could see the tears streaming down Gita-di's face.

They left hastily and, just as I expected, in ten minutes, he called me. He said there had been an accident, and he wanted me to fix it.

So I did. I wiped all the prints. I left some of my own in the kitchen. Then one of the men from the brothel called me. One of the girls there had died. And I knew that I had to get Nandita out. Even if the thekedar let her go, there would be some form of payback. I knew him well enough. He would get me if I tried to bargain with him. He would have me killed, and then my girl, my Nandita, would never escape. I needed to make sure she was safe. When I got out, I would find her.

I found a cheap phone in the kitchen. It was a phone he had given the boys to use. I knew it would come in handy for what I needed to do next. I called a woman whose number I had and told her about the brothel.

Gowda had listened without interrupting. But now he asked, 'But why?'

Krishna smiled. 'The thekedar will never say no to me again. He didn't ask me to confess. I offered to. He likes to think he made me, but he didn't. I created myself. I am Krishna. Besides, he will get me out. I have pictures of what happened on my phone and it's someplace safe. I am the one who can make or break him. I am not just anybody. I am Krishna.'

The door opened and the ACP strode in furiously. 'What's going on here?' he demanded, glaring at Gowda.

'Nothing. I just called him in to say hello and thank him. I was on my way back from settling my stolen calf dispute, sir,' Gowda said, at his laconic best.

'You won't get him,' Krishna called out. 'You'll never get people like him.'

10.00 p.m.

Nandita pulled out the metal lighter from where she had kept it hidden. The night of the raid, Krishna had come into her cubicle and sat with her. He gave her his lighter and said, 'Will you keep this for me?'

She had stared at him uncomprehendingly.

He pressed it into her palm. 'One day I will come for you,' he said.

She flicked open the lighter now and pressed the flint wheel.

A flame rose, tall and steady.

Nandita let it eat into the insides of her palm.

10.30 p.m.

They were all gathered in his living room. Michael and Urmila. Santosh, Ratna, Gajendra and Byrappa.

'He sounds like he's eighty-four ...' Byrappa said.

'What?' Michael asked.

Gajendra cleared his throat. 'Section 84 of the IPC. Unsound mind.'

Gowda pinched the bridge of his nose. 'That he is. And potentially dangerous. He said he would come back for Nandita.' A silence crept into the room.

'How did you know, Borei, that it was Pujary's wife?' Urmila asked.

'So many things: the sight of the men in wheelchairs at the nursery, handling giant pots with ease; the strength of the upper body compensating for the wasted lower limbs; the enclosed garden in Pujary's home that he said his wife looked after. Her shoulders and arms seemed well developed. I saw how easily she handled the full coffee pot when we went to their house; the casual lie about visiting the MLA. When I saw the portrait that Shenoy had drawn, it all fell into place. Dr Khan in his postmortem report had said the injury had been inflicted at a point where the maximum joints were. Pujary is too tall to have hit him there. Then I thought of the wife in the wheelchair. I saw it all in my head and the boy said that was exactly how it happened.'

'So you think she found out what her husband was up to?' Ratna asked.

Gowda nodded. 'When you see them together, you will understand. They are proud of each other and for her to see him fall from grace might have been unbearable. He didn't commit any of the crimes on his own; he was forced to do them. She needs to believe that.'

'The Mumbai police are coming tomorrow,' Michael said. 'The FIR will be written then and they will take the trafficker back once the paperwork is done.'

'And the children?' Urmila asked.

'Abdul's father came in this evening. He will take the boy home,' Michael said, not meeting her eye.

'Tina?'

'A social worker will travel with her once the formalities are complete. And she will be sent to a Catholic home.'

'Why isn't she being sent to her home?' Urmila's voice rose as she glared accusingly at Gowda.

'The mother has gone missing,' Michael said.

For a moment none of them spoke.

'What now, sir?' Santosh asked. 'The boy goes to jail for a crime he didn't commit? And that bastard walks free. The lives he has destroyed don't seem to matter. What are we doing calling ourselves the police? We are useless, sir, we are bloody useless!'

Gowda smiled and rose from his chair. 'There are more ways to skin a cat than one ...'

Michael sat up. 'What do you mean, Bob?'

Epilogue
18 March, Wednesday

9.00 a.m.

Gowda looked at himself in the mirror. He was tired and the fatigue showed, but his eyes were clear. He appraised himself and hoped his appearance reflected the person he was – an honest policeman trying to work within the system.

He had the file ready. He heard the jeep pull up outside.

Santosh and Ratna sat in the back seat. Gowda got in and smiled at them. He pulled his phone out. 'Hello, Stanley, we are on our way to the Inspector General's office. Where do we meet?'

Elsewhere, Michael and Urmila and their child welfare mates were headed to the chief secretary's office.

Gajendra looked at Byrappa. 'Didn't you tell me you know a crime reporter at one of the Kannada newspapers?'

Byrappa nodded.

'Call him,' Gajendra said. 'Let's go talk to him. Let's tell him what we know.'

One way or the other, they would get Pujary. He would be stopped. Human life had to be valued. They had to believe in that. They needed to.

ACKNOWLEDGEMENTS

As always I owe much to V.K. Karthika, editor, publisher and friend, for understanding why this book needed to be written, and her implicit faith in my writing.

Researching this book was perhaps one of the most difficult things I have done, and so much of the information that I collated and my understanding of the sordid world of child trafficking wouldn't have been possible without the support of the following people, all of whom work tirelessly to rescue and rehabilitate trafficked and abused children. I am indebted to them for making time for me despite their busy schedules, for letting me tag along in some instances, and for sharing information and true-life accounts:

Bosco Rescue Unit, Bangalore City Station

Nagamani V.S., Assistant Sub-inspector, Koramangala Police Station

Anita Kanhaiya, CEO, Freedom Project

Meena K. Jain, Former Chairperson CWC to Bangalore Urban

Brinda Adiga, Mentor, GlobalConcernsIndia.org

Suja Sukumaran, Advocacy & Integration Support, Enfold Health Trust, Bangalore.

A CUT-LIKE WOUND

ANITA NAIR

The first in the Inspector Gowda Series

It's the first day of Ramadan in heat-soaked Bangalore. A young man begins to dress: makeup, a sari, and expensive pearl earrings. Before the mirror he is transformed into Bhuvana. She is a *hijra*, a transgender seeking love in the bazaars of the city. What Bhuvana wants, she nearly gets: a passing man is attracted to this elusive young woman-but someone points out that Bhuvana is no woman. For that, the interloper's throat is cut. A case for Inspector Borei Gowda, going to seed, and at odds with those around him including his wife, his colleagues, even the informers he must deal with. More corpses and Urmila, Gowda's ex-flame, are added to this spicy concoction of a mystery novel.

"I loved this book and was constantly gripped. Anita Nair's writing in some moments has photographic qualities, in others the precision of surgeon's scalpel; and always the great inner warmth of the human heart. Truly astounding writing."

Peter James, author of
Dead Simple and *Looking Good Dead*

'Anita Nair is a feminist and highly regarded Indian novelist. *A Cut-Like Wound* is as startling a debut crime novel as you are likely to read this year"
Sunday Times

"Nair captures the seedy side of shiny new India vividly, and Inspector Gowda – with his weary self-knowledge; his secret, wistfully aspirational biker tattoo; his stagnating marriage and his confusion when an old flame re-enters his life – is a welcome addition to the ranks of flawed-but-lovable fictional cops." *Guardian*

"Nair immerses her readers in Bangalore's alluring and sinister mélange of Hindu and Moslem cultures, revealing a people afflicted by the inability to allow unqualified praise for anything or anyone. Complex, psychologically deep characters are a plus." *Publishers Weekly*

£8.99/$14.95
Crime Paperback Original

ISBN 978 1908524 362
eBook ISBN 978 1908524 379

www.bitterlemonpress.com